Wayward

Wrecked

Ellie Pond

Illustrated cover design by SJ Fowler

Object cover design by Melissa Doughty - Mel D. Designs

Copy Editing: The Word Faery

Proofreading by Lori Diederich

Chapter 1

Landing

Easton

The tender bounces on the breakers, heading toward our beach, and the life jacket around my neck smells of its new plastic buckles. I glance behind us, back at the yacht. I can't see Penny anymore. She lunged to get into the tender with us. It took a guard and their chief stew, Kennedy, to hold her back. Penny wanting to get in the tender? Yeah, she can sense something's wrong the same way we can.

I put my arm around Haley. She smiles. But she's worried too. The pirate ship's gone, something we couldn't tell from our cabin. Sunk? Driven off? I don't know, and we haven't discussed it. Dante, Sam, and Calvin have made it clear that we can't talk in our cabin. And they're right. There's no way Z's men aren't watching us or listening to us.

The wind's howling, and it's weird, weird to be looking at our beach from this angle. Weird thinking this is the last time I'll ever see it. My eyes flick over to the guard in the front of the boat, then to the ones on the beach. There's another tender already tied up to the big rock. Three other guards stare at us from behind their Ray-Bans.

There was little talking when Calvin came back into the room, Pepper firmly under his arm. But something happened. There's something going on with Calvin again. He did tell us about the guards picking up the other feral cats on the other side of the island. I didn't sleep much. I thought about making Calvin go off our guard duty, but I know him well enough now. He wouldn't sleep, anyway. He's even more watchful than I would have expected, and his grunting and scowling is at a hundred percent. Dante's right there with Calvin.

We bounce onto the beach. Zane hops out. Holloway, Thayer's chief of security, puts his hand over the gun of the guard next to him. "He's doing his job. He's on autopilot, going back to being a deckhand."

Zane and another of the Rosewood guards tie up the tender. Holloway stands at the edge of the tender like he's going to help us out. Calvin and Dante ignore the male and step into the surf.

"I've got it," Sam says, and he turns back to help Haley. She takes his hand, and I jump out without saying anything to the thick-necked guard.

"Here," a guard says, passing out tubs to each of us. "Collect what you want. Two of you up to the camp."

Haley and Sam go first up the trail to the camp, followed by three guards.

The rest of us sit on the beach, staring at the Rosewood, at least four guards at our backs. My stomach's clenched. My eyes flick to the jungle where Haley and I hid yesterday, waiting for our chance to take the pirates. That was bad, but somehow this feels worse.

It's been a long time. Calvin's leaning into Dante. The wind's at our backs, and I can barely make out what he's saying. But there's no way the guards can hear him with the wind. "Thayer's dad wants us dead."

Sam and Haley are back, tears coming down her cheeks.

"Haley," Dante barks, stepping toward her.

"Wait your turn, chef," the guard yells, stepping between Dante and Haley.

"It's okay—I'm okay, Dante. Just sad." Haley's guard is holding an extra box. They must have decided that Sam and her aren't a threat. The guard takes the box he's holding to the tender and comes back for Sam's and Haley's. "Holloway says the rest of you can go together."

The four of us trudge up the well-worn path to camp. My throat's dry and tight. I'm not going to cry. But this place changed my life. My eyes flick to the gun on the guard closest to me . . . I'm hoping we can all get out of here alive.

Calvin picks up the table. Zane rights a couple of chairs. It's weird. Not only did Mr. Z's crew clean up the body in the middle of camp, all signs of the rubble that dropped on the pirate are gone. Other than the table and a chair turned over, there's not much out of place. We've had worse messes after a heavy storm during the rainy season.

"Try to keep it to a minimum," Holloway says.

I put my Christmas presents in the bottom of my bin, along with my crew jacket that I find on the ground on the other side of camp. Other than that, there's nothing I want here. But then, I have a feeling there's something that Mr. Z is going to want. Though it's buried at the waterfall. I put my box on the table and glance over at my guard. He's staying a respectful five feet behind me. "What does the Z in Mr. Z stand for?"

The guard's jaw ticks.

"Right." I nod. I don't blame him for keeping quiet. Men like Mr. Z aren't going to forgive you when you make a mistake. Zane was the one who noticed what a good job the crew was doing, never having a phone out. He doesn't think they carry their personal phones. I've started looking at their back pockets since then, and I think he's right. The guards all have guns and radios, the deck crew and stews only radios. The Rock Candy had a giant screen that would come down for watching movies. Not that I ever saw it in use, but Zane pointed it out one day. Nowhere on the Rosewood have I seen so much as a TV.

The radio on my guard's belt beeps, and the guards around the camp all stand straighter.

"What's that mean?" I ask, fully expecting to be ignored again.

"Mr. Z's on the beach."

A few minutes later, he strolls up through the zigzag blind. The wire's long gone. Nothing to be afraid of on the beach now. Nothing but him. Dante glares at him. I don't like Thayer, but Dante's taking it to a new level. His glare could kill. Hell, if I were Thayer, I wouldn't eat anything Dante made for me. He's here, next to his guard, wearing a crisp white T-shirt, khakis, and deck shoes. It's like he's about to pull into a dockside bar in Miami. There's just something about the guy. I feel like I've seen him before. Not in person . . . but like on social media. But that doesn't make sense. Men with small army forces don't plaster their faces all over social platforms.

"Whoa, look at this place. You've made yourself a regular Swiss Family Robinson attraction. You could sell this to an amusement park. But I guess that's already been done?" He laughs.

Haley and Sam are behind him.

"Well, show me around, Hal." He glances back at Haley.

"This is it. Three platforms, living room, sleeping, and our version of a bathroom. It's lovely." There's trepidation in her voice, and I fucking hate it. I'm pretty sure it's fear, but there's a chance it's her insecurity sneaking back. I get it. We don't know what is going on with Thayer. And talking about it as a group isn't possible because Dante's right. He set that room up for us. They'll be listening. At least tonight we'll be able to write notes to each other and get a few private thoughts across.

"That's all you want to take, Easton?" Mr. Z asks. I hate that we're addressing this ass who's my age as Mr. Z and he's calling me by my first name. It's getting under my skin. But I'm sure that's another one of his methods: get us off-guard, especially me.

The thing is, Mr. Z isn't here out of the goodness of his heart. No, he wants something. There are three things he could want: The Rock Candy, which doesn't make sense. We don't have it, and anyone who can afford the yacht he has doesn't need it. Second is me. But me alive or me dead? That's the real question. And the third thing is the Pink Phoenix diamond. Seeing that Haley told us Thayer didn't realize Sam floated to the island on the Rock Candy, and the same pirates that took the Rock Candy are the same ones who came to the island, it stands to reason the older Mr. Z. knew about Sam being here . . . and also knew that the diamond wasn't on the Rock Candy. Sure, it's an expensive diamond. And murders happen every day for a lot less. A lot less.

I look to the beach where the Rosewood's anchored offshore. There's something else. Or maybe there isn't. Maybe it's all the things put together. Dead or alive—the words echo in my head like a bad western movie—that's the question.

"Need any help?" I ask Dante. He's gathered things that people made him, and by people, I mean mostly Calvin and Zane. And honestly, it's refreshing. I would have thought Dante would have dusted his hands of everything here. But he's being a lot more sentimental.

"I'm just about wrapping things up." His box is over-flowing.

So is Zane's and Sam's. I climb up the ladder, but my guard doesn't follow. I see why when I get up to the sleeping platform. Calvin, Haley, and two guards are in the room already. And Mr. Z follows behind me.

"Well, isn't this something? You are all really ingenious. I would have spent the year huddled on the beach covered in seaweed, but look at the lot of you. You've got your own little cuddle pile going here." He walks over to Haley's suit-case, and I pray it's locked. "I can see why you wanted to come back and grab more things. That's some impressive luggage." He turns to me.

"Not mine—Haley's," I say.

"A primary gave it to me a few years ago," Haley answers.

Z raises his eyebrows. "That's a nice tip."

Haley shrugs. "She was a nice person."

"I've never been that nice of a person, have I, Hughes?" Mr. Z. asks one of his guards, who doesn't answer. "No really, Hughes, have I been?"

"You're a fair boss, and that's better than nice."

"A true diplomat," Mr. Z says.

More like a man who wants to keep his job and his life.

Haley has a large pile. "I suppose I don't need to take all

these things. But some of them don't belong to me, and I'd like to give them back."

Z reaches down and picks up one of Emily's shirts. My sister's entire wardrobe, even three years after college, has always been T-shirts and sweatshirts from her college and high school. Living in a couple of houses in Miami and an apartment in New York City, she just filled her closets with them. Then when she turned environmentalist, I think she felt bad about the waste and decided to adopt them as her permanent uniform.

Z drops the college shirt and picks up one of Emily's Pine Green Academy shirts. "Oh, I think we can find room for your friend's things." He smiles at Haley but doesn't put the shirt down. Instead, he carefully folds it and rolls it up. Just the way Emily always does. I'm staring at him—Z. It's just a quintessential motion. A lot of people must fold their T-shirts and then roll them. "Let's get Ms. Brewster a third box." He motions for his guard, who radios to the tender. I want to ask him if he knows anything about my sister and dad, but I don't want to give him that power over me. "Anything else here?" Z asks.

"Just this pile," Haley says. She folds her arms over her chest and turns to look around the room. I don't think she's going to cry again, but I might. Fuck. From day one, I thought we would be rescued. Not that I think Z is rescuing us. But this place—yeah, I could just stay.

Calvin's hovering close to Haley. And I see the way the guards are watching us all. It might be my imagination, but it feels like they're all trying to figure out who's with her. I pick up her suitcase and attach it to the rope, lowering it to the ground. Zane unlatches it. I could have carried it, but it was fun to use the pulley one more time.

"Right, well, I'll see you all back on board for dinner.

You'll need to make sure your pockets are emptied. You'll be checked for weapons and any contraband. Cell phones, knives, paper—everything in the box, please. I'll have the stews wash your clothes and deliver them to your cabin." He takes a few steps. "Mr. Rockwell, would you join me on the beach?"

My heart slams into my chest. This is fucking it. Haley grabs my hand and squeezes it.

"Alone," Z says bluntly.

"Anything you want to say, you can say in front of them." I motion to . . . to my friends—my family.

"Alone, just you and me. And Holloway standing off in the distance."

My guard furrows his eyebrows and pushes me with the motion of his eyes.

"That's not exactly alone." I let Haley's hand drop and follow Z.

"It is to me."

I follow him silently out to the beach, where he waves off everyone but his chief and me.

"Ingenious," Z says, sitting on the big rock. He points to the fish weir.

"It fed us most days."

Chapter 2

Murky Water

Sam

I'm bracing myself for the sound of a gunshot. Though it's not logical. Out of all of us, Easton's the one worth something . . . though it has crossed my mind more than once that sinking the Rock Candy would have taken out all the Rockwells.

Shadows flicker on the path. I'm about to let out a sigh of relief, but it's Holloway. By himself. He nods to us men. I turn to Dante next to me. He's glowering, his normal carefree smirk long vanished. There's a vibration coming off him that says he could snap at any minute. I put my box down on the table. It doesn't have much in it. My logbook and the book Haley made me. Penny's things, her life vest and bowls. My Rock Candy jacket with my name on it mocks me from the top of the pile.

Zane comes down the ladder, his box overflowing.

"Here, let me help you," I offer.

"Thanks, Cap." He hands me down his box. It's a mixture of clothes, tools both from the derelict and from the

Rock Candy. His phone lies on top of his clothes. The five of us are gathered around the table.

"It's a good table." I tap the top of it and look over at Zane and Calvin.

"Thanks," Zane says. His throat bobs with a visible swallow. "You need any help, Chef?"

"I'm done." Dante takes his box from the counter. It's packed with precision, things rolled up in banana leaves, the contents flush with the top of the box.

The guard watching Calvin steps up. "Holloway, you want me to start taking the boxes to the tender?"

Holloway glares. "Z said alone. No one goes on the beach until Z says so." Holloway's watching from the opening of the path.

"Copy," the guard says and steps back. I don't blame the guy. I don't want to stand next to Calvin right now, either. There are waves of anger pouring from him too.

This isn't a rescue mission. But why go to the trouble of getting our pets and letting us gather our things? Unless he wants to make Easton think that everything's okay? Is this about the diamond? I glance at Zane. He's got the same focused expression he had when he was working out the codes. We need some time alone. Even back in the room, I can't talk.

Dante moves from the kitchen area over to the chairs next to the Christmas tree. It's been gathering new shells and trinkets since the holidays. "Come here, Sassy." Dante holds his hands out for Haley. She's slow to move from the table. It's weirdly quiet. Like the island knows we're leaving one way or another. It's going to be alone with the boars and goats. The chickens…I glance over at the pen, but someone has already let them out. They'll be fine, filling in the gash we've left on the land.

Haley settles on the arm of the chair Dante's sitting in, between Dante and Calvin. And I'm glad she's there.

"You," Dante says.

"Me?" Haley asks, pointing to her chest.

"It's always you." There's a brief flicker of a smirk. "But no, him." Dante points around Haley to one of the younger guards. "Did you work for—"

The guard cuts him off with a nod.

"You like my Lasagna al Forno. Harris, right?"

"I'm loyal to Mr. Z."

"Didn't say you weren't," Dante says.

It's quiet. I'm not the only one trying to hear what's going on on the beach. When I glance back to Dante, he and Calvin are involved in a nonverbal conversation. Dante touches his right shoulder and flicks his eyes to Harris. Harris has moved next to Holloway, distancing himself from Dante.

Yesterday, silently whispering together, we made one decision: to not ask about the other raft. To not let them hold that over us. I'm a patient man. More patient than the others here. At least, that's how I used to think of myself. But not anymore. I want to know if they're okay. Rocky, Emily, and the crew. But mostly Anders. I've come to think of him as a brother.

Fuck it, it's been bothering me. "Did the other raft get picked up? My crew? Easton's sister and dad."

The guards say nothing. None of them. One rubs the side of his face. He's got a long scratch down his cheek. He glares back but says nothing. The only ones who have talked to us more than "get in," "go here," "get out" are Holloway and the chief stew.

I scan their faces until I get to Holloway standing by the

path to the beach. I hold his stare. "They're people. With families, jobs. Hard workers. Just like all of you."

"You knowing about them doesn't change their fate," Holloway says. The asshole might be right. But it makes a difference to me, and I know it makes a difference to Haley. Her blue eyes flick to me before settling back on Dante.

"Perhaps not, but it would ease our minds."

"Or send you into grief," Holloway counters.

Haley gasps.

"Relax. I don't know anything about your crew." Holloway looks through the blind to the beach. He's got the best view out of anyone, being almost on the path. "Mr. Z's coming." He cocks his head at the other guards. And I fucking don't like how he's phrased it. Mr. Z's coming. Not Easton and Mr. Z . . . but Easton appears in front of Z.

Haley gasps again. She's got a better view of Easton. I have to take a step to the side before I can see Easton's eye is swollen.

"I tripped," Easton says.

Z has a hand in his pocket. "Yes, you should really be more careful about where you step. Hughes, Holloway, and Harris, you're with me and Rockwell here. The rest of you take the boxes to the Rosewood, along with the rest of our guests."

"No," Haley calls out and runs for Easton. She throws her arms around his neck. A nameless guard steps up to them at the same time as Calvin. I'm there too.

"Back up, Green," Easton says before I can.

"You know, Hal should come with us too. After all, she fits right in with Hughes, Holloway, and Harris," Mr. Z says.

"No," Calvin grunts.

Dante's not yelling, but he's a breath away from strangling Z. Like he's a feral dog on a leash. The four of us move to stand beside Haley. I'm ready to grab Dante around the waist. Laying a finger on Z is definitely a way to die.

"Very interesting. It's such an interesting island, Hal. And I hear you know all about the flora and fauna of the land. I insist that you accompany Mr. Rockwell and myself while the rest of you head to the Rosewood."

There's a poke in my back, and it's not a stick.

"Off you go. You first, Captain. Show your men how to behave." Mr. Z inclines his head to me.

"See you soon." I hold Haley's eyes. This is the toughest thing I've ever done, walking away from her. Walking away from her when I know Z is going to use her to get Easton to do whatever it is he wants. The diamond . . . or something else. "Green, Jones, Morris." I step toward the beach. "Go."

Calvin's got his hand around Dante's wrist. I hate this feeling hopeless. Out of control.

On the beach, they've got our boxes in one tender. The other's empty. Haley's box and suitcase are separated from our things.

"Move in a line next to the tender," a guard says. He's young, early twenties. He's got a wiry smile on his face. And I instantly dislike him.

Zane wades in first, then me. Dante's between me and Calvin, whose feet are barely in the water. My heart's dancing around, making its own rhythm while I'm doing the best I can to not show it. I'm still scared as fuck. There's a group of guards behind, six at least, and three in front of us with the punk. He throws the lead at the bow of the tender but misses. It floats in the front of the tender, slapping against the hull. I'm watching it . . . Zane's watching it too. And when it winds back on a wave and brushes against Zane's hand, he takes it. The tender slows its sideways motion.

"All right, Holloway told me you're doing one of two things: You're getting in the tender without causing a fuss . . ." He stares at each one of us down the line. He's a power-hungry punk.

"Or?" Dante hisses out. And I want to push Dante into the water myself. You don't give a lunatic a reason to shoot you.

The punk squints. "Or your little slut's things take their own boat back to the mainland . . . and we kill you. I don't care much, really."

I want to kill the punk.

Calvin grabs Dante's wrist, and the punk laughs.

"Collins," an older voice behind us growls.

"Just having a little fun. Get in the damn tender." Collins motions with his gun. The front of the tender is swaying left and right. Zane's holding on to the lead rope.

I climb in first, and Calvin and Dante do the same down the line. "Get in the boat, Brit." Collins shoots the water a few feet from Zane.

There are grunts and yelling but not from us—it's the other guards. I lean over and give Zane my hand before the asshole does it again. Zane drops the line and grabs my arm around the wrist. I steady him into the tender.

"Fucking hell, Collins," the older guard says.

"They're listening now," Collins sneers.

The older guard throws his gun around his back and picks up Haley's box and her suitcase. He hands the box to Calvin. "Hold this on your lap." The suitcase, he momentarily holds out to Dante, but even I can see what a convincing weapon the metal shiny case is. He places it in the front hollow of the tender, near Calvin's feet. "Collins, stop being an asshole and take the motor."

Another guard slides in next to me while Collins wades in. The weighted tender with only one rope sways to the side and back with a big wave and knocks Collins on his ass in the surf. It's hard to not laugh, but I manage it. But Dante's got a wide smile on his face now.

Collins grasps the side of the tender, and the guard next to me helps him in. He's drenched from his shoulders down. "You think it's funny, Chef?" Collins glares at Dante.

And I'm praying Dante keeps—

"Yes."

Damn it. Listening devices or not in the cabin, I'm having words with Dante. He's going to get himself or someone else killed.

"Shut the fuck up, Chef. You too, Collins," the old guy grumbles. "Move over—I'm going to pilot the damn thing. You'd probably run us aground."

"Whatever, Durant. I know how to drive the tender."

"Sure. And Chef, I don't want to see another smirk out of you or hear a fucking word come out of your mouth."

Dante nods.

"Bunch of fucking babies," Durant says and pulls the cord starting the outboard.

I watch the island slip away. The only good thing about the lunatic Collins is it's made me forget about Haley and Easton being out there on the island—somewhere.

"Toss the rope, deckhand," Durant says, turning the rudder like a pro.

Zane takes the wet bow line and tosses it to the Rosewood deckhand. We're marched up the stairs and down the side deck, Durant behind us, another guard in the front.

"Hold up, Durant—I want to have a word with the Chef

there," Collins says behind him. We're single file. A random guard, Dante, Calvin, Zane, me, and then Durant. The Rosewood's a beast of a yacht, but the outside deck isn't meant for passengers. It's a working strip along the top for deckhands to work the lines.

"Take it up with Z," Durant says. "Keep moving."

"No. I want to teach him to have respect," Collins says.

Metal slaps against the side of the Rosewood. It's a quick click. But I'm fast enough to press forward into Zane. Durant's got Collins' gun in one hand, and his other hand he's got wrapped around the young guy's neck. He headbutts him, and it sounds like a hammer hitting metal. And with a shove, Collins is falling backwards into the ocean. It's a good twenty-five foot drop to the choppy water below.

The splash thuds upward, and when Collins surfaces, Durant is pointing his own gun at him. "You need to learn manners just as much. Now swim before I fucking shoot you," Durant says, following him with the barrel of his gun.

"Hey, everything okay down there, Durant?" a voice says from the crow's nest.

"Good. I'm taking our guests back to their cabin. Have Collins locked up until Holloway gets back."

"Collins?" the voice asks.

"He'll be on the swim platform."

"Fucking kids," the voice says.

"Damn right." Durant slings Collins' gun over his shoulder. "Metal plate in my head from a car accident when I was twenty. Don't drink and drive."

"No way, mate," Zane says.

"Now move," Durant barks.

Chapter 3

Inventory

Haley

I take Easton's hand, my attention glued to the bruise rising above his eye. It's red and swollen with a nasty purple splotch. A trickle of blood rolls down the side of his face. I don't ask if he's okay. He's furious, but he hides it a heck of a lot better than Calvin or Dante. His "swim meet face" is what I call it. Like he's ready to take on world-class competitors.

Harris takes the lead as we walk down the path to the waterfall. Did Easton tell them he buried the diamonds out here? Is that why we're walking this way? It must be. I don't ask questions. But the list of things Calvin taught me about running and keeping quiet in the woods plays on repeat in the back of my head. *Keep your breathing steady, Chiefie—deep in, deep out—so when it's time to run, your legs will listen to you and not to your panic. Watch where you're stepping. Be quick. Remember, doubling back is sometimes the best way to throw people off.* Not that I'm going to run. Not unless Easton gives me a sign.

I do my best to remain calm, but no amount of box-breathing is going to get me through this. Not alone. My heart rattles around inside my ribs, ready to burst out of my body. Breathe in for four counts, hold for four counts, out for four counts . . . yeah.

Harris's shoulders brush along the fronds rattling in front of us. He's staying to one side of the path, keeping Easton in his peripheral vision. I would never have noticed something like that before. Mr. Z—Thayer—is right behind us, and the two other guards are behind him. I'm running scenarios, over and over; is there anything I could do to over-power Thayer? But no. Not with three giant guys with guns. And that bruise on Easton's face? That's most likely from Thayer. His guard came back to camp from the beach fast, so I don't think he's the one who hit Easton. There wouldn't have been time.

"What's this tree, Hal?" Mr. Z asks from behind me.

"Nephrolepis species, I believe, sword fern. At least, that's what I've been calling it." I've named everything from memory, or created names myself. It's going to be almost impossible to unlearn the mistakes I've made. Talking about plants gives me a sense of security that I shouldn't have.

"Violent—I like it. And this one?" He bends the frond down.

"Banana." I smile politely. There are small green fruits hanging above our heads.

"Oh, of course. A banana frond. Did you know that, Holloway?"

"Yes."

"Right, Florida man. Well, not that type of Florida Man," Thayer says without a hint of sarcasm.

Where is Thayer from? He's got a vaguely European accent, but he knows about Florida Man, the joke that men from Florida commit heinously stupid crimes, like breaking into the zoo to wrestle an alligator or calling the police on themselves to report they're high. He knows a thing or two about the States. I have a list of questions I want to ask him, but now's not the time. I need to be alert.

"Sword fern and banana. What about this one?"

"Stop it, Mr. Zzzz." Easton draws the letter out. "Leave her alone."

"I'm just asking her about her degree. Or rather, almost-degree." He's trying to get me—us—worked up. I take Easton's hand and squeeze it. Calm. I try and push at him telepathically. His blue eyes hold mine. And we're quiet for a few minutes, the only sound the rustle of Harris's shoulders hitting the fronds as he walks.

My throat narrows, and I'm back to doing the box-breathing. I don't need a degree to be a stew. I want to defend myself, but that's pointless. He's trying to get under my skin, and letting him know he's succeeding will give him power. Dante told me a long time ago, "Don't give anyone your power." I'm holding my breath until the perfect counterpoint pops out.

"What about the other raft? You know so much about me, about all of us. You must know what happened to our friends on the other raft, to Easton's family," I ask. Sam asked about it while Easton and Z were on the beach, but the guards didn't answer, just gave me a small heart attack when Holloway said it might set us to grieving. Then he retracted it. I'm tired of their games, but I already know that Thayer is a master player toying with his prey. He's come a long way from somewhere to track us down, when a man like him could easily have sent hirelings after us instead.

Easton flashes me a look. He must know already. He thins his lips at me and shakes his head. What does that mean? No, they're dead? No, Thayer doesn't know? I'm not sure which Easton is trying to tell me.

"The other raft? The one from the Rock Candy?" he asks, and if it weren't for the three guys holding guns, I'd punch him. Instead, I keep my lips sealed, just like when the primary in Ibiza asked specifically for Dom Pérignon champagne in her preference sheet. When I poured her a glass on the first day of charter, she went nuts, smashing her glass on the deck because it wasn't Cristal. Later in the day, I overheard her talking to her friend about how you had to be a little crazy to keep the staff on their toes. The rest of the trip, I poured Veuve Clicquot (cheapish, relatively speaking) champagne into a Cristal bottle, and she never said a word. It's good, but nowhere near as good as the other two labels, and anyone who likes champagne should be able to tell the difference between the three of them. Did I feel guilty about it for a month? Yes, but . . . Fine, I still feel guilty about it.

"Thay-er." I draw out his name like I'm scolding a small child or a primary. Which quite often feels like the same thing.

"Yes, Hal." He doesn't bite at my tone but stops and smiles at me. It's smooth. "I know about the other raft."

"And?"

"We'll see how Easton behaves here. Maybe I'll tell him . . . if he earns the knowledge for knowledge, as they say. You've got to give something to get something." His brown eyes twinkle. The curls on the top of his hair blow around lightly with the breeze that's coming down the path from the waterfall. I can almost hear it even from this far away. You can always hear it long before you can see it. Thayer's handsome, I suppose. If you can see past the asshole, godlike demeanor. Which I can't. Power-grabbing asshole is all I can see.

"Life isn't always fair, Thayer."

Hughes makes a noise. Apparently, I'm not to call him by his first name. But I don't care. He's either going to kill us or he's not. I hope it's not. But . . .

"It's Mr. Z, Hal." His right eyebrow goes up like a professor reprimanding a student. "You're right. Things aren't equal. Easton here is going to get me what I want and I won't kill you, not today at least." Thayer's gaze slips from me to Easton, and he slaps him on his back. "Keep it moving, Hughes. Got to keep this H party on its toes."

"Yes, sir," Hughes says and steps out a little faster than we were going before, his shoulder smacking the fronds as he does.

We're almost to the waterfall. It's loud, and today it seems even louder. Like the island is mad, just like my guys. Just like me.

Hughes breaks through the last part of the jungle and steps into the clearing around the waterfall. "Damn, I saw it last night, but it's even prettier in the daylight."

Holloway clears his throat behind us. Hughes steps out of the way and positions himself before us, in a military stance. Thayer's threatened by his employees having thoughts. That's never a good thing. People should have their own thoughts. But maybe not when they are carrying large guns, or at least the person paying you to carry the gun doesn't want you to have your own thoughts. Honestly, if he gets us back to the mainland, any mainland, I don't care what he does to his employees, as long as we're alive. He could have them stand on the fly bridge and quack like ducks for all I care. I just want us to get back to civilization in one piece. All of us. I'll worry about what that means later.

"Holloway, please take the lovely Hal over there." Thayer cocks his head to a tree.

"Haley." Holloway steps around Thayer.

"Don't touch her. I'll get you what you want," says Easton.

Thayer cocks his head to Holloway.

"Serious, Z, I'm getting it." Easton walks around Thayer and Hughes, up the rest of the way, and backs down the path to the big rock. He crouches first at the wrong rock. And I don't mean to, but I flinch.

"What do you know, Hal?"

"Nothing. I don't know anything. I'm nervous because . . . guns." My throat is closing up.

"I see. Such a delicate lady. I can see why they are all so smitten with you." Thayer shrugs.

"Don't touch her," Easton growls. He's still digging under the wrong rock. The right one has a different color to it—it's two below the one where he's digging. Every time we came to the waterfall, I'd stare at it—not for long, but long enough to make sure I didn't forget which rock it is. And I know Easton hasn't forgotten, either. He has a fantastic memory. I told him my mother's birthday once, and six months later, he pampered me all day long, even though I didn't tell anyone on the actual day. Then when we went to bed, he asked me if I wanted to share stories about my mom. So I know he hasn't forgotten. There's no way.

What I don't know is why he's digging in the wrong spot. Does he want more time? Is he not going to give it to them? Easton grabs a chunk of bark and digs deeper and deeper until there's a large pile of dirt around his feet. Thayer's moved over and sits on the ledge above the path.

His white pants aren't going to be white for long. There's an irrational pang of empathy for whomever the stew is in the laundry room.

Thayer kicks his feet over the side. "Do you need some help there, Rockwell?"

"I've got it." Easton glares at Mr. Z.

"Harris, help Rockwell," Mr. Z barks.

"Yes, sir," he says, and I wonder if Dante will be able to make him less loyal to Thayer. Is there even the tiniest bit of connection leftover from their time on the Russian yacht together? I know I always help out other stews that I've worked with. Even difficult ones. Once, in the Med, I gave three bottles of rosé to a stew I had worked with a couple of seasons before. She'd forgotten to order any from her provisioner, and she had ten women on board celebrating a fortieth birthday.

Harris moves closer on the path, but there's not enough space for the three giant men.

"It's a small hole, Z," Easton says. "I think I have the wrong rock. Let me try this one here." He pushes the dirt back into the hole and takes the rock one up from where he had been digging, farther away . . . and now I'm wondering if he really has forgotten where the diamonds are.

Mr. Z cocks his head at Harris, and he moves away.

Chapter 4

Rocks Ahead

Easton

I'm at the reasonable bottom of the third hole. The undersides of my fingernails are black with dirt. I'm dragging this out as long as I can . . . and Z's losing his patience with me. I don't glance up, but I know he's glaring.

Haley is crouched twenty feet away with Holloway leaning on a tree behind her. Hughes is looking at the clouds coming in and out of the jungle canopy. I've caught Harris more than once watching the waterfall instead of me. It's a fine line between getting shot and distracting them enough with boredom that they don't notice when I find the bag.

"Yeah, it's not this one either. I know it's one of these rocks. Sorry." I say it convincingly. It's not an excellent trait, but in a pinch, I can lie with the best of them. *"No, Susan, I don't know where your good scissors went—I don't even know what they look like"; "Dad, I'm training and there's no way I can come for a week on the Mermaid's Tale with you."*

Fuck, that last one I wish I could undo. I'd give anything to spend a week with my sister and my dad now.

Z stands. "Harris, keep an eye on him. I have to go to the banana tree."

"Yes sir!" Harris says, though he's startled.

Z cocks his head at me and brushes off his pants. And this is my opportunity. Holloway and Haley are far enough back that they can't see the bottom of the pits when I dig them. The second Z turns around, I casually push the dirt into the last hole I dug, moving the next rock—the right one—aside. Holloway's watching me, but the other two are watching Z leave.

"How long are we going to be here?" Harris raises his chin at Holloway.

"Until Z says we're done," Holloway growls.

I check to make sure Z's really gone. Haley catches my eye. She sees that I'm on the right rock. I give her a quick wink and cock my head slightly at Holloway as I make my way through the dirt. It's not as loose as I thought it would be. The rainy season has compacted it down, but it's still a lot easier digging than the other holes, and I'm almost to the bag when I flash my eyes to Haley.

She gives the tiniest of nods back and sneezes. It's an adorable sneeze.

"Bless you," Hughes says.

All three of the guards are looking at her as she holds up her hand.

"Thank you." Two more high-pitched adorable sneezes come out of her, and then she coughs. But the funny thing is, that's really what happens to her when she sneezes. Then, through her cough, she says, "Do you have any water?" Right on cue.

"Sure." Holloway looks down at his belt. I scratch

through the last bit of dirt and fight with the knot on the top of the bag. But it comes open, and I slip my hand into the bag and take one of the diamonds out. The real one? The fake one? I have no idea. I just know I've got a 100% shot of having something to barter with later. And those years of practicing magic during middle school swim practice . . . This is far better than impressing people at poker games with my fancy card shuffling abilities. I palm the diamond and slip it into the waistband of my shorts. I'll have to find a place to hide it. I push dirt over the bag and poke at the side of the hole, waiting for Z to come back. Which is taking a lot longer than I thought it would. I'm digging beside the covered bag with Holloway watching me when there's a crunch of gravel behind me.

"What's that in the bottom?" Z's voice bottoms out.

"There it is. I told you." I pull out the bag, shake the dirt and clay off it again, and hand it to Z.

Z raises his eyebrow and purses his lips. "What's this?" he asks. And I'm momentarily nervous that he's a gem expert.

"It's the Pink Phoenix," I say with as much conviction as I can.

"Very good, Rockwell. I can see that, but there are other diamonds in here, and a necklace."

I swallow. The necklace was my mother's. A sentimental piece that I know Emily would want to have back. Even though she doesn't like flashy jewelry, it was Mom's. "The necklace belonged to my mom." I'd slipped it in at the last minute along with the loose diamonds.

"Oh, Susan." Z nods, like he's some long-lost friend.

"She was my stepmother. I'm talking about my real mother. The loose diamonds were Candy's."

"Candy. Interesting taste in woman, your father had," Z

says. *Had* as in past tense. My shoulders tense, and I want to throw up. He's referring to Candy, not Dad. Not Emily. I have to believe that.

"He tends to . . . not see the problems in people. Do you know him?"

"Not directly. No."

"Indirectly, then?" I push.

"On paper. I like to be thorough. I'm not a fan of surprises."

I'm guessing he doesn't like playing by other people's rules. Well, fuck him. He might have the guns behind him, but we're going to figure out how to get out of this. I might have played by the set of guidelines he gave me back on the beach, but I'm done having fists connect with my eye sockets. I wince as I think about it. It's tender. There's an urge in me to touch the side of my face where it's swelling. But giving him the satisfaction of knowing he hurt me isn't going to happen. "Surprises can be a lot of fun."

He walks toward Haley holding the Pink Phoenix up in a spot of dappled light. Did he hear me? His lips part, and he drops it back into the bag. "Surprises are never fun."

"What about surprise parties?" Haley steps closer to me.

"Hate them," Z says.

"That's sad. But I understand." Haley smiles at him, and I can hear her thinking how sad it is that he doesn't like spontaneous fun. "What about puppies?"

"No."

"Gifts, presents?" she asks.

"I can buy whatever it is I need," he fires back.

"There are some things you can't buy."

"Like what?"

"Expecting your coffee to be cold because you forgot to drink it, but it's still warm."

He raises his eyebrow at her, and she smirks back.

"Okay, that's a minor surprise, but it's still nice, like seeing a rainbow or a shooting star. Having someone remember and make your favorite meal for you, or having someone bring you a coffee when you didn't ask for it. Surprises don't have to be adrenaline-rushing horrible events."

"Yet they usually are horrible things. Wouldn't you rather know you're in control of your surroundings? That's the perfect ideal, really. Knowing what's going to happen. That you'll always have what you need when you need it. The Rock Candy having issues? That certainly was a surprise for you."

Haley has her stew face on. But I know there's more she wants to say. I can see it in the way her shoulders arch up, the angle of her head. She wants to unload her tank of never-ending optimism on him. But I know the type. He's got the mini army and the black AmEx card to make the world move the way he wants. She could name a thousand positive little things. Like waking up and listening to a rainstorm in the middle of the rainy season. And thinking you were going to have to check the fish weir in the rain, but then the din of drops on the old metal slows and stops and the sun comes out. Or turning the corner on a trail you've taken a hundred times and spotting a new coconut tree laden with ripe fruit. He's never going to understand. He's had everything he wanted his entire life. Yeah, I know who Z is . . . he's who I used to be. Who I never want to be again.

"If you hate surprises so much . . . why don't you tell us what's really going on here?" Haley puts her hands on her hips.

"Well, Hal, I might hate surprises, but you both seem to like them so much I think I should keep something for later. Now go. It's getting to be midday, and the captain wants to be away from the island." Mr. Z holds out his hand, ushering her down the path.

When we're back on the path and about to step back into the thick of the jungle, I can't help but take in the beauty of the waterfall. One last time. Taking in the things I learned here. If I could, I'd . . . I'd never leave. My chest fills with a large breath frozen in my chest. The feelings of this place are what I need. Haley's what I need.

I need her safe.

Safe.

Fuck.

Hughes presses the muzzle of his gun into the middle of my back. "Move."

Holloway's behind him. Harris and Z are in the lead.

I take Haley's hand; it fits in mine so perfectly. I give it a squeeze and add a wink.

"Move," Hughes barks again. "You heard Mr. Z."

"Indeed," I say. Stepping out, I guide Haley in front of me. Harris's gun disappears from my back. The stream's flowing next to us as we trudge back to camp. It's got to be close to a hundred degrees, but I don't even feel it anymore. Z's guards, dressed all in black, have sweat glistening on their faces.

We're almost past the side trail to one of the boar traps, the one that killed the pirate, when Hughes behind me clears his throat loud enough to make both Haley and me turn.

"Oi, what's up with the lot of you? I thought she was with the big cranky one?" Hughes asks.

"Hughes," Holloway growls at him.

Z stops. "That is a good question. I'll allow it," he declares, like he's some sort of judge on a gilded platform. My blood is boiling, and if they come down on Haley . . . If the ass calls her anything but what she is—the love of my life, the most amazing woman on the planet, the soul that saved me from myself—I'm going to end up dead, that's for sure. There's nothing I wouldn't do for this woman. I squeeze her hand tightly. But she shakes her head.

"We're family," Haley says in a clear voice. Like she's announcing a menu with no options. End of statement.

"Well, my family doesn't share a bed," Hughes says.

"Family," Z says and starts back up the trail. "You know, whatever worked for you on the island worked for you on the island." Z doesn't turn around.

"They will always be my family." Haley squeezes my hand again, and it ricochets through my body.

Fuck this.

"I love her. We all do."

"Interesting," Z says without turning around.

Haley squeezes my hand again. Though there's a giant hole in my stomach that I've opened Pandora's box. Sure, they already knew, but now I've given Z even more to hold over our heads.

Walking through camp, Haley has my hand in a death grip. Her head's down, staring at her feet. And I get it. It's so different. Dante's workstation's disassembled. The shutters on the treehouse are shut tight. The driftwood tree is empty. Even my sad ornament, that had mostly fallen apart, is gone, packed in Haley's tub of things.

Haley leans into my arm. "I can't look. It's too empty."

"Are you serious—" Hughes starts off again, but there's a thud and he stops. Holloway must have smacked him.

Haley clings to my arm as we leave the camp, her forehead to my skin. I help her into her life jacket, click it around her waist. There are tears welling on her lower lashes. "Come on, Firefly." I help her into the raft, and she doesn't even mind. There's no "I got it" or rolling of the eyes that she's as capable as one of the guys. She snuggles into me again. But I lift her chin to the beach and lean into her ear. There's no whispering, not with the motor, not with the breaking waves over the reef. "It was a good home. But you're my home. As long as we have each other, it's going to be all right." I put my arm around her and shield her from the wind the best I can with our bulky life jackets.

Her eyes flick to the gun that Hughes is holding. The way he's glaring at us . . . And I get it—our home is under attack. We have no home. Not yet. Civilization has found us, and we're far from safe.

Chapter 5

Cartographer

Dante

"**Y**ou could move your giant head, Green."

"I could, but why would I?" He doesn't move.

I can hear Haley. *It's okay to sometimes count in your head before you say something that might not be the best thing.* Fuck it. "Because you're being a selfish prick."

"Not helpful, Dante." Zane stands and leans flush with the wall. He's been going over the wall to see if he can find a camera. "This is helpful." He points to a seam in the wall.

"There?" Calvin asks. His huge head leaves the glass, and he makes his way to the wall where Zane is looking.

Sam looks up from where he's not reading a ten-year-old paperback novel on the sofa. "Here too." His index finger points to the seam on the sofa.

I plop down next to him and place my hand over the seam, feeling around until my fingernail catches a small metal button, maybe a centimeter wide. It's not a button, though. The seam's open. That's got to be one heck of a view.

Calvin thunders over to where I have the one on the sofa under my hand. I lift my palm, and he places his hand on top of it. "Fuck."

"Small, just like you." I hold his blue eyes, and he shakes his head.

"Fuck you, Chef."

"No, thank you. Did you see anything out there?"

"No."

"They lifted the anchor a while ago," Sam says. "We're sailing soon." The engines are running.

We all feel it, even me. But none of us have said anything about it. It's not something any of us want to think about, leaving here without Haley—or even Swimmer Boy.

"They'll be here soon." Zane goes back to combing the wall. I don't see any point. One camera, two, three, or five thousand. They all mean that anything we talk about is something that Z will know about.

"Let's pass the time. Take off your shirt." I glare up at Calvin.

"Fuck no," Calvin says.

"Just do it. Lie down on the bed, face-down."

"No."

"You do it, Zane."

"I'm not gonna." Zane crosses his arms in front of his chest and leans against the small device in the wall.

"For fuck's sake, it's not sexual. Just lie down. And the two of you twats gather around."

"Dante?" Sam says.

Working for the Russian, I learned not to trust anyone. That's been something I've had to unlearn this year. Trusting and being trusted. Worrying about someone other than myself. Other than my sister and her kids, my mom, I don't care for anyone. Yeah, that's been a lot. Z's taken a page from the Russian.

There's nothing in this room we could write with, nothing to make a weapon out of. Well, I suppose give Calvin enough time and he'll figure out how to take apart the bed frame and whittle some kind of weapon. But that's the thing with guys like Z. Time is theirs, not yours.

"We haven't had a proper bed in forever. I'm going to show you the muscle groups to give a proper massage." I say it with enough confidence that I almost believe it myself when it's utter bullshit.

Zane drops onto the bed. "I like it a hell of a lot more when Haley does this."

Sam and Calvin are hanging back.

"Get closer, you fuckers." I drag a finger down Zane's spine. "This is the spine. These are the ribs." I write an H with my index finger on Zane's back.

"I know that." Calvin looks at me like I've lost my head.

And I draw the H again. "Do you?"

"Haha," Zane says with annoyance. He's clearly gotten the idea of what I'm doing.

I turn to Sam, who hasn't come that close to the bed, and hold his eyes as I do it again. I flash my eyes as I do it.

"Haha," Zane says again.

The blinds go up in Sam's eyes, and he sits on the side of the bed. Shielding one side of Zane from any cameras.

Calvin wrinkles his forehead.

"You're the anthropologist, Calvin. What muscle is this?" Sam writes H-O, and I move closer, leaning over Zane, keeping the view of his back from two more sides.

"Right, that's Latissimus Dorsi." Calvin covers the other side, leaning over Zane's legs.

Sam's writing speeds over Zane's back now. *How do you know Z wants—*

Calvin moves Sam's hand. "This is the Trapezius." *Heard him on phone with dad—who wants us dead.* "This is the Iliocostalis Lumborum. I think. It's been a long time."

How, I write back.

Cat ran back deck. He no see me. I hope. Calvin looks up at me and over to Sam.

"Are you understanding the muscle groups, Zane?" Sam asks.

"Enough to pass a test that we're all going to fail." Zane turns his head on the pillow. "But I do have a question about the muscle groups on my chest."

"Ah, yeah. Those are important." Sam moves back, letting Zane flip.

"Like, what are these here?" Zane writes. *How keep Haley safe?*

And the door opens.

It's the old guard, Durant, the one who pushed the punk off the boat. "What the hell are you doing?" You know what? I don't fucking care. Just get up. Z's back, and he wants to see you."

Zane grabs his shirt, and we're out the door and into the corridor.

I don't gawk at boats. I've been on all kinds of yachts. New ones that you have to peel the plastic off the appliances, old ones that you have to scrape years of grease out of from chefs that had no idea how to keep a galley clean. And I don't give a shit. Because a new yacht can be a piece of shit, just as well as an old one—the Rock Candy as an example. Though we've got enough evidence that proves the mishap on the Rock Candy wasn't the mechanics of the ship's fault. More like the elder Z's fault. But damn, the Rosewood is fine.

And it pisses me off that I'm even thinking about it. I'd like to see the galley . . . but what I'd really like to see is a lot of us not on it. Back in Miami, maybe catching a gourmet meal at the food trucks at the beach. Or just sleeping in a soft, huge bed. Air-conditioning, a stocked fridge, sleeping in safety—that's what I want. Haley tucked away. Fuck the galley of the Rosewood.

A guard drops in behind Calvin, who's behind me. Zane's in front of me, following Durant. We take a turn and go down a level. So far, I've only been on the top level and this one, where our cabin is.

"In you go," Durant says, pointing with his beefy fingers, his other hand resting on top of his compact assault rifle. It's the same type my old boss used to have his guys use. Though he wasn't nearly as well organized as old Z, and I'm thinking Z's got more money behind him. Things are top end. Everywhere.

The walls of the room are polished ochre honey mahogany—floor to ceiling. Overhead lights fill the port-hole-less room, which must have been designed as a media center. But this one is decked out like a weird boardroom. Ten tall-backed leather desk chairs surround a long black table.

"Have a seat," Durant says and leaves the room.

"Where do you think Easton and Haley are?" Zane asks, no trace of his normal smile around.

Sam puts his hand on Zane's shoulder and pulls out one of the leather chairs on wheels. He sits and motions for us to sit too.

But I've got other things I want to do. At the head of the table there's an intercom, and next to the intercom, there's a stack of small notepads and pens. With the guards outside, I take two of each, slipping a notepad and pen into my pocket. I sit across from Sam. Zane's next to him. I draw a bird, then a house. When I look up, I realize that Sam and Zane are studying what I'm doing. "Just drawing."

"Oh." Zane's shoulders drop. He takes one, and his pen strokes are different from mine. Assured, a real house appears compared to the one on my page. Mine looks like a preschooler drew it. But that's fine. I push a notepad to Sam, but then pull it back and split it in two. If they don't know how many were here, perhaps they won't miss the one I took.

"What are you drawing?" Sam asks.

"Nothing," I say.

"Not you. Zane."

I shrug but glance up. On the second page of Zane's notepad, he's drawn the blueprint of the Rosewood—or the little we know about it. Haley's seen more than the four of us.

He's sketched out five decks. Sam taps the paper. "Six."

Zane's eyebrows shoot up. "Really?"

"It's modified."

Zane's pen moves across the page. He lifts the pen every so often, filling things in with a lighter line that are guesses. I have no idea if it's going to help us, but fuck, we have to try. We're at it long enough to fill in the whole diagram. There's no way they're going to let us keep it. No way they're not watching us as we do it. But we finish the whole thing.

Calvin's finger slides across the page. "Cat room, boiler, engines, lounge."

We're done after a few minutes, and we're studying the schematics. But what's the point? There are too many men, too much firepower. These aren't a bunch of unorganized pirates. They are a highly trained killing force.

I lean back in the chair and close my eyes, calming my system. In a way, being locked in a porthole-less room is more soothing. I don't have to fight the Viking for window access to see if Sassy is on her way back to the boat. I'm more on edge than ever. And there's no surprise to me. Being on the ship reminds me too much of how I hated working for the Russian.

The door opens, and I jump up.

Holloway's there. But no Sassy or Easton. "Sit down," the beefy guard says.

Kennedy is behind him, wheeling a cart with covered dishes. "Lunch." He places the plates in front of the four of us.

"Where's Haley and Easton?"

Kennedy nods at us, his eyes flashing at our little art projects around the table. He doesn't take them. "Enjoy." He pulls the door closed with a firm click.

The food isn't bad, but it's not good either. Boring. Lacking imagination and zest. But maybe their chef is as eager to get away from Z as I was to get away from the Russian.

With the plates stacked, the table shakes with the bounce of Zane's leg. "You good?" I ask.

"No. I want to see Haley. Easton too." He pushes back from the table and bangs on the side of the door with his fist. "I need to use the loo." His accent is ten times as strong as normal.

The door opens. "Can you wait?" Holloway asks.

"Do you have a bucket?"

"I'll take that as a no. Fine. Let's go." Holloway takes Zane, and the door shuts with a click.

"Fuck." Calvin stands and paces.

"Sit down, Green. We need to keep our shit together."

"We need a plan." Calvin paces behind me.

"We need to keep quiet." Sam points above my head. And he's right. There's a speck about the same size as the one we found in our cabin, behind me on the wall.

"I'm fucking done with being quiet," Calvin yells, and the door slams open.

Chapter 6

Code Breaker

Zane

Holloway hands me off to another guard, one I haven't seen before. There's a shit ton of them. Holloway, Durant, Collins, Hughes, Harris, and at least five others. Ten or more, total. But with as many deckhands and stews as a ship this size requires, how many more can there be? There has to be a maximum. The Rosewood's big, but it's still a bloody boat.

The guard takes me three doors down on the right, not back to our cabin. "Go in. Be fast, and leave the door open."

"Fine, but I'm warning you: I haven't had proper food in a long time, and it's not agreeing with me." There's a little pang of disingenuousness, as Dante's food is more than proper and this is back to normal for me. But I really just want to see if I can find anything out about Haley.

His forehead furrows, but he gets my drift. "Right, then fucking turn on the exhaust too." He pulls the door shut.

The WC has another exotic, dark veneer on the walls and a mirror that goes from the ceiling to the marble-topped counter. I flick on the vent, turn on the water, and make my way to the small porthole above the window. A quick yank, and the wooden blinds are up. We are underway, but I knew that already. There's no land to see outside. I drop the blinds and do what I need to, then wash my hands and leave the water running while I flush. I search under the cabinet, but there's nothing there but a stack of neatly folded towels. And unlike so many other yachts, there are no sanitary products for women. It's weird. I guess there's no women on board at all. There aren't even spots for normal things like cotton buds or cotton balls—standard on all the yachts I've worked on. And nothing to use as a weapon.

The guard pounds on the door. "Are you done?"

I turn the water off and open the door. "I'm good, mate."

"Not your mate," he growls at me.

"It's an expression."

"Yeah, still not your mate or your friend."

"Yeah, you're loyal, like Harris."

The guard scoffs but then schools his expression.

Interesting. "What's the deal with Harris?"

"Nothing." He scowls at me.

I shrug and turn my attention forward down the corridor, away from the conference room. The doors are all closed, and no one is walking around. "You must be happy to be heading back."

He grunts. Like he's upset with himself for letting something slip. He wasn't back at camp when Dante confronted Harris about working with him on the Russian boat.

There are footsteps back toward the conference room. Our heads snap that way. Haley's there, Easton behind her. She's wearing different clothes than she had on this morning. Easton too. There's a bandage over the top of his eyebrow.

"You good?" I'm moving toward them before my guard tells me to move. But he doesn't tell me to stop. And neither does the muscle behind them, another guard I don't recognize. That brings us to at least eleven. He opens the door to the room and ushers Easton and Haley in. I don't know which of them I'm asking, Little Bird or Easton with his bandage.

"We're good," Easton answers for the both of them. His hair is wet and slicked back.

Haley pauses at the door and takes my hand. She flinches when she sees the room. "This is different, quite the private conference space." So it's not the place she had dinner with Z last night. Crazy to think that was only last night.

"It's private, to a point," Z says, his voice bouncing into the room. He's appeared in the doorway like a king scoffing at his subjects, and I want to punch him in the throat. Maybe more of Green and Rockwell has rubbed off on me than I thought. "All right, class, pens down. You can pass your little drawings to the front of the room." Z glares at Calvin, who's sitting at the end of the table.

"Assigned seats?" Calvin pushes back and stands. "By all means, it's all yours."

Z and Calvin stare at each other eye to eye. Calvin's got Z by a couple of inches, but their shoulders are the same width. They've both got their an asshole glare going on.

Haley clears her throat, and heads turn to her. She sits and pulls the chair next to her out for Calvin. Without taking his eyes off Z, Calvin sits next to her. And I take the other side. I grab her hand under the table. I want to feel relief, but it's too soon. From what Calvin told us back in the room, Z's dad wants us dead. So the younger Z is toying with us. Having some sort of sick, twisted fun.

"All right, how was lunch?" Z flips through the pile of papers that one of the guards collected for him. "Some of you have drawing talent, and others . . . not so much." He tosses Dante's notepad with the bird on the smooth table with a slap, and it slides to a stop in front of Haley.

"Oh, I think this is lovely," Haley says, turning to Dante.

"You sound like a toddler's mother, Hal." Z chuckles.

"Just kind."

"This one, *this* one I can get behind." Z holds up the picture that I see in my sleep of the house I designed for Haley. The one for the beach. "A natural talent."

"Nothing natural about me. I had to learn to draw," I say. It took me a long time.

"I like it." Then he flips the page. "Making plans. Of course. Hal's troop of superheroes wouldn't have survived without hope." He crumples up the page and drops it on the floor. "Hope's not here, I'm afraid. Not on the Rosewood." He places the Pink Phoenix on the table and spins it like a top. Reflected spectrum light dances on the table.

It's an expensive diamond. But the cost of coming after us, the cost of what they did to the Rock Candy . . . it doesn't add up. There's more to it than him or his father wanting the diamond.

"Business is business," Z says, but it's like he doesn't mean it.

"What sort of business are you in, Mr. Z?" Sam glares at him.

"Family business. A very long line of a family business." Z twists a signet ring on his finger. There's a crest and four giant rubies in each corner.

"Nice ring," I say as the diamond stops spinning.

"My grandfather's. Now mine."

"A family business," Haley repeats.

"Yes." There're furrows on Z's forehead.

"What sort of business?" Haley cocks her head to the side like she's run into him at the market and is inquiring about his family.

"The kind with a deep history."

"That answers nothing," Dante says. It's the sort of thing that most would say under their breath, but Dante just says it out loud, gunmen or not.

"Yes, rather vague, isn't it? But I don't have time to give you the confessions of five generations. Or maybe I do. Seeing that we're in the middle of nowhere."

"Where exactly are we going, Mr. Z?" Haley asks.

"First? To find a cat shelter before my engineer throws me overboard." Z laughs again, but then his face turns hard and he stares at each one of us around the table.

"What do you want with us, Z?" Calvin growls.

Z glares back. And it's the first time I realize that he doesn't know what he wants with us. Well, other than maybe for us to not be us. I've been on ships for a while. Granted, not as long as Calvin or Sam—or even Haley—but I've learned that rich people aren't people. That's wrong—of course they're people. But some of them have a habit of thinking that everything's going to just work out for them. They make a plan, toss enough cash at the problem, and presto, the plan works. Then when it doesn't, some of them, or rather the second generation of money, don't have the fortitude, the grit to make things work. Or make things work without money. There's something about us that's holding Z back from carrying out his father's orders. Something more than the goodness in his own heart. Though a guy that rescues a bunch of feral cats from an island has to have something in his heart. A guy that lets us go and get our things, Penny. That's not the kind of guy who's going to kill us around a table in the conference room of his ship. At least, I hope so.

A wall slams down over Z's face. A mask. A shiver runs through me. "Stand up. Out." This isn't good. Far from good.

Holloway opens the door, and Z leaves. Easton stands first, following him, and we file out behind him. There's a pit in my stomach. I want to grab Haley and run, but where? How? There is confusion in the corridor with us bunching up. The guards don't know if we're to follow or not. Holloway catches up with Z. They're far enough away that I can't hear what he's saying.

"Follow him." Holloway points. And we're a train after him, though Easton's in no hurry.

I grab Haley's hand. Sam takes her other one. Calvin's behind us, Dante in front. Holloway and the other guard from my bathroom trip are behind him.

There are things I haven't talked about. I've uncoded a lot more of Rocky's book than I told anyone. I'm not quite fluent yet. But close. One thing missing from my stuff when I packed it up was Rocky's book. I'm guessing they had already taken it. But they didn't have the cipher. Still don't. That's back in the ceiling of the treehouse.

A month or so ago, I took it out of the book and hid it in the rafters of the treehouse. In one of the few moments that the guard covering me wasn't looking, I ran my hand over it. It's still there. I took it out of the book because . . . what I know . . . I didn't want Easton to know. There was no point. Not while we were on the island. I found some shit out about my dad after he died—nothing like this, but stuff I'd rather not have known. I still love my dad. He was a good man. When you love someone as much as we both love our dads? Easton didn't need this hanging over him on the island. Now, though? Fucking wish I could tell him.

We're marched through the grand salon, past a fire in the fireplace, and not a gas fireplace but a wood one—craziness—and out onto the sundeck. There's a table and recliners and stairs down to the swim platform.

Z stops on the swim deck. "Head on down there, Rockwell." Z points at Easton.

My heart squeezes against my chest.

Holloway stands next to Easton. "Down you go."

"The rest of you too," Z says.

Easton turns back to Haley and then to Z. Easton's eye twitches. "No one cares about the rest of them. There's no reason to hurt them. You don't need to—"

Z cuts Easton off. "So, they just show up in the middle of what? Singapore or Tokyo? Found, and no one needs to know anything? No loose ends. You know how it has to be, right, Chef?"

Dante glares. "There's more than one way to keep a person quiet. You always have options."

"Right. If it was only that simple. I should pay you off to keep you quiet? Put you back on the island for someone else to find?"

"You could have left us there. We could have died on our own. Less guilt for you. Turn the boat around, and no one will be the wiser," Sam says.

"Oh, there's always plenty who will be the wiser." Z motions to the other guard.

"Move on down. The whole lot of you." There's nothing behind the guard's eyes.

"You don't need to do this." Haley's on the verge of tears. Rightly so. There were plenty of times I thought one or all of us might die in the last year. On the raft, Easton being shot, me almost drowning. The bloody damn boar. The pirates . . . so many times, but I sure as hell didn't think it would be from being assassinated on a swim platform.

"You don't know what's needed—"

"Your father." Calvin's shoulders are back, his head square. He's standing in front of Haley.

Z nods. "Perhaps you do understand."

The problem is, I understand better than all of them. Maybe even better than Mr. Z, seeing as how he hadn't known that the Rock Candy had been found but his father clearly had. "You have Rocky's diary," I blurt. "The book with the numbers—not the phone numbers, but the other one."

"Yes, it's gibberish.

"No, it's a code." Gibberish? "I can read it. I can read it in exchange for letting us go." I turn to Easton. "All of us."

Chapter 7

When in Rome

Haley

I'm not going to fall apart. I want to. I so very want to break apart and fall down on the deck crying in a sobbing mess. But if they're going to shoot me, I don't want to make it easy. I want them to have to look me in the face. Thayer told me he had no problem killing a man. But not a woman. That's why he doesn't have any on his crew. That, and his father sounds like a real womanizing asshole. If he won't shoot me, I might be able to save the guys.

Thayer stares at Zane. Mist from the engines sprays over our backs. It's colder here than on the beach. But I'd give anything to go back. For it to be New Year's Day again. To watch the sun rise over our beautiful beach. To eat nothing but fish and pomelos for another year. I don't want to die. But I don't want my guys to die, either.

"You can read it?" Thayer narrows his eyes at Zane.

"Yeah. It took me fucking forever, but I've recently had a lot of time on my hands." Zane cracks a smile. It's not his real smile but one I'm sure he uses with hard-to-handle guests. Thayer's not a hard-to-handle guest. He's something all on its own. One minute I think he's a reasonable guy, and the next, I'm standing on a swim platform waiting to have a bullet sunk into my head.

Thayer laughs. And I have a moment of hope. "Why should I care?" he growls.

"Because it says things. About Rocky, his partner, and someone else. I had problems figuring it out—I even asked Easton if he knew of an Ed. But Rocky didn't mean Ed, did he? He meant Zed, as in Z. There's more, though. About a Swiss bank account. He was stealing money from the man he was helping launder the money. But there's more. And it took me months to figure out the code."

Thayer flinches. He's so polished it's hard to tell if he knows he flinched. But there was definitely a moment when something Zane said struck a chord with him. Thayer shakes it off quickly and nods. "Without a computer, it took you what? Five months? I'll be able to do it in no time."

"You're a cryptographic code breaker?" Zane's got his arms crossed over his chest, his head cocked sideways like this is a normal afternoon chat.

"You're a bosun." There's a bit of disbelief in Thayer's tone.

And I want to smack Thayer. Dante grabs my wrist like he can read my mind. "Sassy," he whispers.

"And a damn good one. But my hobby is solving cryptograms and puzzles. I can get you the information you need. I know things already that no one but the older Rockwell knows."

My eyes flick over the guys. Sam leans in hopefully. Calvin and Dante are stone-faced, probably planning how to kill everyone. And Easton? Easton's doing his best to conceal his anger and confusion.

"Get me the book," Thayer says to Holloway.

"Yes, sir." Holloway picks up the radio.

"No, you get me the book," Thayer barks. "No one but you goes into the room."

The room. What room?

Now I want to go into the room.

"Do you want a second guard?" Holloway lingers in the doorway between the grand salon and the back deck.

"No." Thayer waves him off and stares at us. The six of us and one guard. Calvin taught me a lot. All of us, really. I'm waiting for him to give a signal. I'm not the only one. Sam and Dante are watching him too.

Calvin's jaw twitches. "You can relax, Z. You're in charge. You and your firepower can rule the world, or at least this corner of the South Pacific."

"You're really something, Green. You would have made one hell of a CEO."

"I make one hell of an engineer. But again, you didn't bring us on board out of charity. You want something."

"Green," Sam growls.

"Shut the fuck up, Green," Dante adds.

Thayer's hazel eyes sparkle in the afternoon light. Calvin's right. There's something there. Thayer's rich and arrogant, but he's also wounded. And maybe not all that bad? No . . . no, he's all that bad. He was about to kill us. Have us lined up and shot off the end of the boat. Because he doesn't have women on his boat for his dad to sexually assault, and he doesn't like killing women employees, but he's still willing to kill the men who work for him. Ones that don't do what he wants them to. And Calvin's pushing him.

I've spent a year thinking that Calvin could fix anything. That he'd save us from ourselves and starvation.

He did, though. The fish weir provided for us. But he's a man too. Not a god. Not infallible.

"Please," I say. The word has power with my guys. So much so that I try not to use it. I don't want to beg Thayer. Not for my life. But for the guys? Yes, I'll beg as much as I have to.

"What will you do for me, Hal? With your please?"

There's an echo of noes behind me.

Boisterous laughter rolls from Z. The tension's cut, so much so that the guard behind him squints in confusion. And I have to agree. "You and your family, Hal. It's beyond interesting. I would never have thought of something like this . . . that something like this could work. You know . . . Fuck. Take them back to their room. All of them but the bosun and Hal, here. I'm going to have a fireside chat with them," Z throws over his shoulder to the guard as he walks away. The lounge doors open, and two other guards walk out as Z walks in. So much for being able to overpower the remaining guard and take down our host. I glance at Dante, and he smiles.

"You're developing a violent streak, Sassy?"

"When in Rome . . ."

"I love Rome. Have you spent much time there?" Dante moves as a guard points at the stairs with his gun.

I'm nowhere near as good at pretending I'm not scared to the point of passing out as Dante is. My heart is still slamming out a questioning beat. Like it's asking me what the hell is going on. Honestly, I have no idea. "No, Dante, I haven't spent much time in Rome. It's on my list. I've been to Portofino, Sardinia, and Genoa."

"Ah, don't get me started on pesto alla genovese. So good. I'll make it for you. You have to try it—it's this silky, vibrant green sauce made from the freshest basil, garlic, pine nuts, Parmesan, and olive oil, and it tastes like the heart of Liguria in every bite."

"Fuck, I want that," the guard standing next to me says.

Dante and I both glare at him, and Dante's smile turns to a smirk. I hope the guard doesn't see it for what I do: Dante's pushing in. A crack to manipulate. "You'd love it. I'm not sure if I made it for the Russian, but you should ask Harris about my lasagna. Homemade pasta and homemade ricotta make it out of this world."

"Rosewood chef uses canned sauce for us."

"That's not right."

"Exactly what I said." The guard cocks his head to the doors. In the lounge, Holloway is back and has Zane, Sam, and Calvin next to him already.

"You done chatting?" Holloway's eyebrow pops up.

"Yes, sir." He drops back, his shoulders square.

"Good, now take the guests back to their cabin before I tell Chef what you think about his food."

The guard gives a sharp nod. That's something the canned-sauce-giving chef has in common with Dante—with all yacht chefs. They are a little unhinged and vastly protective of the reputation of their food.

"Be good, Sassy. You know we love you."

The other guys each give me their version of I love you. And Dante, Calvin, Easton, and Sam vanish down the hall with three guards, leaving Zane and me standing behind the sofa. Z has Rocky's journal in his hand. He slaps the back of it three times. My brain is spinning. I'm completely overwhelmed. But then, I'm not here for my brain. I'm here to motivate Zane. And I hate it. I absolutely hate it. All of it, all of this. But what can we do?

"Come on, sit down." Thayer motions to the sofa across from him.

Zane holds out his hand to me, and I take it. He pulls me close to him.

"Go," Thayer barks at Holloway, who stands in the corner. "I'll be fine, won't I?" He looks to Zane for confirmation.

"Sure, I'm sure I can keep Little Bird from taking out her aggression on you."

"Little Bird, Sassy—you certainly have a lot of names, Hal."

I nod.

He leans forward as if he's about to say something, but stands instead. "Where are my manners?" He steps behind the bar. I expect him to fumble around, unsure of where anything is, but he moves with practiced ease, pulling out three short glasses. He pours two fingers of expensive Macallan scotch into each one, expertly dropping ice into two. With two resting in his left palm and the iceless one in his right hand, he crosses the room. He holds out one to Zane and the other to me. I'm not a scotch person. It's too strong for me. Though I've taken classes. Three years ago, a primary's grandfather wanted me to try some of his Macallan, a twenty-five-year-old aged sherry cask. But my captain got me out of it, saying I couldn't have any.

"I'm not much of a drinker. But thank you." I take a small sip, the smooth warmth of the scotch spreading across my tongue, its rich notes of dried fruit and spice lingering as I swallow. It's not as horrible as I remember scotch being, but I'd rather have the two thousand dollars in my bank account and have a glass of water. I hold it gingerly on my lap.

"I'm not either." Zane puts his down on the sofa table. "Let's get down to business."

"Right, see, I told you. You're meant for more than being a bosun."

"Don't diminish my career. It's important. The safety of the boat and the passengers on her is important. And like I said, I'm a damn good bosun. And cryptogram and puzzle wiz."

Z flips open Rocky's book and thumbs through the pages. "All right, then tell me what you know."

"When we're back on land. And away from the Rosewood." Zane glares. "Not until then."

"No." Thayer shakes his head. "It's not that simple. A man of puzzles has to understand that."

"The information about the Swiss bank account isn't in one spot. It's spread out over a number of pages. Mixed in with actual words and thoughts. That's one of the reasons it took me so long to decipher it. One of the many reasons it took so long."

Somehow, we all sort of let the code slip away. One day Zane was working at it for hours on end, and then it was gone. That must be when he figured it the rest of the way out. I wish he'd told me. Or maybe I don't. I'd like to think I wouldn't have spilled all the details. But it's certainly easier not knowing them.

"You want a sample of the goods?"

"More than a sample. You made some strong claims. That Ed is running money through Rockwell-Harding."

"Ed." Zane nods. "So, not Zed?"

"Ed to his friends."

Chapter 8

Decoy Maneuver

Calvin

Dante's glaring at me as the door closes. I know that look. He's going to say something fucking stupid.

"We could have—"

There it is.

"Gotten killed. The remaining guard would have taken us all out before we could have tackled him to the deck. I'm not stupid," I say, throwing my hands in the air and announcing it to whoever is watching and listening in the control room. Wherever it is. "And I thought you weren't either. You're not thinking. He's not the Russian." I shove Dante's shoulder, and he stumbles back a few steps. Hell, from the way Dante talks about the Russian, we'd already be dead if someone in his organization wanted us dead.

"What the fuck?" Easton steps between Dante and me. Easton's hair stands up, and his eyes dart around the room like he's wired on Red Bull and speed. "Can you just stop?

Both of you. There are more important things to worry about."

Dante and I, in unison, turn to him. "Like what?"

"What's more important than getting ourselves off this floating prison?" I continue.

"Like what's going on with Haley and Zane." Sam grabs my arm. Dante's too.

"Sure, sure. I think we all know what's going to happen there." Dante shakes off Sam and steps around Easton. He slams his palm into my shoulder, leaving it there. But I don't budge. Though the chef doesn't lack force, he's no defensive linemen. "You know what, Green? You're a coward."

I'm not a coward. I wasn't any more scared than they were. Hell, I may be more scared now than I've ever been. Mostly because I think I finally realized what I have to live for. What I have to lose. And if they so much as harm a hair on her head . . . I'd willingly give my life to take them out. But what good is that if it only gets us so far? We're still stuck in the middle of the damn South Pacific. Taking over the pirate ship—that might've worked. But the Rosewood? No way in hell. I'm a realist. I might have been wrong about getting off the island alive, but this doesn't feel a hell of a lot better.

"We wait," I say.

"What's going on out there might not make life worth waiting for." Dante drops his hand off my shoulder.

He might be right. Z could torture Haley in front of Zane until he gives him everything he wants. And then he'll just kill them both. And fuck, maybe we should have just taken the risk and captured Z, taken over the Rosewood. That's the thing with calculated risk.

You have to do the calculations.

And I did.

It wasn't worth it. Not then, not a full-out attack. They . . . Z has to think we've given up. "I'm not a coward, but I'm not willing to get us slaughtered for no reason. And going after a well-trained guard is nothing but assisted suicide." And Dante, with all his spouting about the Russian, he should know that already. "But you want to call me a coward—fine. I'll call you a fucking idiot." I spin around. Let the cameras see I'm losing it. Fuck, it's better if they think we're at each other's throats, anyway. I'll turn it up a notch. I punch at the air, waving my hands around, then drop on the bed and pop back up again. We play along. Let Z and his men get used to being sheep. Then we hit them. It's only half of a plan. "It's over. No point in even trying anymore." I spin again and punch Easton in the stomach. Not hard. He knows what hard is.

He doubles over, holding it. His blue eyes flick up to mine in confusion.

"Calvin!" Dante yells.

Penny barks, jumping around at my feet.

"Stop it!" Sam yells, cutting through my foggy thoughts. "This is not who we are. We're a crew; we're family. This isn't how we're going out. This isn't how this ends. I refuse to believe that."

I glare at him, but I think at least Easton's picking up on my excellent acting ability. We can't just give up. But I'm not lining up for a firing squad again. We're going to have one chance to sell it. And one chance only.

Sam paces across the small cabin, his voice strong and certain. "No. We're gonna make this happen. We're gonna get home. And if we can't fight them . . . there's another option." He sits down heavily on the side of the bed, leaning forward as if the weight of the world is pressing him down.

"What do you want to do?" Dante asks, taking his hand

off my shoulder. His tone is sharp, challenging. "Invite them over for tea and crumpets? Last I checked, we have neither tea nor crumpets."

Sam shrugs, unfazed. "If you can't fight," he says simply, "you can always join."

I smile. Two down.

The room falls silent. Easton, the one who hasn't said a word this whole time, just leans against the wall. Dante glances at him, then shrugs.

"What choice do we have?" Dante says, his voice quieter now. "We've got no other way."

All eyes flick to Easton.

"Don't look at me," he snaps. "I have no fucking clue about anything anymore. Zane could've told me what was going on. Why the fuck didn't he tell me?"

"Maybe he could have." Dante places his hand on Easton's shoulder. And turns to me. "But I'm alive, and so is Haley. And you are too. Though you don't seem to care."

I move closer to Easton.

"For a minute. We're alive for a minute. You think the second Z gets whatever Zane knows out of him he isn't going to kill every last one of us? They went to a lot of trouble to come and find Easton," I say. And I still don't get it. But then, maybe the elder Z was told we were alive, and he figured it was only a matter of time before someone found us. And he didn't trust the pirates with the diamond or the kill. I'm not sure which, but I'm thinking it's most likely the kill, as I've seen how much it is to fuel up a yacht like the Rosewood. Taking a ship like this halfway around the world? Fucking expensive. This isn't something you do for the fun of it. There's a really good reason.

"And the diamond," Easton says.

"Right, the diamond." Dante's eyes are still focused on mine.

But Easton's cupping something between his hands. Like a baby bird. A small crack in his hands, too small to see anything from a camera. "Though the diamond is just extra. They wanted me dead. That's the big reward. It has to be. The bastard billionaire bending every detail to his will. And you know how he's going to do it?"

Dante shakes his head at Easton. I'm pretending to have lost it, but there's genius in the flash of Easton's wild eyes. It draws me over to him. He's not making sense. His head bows to his cupped hands again. And I look in. The Pink Phoenix is a dark speck—well, a frigging huge speck—inside his dark flipper hands.

"Fifty-fifty," he says with a shrug and swipes his hand behind his back and then flutters both like some weirdo magician. "Nothing to see."

How the heck did he swipe the diamond from Z? Or . . . did he find a way to separate the true diamond from the fake and take one back on the island when he dug it up with Haley? Damn.

"You live with a guy for a year and you think you know him. When did you learn the tricks? You know what, never mind." Dante's got the same look on his face that I do. He crosses the room to the porthole.

"You talk enough about the Russian. You must have seen things. Calvin's right. It would have—" Easton says.

"We'll never know now. And no, I didn't see a lot of things working for the Russian. I worked hard not to. Stayed in the galley or my cabin. But what happened on the aft deck? That's all you have to know. Maybe we'll see Haley and Zane again before they drag us out back. I hope they shoot me before they drop us over the side."

"Dante," Sam growls, cocking his head at one of the microphones we know about.

"Fuck it. I've had it with note passing and finger painting. This is just like when I came back from the other side of the island and immediately told you all about the orchards and huts?" Lies you can understand, you dumb jock. I see him take in what I'm saying. Dante too. Because no, I don't think we can take over the boat. And yes, I do think trying to overpower them is suicide. "So we go with Sam's idea and join them." We need to fight.

Dante's eyes are slits. "You know, Green, I've never really liked you all that much." And now I'm not sure if he's acting or not. But I suppose it doesn't matter. You can hate family. As long as he's good to Haley and stays mostly out of my way, he can go on truly hating me or fake hating me. I don't care which it is.

Easton's looking over my shoulder like the answer's going to come out of the ether. The door opens, and Haley's shoved in. She stumbles a few feet and lands in my arms. Her eyes are clear blue, the color they get when she's been crying. Though they're not red and puffy. Her hair's out of her ponytail. I help her up and scan the rest of her. Clothing intact, no marks on her skin.

"What the hell, Sassy? Are you okay? Did they hurt you?"

We surround her.

"No." Her lip quivers. There's more to that no. I want to rip it out of her. Fuck that, I want to strangle Z and rip it out of him.

"Zane?" Sam asks.

"He's okay." But her tone says he might not be for long.

"What did he tell Z?"

"Honestly, not much more than he'd already said on the

deck. There's a passage about an Ed. Rocky wrote that he figured out the quarterly figures weren't what they should have been. Enormous sums of money going in and out. Then there's a passage about him hiring a second forensic accountant, one that no one in the company knew about. Another where he questions if this Ed caused the stock price to artificially inflate. That the company's evaluation is off. But Rocky couldn't pinpoint where. And his accountant was still working on it when they boarded the Rock Candy. There's a line where he thought about postponing the wedding trip until he had answers. But Candy didn't want to wait."

"Did Candy know?" Easton asks.

"I don't know. I'm not sure if it says. If it does, Zane didn't translate that part."

"Right." Easton takes Haley's hand.

"There's more, but Zane didn't give it to Z. Said he'd have to recreate the cipher key. That there are sections where the code is off. Like Rocky changed it enough to make it different. That there are more specifics about who was involved and why. But it seemed like Rocky was finding it out in real time in the diary. That he'd only really pieced together the last bits over the final few weeks before the trip. Zane also came out and told Z that he hadn't translated the whole thing. That's when Z got mad and had me brought back here."

Chapter 9

Standing By

Easton

"Shit," I say under my breath.

"He's going to be okay. He has to be." Haley wraps herself around me. My stomach tenses. The world around me darkens. I shake my head, clearing away the doom. I have to believe that my dad hadn't gotten involved with guys like Z. That's not the man I thought he was—is. No fucking way I'm letting this take me down. There's enough other shit to worry about. What the hell is one more thing?

"I'm good," I say before she can ask.

"No, you're not, and it's okay. None of us are. And you've got it doubly so. The thoughts of your father." She's right, but what my dad did or didn't know . . . I can't let it matter. Though with Calvin's odd little plan, or at least I think his plan . . .

I glance up and Sam's the first person I see. With his arms crossed over his chest, he looks just like himself. There's a crease in his forehead.

"Nope, I'm fucking not fine either. None of us are. Haley's right." Sam cocks his head at me, and for a second I wonder if this is part of Calvin's big ruse. But he stares at me and it's not. I sink to the side of the bed.

"I just want Zane back here." Haley sits next to me, her thigh against mine. She lays her head on my shoulder and stretches her arms around my body.

And then the waiting begins. And continues. My head's spinning with the idea of how we get off the Rosewood alive. How to make them believe we'll do anything. That we're not going to fight. Which we haven't been doing, anyway. We've been good little hostages.

Haley's stomach rumbles loudly.

"You hungry, Sassy?" Dante crosses the room and sits on the floor in front of her. It's close enough to dinner that I wonder if they're going to give us anything. Another hour passes. Even Penny's not moving. Pepper hasn't come out from under the bed since we got back. Calvin has checked on her a couple of times. Shadows move across the floor after another hour. A fast knock vibrates the door. It opens, and a guard drops a paper bag on the floor, then slams the door shut.

Dante opens it. "It's sandwiches, if you could call them that." He pulls out two slices of sandwich bread with some cheese in it. He flaps them from side to side.

"Guess the chef heard about the canned sauce comment." Sam reaches into the bag and takes one out. "Haley?" He holds it out to her.

"I'm not hungry."

"You should eat, Haley." Sam holds the sandwich in front of her.

"Okay." She takes it and perches it on her lap, while Sam passes the rest out. "Is there one in there for Zane?"

"Yes." Dante hands one to me and sits on the other side of Haley. "This is delicious," Dante says to the mike in the wall. "So good." He eats it in three bites and dusts his hands off.

"Eat." Calvin looms over both Haley and me, and I'm not sure who he's talking to, but it doesn't matter. We both follow orders. And shit, this might be the last straw for me because normally when Calvin tells me to do something, I want to do the exact opposite. It's bland, and the bread is stale, and for a half second, I wonder if Z would poison us.

We wait as the sun goes down. No one starts foaming at the mouth. Someone turns on the bedside light.

Haley stands and stretches. "I could shower." My dick jumps. Even now, I want her. The idea of some thug watching her shower on a grainy surveillance screen has me wanting to punch the wall. She settles back down on the bed between me and Dante. "But I'll wait until Zane's back. He'll be back soon."

"Sassy." Dante pulls her feet onto his lap.

"That feels nice." She moans, and her head slides down my chest.

I'm holding Haley tightly to me when the door opens and Zane staggers in.

"Holy shit, Zane. What happened?" Sam grabs him by the shoulder and tilts his head up to face him.

"I'm good, mate. I'm good," Zane says, his voice low and strained. "I'm just really, really tired. Z is trying to get me to duplicate the whole code in hours when it took me, what, six months before?" His eyes dart around the room, avoiding ours. "And cherry-picking the data to make it take as long as possible . . ." Zane lets out a bitter laugh. "It's draining on the soul."

There are so many things I want to ask him. So many

things he hasn't said. Like why he didn't tell me about my dad knowing about the money laundering. Was he involved in it? Why didn't he report it? And why didn't Zane speak up at all? Did he really think I'm that weak? That I would just fall apart?

Haley moves to Zane's side, placing a gentle kiss on his cheek.

"Hey there, Little Bird." Zane pulls her into a big hug. "I'm okay. I'm okay." His words are meant for himself as much as for her, but it seems to comfort both of them.

Her blue eyes lift to meet his. "Do you think he's really going to let us go?"

Zane shakes his head, a pained expression crossing his face. "I don't know, Little Bird. I don't know." He exhales slowly, straightening his posture as though gathering strength. "But maybe . . . maybe. I'm confident about one thing."

"What's that?" Haley asks softly.

"He won't be able to crack the code with a computer, even with what I'm giving him. That much is true," Zane says, his voice rising slightly as he glances toward the ever-present cameras and microphones, the surveillance equipment that has infested every corner of our lives. "I'm giving him the absolute truth—data that's accurate—but not in any order that would make me disposable. That would make any of us disposable. The second he lays a hand on any of you, I'm done. I won't tell him another thing. I've given him enough to prove I can read the book and enough to keep him guessing. But the couple of big things he really wants—the things that would actually be useful? He's not getting them. Not until we're safe. Out of his hands, out of his grasp, and far, far away from his world."

Dante's eyes go wide. And I can read what he's thinking, that there are a lot of ways to get what you want out of a man. And men like Z, they live in a different world, by a different code. Zane's gaze shifts to me, his expression hardening. Z's world. My family's world, too, now, I suppose.

"You could have told me, man," I say, my voice sharper than I intended.

Zane shakes his head, a faint smirk tugging at his lips, though it doesn't reach his eyes. "Why? What good would it have done? You would've been mourning—grieving your dad and your sister, not knowing what really happened to them—and angry at your dad at the same time. What good would that have done? We've had enough spirals. Enough sadness. It was enough that I kept it for us."

I tighten my abs, pushing the frustration down, but the questions still hang heavy in the air between us. I'm not that fragile.

"You fucking worship your dad, mate. I made a call. I did the best I thought I could for you. I would never intentionally hurt you. Any of you." Zane's half yelling.

"I know it, man. I didn't mean . . . Thank you. Thank you. You and that bulging brain of yours saved our lives. Saved Haley's life." I pull him in for a quick hug.

Zane steps back, his normal smile on his weary face. "Bulging brain, huh? I am rather brilliant."

"You fuckhead." Dante lightly smacks at Zane's back.

"We all need to relax a little. Tomorrow's going to be another long day." Zane grips the back of his neck.

"Here, let me do that," Haley says, rubbing her fingers on the side of his neck.

"Are you hungry?" Dante holds up the bag with the sandwich.

"No, they brought me dinner." He peeks into the bag. "This is what you got?"

"Yup."

"What did you get?" Dante leans in.

"I had the same thing as Z. Steak, mash, cheesecake, but I didn't eat it. The cheesecake, that is. My stomach has been a bit dodgy."

"Cheesecake," Haley says, a far off look in her eyes.

"I'm with you. Cheese barely has a place in savory, let alone dessert." Dante sits down on the bed.

"Right, that's what one of the . . ." He shakes his head. "Come here, Little Bird." Zane takes Haley's hand. "You, too, Rockwell."

Haley takes me by the hand, and Zane leads us into the bathroom. It's dark until he flicks the lights on. He puts his finger on Haley's lips and shuts the door. Zane points to himself.

"You," I say.

Haley and Zane's eyes go wide. And Haley cocks her head at me. Ah, right, we're playing charades. A hand cupped around his ear, he nods and continues on. I wait until he's finished. He might be bloody brilliant, as he says, but he's trash at charades.

I mouth, "There's no camera in here?"

Zane nods and wiggles his eyebrows.

I flick on the water for the shower and then the sink too, while Haley's jaw drops. When I turn around, Haley's top is off and Zane's naked. Her arms are linked around his neck and they're kissing. The skin on the nape of her neck is velvet under my fingertips. A wave of goosebumps follows my fingers down her arm. I nibble on her ear. It's not loud, not loud enough to be heard over the water. And damn, I'm not sure I would care if they can hear us. I'm rock hard. Just having her here, in one piece. I need to touch her, feel her. And fuck it, have her yell in my ear as she comes over my cock. Hell, I'm not even picky at this point. It could be Zane's cock.

I suck her earlobe into my mouth, loving her softness. She shivers in Zane's arms. The need to make her vibrate and let all the tension from the past days vanish rushes through me. I explore her skin, tracing the curve of her hip.

Zane's hands glide down her other side. He crouches, pulling her pants and underwear down with one jerk. She leans back into my arms, and I savor the taste of her skin and neck.

Her back presses against my chest. I pull her closer, my hands gently caressing her waist. Zane pushes his head between her legs. My hands find their way around to the front of her chest. One rolls and pinches a nipple while the other settles underneath her sternum. Her heart's rhythm pounds against her skin. My lips trail down her neck, then her chin. She turns enough that our lips crash. Tasting her. It's like nothing I've ever known. Haley. I'll never get enough of her.

Zane lifts one of her legs, and I'm holding her up. She's moaning into my mouth now.

Chapter 10

Swabbing Down

Haley

I'm on fire. I'm trying my best to be quiet and to believe that what Zane found out is true. That there are no cameras in the bathroom. Though it tracks with what Thayer told me. I can't imagine him wanting his crew watching me in the shower. I rest my hand on Zane's head. I don't understand Thayer, and I certainly don't want to be thinking of him. Not now.

My attention focuses on the heat building between my legs. Zane's mouth is magic, sending electric pulses throughout my entire body. I could forget about everything and everyone else if it weren't for the fear of being heard. I squeeze my eyes shut, trying to block out the world outside this bathroom, imagining we're anywhere else besides the Rosewood. I tilt my head back, giving Easton more room to work with. My back arches backward, pushing into his touch. Every nerve ending screams in pleasure; every muscle tightens in anticipation.

My heart is pounding in my chest, and I can feel the

sweat on my forehead. I want this to last forever, but I also know it can't. The tension is too high, the danger too real. But for now, at this moment, I'm just a woman being pleasured by my guys.

Zane's touch is skilled and precise, his lips and tongue doing wonders to my most sensitive spots. My breath hitches as he moves his fingers inside me, finding that sweet spot that makes me moan his name. I grasp at Zane's shoulders for support, my legs shaking with the intensity of my pleasure.

Easton, meanwhile, holds me close from behind, his hands exploring my body as he watches Zane work his magic. His touch is firm and reassuring, a comforting presence during this otherwise intense experience. His touch tells me all the things I want to hear. Zane's tongue hasn't stopped his assault on my clit. A finger pushes into my pussy, then another. I whimper, desperate for this moment to last a little longer.

There's a rush of cold air, and Dante's laughter fills the room. "Close the door, Green, you don't want Sassy—"

"Shut the door," Easton says.

"Fuck," Dante calls out, his voice echoing through the room.

"And shut up." Easton pulls me closer.

I twist in Easton's arms. Dante, Calvin, and Sam fill the doorway. Dante's eyes widen as he watches the scene unfolding before him. It's both weird and hot to see him there, witnessing this intimate moment.

"Hey," I whisper, my voice barely audible over the shower. "I'm just brushing my teeth." It's the first thing I can think of. "I'll be done with my shower soon," I say clearly.

"Well, tell Zane to save some mouthwash for me."

Dante pulls his shirt off, and it lands on the floor next to me. "And I know you and your bathroom time, Sassy. This could take all night."

Zane lifts his head. "This is all mine," he says in a quick breath. His tongue is back at my core.

"I don't know about that, Morris. There are five of us and only one shower." There's a catch in Sam's voice. "But I think someone should stay in the other room."

"Thank you for volunteering, Captain," Dante says.

Sam leaves the door closed tightly.

Calvin brushes my hair away from my face into a ponytail. He holds it firmly, staring into my eyes. He raises his chin at me, and his mouth crashes down. "Save some hot water for me, Chiefie." He lets go of my hair, and my head crashes back to Easton's chest. Dante steps beside us, and I hear the click of the door shutting as Calvin exits too.

"How did you get so dirty, Haley?" Dante smirks down at me. He's stripped his clothes off, and he runs his hand down his length.

"It's hot outside," I gasp, my breath hitching as Zane continues to work his magic on me.

Dante chuckles, his eyes fixated on the scene unfolding before him. "Well, it's hot in here too. Steamy, in fact." He grabs my hair and turns my head. Our lips crash together.

I moan into Dante's mouth, feeling Zane's fingers inside me and Easton's hands on my chest, grasping and pinching. I reach for Dante's cock, but he's too far away.

"Now, Sassy." Dante wiggles his eyebrows at me. "You need to get nice and clean."

"All right," I say, trying to catch my breath. My mind is reeling with what's happening, but my body is begging for more. Easton holds me steady. I should stop this. But I can't.

I need them, and after the last two days I know nothing is promised.

I turn my attention back to Dante, and he smirks down at me, watching as Zane continues his ministrations. "You missed a spot. Just right there," he says in a deep voice filled with anticipation.

Dante skims his hand down the side of me and over my butt cheek, creating a magical feeling of exposure. "Here." His voice is low and thick as he pushes a finger into my ass.

I concentrate on my breathing, trying to slow it down, but every time Zane's fingers brush against that hidden spot, I gasp and moan. He steps closer to me, and I reach up to wrap my fingers around his cock.

As I stroke him, Dante leans in close, whispering in my ear, "Remember what I told you earlier? About saving some hot water for me?" I nod, feeling the tension building between us. But I have no idea what he's talking about.

Dante pulls on my hair while Zane sucks hard on my clit and Easton rolls my nipple . . . and I'm lost. My body begins to shake, the heat building between my legs threatening to consume me. Zane's fingers move faster, inside me and outside, kissing and sucking on the delicate skin that he can reach. Easton's hands never stop moving, one pinching and rolling my nipples while the other trails down my stomach to trace circles around my belly button. I shatter. My body shakes violently, a tidal wave of pleasure. My walls constrict around Zane's fingers, and I gasp, moaning his name. There's no holding back. No one muffles my cries. And I don't care. My head falls back against Easton's chest as I ride the wave of my orgasm.

As my body slows down, Zane kisses down my leg and places my foot on the ground. He stands, his lips glistening with my arousal. "That's what you get for being so dirty,

Little Bird." His smile lights up his face. I want to drop to my knees and take him in my mouth. It must show in my eyes.

"Not now, Little Bird. Let's get you cleaned the rest of the way." Zane lifts me out of Easton's arms and into the shower.

The three of them pile in after me. I'm tired, but there's no chance of me falling over now. There's so much skin in here. Dante rotates me by the shoulders and positions me in the prime spot of the water spray, then takes the shampoo and lathers my hair. His fingertips are a blessing on my scalp. I can't help but moan in pleasure. I clasp my hands over my mouth.

"I don't think it matters anymore," Easton says, scrubbing me with body wash. His touch is firm, yet tender.

And he's right. There's no disguising what just came out of my mouth. So forget about it. I drop to my knees. It's like a forest of redwoods around me. They're all so tall. I take Easton in one hand, Dante in the other, and go in for Zane. I was never good at bobbing for apples as a child. And now is no different. Zane's warm laugh fills the shower, and he holds his cock out for my lips. I glance up at the other two. They're watching me carefully, their expressions a mix of arousal and concern.

"You doing okay, Sassy?" Dante asks, his voice a gentle rumble.

"Mmm hmm," I mumble around Zane's cock.

"Fuck," Zane says. The vibration in my voice has him jumping in my mouth.

"Good girl," Easton murmurs, his fingers in my hair.

Zane groans, his hips jerking uncontrollably as I suck him deep into my throat. He thrusts into my mouth, hitting the back of my throat and sending waves of pleasure radiating through me. His hands overlap with Easton's in my hair, his fingers digging into my scalp as he fucks my mouth.

My hands are moving up and down Dante's and Easton's lengths. Luckily, Easton's large back is keeping most of the water from rolling over me.

"That's it, Sassy."

I flick my eyes up to Dante, and he puts his hand on top of mine. There's a twitch under my hand, and he's coming. Streams coat my shoulders, and Zane comes hard down my throat. I'm choking on it until he pulls out of my lips. I turn to Easton. His blue eyes glow down at me.

"Suck him, Sassy," Dante orders, his voice gruff with desire.

I oblige, wrapping my lips around Easton's cock and enjoying the taste of Zane still in my mouth. It's a sinfully delicious cocktail of flavors.

Zane reaches down and supports my head, guiding my movements as I pleasure Easton. "That's it, Little Bird," he groans, his breath catching in his throat.

I hum around Easton's cock, feeling the vibrations in my throat as he nears his release. He hits the back of my throat. "Yes," he hisses, thrusting into me one last time before tensing up. His cock twitches in my mouth as he releases down my throat.

Easton helps me up and kisses me. It's demanding and passionate. He twists me around under the water jet. Hands scrub at my skin while Dante and Zane wash me all over again.

"Now you're good and clean," Zane says.

"There's nothing clean about Sassy." Dante shuts the water off and puts a finger to his lips. He's right. Best to not overdo the chatter now that they'll definitely hear everything we have to say.

"That's not true." Zane holds up a towel for me. I wrap myself in it.

Easton slips out the door and returns a few minutes later with a clean T-shirt.

"Underwear?" I ask.

Easton cocks his head to the other room and shakes his head.

"You're not going to need it. Wait until you see what Calvin and Sam . . . Just come and look."

I slip the shirt over my head and hang up the towel. Easton's laughing. Zane steps into the bedroom for a second and comes back in, shaking his head.

"What?"

"You're going to love it. Fuck, I love it," Zane says.

Dante's out the door and calls back. "Fuck, yeah."

I step out into the room. "Whoa."

Chapter 11

Old Salt

Sam

"You like it?" I ask.

"I love it."

I take Haley's hand. "Let me show you around. Calvin's already inside." I pull back the sheet of our cobbled-together tent. Green's in the middle of the main bed in the cabin, with sheet "walls" all around the sides.

"Wow, you made this?" Haley gushes. "I would have loved it as a kid. Heck, I love it now."

"Hey, Chiefie. I may hate my brother, but I'm fucking amazing at building forts for his kids."

"It's wonderful." Haley crawls in toward Calvin.

"The thing felt a heck of a lot bigger before Green got in it." I crawl in after her. I've already ditched my shirt and shorts on the floor next to the bed. "We can just sleep."

Haley's hand lands on the front of my chest, her back pressing into Calvin's front. She leans in and whispers, "Need you."

Fuck, I need her more than air. Watching her hair blow around on the back deck, thinking that was it—that they were going to kill us. Kill *her*. I was a second away from running straight at the guard.

"I love you." I don't whisper it. I don't give a shit what they know about us on the ship. She's it for me. And the rest of the world can fucking explode for all I care. Her fingers trail over my chest, down past my stomach to my growing erection.

Our eyes lock. "I love you too, Sam." Her fingers slip beneath the elastic in my underwear and down my groin. I grip my teeth at the anticipation of her touch. My cock jumps into her hand.

"Lift up, Chiefie."

Haley lifts her shoulder, and Calvin pulls her towel away. Her breasts skim my side, but it's only a second before Calvin has one in his hand.

She gasps, but it's only for a moment before her breath hitches. Her eyes flutter shut as Calvin's fingers dance around her nipple. Haley rocks with a shiver. Her hand slides all the way down my cock. She pulls up once, then twice. I wrestle my underwear off and seal my lips to hers.

With some squirming, she has her other hand free and around my neck. Our lips crash against each other. Her fingernails comb and scrape through my hair. Zips of electricity fly around my body.

She breaks the kiss, and her blue eyes flash at me in the low light. "Sam, I want you."

Calvin's hand lifts from her breast to her chin, moving her head until their lips meet. I'm a beat away from smacking him away when he breaks their kiss and lifts her and himself in one fell swoop. He's twisted all of us. Haley ends up straddling me, with Calvin behind her.

The sheet walls shake and flare but settle around the sides of Calvin's shoulders. There's a soft light on in the cabin, and the white sheet behind Calvin glows.

"Sam." Haley's lips are on mine again, her fingers pulling at my hair, running through my beard. She's grinding on me. Taking what she needs until she's not.

"Just a second," Calvin growls. He's pulled her up onto all fours.

Haley bites her lip. Her eyes flick to the top of the tent and back to mine. I'm mesmerized by her. Her lightly tanned skin hovering above me. Calvin's arm's around her waist, holding her up. My eyes trail down her body to her pussy. And I'm shaken awake by the importance of this moment. It's rash, doing this now. But it proves we're alive. Proves that they can't take away what we made.

I push up onto my elbow and reach for her with my other hand. My thumb rounds her clit, while Calvin's working her other side.

"You good, Chiefie?"

"Yes." Her breath hitches. "All good. Sam." She reaches for me, and in a quick motion she slides onto me. My hand is knocked out of the way. My eyes roll to the back of my head.

"Damn, Sugar."

Haley grabs my neck again. The Rosewood's shower gel can't hide how much she smells like home. Our lips join, and she tastes like home too.

Calvin moves, setting a rhythm as he slowly penetrates her. Haley's eyes close, and she lets out a soft, guttural groan. I can't help but match her intensity with my own, kissing her deeply and passionately. The sheets tremble above us with each thrust from Calvin.

The three of us are lost in this moment, united in more

ways than just our bodies. She lifts her head and twists back to Calvin. "So close."

Calvin slows.

"No," Haley protests. And I have to agree. I'm trying not to release. Not yet. "Calvin," she moans, desperation and grit in her tone. Her eyes search mine.

"I've got you, Sugar." I tighten up and thrust into her from below.

"Cheaters never win," Calvin growls. He picks up the pace again, his rhythm syncing with the pounding of my heart. The Rosewood's rocking doubles down on our rhythm. Being surrounded by Haley is the only thing that matters. The rest of my brain has melted into oblivion.

"That's it," Calvin growls, his voice low and intense. "You like that, don't you? Both of us, fighting for control."

Haley's breath hitches. Her eyes are wide and glassy with desire. "Yes," she says, as her fingernails grip my biceps. She's holding on for dear life.

"You're the boss, Sugar. We'd do anything for you."

Tension wracks her beautiful face. "Now, please. Now, more."

Calvin lets out a low growl, his movements becoming urgent and intense. The sheet wall around us vibrates with energy, threatening to crash down. But I'm focused just on Haley, her eyes, her lips, the tilt of her chin as she's chasing her orgasm. She's mine. She's all of ours. I never want this to end.

"Come on," Calvin urges, his voice gravelly with arousal. "Give it to us."

Haley's body shudders, and she calls out our names. There's nothing discreet about it. The intensity of the moment washes over me, and I can feel my own release coming closer. Calvin jerks erratically, pushing me deeper into Haley.

"That's it, Haley," I murmur, my voice hoarse with desire. "Give it to us."

She tenses. Her body tightens around my cock. "I'm . . . I'm . . ." I surge up and kiss her, swallowing down her moans. Eating her words. I crash over the edge with her. Electrical shocks burst through my body. My vision goes black.

Her head lands on my chest. Fuck, I love her. But I also love breathing. Something that's really hard to do right now. "Move, Green."

He slides off, pulling Haley between us. There's a ripping noise, and the top of the tent flutters down over our heads.

Haley laughs.

"You okay?" Easton says.

I'm fighting with the sheet to pull it off our heads, but it's the roof and the sides and goes on as long as a rope of scarves pulled out of a clown's pocket.

"I'm good. Good." She giggles.

And it has my cock starting to harden again.

"Here we are." She's the one who pulls it the rest of the way off our heads.

"Peek-a-boo, Sassy." Dante's dressed and looming over the side of the bed.

"Hey." Haley tucks the sheet under her chin.

"I've got first watch." Dante nods at Calvin and me.

Easton and Zane are lying on the cots on the other side of the room. Easton's blue eyes catch the soft light from the closet, but Zane's asleep.

Calvin grabs Haley's towel from the floor and heads

into the bathroom. I hold Haley to my chest, watching her slowly spiral into sleep while I wait for Calvin to finish.

When I'm done with the shower, Penny's staring at me. She chuffs and scratches at the cabin door.

"Sorry, girl," I whisper. I take her into the bathroom and convince her to do her business on a dirty towel. If you've never been judged by a dog, you just haven't lived.

Back in the room, she jumps up on the bed and manages to wedge herself between Haley and Calvin.

Dante cocks his head at me. He's sitting on the floor, leaning against the wall next to the door, Pepper curled in his lap. I smile.

"Want me to take over?"

"I've got it," he says.

The ship shakes, changing course. Not a lot, but it's definitely a shift in direction. And then the engines kick it up.

"Whoa," Dante whispers.

"Yeah."

"You think we should wake them up?" He lifts his chin to me, then shakes his head, answering his own question.

"No point," I whisper and pull on my pants. I hang the towel up and head to the porthole. There's nothing out there but the moon on the water. Fuck, I used to love watching the waves from the bridge. The quiet of the night. I'm staring out at the waves, but there's nothing now but dread. The dread of being under Z's control. Having him pull us out to threaten us. There's a click behind me.

I turn to hear Penny growling, the light from the corridor shining across the foot of the bed. Calvin bounds to his feet, but the others don't move.

"Come with me," Holloway says, pointing at me.

Calvin takes a step toward the door.

"Just your captain."

I follow Holloway out the door, and Penny leaps to come with me. "No, you stay."

"Come on, Penny." Dante pulls her back in.

Holloway closes the door with a click. One of the nameless guards stands on the other side of the hall. He looks away, his face blank. But if he's been standing there for the last few hours, he's heard some things.

"She's a good dog," Holloway says to the closed door. He takes long steps to the stairs at the end of the hall.

"Thanks, she is." I leave off all the things I used to say, like "when she wants to be" or "she's stubborn." Because no, she listened to Calvin when he told her to go home. "She's the best dog there is." There's no point denying it. They have enough things over my head to keep me motivated. "Where are we going?"

"Wheelhouse." He doesn't slow.

"Okay. Any reason why?"

"I didn't ask."

"Probably for the best."

"It's always for the best." We step up the last step. He points me to the wheelhouse. "Don't do anything dumb. Captain carries." Holloway angles his head to the wheelhouse's side doors on the port and starboard. Large backs fill the window in each door. Holloway pulls the interior door shut behind him.

And I'm left staring at the back of the uniformed captain. He's tall with square shoulders, his elbows sticking out from his sides, a bulge of the weapon he carries on his right. "Hello," he says with a strong Scandinavian accent. He turns, dropping a pair of night vision binoculars on a stack of charts at the back of the wheelhouse. "Thank you for coming." The crewman next to him, holding the helm, doesn't turn.

I swallow down my smirk. Like I had a choice.

"Right, so Mr. Z has cleared me to talk to you about the drifting of the Rock Candy. I'd like to know more about the current that brought you to your island. I like my charts to be complete," he says in the gruff sing-song voice that so many older Nordic sailors have. He doesn't say his name. But there's something familiar about him.

"Well, I don't have my charts. They're still with the Rock Candy. Wherever she is. And Z has my logbook."

The captain pulls it out from under a chart. "*Dis, ja?*"

"Yes." I hold my hand out and take it. "Thank you. May I sit?" I motion to the bench next to the table the charts are on.

"Please." He clicks on a map light. "Humph, it would be better to have more light." He yanks open the door back to the corridor. "We are moving to my office." He snags the charts from the table. "*Nei,* I need that one." He points to the stack next to me. "Take those."

I take the stack and follow him out.

Holloway has an eyebrow arched.

"If I'm going to understand the charts and his logbook, *ve* need more light."

"Fine," Holloway says.

The Rosewood's captain opens the door next to the wheelhouse. It's a large office with a closed interior door toward the aft of the boat, and his cabin. He moves a few things from his desk and puts the ones he brought in down. I place the ones on my stack down on top.

He flips through the charts until he finds the right one, where the Rock Candy lost power. "Here?" The Rock Candy is marked on the map. His hand slides down from where he pointed, down the side of the chart to the edge where it's stamped with a rose. He holds his finger next to the rose, where a name is printed. *Captain Haakon Lind-holm.* He glares up at me. And it takes a minute.

Fuck, yes!

I give a single nod. And do my best not to jump up and down.

Chapter 12

Chow Boss

Dante

It's been at least three hours since Sam left. Calvin's taken over watch, and I'm fighting with Penny for a few inches of bed. And when she kicks me in the groin in her sleep, dreaming of chasing a rodent, I'm sure, I roll off the bed and pull on some clothes. I don't give a fuck about the cameras. Never have. I make my way over to the porthole. Calvin's leaning next to the door, his ear almost pressed against the wall. There's a sliver of pink across the horizon. But there's more than that—there are lights. They're far away, but it's too soon to know if I'm looking at a swath of tankers, an island, or a main body of land.

"What?" Green's at my side before I can say anything. "Fuck." I can see the wheels turning in his head. "Everybody up. We've got lights outside."

Zane jumps out of bed. Easton's slower, but Sassy? Sassy bolts past me like a cheetah, her oversized Rosewood pajamas slipping down her waist as she does. "Land, land? That's fantastic."

I curl my fingers around her shoulder. I don't want to squash her excitement, but this isn't going to be good.

"Wait, where's Sam?" Sassy pivots from the lights out the porthole, her hands landing on my chest.

"Holloway came and got him. I'm sure he'll be back soon." I give her shoulders a squeeze.

She nods because, really, what else can she do?

"It's early, Sassy. Go back to sleep."

"I'm not tired, but I can try. Have you slept?"

"Some." I eye our four-legged bed hog, who's now sitting pretty like she didn't do anything, leaning against Haley's hip. "Come here, Sassy, let's snuggle." I take her hand and lead her back to the bed. There is a pounding on the door, and it swings open.

"Chef?" one of the unnamed guards says. There's another guard in the hall.

"Yeah?" I straighten my shoulders, but Haley's clamped onto my hand.

"Come with me."

I kiss the top of Sassy's head. "Love you."

Green's blocking the door. "What do you want with him?"

"Move." The guard puts his hand on his gun.

Green steps to the side, and I head out. It dawns on me that he's the same guard I tempted with my pesto alla Genovesa. "So, where are we going?" I ask, though I have a pretty good idea. We're up one flight and halfway down the main body of the ship.

"Here." He nods.

The galley. My home, normally. But this one's been set up by a blind mongoose. What the hell? There's shit all over the counters. Bins of lentils next to flour, a tray of twenty-five different hot sauces, and mounds of dirty pots in the sink. "Great, why am I here?"

"I told Z about your pesto all genie—"

"Genovesa."

"Whatever, and Z wanted the chef to make it your way with the homemade shit."

"Let me guess. He told you to go to hell?"

"Yes." The guy swallows hard. His Adam's apple bobs.

"So I'm making pasta at dawn?"

"Yes."

"No."

He lifts his gun. And I glare at him. We stare at each other for a good two minutes.

"Make the pasta."

His story doesn't add up. If the chef refused Z, then he's not going to let me use his galley. Maybe this guy is the one who wants the pasta, and neither Z nor the chef know I'm in the galley. "You don't think this is going to make the chef testy?"

"No, I don't think he's going to be anything anymore." The guard raises his eyebrow. And now I'm wondering who the true crazy is. Did Z order the chef killed, or did this guy overstep?

I scan the mess I have to work with. I suppose it doesn't matter. If my cooking can help us get out of here . . . or if I can slip a knife back into the cabin . . . Either way.

"What's my timetable?" I search around the space for an apron but settle for a clean kitchen towel tucked into my pocket.

"What?"

"When do you need it? Forget that. I need two and half hours."

"What? Z wants it as soon as possible."

I'm a little shocked he said Z. I was starting to really believe that he'd come up with this plot himself. "Two hours. Fresh pasta has to rest." I'll make it in an hour and a half, but I have to give myself some sort of buffer, as I don't know where anything is in this cyclone of a space. Is the pantry stocked with the things I'll need? I glance at the cupboard that seems most logical to house the dry goods.

"I'll tell him two hours."

"Does he not sleep? Pasta at dawn?"

"No." He picks up his radio and calls another guard.

Collins, the one who shot at Zane, of course, is the one who shows up. He scowls at me. "What the hell, Dakota? What's up with this asshole up here?"

"He's making pesto alla Genovesa for Z."

"Where's Chef?"

"Not here."

"I can see that."

"Just watch him while he cooks. I need to go tell Z when it will be ready."

"Copy that."

Dakota leaves me alone with the psychopath. I glare for a second, then get down to work. I wash the dishes in the sink as fast as I can and clean a section of counter big enough to work on, relocating a hundred bottles of hot sauce and hot sauce packets. "Your chef has a thing for hot sauce."

"The hotter the better," Collins grunts.

I nod. Heat is good, but it needs to be layered, not blasted. Whatever. Inside the chaotic fridge, I find good enough cheese and fresh basil. I take a moment to smell it, huff it even. But I've got pasta to make. I search through drawers and things. But someone's prepared for my arrival.

There's only one small paring knife on the magnetic knife board.

"Chef keeps the food processor over there." Collins points to a set of double doors.

I nod, because I don't need a food processor when making pasta for six. But I slide the knife off the board and move over to the doors. With my left hand, I rummage about with the food processor while I slide the knife into my pocket. I bring the processor out and set it on the counter. "Fuck, this is filthy. I'll just make it by hand."

"Cool. Put the knife back on the counter," Collins says, his hand on the grip of his gun.

I take it out and put it in the sink.

"Get busy, clock's ticking."

I'm forty-five minutes in. The pasta is resting, and the sauce is done. It's coming out fantastic. And more than once, I almost smile. I whip up a second batch. Because I have a feeling I'm going to need to feed more than just Z.

The second batch of pasta is resting and I'm cleaning underneath where the forty-seven hot sauce bottles had been when Z saunters in.

The water's boiling, and I've got plates ready to go—plates that I rewashed.

"It smells good in here." He stops next to Collins. "You can go." Z cocks his head to the door. Holloway's standing in the stew's pantry.

"Yes, sir," Collins says.

I glance at the clock. It's five. If I was the chef of this yacht, I'd be up now, making muffins and fresh croissants.

It's occurred to me more than once that I might be making my last meal. There's a quick flash that I should have taken more time doing it. But fuck, I always take the right amount of time doing what needs to be done.

"I'll have a plate for you in two minutes." I drop the pasta into the water.

He leans over the stove, watching the pasta swirl around. "Just a small taste."

"Is this breakfast?" I ask.

"Is there ever a wrong time for good Italian food?"

"No, there's not." I plate him up a heaping portion and slide it over the counter. I haven't seen a stew since I've been in the kitchen, and I haven't found the eating utensils either.

Z ducks into the stew pantry and comes back with two sets. I plate up three more plates.

"Expecting friends?" He cocks an eyebrow.

"Habit," I say.

"Holloway, you want one?"

"I'm good." The guard crosses his arms over his chest.

Z twirls his pasta around in his spoon and takes a bite. "Mmm, that's fucking fantastic. Holloway, take this." Z picks up an extra plate and shoves it at Holloway.

"Yes, sir." Holloway frowns at the plate, and then his eyes flick to me. He's not won over, not yet. But he hasn't tasted it yet. He takes a bite.

"Good, right?"

"Yes. It's good." He puts the plate down on the counter in the stew pantry.

"This is fantastic. I can see why the Russian raved about you so much." Z takes another bite. "Why did you leave him, anyway?"

"Stylistic differences." I'm not going to say anything else. I'm still not sure if he's close or just in the same line of business as the old bastard.

Z nods. And I'm fucking grateful he doesn't push harder. "You know why I had you make this?"

"You were hungry?"

"No, I needed your genius bosun to have more motivation to translate the rest of Rockwell's notebook. I ordered Dakota to take you to the swim deck and shoot you. He agreed, but there was a twitch in his eye. Something I hadn't seen before. I inquired. And he said he'd never get to taste your pasta la genie. I was hungry, and now here we are."

"I see." I fucking wish I had that knife now.

Z cocks his head from side to side. "But the chef heard about your detour and burst into my office, making demands. Saying I couldn't do what I wanted to do on my own yacht. He got steamed up. Made more demands and ran at me. It was a tragic accident he had. Crew breakfast is at six, lunch at twelve, and dinner at six. Don't disappoint me, or I'll find someone else to give you some motivation."

"You want me to work for you?"

"Sure, let's call it that. Only until I hire a replacement."

"And you're threatening my friends, my family?"

"It's not a threat. I'm telling you to do what you're told to do or others will pay for your insubordination."

"Where's Sam?" My heart slaps around my ribs. If he was going to kill me, he might have already killed Sam.

"The captain of the Rosewood is questioning him about the currents the Rock Candy drifted in."

I study Z's posture. I'm not a human lie detector, but I like to think I can read people. He's telling the truth. I turn away from him and grab an empty box from the pantry.

"What are you doing?"

I take the side of my arm and sweep the hot sauces into the box. "I don't need to burn people's taste buds off to give them a quality meal."

Z laughs. "Take him back to his cabin."

"No, if breakfast is at six, I have a lot to do."

"I'll leave you to it." Z stands but then doubles back and takes a second plate of pasta.

Between the galley and the stew pantry, I find a clean bucket. I quickly scrub the counters, floor, and everything else dirty. Then I get down to business throwing away expired food. My head's in the freezer, taking stock of what's there, when someone taps me on the shoulder.

Chapter 13

First Light

Zane

Easton, Haley, and I are huddled together in bed. There's a pink line of light on the horizon and dots of light in the far distance. A knock shakes the door, and it bounces open.

"Green, Morris, both of you come with us." Holloway's growl rattles through the room.

"Where are you taking them?" Haley shakes her head.

I kiss her cheek and hold on to her. "I'll be back," I say, not knowing if it's true. I only let go of her so Calvin can give her a hug.

"Let's go," Holloway barks. "Move it. Now." The man's done with this, and us. His hand rests on his gun. It's casually threatening.

"Happy to oblige." I dip my head to him.

"Just move, man." Holloway gestures with his left hand.

I step out into the corridor. Calvin's behind me, and our cabin door closes with a thud. A lump rises up my throat. My eyes lock with Calvin's, and I mentally push at him: *Be*

99

Helpful. But what I want to say is . . . is fuck this. Going along with what Z and the *Rosewood* crew say was Calvin's idea.

Calvin's chest expands, and the most uncomfortable smile appears on his lips. "Where are we going, Holloway?"

"You're going to clean up cat shit, Green. After I drop Morris in the galley to wait for Mr. Z."

I'm going to decipher the book with Haley not around again today. I'm not sure if that's a good thing or not.

Holloway winds us through the crew stairwells—where we don't come across anyone else. It's barely light. But that doesn't mean anything on a ship. Where is the *Rosewood* crew? There's always something to be done. My eyes flick over to Calvin. But the plan isn't to try and take over the boat. At least not yet. And certainly not with Holloway. I have a really strong feeling if I even flinched at Holloway, I'd be shark food.

He yanks the galley door open. Sam's sitting on the other side of the counter with a cup of coffee in his hand like we're not prisoners on a madman's yacht.

"Sam." Calvin lifts his chin at Sam, waiting in the doorway.

I jump when Dante steps out from the pantry, an apron over his borrowed *Rosewood* pajamas.

"What's going on here?" I raise my eyebrows at Dante.

"Well, they had an unexpected opening on the staff." Dante rounds the counter to a pantry on the opposite side of the cooking space. What would normally be the steward's pantry. He takes two coffee cups from the cabinet and pours coffee in both. He holds the first one out in front of Holloway.

"I'm good." The guard waves him off.

"The water filter hadn't been cleaned since the *Rose-*

wood hit the water. You might want to change your mind." Dante continues holding the mug out.

Holloway takes it. And fuck me. It's a good thing we're all on the same page of waiting because this would be a good time to try and take out the lead muscle of the ship. Four of us, one of him. But instead, I watch the head of *Rosewood* security sip the coffee. His eyebrows shoot up.

"See, I told you. Paying attention to what you're doing makes a difference." Dante moves around the counter to the center of the galley like it's always been his domain.

"And where did you go?" Calvin asks Sam.

"*Rosewood* captain, Haakon Lindholm, wanted to see me about his charts and where we went dead in the water with the *Rock Candy*." Sam says it so monotone that it takes me a minute to register what he really said. My heart thuds in my chest. Because Haakon Lindholm sounds a hell of a lot like Hawk Lindholm, the deckhand who spent the last few seasons with us on the *Mermaid's Tale*, Rocky's old boat. I'm watching Sam carefully, but then so is Holloway.

"Were you able to help Captain Lynholmes?" Calvin mispronounces Lindholm the same way Hawk always hated it.

"I told him what I know. Which isn't much."

Fuck me, I'm jumping inside—the captain of the *Rose-wood* is the father of one of the most decent guys I've ever worked with. In fact, the only reason he left this season was he was ready to be bosun. And with me and Anders in his way, there wouldn't be anywhere for him to move up to for the long haul. Damn. I can't even imagine what would have happened if Hawk was on board with us. I study Calvin, but I can't tell if he's thinking the same thing. Maybe he is. Dante, however, hasn't a clue, and it's going to have to stay that way. If Hawk's dad is going to help us, there's no way anyone can know he has a tie to us. But fuck, if he can at least get Haley to safety? Though he didn't step in yesterday. So how far is the Norwegian captain really willing to go to help some friends of his son? And honestly, he probably doesn't even know about any of us, only that his son was a sailor under Sam. Sam and Hawk weren't close. It was two years of sailing with Hawk before I even knew his dad was a sailor too. Though I guess I know why he kept it to his chest now. There's no reason to go bragging about your dad if he's working for a criminal. Hell, I don't even know where Hawk's working this season . . . I swallow hard. They have my phone. And it's a damn good thing it's locked. Because there's two years' worth of photos of me, Sam, Anders, Calvin, and Hawk all over the bloody Med and Caribbean.

But then, I doubt Mr. Z's versed in his crew's families. And I don't plan to find out. I'm only hoping that Hawk's dad is willing to do something to help us get the hell out of here.

Dante hands the other cup to Calvin before pouring a third and handing it to me. It's the first cup I've had in months. Since we had our last pot over the holidays. When I thought it would be the last cup I'd ever have. Honestly, I didn't think we'd ever get off the island. And I certainly didn't think we'd be sipping coffee in a galley wondering when and how we'll escape. More than once, I pictured being found by a cargo ship or a fisherman. Leaving the island surrounded by stinking fish.

"There's lights out there." I nod to the small port window above the counter.

"Yes, we're coming up on Kaohsiung, Taiwan for fuel," Sam says.

"Captain Lindholm told you that?" Holloway puts his empty cup down on the counter.

"No, we were looking at charts so he could fill in the log about the *Rock Candy*, and I figured out where we were." Sam puts his coffee down and turns to Holloway. It's a quick interaction but one that's sincere, and it must be enough for Holloway.

"Leave your mug. Time to work, Green. Stay here, Morris. I'll be back in a minute to gather you." Holloway points for Calvin to leave through the stew pantry.

Calvin waves and ducks to get out of the galley. It was easy to forget how big he was on the island. But it's not now. Holloway is big. Calvin's massive.

I raise my eyebrows at Dante and Sam. But Dante's not looking; he's chopping onions with the smallest knife I've ever seen. I guess they're not fully ready to trust us yet.

"How's that knife working for you, mate?" I ask.

Dante puts the blade on the cutting board and gives me a middle finger but then turns his hand to the side and shows me a blister the size of a two-pound coin.

"Fuck."

"No thank you." Dante picks the knife up and keeps chopping. "It's going to take all day to finish this, no time for fucking."

"Let me take a go." I move around the counter to wash my hands—and yes, I'm still taken aback by running water and soap.

Dante hands me the hilt of the knife. And I wish there was some way of telling him about Hawk.

"Yachting's a small world," I say and nod my head at Sam. There's no guard with us right now. In the galley, the cameras aren't hidden. There's not one but three green lights glaring at us from different parts of the kitchen.

Sam clears his throat. "I should have offered before. Let me have a turn." He takes his coffee cup to the sink and washes his hands. And he's right. There's no way of telling Dante. Not now. Not without endangering anything Hawk's dad might be willing to do for us. Sam's looking out the porthole while I'm trying not to cry from the onions.

It's only a few minutes before Holloway is back. "Let's go, Morris."

"You want another cup?" Dante asks the guard.

"Yeah, sure." He takes the seat Sam vacated.

I glance over my shoulder. Sam's peeling carrots in the sink. *Oi. I bet we could do some damage with a peeler and the world's smallest paring knife.* I raise my eyebrows at Dante, but he's not picking it up. And that's not the plan, anyway. I guess living with Calvin for a year has really ruined me.

Holloway drains the bottom of his cup. "Let's go, genius. You're too smart to be a peeler goblin."

Dante lets a laugh burst out. "You're not so bad, Holloway."

Holloway's face drops. "Move, Morris."

I nod at him. But I'd rather slice onions for ten hours than translate Rocky's journal. Especially while making it take long enough that we have a chance of getting off this yacht in one piece.

"I'll be back for you." Holloway points at Sam.

"Don't take both of my peeler goblins," Dante says.

Holloway stops. "I'll see what I can do."

"Though I'd rather have a goblinette helping me out."

"Yeah, Z has a strict policy about that. You can have the old guy for a few more minutes."

"Old guy," Sam mumbles as we leave the galley.

"This way." Holloway turns me away from the grand

salon I was in yesterday and back to the windowless conference room. The journal's on the table along with my notes from before. "Z will be in. Make progress." And he closes the door with a click.

"Right." Make progress. But not too much.

I flip through the journal. That's the problem. The second time you do a puzzle, it comes a lot faster. I could read him the whole thing right now if I wanted to. Like the Swiss bank routing and account numbers where all the money Rocky syphoned off went. Along with when Rocky figured out that Harding was laundering money for Ed. But there's something else, something that doesn't make sense. And I want to talk to Easton about it first. But not now, not when Z or anyone else can hear it.

Chapter 14

Foul Air

Calvin

I bang loudly on the inside of the door like Holloway told me to do when I'd finished cleaning everything up. And it was for at least thirty seconds, before a cat did its thing again. The door opens, and an engineer scowls at me. The head engineer, by the stripes on his shoulder. Do I blame him? Fuck no. If someone took my workshop away to house a dozen cats, I'd be pissed as hell as well.

"You're finished?"

"Yeah."

"Already?" He steps into the room to inspect my work, and it takes every ounce of me to not take one of the wrenches from the wall and clobber him over the head with it.

"Yeah, what's the point of doing a job if you're not good and quick?"

"Hmm, yeah, true. Good enough for now. Put the garbage bags in the hall." He peers around the room, putting his foot up to stop a large tom from jumping into the hall. He stands and watches while I place the full bags next to the door. "Come on, then. You can wait in the engine room for someone to come pick you up."

"I appreciate it." I more than appreciate it. It gives me a chance to scope out more of the Rosewood. Because while I'm all in for playing nice right now, that's not going to last for long.

He radios for someone to come get me and motions for me to move down the hall ahead of him. He's carrying a gun, judging from the bulge in the back of his belt. Not something I'd want to have strapped to me in an engine room. But then, I'd never work for a guy like Z. And I sure as hell wouldn't stay somewhere an ass like Collins is welcome.

I haven't seen much of the deck crew, but I'm wondering if they care as well. Kennedy the chief stew doesn't appear to.

"Sit there. Don't move." The engineer points to a small stool against the wall, away from the control panel. There's a crowded counter and shelf behind me.

"Got it. I'm Green, Calvin Green." I sit on the stool next to a small bench. There are two other engineers monitoring stations on the other side of the room. I take in a breath.

The old guy nods without giving me his name and wanders away.

But there's something up. Something's not right. Then again, maybe it's just my nose coming out of the cat room.

My eyes flick around the engine room. It's state of the art, for sure. Clean. But I still can't shake the feeling that something's off. "Nice engine room."

"Aye." He nods without looking back at me.

"Stopping for fuel soon?" My eyes run over an open logbook on the counter next to me.

He glares over his shoulder and purses his lips. He doesn't say anything. But he doesn't deny it. I skim the page the logbook is open to, finding documentation of the transfer of fuel from one tank to the other. The last date is from yesterday. Or at least what I think was yesterday. And both of the primary tanks are low.

The chief engineer lumbers across the room and shuts the logbook, moving it to the shelf above the table. "Keep your eyes and hands to yourself."

I suppose Hawk's dad is going to be the only friend we have on the yacht. Fucking Hawk. How did he not tell us his dad is the captain of the *Rosewood*? Like we would have said anything. It might have made a difference. Then again, it might not have.

I take in another breath while waiting for my babysitter. "Do you smell that?"

"Cat shit? Yes, I can smell it. I've been smelling it since the howling things were brought on board." He sneezes on cue.

He's right. It smells like an underfunded animal shelter down here, but there's more. "No, it's a faint scent of acid. Have you checked the battery rack?"

One of the guys near the back takes off his hearing protection. "What did you say, Tom Hanks?"

I run my hand over my beard. Tom Hanks from the movie *Castaway*. Whatever. Our experience is going to have people saying that over and over to us. I get it. I shrug at him and run my eyes over each part of the equipment around the room.

The head engineer steps closer to me, and for half a

second I think he's going to punch me, but he swings around and faces the inside of the engine room and stands with his hands on his hips, his chest pointed upward. "You know, I do smell something, now that you mention it." He heads over to the battery rack. "Fucking hell. Shut the engines off."

"No," I yell. "Don't do that. You need to vent the room first. You might have a buildup of hydrogen, depending on how long they've been leaking. Shut the engines off, and you could get a spark."

"Damn. Belay that order. Get the room vented," he yells and glares at me. It's half thank you and half shut the fuck up.

The three of them are moving. Doing all the things they should. Turning off nonessential equipment, opening the louvers. Soon they've got the door propped open, and a fan appears from a storage area.

The old guy is talking to the bridge. It's killing me to not help. More engineers appear and then a guard. Of course it's Collins, the asshole who fired at Zane.

"Did you cause this?" Collins grabs my arm.

The head engineer stops in the middle of talking to a level one engineer. "What the fuck. No, he's the one who noticed the problem." He scowls at Collins.

But the asshole Collins has half of my bicep in his hand. "Sure."

"It's true. I'm Turner. Thank you, Green. I'd like to say that I would have smelled it as soon as you did. But . . ." The engineer shakes his head. "Thank you."

I nod. Because I get it—he's going to be reliving today for a while. Just like I've revisited the issues with the *Rock Candy* in my dreams for a year. Only this time it wasn't sabotage, just a bad battery and a room full of engineers with allergies.

"Whatever. You want him as a crew member? You'll need to fish him out of the water when Z has him sinking to the bottom."

The old guy's glaring at him. But there's no point. Hotheads like Collins never see anything but what they want to see.

"Thank you," the engineer says to my back.

I glance back and incline my head to him. He does the same back to me. Maybe I've won him over. Saving his job might have something to do with it.

Collins takes me up to our cabin. He opens the door and tries to push me in but doesn't have the muscle to move me any faster than I want to.

"You're back!" Haley jumps up from the port window as the door to the corridor slams shut.

"Yes." I wrap my arms around her neck and kiss her cheek before she buries her head in my chest.

"The yacht's slowing. We're docking. I'm thinking we need fuel," she says into my shirt.

"Yes, they're taking on fuel. We're somewhere in Taiwan." I let her go, and we join Easton at the porthole.

"How long will this take?" Easton asks. "The fueling, I mean."

If he'd ever come on a trip with his dad for more than a day, he'd know fueling takes forever. "At least eight hours."

Haley nods and raises her eyebrow at Easton.

"I didn't doubt you." Easton pulls Haley to him. "Honestly."

"What did they make you do?" Haley asks.

"Nice one, Swimmer Boy. Don't ever doubt Haley." I laugh and grab Haley's waist. I press my nose into the crook of her neck and try not to think about what might have happened if I hadn't detected the acid of the batteries. They would have noticed soon enough. Right? Of course they would have. "Cat boxes. Dante's the new *Rosewood* chef, and Sam was in the galley too."

"And Zane?" Haley sinks to the bed.

"He was in the galley when I left. Holloway took me down below, but he said he was coming back for him."

She nods and moves over to the window again. We slowly approach the dock. We're on auxiliary power and are inching along. I can almost see the port, if I squint. This has got to be frustrating to them too. The crew of the *Rosewood*. Because they're not going to fix the batteries and take on fuel at the same time. Though now that they know there's an issue, it's not a hard problem to fix. Fuck them. I don't give a damn about them.

Even when Haley moves to the bed, I can't pull myself away from watching the approaching port. And that's the problem. The closer it gets, the more I realize that this isn't going to be a place where we can blend into the landscape. The fueling station is a concrete building a long way down a pier and nowhere near land. It's discreet. Just the type of place a yacht like this would want to fuel. Our porthole is below the dock. Above us, I can see the legs of the crew moving along. They're taking on supplies too. It's hard to tell from this angle. I keep waiting for one of the other guys to appear. But then, if they're taking on food, that will keep Dante busy for a while. There are long shadows of what I'm assuming are guards along the edge of the dock.

Fuck.

After a few hours, the yacht rocks while being tied up. And Easton and Haley appear back at my sides.

"Do you think?" Haley looks up at me. And I know what she means. Do I think we can escape here? I want to tell her about the *Rosewood's* captain. But there's no way.

I'm not writing it, or even spelling it on her stomach. If Hawk's dad is going to help us out, it could mean his life.

"No," Easton and I say together.

"But we could—"

The door opens, and Z's standing there with his hands on his hips. Several guards are behind him, but it's the scowl on his face that worries me more.

Chapter 15

Waylaying

Haley

"Thayer," I say, holding my head high. There are dark circles under his eyes, and his hair is standing up on end. He's not wearing his normal button-down linen shirt but a polo instead. There's no logo on it—custom, no doubt. I'm not sure if it's seeing him in our cabin or the change of clothing, but he's disarmed. Like he's a normal guy. A normal, worried guy.

"Come along now. Move." There's an edge of fear in his usually calm voice.

I step forward, but Calvin and Easton haven't moved.

"Now." Thayer grabs my upper arm and jostles me into the corridor. But I catch the look in Thayer's brown-flecked hazel eyes. He's pleading with me.

It's Calvin's plan to go along with what they want, but right now there's empathy rolling off the man who had us lined up on the deck for death just a few days ago. "Easton, Calvin. Just do as he says." I twist my neck. Calvin and

Easton stand with two guards, arms crossed and faces stoic, far from willing to go along with it.

Thayer takes my arm and leads me up the stairs. Easton and Calvin are right behind us. And my heart sinks. This is the way to the back deck. I hold my breath, but I want to scream.

I must have taken a gulp of air, because Thayer glares down at me. "I need you to be quiet. Do you understand me? Your life depends on it. Do as I say, Hal."

I bite my lips and nod. I'm doing the best I can to keep my fear pushed down. We're past the windowless conference room. Down the hallway and not quite to the grand salon. He punches a code into a pad next to a door and opens it. It's a stateroom. The owner's stateroom, if I'm not mistaken. The walls are dark cherry and the linens on the king-sized bed a deep brown. There's a deep scent of cloves and eucalyptus in the air.

"That's good enough," Thayer says. He holds up his hand, stopping the guards from coming into the cabin. They linger in the corridor like well-trained dogs. *Penny.*

There is a pause until Thayer motions them away and closes the door with a button next to the nightstand.

Thayer clears his throat. "The crew I've got on board is loyal to me. But I've been surprised with some of my father's men waiting for us here. They've asked for a ride to our next port."

"And this complicates things," Easton states.

"Yes, spoken like a Rockwell. This complicates things." Thayer pushes another button next to the bed, and a panel next to it opens. "You've had a downgrade in accommodations."

I glance over at Calvin and Easton.

"Don't look at them. They follow you, Hal. And if you want to live, this is the way to do it."

"Okay." I step inside the space. It's a massive closet with an array of Thayer's expensive shirts and suits.

"Back here, Sassy." Dante slides a hanger to the side and opens his arms to me. Beyond Dante, there's another open panel. Sam and Zane are standing in front of the open panel with their arms crossed over their chests. We're all here.

I turn to Thayer. "I'm glad we're together, but why are we here?"

"According to my crew, you've all been killed and are at the bottom of the ocean now. My father's trying to kill all the Rockwells, and the rest of you can't be alive if the younger Rockwell isn't." Thayer says it like he's ordering a bottle of Macallan at a Michelin star restaurant. "Fill them in. And no 'family time.' He cocks his head when he says it, staring at me.

Warmth rushes up my neck in what I know is a strong blush. "Got it." I nod and turn away from him. "Wait. Thayer, where are you giving them a ride to?"

Thayer shakes his head. "Sorry, Hal." Thayer motions Calvin and Easton behind the line of suits and closes the door.

"So fill us in," Easton says, taking a seat on top of a Rimowa extra-large metallic suitcase.

"There are seven little spaces. And enough scratch marks to know they've been used more than once," Zane says, giving a shiver.

"It's disgusting," Sam adds.

"Also kind of genius." Calvin ducks his head into the chambers. "What?" he says when we all stare at him like he's lost his head.

"It is. I mean, yeah, disgusting. That the ship has a

secret compartment for something like this. But also, most of these things are built into the bilge where the Coast Guard or any other maritime agency are trained to look for them. But the owner's cabin? Yeah, they walk in here, move a suitcase maybe, and that's it. Unless they're looking for something small. But people? Not small. Plus, if it's his father's men we're really trying to steer clear of, they're not going to come looking for us in here. His own guards didn't want to come in here. So, gross on a moral scale but good for us. Also, we're not going to smell like bilge or . . ."

"Cat piss," Dante says.

"Yeah, or at least *you* aren't." Calvin laughs and sniffs his shirt. "Guess I should have taken a shower when I had the chance."

"What about Penny and Pepper?" I turn to the closed door.

Sam takes my hand. "Thayer said he would have someone feed and look after them. Apparently, his dad has a thing for animals and would have been more upset if they were gone."

"That's good? I guess." I move closer to Sam.

"Yeah, it is." Sam pulls me onto his lap.

"Here, Sassy." Dante takes a sleeve of crackers from the floor and hands it to me. "I grabbed these on my way out of the galley."

"Thank you." I take a few and pass them to Calvin and Easton.

"There's bottled water in the cubbies back there. Along with a bucket for . . ." Sam trails off.

"Thanks. He wouldn't have cameras in here, would he?"

"No, I don't think so. But you never know with Z."

Calvin steps into the cubby and comes back with a bunch of bottles of water. He hands them to Easton and me.

"If that light there above the hamper clicks from clean to dirty, we're to move into the wall," Sam says. I kiss his cheek and stand, moving into the main part of the closet. My heart rate is beginning to return to normal. It's the stew in me.

I can't help but look through Thayer's suits. They're all custom or high-end off the rack. There are several drawers full of ties. I've been a stew for single male owners before. Most naturally stick to half the closet. Like there's some sort of invisible barrier keeping them off the side of their future partner's turf. Thayer doesn't have that problem. He's taken over the entire space. I open a tuxedo jacket. It's clear it's never been worn, but it's pressed to perfection. The *Rosewood* stews are good at what they do. And it ticks me off a little.

"Little Bird?" Zane wraps his arms around me. "You doing okay?"

I nod. He spins me around and stares into my eyes. And my heart stops beating for a second. Without words, he's telling me that listening up is important.

I nod again. "We're in Taiwan. Right?"

"Yes, Sassy." Dante raises his chin to Zane, in the same subtle *listen up* way.

"Do you remember when I showed you the pictures from last year?" Zane asks.

"Yes."

"Last year's crew at Portofino?"

I nod at Zane. "Yeah. You climbed it with some of the deckies who didn't come back after Rocky changed boats."

Zane turns to Sam.

"I spent time with the captain. Hawk-on Lindholm,"

Sam says. It's a weird change of subject, but I'm getting that somehow the two are connected. "About where the *Rock Candy* went dead in the water. He's about sixty. How old is your mom, Zane?"

"Fifty-eight, but if you meet my mum, I didn't tell you anything." Zane smiles.

This is beyond a little weird. Then it clicks. I remember Zane talking about a deckhand named Hawk. A tall, lanky twenty-one-year-old who could outdrink the rest of the crew.

I nod and give it a few minutes. Dante's listing all the supplies that were brought on board before he was removed from the galley. ". . . watercress, swordfish, Wagyu in all sorts of fucking cuts. Tomahawk, top round . . ."

"The elder Mr. Z is interested in yachts, just like Thayer. It does seem that there are a lot of yachting families."

Sam breaks out into a smile. "Exactly, Sugar. Exactly."

I try to contain my excitement. But I knew that Calvin was holding something back when we were in the cabin. The captain of the *Rosewood* is going to help us. Or at least hopefully doesn't want us dead. "Did Thayer say anything about how long we're going to be here when he brought you in?" I ask Dante.

"No, Sassy. We just got the lowdown on the water, bucket, and glowing light."

"He told you about his father's men?"

"Yeah, and that the *Rosewood* is being used as an Uber by Daddy Dearest." Dante pops a cracker in his mouth.

Sam stands. "We're in Taiwan. Let's talk this through. Where are there ports big enough for the *Rosewood*?"

"More like where is the hot yachting scene within a week of here?" Zane adds.

"Fuck-ton of places," Dante says.

"Gold Coast, Hong Kong . . ." Zane cocks his head.

"No, no way a family like Z's is going to hang out in Hong Kong. There's too much competition, and the government is . . ." Dante dusts his hands together.

"There's Singapore, and the popular areas around Phuket, Thailand. But the real problem with a boat like this is where the fuck do you dock it? Were you guys able to look outside at all when we first docked? We're at some sort of strange outstation fueler." Calvin's pacing, and the small space feels even smaller.

"Yeah, we saw it for an hour or so while I was unloading supplies into the pantry." Dante runs his hand down the side of my arm.

I breathe out. I'm not claustrophobic. Heck, I don't think I'm even afraid of storms anymore. But this space is enough to give me a whole new set of fears. And most of them come from Thayer's dad. "Why does he want us dead? What possible danger do we pose?"

"It's not us, Little Bird."

"It's me," Easton says.

Chapter 16

Dead Weight

Easton

Zane nods at me.

"What else do you know? Because you damn well know more than you're telling me. You don't need to protect me. Leaving me and everyone else in the dark isn't going to help anyone."

"Zed—Ed—the elder Mr. Z, whatever you want to call him—he wants your family dead. There's another player, but I haven't been able to figure out who it is. If you, Rocky, and Emily are dead . . . this person gets everything."

"Harding." I want to smash my fist against the wall, but I don't.

"Your dad's business partner? I don't think so. I don't have Rocky's book in here, but there are a few pages where he's trying to figure it out. Harding knew about the laundering, of course. But he's not the one who started it. At least, that's the impression I get." Zane puts his hand on my shoulder. "You're right. I was trying to protect you. Because knowing your family is in danger and not being able to do anything about it? Bloody hell, if I knew someone had it out for my little sister, I'd go batshit mad not being able to do anything about it. And fuck me, I didn't want that for you. You already didn't know whether they made it to land. I didn't want to add another layer of worry."

Bile rises up my throat because he's right. My face tightens, and I squeeze my hands over my eyes. But then Haley slides under my arms and up my chest. I inhale, letting her coconut scent surround me. My hands drop to her back, and I pull her to me. "Sorry, right." I pry my eyes open. "You're a good friend, Zane. Thank you. I'm sorry my family has wrecked your lives."

Dante scoffs. "I mean . . . thank you. But this has been pretty fucking awesome."

"Dante, we're locked in a closet," Haley says into my shoulder.

"This is a pretty damn good closet to be in." Dante laughs. "No really. All in all, this has been a fucking amazing year. Though there are some things I could have done without."

"Wild boar," Zane says.

"The rainy season." Haley peppers the underside of my chin with kisses.

"The fucking pirates," Sam adds.

"Thayer," Calvin says.

I've already told them a hundred times how the last year was one of the best things that ever happened to me. And I'm the fucking worst thing that has ever happened to them. No matter what happens to me, I'm going to make sure they all come out of this okay. Or at least alive. Fucking alive.

"You know what this means . . ." Haley lifts her head. Our eyes lock.

"No, what does this mean?"

"That Emily and Rocky are alive. Thayer would have said something like you're the last piece in his father's way. But that's not what he said." She cocks her head.

"You're right. It's not proof that Emily and my dad are alive, but . . ."

"There's hope." She squeezes me.

"Okay, I can try and have hope." I kiss the top of her head.

I've slept in a lot of horrible places in the last year. On the beach, in the damn damp plastic raft, sticking to the floor, swaying in the ocean and then again with sand rubbing into my face on the beach, the floor in the abandoned hut on the other side of the island, the treehouse, and then on the pull-out cot in the cabin downstairs. But nothing has prepared me for sleeping in a trafficking closet. We decided that two people would keep watch and four of us would sleep.

Z dropped off some fruit and bread a while ago and graciously let us each take a silent turn using his bathroom instead of the bucket. Now I'm leaning against the back wall, and Haley's nestled between my legs using my stomach as a pillow. I'm pretty sure I've slept only a handful of hours in the last few days. But I'm glad to be assisting Haley. My head's spinning about my sister and dad. And fucking getting us out of here.

Calvin pushes in, Sam too. "The light's on dirty," Calvin whispers, shutting the panel behind him.

My heart thuds at the shouting coming from the main cabin. It's muffled, with the walls and the clothing between there and where we are. But there are at least two male voices. Z's, I think, and another one, maybe two, possibly three.

I lean over Haley and rub her arm. "We have visitors," I whisper.

"What? Oh, oh . . ." She moves to her feet. The space is a little wider than my shoulders. There's light, but it's tinged red and dim. To not be seen through any cracks, I suppose. The conversation I had with Calvin yesterday runs through my head.

He had scratched his beard and scrunched his face like he does before he comes up with a doozie. "If Ed's men are the reason why we're here, but trafficking is part of his business while Z seems . . ."

"Not into shooting us," I said.

"Exactly. Why wouldn't Ed's men know about the chamber in the owner's closet?"

I glared at Calvin. "Shit if I know. Is this Thayer's yacht or Ed's?" I cocked my head at Calvin. Because he's smarter than I'll ever admit he is.

"Thayer's what . . . thirty? Think Dad paid for the yacht?"

"Yeah." I think back to my own finances. Emily and I have trust funds, and different amounts of money vests at different ages. A way of keeping the kids in line. Though I've never actually cared about my dad's money, I'm not as much of a free spirit as Emily. "I couldn't afford to buy the *Rosewood*, not on my own."

"So, his dad did. And if his dad did, wouldn't he have his men search it?"

"Yes," I said.

Now Calvin's voice hisses in the quiet compartment. "Wait for the signal . . ."

Haley's shaking. Vibrating. If she wasn't holding her jaw just so, her teeth would be chattering.

I hold my lips above her ear and whisper, "It's okay." I have absolutely no idea whether it's going to be okay. But at least we've come up with something. Though I'm vibrating on my own.

The overhead light flicks on. Calvin moves the panel to the side, and we all file out. The door to the closet is open. I'm to go first. I have an important job to do. I poke my head out into the main cabin. The door's cracked open. I throw a thumbs-up behind me, and we all move across the primary cabin to our hiding spots. Thayer's voice echoes in the hallway. Calvin and I will hide in the bathroom while Dante, Zane, and Sam hide under the bed. Haley will be in the best spot, the chest at the end of the bed. It's just big enough for her. I stop at the chest and hold it open for her while she contorts herself. I give her a smile and close the lid. Calvin's standing in the doorway to the bathroom when I get there. There's enough space behind the door for the two of us to stand. As long as the door doesn't get thrown open, we should be good. Calvin pushes me back, taking the front position. He wanted Haley in here with us. But she's better off in the chest. It's small enough that they're not going to open it. Especially after they've already searched the room. Calvin had brought up the issue to Thayer, that Ed's men would want to search the lockers. And we all came up with the plan together. Thayer would let them search the room, take them out into the hallway and acquiesce about letting them search the lockers after giving us time to move.

"Fine," Z says, too loudly. But I'm hoping they don't figure it out. Nothing we can do about it now. "Search it. But I like my privacy too much to ever let someone stay back there."

"I heard you've hardly been in here for the last few days. Staying in your office."

"I'm a workaholic, just like Ed."

"Right," the deep voice says. "Then you don't mind showing us."

"Fine," Z responds. "I'll remember this."

Through a small opening in the hinge, I see a flicker of a dark-clad security guard and then . . . nothing.

"Nothing. Exactly as I told you," Z says a few minutes later.

I'm holding my breath and keeping as still as possible. Wishing I wasn't as close to the hinge as I am. But I'm not moving now.

The door slams shut. We're not supposed to move back until he comes into the cabin again. Which could be a hell of a long time. I find myself watching a shadow slowly moving across the floor.

It's been over an hour when I lean forward to Calvin. "We need to get Haley out of there."

"It's made of wood, and there's a crack in the side," he whispers back.

"She's not going to be able to walk straight."

Calvin glares back at me, and the shadow inches forward, hitting the shower door. Thayer made it clear: don't move from where we're hiding until he comes back. But this is becoming fucking crazy, and I'm worried about Haley. Though sore is better than dead. I school my breathing and wait.

The yacht shakes. We rock left and right, and then it stops.

"We've docked," Calvin whispers.

I nod. Because I'd figured that out on my own. But where are we? And what now?

Chapter 17

Monsoon Bay

Sam

"We've stopped moving," Zane whispers to the right of me.

I nod.

I can't stop thinking of Haley in the hutch. We should have brought her under here with us. And I've had enough. I'm not sure the last time I squeezed under a bed, but I definitely had more space when I did. Hide and seek with Charlie, maybe?

"Sam?" Zane whispers.

I hold my hand up to him to say wait, but straighten myself up. Easton's already at the end of the bed, pulling Haley out of the box. Dante and Zane pop out of the other side of the bed.

"I thought it would be a good space," Haley whispers and then winces when she tries to put her foot down. "My foot's asleep."

Easton picks her up and turns to the bathroom when the door opens.

"Well, I see you all fucking listen well. I said stay hidden. Fuck me," Thayer growls and shakes his head, closing the door behind him. "We've anchored. I've made arrangements for you to be taken to the main building. My father's men have their own facilities on the other side of the property. You'll need to be out of here fast. Holloway will come get you. I know this isn't what you want. But in my own way, I'm keeping you safe. So don't fuck me over." His eyes narrow, and he glides through the door with a click. Honestly, I'm not sure what to think of him anymore. Is he even telling the truth? Mostly I have no idea what's in it for him.

"Sam?" Haley wraps an arm around my waist, rubbing her calf with the other hand. "Are you good?"

"No. But yes. What do you think is in it for him?"

"Thayer?" Her eyebrows rise. "I don't know. But you know, I don't think he knows either. He's like a hurricane, not sure if he's going to rain down over the coast of Florida or save it all for the Carolinas. Ya know?"

"Yeah, that's perfect."

We debate about going back into the closet, but we're all sick of it and end up sitting and sprawled over the massive bed. Haley's still trying to stand when the door opens again. We pop up, a wall of men between the door and the bed.

Holloway has a sack over his shoulder. "Here, black clothing to match the rest of the security team." He tosses it down on the bed and shakes his head. Like he too can't figure out how we're still alive. "I'll be back in five minutes. Be ready. Single file. There are some guns in the bottom of the bag." I must have given him a reaction because he laughs. "No ammo in them. But it would look weird to have a boat full of unarmed guards coming ashore. And Hal, cover up your hair."

"Got it," Haley says behind me. I turn to find her still rubbing her leg. Her wide blue eyes hold mine.

"Be ready." Holloway shuts the door.

Soon, we're changed and standing with our empty guns strapped to our bodies. Haley found a black T-shirt of Thayer's and has it wrapped around her sun-bleached hair as a scarf with a ball cap over top of it.

Holloway's back in the room in no time. "You're a sorry looking bunch of recruits. But let's go. Anyone talks to you, you let me do the talking." Holloway moves over to Calvin. "Do you understand me, Green?"

"I've been a good little prisoner."

"Fuck me. Move." Holloway opens the door and we're out. Through the main salon where the odd wood fire is crackling, out onto the back deck, and down to the swim platform where there's one guard—the older guard who threw Collins into the water—and the head steward Kennedy. I step up to the tender. Calvin has already climbed on board.

"What's wrong with him?" Holloway points at Haley. We're moving quickly, and Haley's limping.

"My foot's asleep." She lowers her voice, just like she did back on the pirate boat.

"Well, cut it out," Holloway growls.

"I'm trying," Haley huffs out.

I step onto the tender and turn back to take Haley's hand to help her aboard, but she shakes her head. I drop my hand because she's right—Thayer's dad or the security team might be watching. I take a seat in front of Calvin, moving all the way to the end of the bench. Haley sits next to me and slides down.

"Hurry up." Holloway glares at Easton, Zane, and

Dante. "I'm not sure which I'll be happier to have gone, you or the damn animals."

I look back at the *Rosewood* and at Holloway. "Penny, my dog?" Fuck, after all of this . . . to lose Penny now? She's half of the reason I didn't lose my mind when I was adrift on the *Rock Candy*. I'm trying to forget my drunken nights on board, the hours of spying for a speck of light on the horizon. Praying that anyone I came across didn't want to shoot me to salvage the *Rock Candy* for profit.

"And Pepper?" Haley asks. Haley's the other half of what kept me alive all those days. Staring at her picture kept me from losing my shit altogether. Hoping, *praying* that she was okay. Picturing her back in Miami, alive, kept me going through those long days.

"They're already in the main house. Mr. Z had me bring the two of them there. After the animal shelter picked up the feral cats," Kennedy says.

My head snaps to Kennedy. "I want her back—them back. Penny and Pepper, not the feral cats," I say to be clear.

"Good luck getting them back from Esmeralda. When she finds something she likes, she doesn't let go. She can be a bit—" Kennedy cuts himself off with a look from Holloway.

What the hell does that mean? But I keep my questions to myself. Haley's more important. As much as I love that damn dog, I'm not putting Haley's life in jeopardy. We'll find a way.

I glance across the water to the beach. We're about three hundred yards out. At the shore's edge, there's a long dock with a boat shed. Beyond the dock, there are several long flights of wooden stairs up to a structure that climbs the hill. Pops of red metal roofs flash through the deep foliage.

It's steep enough that I can't see the tops of the buildings from this angle. "That's the main house?"

Dante slides in next to me. Zane sits next to Calvin, and Easton sits in the row in front of us.

"Yes, but you're not going there," Holloway says as he boards and takes the tiller from the old guy.

"Good luck." Kennedy tosses the lines from the *Rosewood* and we're off. I'm not sure if his wish is a warning or genuine.

I'm glaring back at Kennedy when Dante catches my attention over Haley's head. "Esmeralda? She better give us our animals back. We'll make it happen," Dante says.

I wish I could be as confident.

Holloway pilots the tender toward the house and its massive dock. There's a bit of chop in the water. Until we're over the breakers, water sprays over the pant leg of my too-large pants with each wave.

Haley points at the house on the hillside. "Whoa."

I've seen some mansions in my day. This one goes up the side of a steep cliff. Each story has a balcony, and every level up steps back. The structure's sienna-colored wood glistens in the midmorning light, and the red roofs flash. If I was cruising by, I'd think it was a private resort, not a family compound.

Once we're through the breakers, Holloway changes course and veers away from the house and the large dock. Away from the pristine beach, out of sight of the main house, stands a utilitarian concrete building halfway up the hillside. There are no glamorous teak stairs here, but rather a well-worn path along an eight-foot-high fence topped with barbed wire. In the span of a couple hundred feet and a vegetation screen, we've gone from an upscale five-star resort to Alcatraz. There's a small wooden dock fifty feet or so out from the shore. It has more missing boards than ones still intact. I peer over the side of the rubber tender. The water's deeper than I thought it would be, twenty feet at least.

Holloway turns the tender to the side and comes along the crumbling dock to a waiting guard.

"How's your leg?" I rub the lower part of Haley's calf. "Can you feel it yet?"

"It's still pins and needles." She tries a smile. "We need to get Penny and Pepper," she whispers to me.

"Good luck with that." Holloway laughs over the outboard engine, stands, and tosses a line to the guard.

Dante's out first. I step up and around him, turning back to help Haley.

"Why?" Haley steps tenderly on her foot on the dock and winces.

"Here, Sassy. Let me help you." Dante holds out his hand.

"It's Hal. And I've got it." She steps on the dock, but Dante's not moving. His hand stays stretched out to Haley. They're having a standoff. And I know who's going to win. I step over the row of seats in front of me and up onto the dock next to Easton. Haley's climbing out with Dante standing over her. I take another step back without looking. There's a crack. And then I'm through the dock. Somehow, I have the presence of mind to clutch my hands to my torso as I go down.

Down.

Water.

Seaweed.

Splintering boards follow.

There's a rock at my feet. Sharp rocks on my leg.

I flail my arms. Splinters of boards mix with seaweed and barnacles.

I turn onto my side and give a few hefty kicks. I'm out from under the shitty dock when I burst through the top of the water. Sputtering.

"Sam!" Haley screams, all discreetness in her voice gone. "Sam."

"Fuck, Sam, are you okay?" I'm not sure which guy yells it. I am glad to hear that Haley didn't fall in behind me.

"I'm good." I bob up and down, grateful to be wearing the too-big shoes. Coral, barnacle, and rocks claw at my legs. Flotsam and jetsam swirl around me. I take a few strokes toward the dock but stop short. There's no point going back up there. "Get off there. Carefully. I'll meet you at the shore." I switch to shallow strokes, swimming on my back.

"Sam, your arm," Haley says when I get closer, a concerned edge of panic in her voice.

I don't have to look to know I'm scraped to hell and full of adrenaline. "Watch where you're going."

They're bunched up on the dock. I turn on my stomach and swim until I can stand—taking my own advice. It's tough going as the rocks are uneven and I'm fighting clothes that are a few sizes too big for me. I grapple over the wave-battered rocks. Calvin's wading in to meet me. "I'm good. I'm good."

"Shut the fuck up and let me help you," Green says.

I nod and throw my arm over his shoulder. "Thank you."

"That's what family is for." He half carries and half yanks me over a few yards and helps me up to the path where Holloway is keeping everyone else from coming down.

"Let me go." Haley rips away from Holloway. "Sam, oh

god." She touches my arm and drops to her knees where my pants are sliced open.

"I'm good, Hal." I stress her name. "Thank you, though."

"Can you walk?" Holloway hollers from the path.

"Yeah. I can walk."

Chapter 18

Dead Calm

Haley

It took me more than a second to recover from Sam breaking through the dock. I had to fight my way through Dante to get onto the dock. And now that I've got my hand on his leg, and there's blood trailing into his shoes? I want to shout, "You are not okay. None of this is okay." But I don't. Because what good would that do? Nothing.

"Haley, Hal." Sam puts his palm on my shoulder. "Really, I'm okay. It's just a tiny scratch."

I gently lift up his pant leg. There's a pair of long, deep gashes, with several others around them. I flick my head behind me and hold Calvin's eyes long enough for him to know that this is more than just a tiny scratch.

I tilt my head up to Sam and purse my lips. "Well, this tiny scratch needs Easton's attention."

"Do you have a medical kit?" Easton's at my side.

"Can we get the lot of you into the building?" Holloway

growls, but he's not looking at us. He's looking up the path, next to an ominous chain-link fence with barbed wire. I've been to some really crazy-expensive mansions before. But none of them had fences with barbed wire.

"Yes, I'm good. Let's get inside." Sam pushes past me and onto the path. Calvin's at his side. He's not holding him up, but he's got his hand out in case he needs to help Sam again. "I'm good, Calvin."

"All right." Calvin puts his hands in the air.

"Lead the way, Holloway." Sam says, limping and leaving a trail of bright red behind him.

"Fucking hell, man, we didn't even last thirty seconds on land before one of us got hurt. It's amazing we didn't die back on the island." Dante half slaps Sam on his back, but then he doesn't move his arm and Sam puts his arm around Dante's shoulder.

"Well, if you hadn't been fussing over Hal back there, I would've seen the— Forget it, that's not right. That's the scratch talking." Sam looks back at me. "This is not your fault, Haley. You either, Dante."

"You mean Hal," I say. "No, it's Thayer's. Or Ed's. Or whoever orchestrated the sabotage of the *Rock Candy*, and now you're hurt. This should be the biggest and happiest moment of our—" I was going to say lives, but that's not right, not anymore. There were so many moments back on the island that were so perfect, but the second we touch the mainland, or as close to civilization as we've been in over a year, *this* is when one of us gets hurt? I don't like what the universe is trying to tell us. I don't like it at all. My stomach twists looking at Sam's leg. He's lucky it wasn't worse.

Zane grabs my hand. "Don't go putting too much meaning into this, Little Bird. It's just deferred maintenance and a rich asshole not thinking about the people who take care of him, spending all his money on his fancy boathouse and nothing on the security team that keeps him safe."

"I know," I say, but I don't mean it. We're halfway up the well-worn path to the concrete building with a mismatched metal roof. It looks like something built fifty years ago and never maintained, not something that should be on Thayer's estate. But I guess it matches the dock.

Holloway holds the door to the old building open for us. Inside, it smells like mold and stale cigarettes. The fluorescent lights are only half working. There's a metal table in the corner, and a broken cabinet holds a sink and a hot plate on the other side. Mismatched chairs line the back of the room.

"Now what, Holloway? You don't expect us to get Sam cleaned up here, do you? He'll end up with a staph infection. This place is filthy." I cross my arms over my chest and glare up at the big guard.

He glares back at me. "No, that wasn't part of the plan, but neither was falling through the dock. I was to hold you here until sunset and then take you up the back way to the main house. Thayer will be waiting for you. Only the caretaker guards use this building. They're a couple of old locals who have worked for the Zambranos forever. So no, I didn't expect us to be doing any triage in here, but that's what we've got. I can't risk taking you up to the main house during the day. The elder Mr. Z's guards will definitely notice. And that's not something you want. So stay tight. I'm gonna go get some stuff. I'll be back. I don't know. See what you can find around here to clean up a bit if it bothers you that much. But don't move. Don't leave this building. If you do, I can't protect you." Holloway's out the door.

Zane peers out the door after Holloway.

"And stay away from the doors and windows," Holloway yells back.

Zane turns back to us. "He's halfway up the path out of sight. We should move."

"No, we're not going anywhere," Easton says.

Calvin goes to the sink and turns on the faucet. The water runs light brown.

"Ew, that's not good," I say.

"Let it run for a while." Dante helps Sam sit. "I worked a couple of weeks in a restaurant here in Thailand. Older buildings can have bad pipes, but if you let it run, it'll clear right up."

I shake off the fog of shock. My adrenaline's crashing. We've got to get Sam cleaned up as well as we can. "Take your shirt off," I tell him. Sam pulls off his shirt with a grunt. There's not a mark on his chest and only a few light scratches on his shoulders. His arms, however? The outside of his forearms on both sides are scratched with light abrasions. His left elbow has a deep gash. "Pants too."

Sam stands next to a chair. He drops his pants, holding on to the side of the chair for support, and I try not to gasp at his injuries, but they look worse than when I first saw them. There are a few scratches on his left, nothing big. But on his right leg, there are two long gouges, two inches apart, from his knee down to his ankle bone. There are some on his thighs too. But they're not as deep.

"Bloody hell, Sam. You're gonna need a tetanus booster shot for sure," Zane says.

Easton's eyes flick to mine, and he swallows. "We've seen worse. And there's medicine here. I'm sure Holloway can maybe go get us a tetanus shot. And as long as he has a kit for stitches, I'll have you cleaned up in no time." Easton nods up at Sam.

"Let me help you get your shoes off," I say.

Zane finds the cleanest of the chairs and places it next to Sam. "Sit on the edge of this."

He does, and I take a lopsided chair and sit next to him. I hold out my hand, and he takes it.

"This isn't how I thought things would go down either, Sugar."

"Yeah, but it's not that bad." I kiss the top of his hand. I'm trying to convince myself more than Sam.

"It's clear," Calvin says from the other side of the room. "And the hot plate even works."

"There's got to be a pot or something around here. Let's boil some water." Dante crouches next to Calvin's legs and rummages around in the cabinet until he comes up with a pot.

Twenty minutes later, the water's just starting to boil when Holloway comes crashing through the crooked door with the supplies we need.

"Took you fucking long enough," Dante says.

I cock my head at Dante because, while I love him, he doesn't need to antagonize the one person who has shown us some kindness.

"Thank you, Holloway," I say, taking the kit from him. I spread it on a corner of the table that we've cleaned while waiting for the water to boil.

Holloway pulls something from his back pocket. "I brought this too." He hands a bar of soap to Easton.

Hands washed, Easton begins the long process of cleaning out the larger scratches and stitching them up. After twenty, I lose count of how many stitches Easton makes. It takes a good couple hours to get Sam bandaged up, even though we run out of bandages for some of his smaller scratches. It's well past dinnertime when I get the last bandage on Sam's leg. His stomach starts rumbling.

"Excuse me," he says.

Holloway has been standing in the corner watching. "I can't bring you guys anything to eat right now. But it'll be dark in another hour."

"I've gone longer without food. It's not a problem. Thanks for the supplies, Holloway," Sam says.

I wrap my arm around Sam as we watch Holloway leave. "How do you feel now?"

"Not bad. It stings, but it's not horrible."

The door squeaks open, and I jump. We're not expecting anyone to come in since it's not nearly dark yet and Holloway just left. A tall gray-haired man with a square jaw and deep wrinkles, the kind you get from decades of being out in the sun, stands in the doorway.

"Hey. Excuse me, I didn't mean to startle you." His voice is deep with a thick accent, something Nordic—like a lot of officers in yachting. And I can't help wondering if this is Haakon, the captain of the *Rosewood*. "Sam, are you hurt?"

"I'm gonna be fine, just fine. Our resident medic has fixed me up. It's nice to see you again, though."

The *Rosewood* captain glances over his shoulder out into the twilight. "I'm sorry I can't help you more. But I do have this for you." He hands Sam an envelope. "Holloway should be taking you to the house soon. When you get there, what you find in the envelope should help you. I wish you the best of luck. Once again, I question the decisions I have made in my own life, and I know Hawk will never forgive me for not doing more." The captain looks down at the dirty tile floor, and he shakes his head and disappears back out into the early evening.

Sam holds the envelope in his lap.

"Bloody hell, Sam. Aren't you gonna open it?" Zane's eyebrows shoot up.

Chapter 19

Paper Beats Lock

Zane

I want to rush across the room and rip the envelope from Sam's hand. "What is it?"

"It better be six plane tickets back to Miami or I'm gonna track Hawk down and tell him exactly what an asshole his dad is," Calvin says.

Sam cracks open the seal of the envelope and peers into it without revealing the contents. His eyebrows shoot up.

"What is it?" Dante storms across the room. And I expect him to rip the envelope from Sam's hand, but he doesn't. "Show us. Holloway could be back any second."

Sam holds up a fistful of cash. It's mostly American money, but there are some pounds and probably what's local currency mixed in. "There's a note too. It says, 'Esmeralda, these are good people. Do what you can, and I will owe you one, whatever you want.'"

Dante lets out a laugh. "I wonder if what Esmeralda wants is the *Rosewood*'s captain?"

"Well, I don't care what she wants as long as she helps us," I say.

"Here, Haley, you hold the money. Z seems to have some pretty strong rules about what his guards can and cannot do to women. It'll be safest with you."

"It better be, or I'll tear them to shreds." Calvin moves from where he's been standing next to the door. "How much is there, Haley?"

We watch her count it in silence for a few moments.

"That's great and all, but what use is money if we can't get by Z's guards? And more importantly, Ed's guards?" I crouch next to Haley, and she stops counting.

"Maybe Esmeralda holds our get out of jail free card." Easton gathers up the medical kit from the table.

"You played Monopoly?" My voice rises. Easton gives me the look. It's his I'm-thinking-about-Emily look. "Sorry."

"No worries. We did use real money, though." He smiles.

"Shut up, Rockwell," Calvin says, staring back out the window next to the door.

Easton cocks his head at me. "Susan won a house in the Hamptons from my dad when I was on Christmas break my freshman year."

"Fucking—"

"—rich people," Easton finishes for me. There's a moment of laughter. A moment where we're just us back on the island.

"How much, Sassy?"

"Excluding some of the Asian currencies I don't know the exchange rate for, it's about 3000 USD." Haley shoves it inside her bra.

"Well, we've got cash and a note. It's the start of a plan," Sam says as he stands. There's a twitch in the corner of his eye. He's in pain, but he's trying not to show it as he paces along the windows.

Haley hasn't moved from the chair next to where Easton stitched Sam back together. Dante's wiped down the counter around the hot plate with some rags they've boiled. I'm resisting the urge to mop the floor. Instead, I sit in Sam's chair and hold Haley's hand. "You all right, Little Bird? Forget that. None of us are okay. But we will be. We've got cash and an IOU."

She wraps her arms around my neck and hugs me. "Thank you, Zane." She squeezes me tightly. There's a squeak, and Haley jumps in my arms. Her chair clatters to the ground.

Holloway's frame fills the dark doorway. "Let's move out." He waits for all of us to exit the building before locking the door behind us. "Keep quiet and move quickly." He stares at Sam, who returns the decisive nod.

Holloway leads us up the path a hundred yards or so, and we end up walking alongside a more modern building. He's not a good tour guide, but from the looks of the building, it's what replaced the building we've been sitting in for the last few hours. A lit crisscross path through the manicured jungle eventually runs up to the side of the mansion.

He holds open the hearty-looking wooden door until we're all through. It's clear that this isn't the main entrance of the mansion. But it's also not the staff entrance; the trail we were on continues upward to a utilitarian door, forty feet up the path. "Turn to the left when you get in and wait for me."

I'm the third one in behind Calvin and Haley. The corridor smells like incense or jasmine, a relief from the stench we've been sitting in. And it's a lot cooler. The walls are dark, polished wood, and the floor shines. You can tell there's money here. Even though there's no impressive art on the walls, the architecture itself is enough to stand out. This is exactly the sort of place that, if we weren't running for our lives, I would like to explore. Once everyone's in, Holloway takes the lead and we're down the hall and up half a flight of stairs, down another corridor, then left. I catch a few glimpses into some rooms. They're all inspired by Thailand, not like so many rich people who want their mansions to look like a London flat. It makes me mad that I'm having positive thoughts about the Zed family at all.

Holloway leads us down a long, narrow dark corridor. The walls, ceiling, and floor are all the same polished dark wood. Identical doors pepper the corridor every twenty feet. He stops at the end of the hallway and opens a door on the interior side of the building. "Stay here until I come get you. I'll see if I can find some food. And no noise, nothing at all. Try not to breathe if you can." He pulls the door tightly shut behind him. The handle rattles.

Calvin tries the handle, but it doesn't turn. "Locked."

"Had to try," I agree.

Haley finds the light switch, and a hanging brass lantern illuminates orange velvet cushions scattered around the middle of the room. On the far wall, there's a single long shelf with leatherbound books. The right-hand wall has a small horizontal window at shoulder height, and across from it there is one sleek modern recliner. It could be worse.

Haley pulls a few cushions together. "Here, Sam, you take the chair."

"I'm good. I don't want to put any pressure on the new stitches."

"I could hold your legs up," Haley says with a laugh in her voice.

"Thank you." Sam kisses the top of her head. "But I'll stand for now. You take the chair."

Calvin and Dante are right at the corners of the room, running their hands along the wall, looking for cameras.

Easton's at the bookcase. "Did you catch what Holloway said?"

"Zambrano," Haley says, pushing up onto her elbows on the cushions.

"That's what Zed must stand for." I sink onto the floor next to her.

Easton's got his back to us, flipping through some books. "It feels like I should know that name, for some reason." He turns, holding the book open in his hand. He looks like a preacher the Sunday after a rock festival.

"There's a Zambrano's Pizza in my old neighborhood." Sam takes a book and flips through it.

"It's not that uncommon of a name. But Rocky knows Thayer's dad. So maybe you heard it from him." Haley's rubbing her calf again. She should never have been in that chest for so long.

"I don't think there's any surveillance in this room," Calvin says after a good few minutes of searching.

"Zambrano's Pizza? Bet the crust was limp." Dante drops on the cushion on the other side of Haley.

"It was hit or miss," Sam says.

"That tracks." I take over, rubbing Haley's calf. Because just when I think Z's a decent guy, he shits on us again.

The door eases open. "Remember, I said no talking." Holloway places a tray in the middle of the floor. There's a loaf of bread and a half dozen water bottles. Sam stops his pacing behind Holloway, the book behind his back.

"Bread and water," Dante says with a cock to his head.

"That's all I could get quickly. The kitchen is super

busy. Listen, I don't like this any more than you do. I don't want to have to shoot you, so don't make me. Esmeralda would kill me after she got the bloodstains out of the floor."

"I'd like to meet her," Sam says.

"No, you don't." Holloway shuts the door.

Sam's leaning against the wall next to the door. "Who wants to do the recon?"

"Recon?" Easton asks.

"I'll stay here with Haley. Calvin, I don't think you should go. I know you can walk softly but . . ." Sam twists the handle. There's a muffled noise, and the door opens.

"Don't be mad at me Haley, but I've defaced a book." Sam holds open the book with a ripped corner missing. "I pushed some paper into the lock keeping it from latching all the way."

"Zane and I are going. The rest of you stay here," Calvin says.

"He's right. They're both quiet when they walk, and Calvin's good at combat. I'm faster, but I'm not going to blend well here. I have certain other assets. Go." Haley touches my leg and gives me a quick kiss on the cheek.

"I'm going too," Easton says.

I look at Calvin and back at Rockwell's clown feet. They might have helped him win some gold medals, but the bloody things echo.

"I can be quiet."

Calvin shrugs and cocks his head to the door.

"I'm leaving the paper in the lock so you can get back in," Sam says, then silently pulls the door shut behind us.

The Viking takes the lead. I'm next, and Easton takes the rear. There's a trickle of sweat running down my neck, even though a breeze blows through the corridor.

"Silent but like we belong," Calvin whispers. Which

might work as long as we don't run into any of the security team from the *Rosewood*. He takes us back to the beginning of the hallway and turns away from the door. Ten feet in, we have a choice to make—down a flight of stairs, through a door to the right, or up the stairs. The current of air shifts, and the scent of food rises from the floor below.

No one has said what or who this Esmeralda is, but if she's the house manager, she's bound to be around the kitchen.

"Down." I point.

Calvin shakes his head and points up. But then there are footsteps coming up the stairs and Easton opens the door and yanks us both through it with him.

Chapter 20

Set a Course

Easton

I grab Zane by the arm and give him a firm yank into the room. Calvin moves on his own, even though I'm holding on to his arm as well. I don't even check what's in the room behind us. It could be full of guards, Holloway, or Z himself. It doesn't matter. It's better than being exposed to whoever is coming down the stairs.

Calvin shakes me off his arm and closes the door with a silent click. The room's dark, and it takes my eyes a minute to adjust. There's a massive antique desk facing into the room, with a green-shaded lamp. Behind the desk is a wall of bookshelves.

It's different from the other rooms we got a glimpse into on the way in. It's all western decor, leather furniture. On the far wall, there's a low sofa with a table behind it. The light's pretty dim, but there are at least thirty framed photographs in different sizes. I pick one up. It's a view of Central Park from a building, the balcony's cement railing in the foreground.

The scrape of a shoe on the floor spins me around.

"Sorry," Zane whispers. He's by the desk.

Calvin's by the door, on guard, waiting for it to open to choke whoever is behind it to death with his bare hands.

Zane moves behind the desk and motions us over. "Come on. If someone comes in, we should hide."

Calvin glares and puts his finger over his lips. He's listening to whoever is moving around in the corridor. We all freeze until he nods. "Anyone who comes in here, we're going to need to fight them," Calvin whispers back. "We'll stay here for a few minutes, see what you can find."

Zane clicks on the desk lamp. There's no computer, but a collection of fountain pens in a case sits in front of other supplies. Zane tries the drawers, but they're locked.

With the light on, I can see the pictures behind the desk more clearly. They're all landscapes. A few are artsy black and white; others are color.

My stomach twists. I can pick out exactly where most of them were taken. I don't like being anything like the Zambrano family. But I can't change that I was raised in privilege. That's the past. I pick up a picture. It's definitely London, Oxford maybe. Another one is a ski resort in Switzerland. I've been there once. One of the times that Emily dragged me along to go skiing.

I grab another. I've definitely seen this one before. Maybe it was thinking about the ski resort and Emily, but this is Emily's high school in Vermont, a picture of the main building. It's like a stone castle. I'd know it anywhere. In the background is the mountain that the freshmen climb on their first day, and then the seniors climb again down the other side of the mountain the day they graduate. And that's when it hits me.

Zambrano. Thayer Zambrano. He's that asshole boyfriend of Emily's. The one she had her freshman year. He was a senior. Fuck me. How could I have forgotten . . . I was training in Utah, but still. He told her he loved her and then dumped her when he graduated. Just like I said he would. Because Thayer and I were—are—the same age. And I know the type. Because I was the type. Damn. She sent me links to sad YouTube videos the entire summer. Dad took her to Europe to cheer her up. But she wanted to go to Thayer's apartment in London and convince him to not break up with her. He wouldn't see her . . . fucking hell. That's how my dad met Ed. That's how this whole hell started.

"Whoa, mate," Zane says, not in a whisper.

"What?"

"You're bleeding." Zane takes the broken picture frame out of my hand and turns in a circle. "I need to stash this somewhere."

"Give me that picture," I say.

He puts the frame on the desk and hands me a tissue. "Stop the bleeding first." He raises his eyebrows at me.

It's not a big cut. I'm able to wrap the tissue around my finger and slow the bleeding.

"What makes you so mad about a castle? Not even a bloody good one. Well, I guess it's bloody now." Zane's working on extracting the picture from the broken frame.

I ignore his joke. "That's how the Zambrano family met mine, or rather Emily. It's her boarding school. Their school, I guess. Thayer's an asshole she dated in high school. He broke her heart, and my dad took her to some estate in Switzerland—no, Albania."

"Well, at least we know now why he's not killing us. He's still got a thing for Emily," Calvin says. "We don't need to worry about it now. The coast is clear." He has the door cracked.

I can't look away from the array of photos behind the sofa. I step back over to look at them again.

"Here." Zane hands me the scratched photo, then crouches down and shoves the broken frame under the desk. "Hold up. There's something down here." Zane pushes on something, and a wood panel drops, clanking loudly to the ground.

"What is it?" Calvin asks.

"Not sure. A file." Zane puts it on the desk, flipping through it. "Why do rich people think that paper is more secure?" Zane's forehead creases in his code-breaker stare.

"Because it usually is. What did you find?" I tuck the picture in my pocket.

"This is Ed's office. And this is a list of people with marks next to each name. Pound signs, check marks, and downward arrows. I'm not sure what they mean. Should I take it? Fuck that, I'm taking it. The head asshole has tried to kill me at least three times now. I might as well give him a reason. The wanker." Zane tucks the file into the back of his pants.

"Are you two ready?" Calvin glares at us.

"Yeah." I nod. "No, wait."

"Wait? Why?" Zane asks.

I take a couple more of the framed pictures and bring them over to the light on the desk. I can't shake the feeling that there's more here. "This one. This one is the same cross that was in the black and white photo we found on the *Rock Candy*." The picture is of the inside of a simple cathedral. But the rustic cross matches the one in the other picture.

"Maybe? It's clear that Ed is the one who set up the sabotage of the *Rock Candy*. Though I'm still not sure he's the one who ordered it." Zane takes the photo from me and hands it back. "Creeps me out, mate."

This time I slide the photo out of the frame. I fold the photograph and put it in my pocket next to the other one of Pine Green Academy.

"We need to get going. I don't want to stay anywhere for too long," Calvin says.

"Agreed." Zane moves to the door next to Calvin.

Calvin puts his hand on the door handle. "Up or down the stairs?"

"Down. The kitchen is definitely down, and that's where we're going to find Esmerelda." Zane turns and asks, "Your finger good?"

"It's fine." It's mostly stopped bleeding.

"You've got some rage in you. Save it for Zambrano's men." Calvin opens the door and walks out into the hall like he belongs here. We're down the worn wooden stairs. The hallway here steps away from the hillside. But Zane was right—this is the direction of the kitchen. And my stomach is turning traitor.

The corridor opens up into a small commercial-style kitchen. There's a lot going on. Four Thai males hustle around. A tall woman with gray hair in a chef's jacket and floral scrub pants is chopping so fast her fingers are a blur. She's absolutely not from here.

She turns and glares at Calvin. "You new? Ed's man?" She puts one hand on her hip, a knife in the other one. And I'm wishing Dante was here to speak to her, chef to chef.

Calvin raises his chin in an affirmative.

I widen my stance and act like any of the security guards my dad has hired over the years.

"What the fuck? You're not due until midnight. All twenty of you are already here? I'm not going to have enough dinner for you. I have to feed everyone on the *Rose-wood* too. Along with all the regular staff. And Mr. Z." She shakes her head. Her accent is odd. American, maybe, but twisted from years of living abroad.

There's a high-pitched bark, and Penny comes running from across the kitchen. She's in full play mode, barking and jumping, first on Calvin. But when he ignores her, she moves to Zane, who has never ignored her. Zane rubs her behind her ear. Her foot starts thumping.

The thump of Penny's foot matches my heart. I scan the kitchen for a weapon. There are lots of options, but no knives near me.

Esmeralda says something in Thai, and the four men scurry out of the kitchen. "You're not Ed's men. You're the ones who're supposed to be dead. The crew of the yacht that was lost last year." She looks from Calvin to Zane to me. She holds up a chef's knife.

"Yes," I say. "We have a note."

"A note?" She laughs. "A note? You think that's going to keep me from calling the guards in here?"

"Why didn't you already?" I ask. "You could have. Instead, you let the kitchen staff take a smoke break."

"I like your dog. Cat's okay. A bit of a demon. But she's coming around. And my sous chefs? They would have knocked over my broth on their way to get out of a fight anyhow. Now, what's on this note that makes you think I'm not going to call someone who won't run away?"

Penny nuzzles my hand until I start petting her, even though I'm not looking at her but at the knife Esmeralda's holding.

"The note." I cock my head at Zane.

"Right." He pulls it out of his pocket. "Here." He hands it over to her.

She reads it and purses her lips. "Well, I guess that answers my question about what I'm going to do." The knife drops to the counter with a clatter, and she takes long steps over to a disheveled desk in the corner of the room. There are stacks of paper and open cookbooks mixed with receipts and at least ten open energy drinks. She grabs a piece of paper. "I'll give you the information, but it's up to the lot of you. Aren't there more of you?"

I nod.

"Right." She draws a map on the paper. "This is the staff path to the main dock. There's a boat in there. Keys are in a locker on the wall."

"Where's Pepper?" I ask.

"You're going to take the dog and cat with you?"

"Yes," Calvin says.

"That's the dumbest thing I've ever heard. You're going to get them hurt. No, they stay. You go. You know the way?" She shakes the map at Calvin.

"Yes," Zane says.

"Right. I'm not letting you keep this. But here's my email address. You actually get yourselves back to the states, or England, or wherever the hell you want, contact me. I'll find a way to get you your animals. Because they don't need to die with you. Okay?"

I'm about to go to town on her when Calvin puts his hand out. "I have your word?"

"I swear to the Philadelphia Eagles that I will take good care of your pets until you let me know you're safe." She shakes his hand.

"I expect you to stick to your oath even though you're an Eagles fan," I say.

She laughs. "So, what are you going to do? It's up to you. But if it were me, I would get the hell out of here."

Chapter 21

Below Deck

Calvin

A sliver of light comes from the room with Haley and the guys. Easton's about to push open the door when I grab his wrist. With my other hand, I put a finger to my lips and raise my eyebrows. We don't know if anyone else is in there.

He nods at me and checks. "Clear." He pushes into the room.

"Let's go," I say.

Sam and Haley are sitting on the floor near a blanket with pillows under it that looks like someone could be sleeping under them.

"Where?" Dante asks from next to the window.

"The dock. Now." I hold the door open and usher the three of them out into the hall with Easton and Zane. I remove the wad of paper Sam stuck in the lock and pull the door tightly shut. I hold the paper up to Sam before I put it in my pocket. "Let Holloway think we can walk through walls."

Sam smiles.

"This way." Zane beckons to Haley.

"Keep looking for cameras, and turn your face away if you see any," Dante says.

I'm watching every limp Sam makes as we wind our way through the mansion. The damn thing has more flights of stairs than the nosebleed seats at Wrigley Field.

"I'm good. Keep going." Sam lifts his chin at me.

We have to duck into what's clearly a guest bedroom to avoid a trio of security who are moaning about the arrival of Ed's men.

Haley's got her hair wrapped up again, and we're walking single file in the best formation we can. But we're not going to fool anyone up close.

Zane holds open a door. From Esmeralda's sketch, this should be the exit to the dock. Dante called it. There's a line of cameras outside the door. No way they won't know we're on the way to the dock.

"Hustle but don't run," I say in a low voice. There's a good hundred yards of landscape and beach before we hit the main dock with the boat shed on it. This dock isn't falling apart but rather oiled teak. It's long, but we make good time. Zane stops at the corner of the building before anyone can see us through the door. I move in front of him.

I use the hand signals we practiced back on the island when we were prepping for the pirates.

The others are lined up behind us, Haley and Sam in the rear. I turn the handle and open the door, but the boat shed is empty.

Fan-fucking-tastic. We need to get out of here before Ed's men arrive. We're extraordinarily lucky the boat shed doesn't have any security guards or anyone in it. But it does have three fine-looking boats. Two of them are high up on lifts, and the last one is hanging as if it's about to kiss the water. "Esmeralda said the keys were in a lockbox. But more importantly, we need to find the controls for the slings and hope the tides are right to put in. Then there's getting around the guards on the *Rosewood*. That's something we can figure out next."

"I've got the box and the keys to the Riva Aquariva Super." Zane waves the keys at me. It's a high-speed boat. Something out of a James Bond movie. You see assholes zipping around in them in Monaco, showing off for supermodels in bikinis. Cutting off yachts and crashing into sea walls because they've had one too many espresso martinis.

"No," Sam and I say together. "Sunseeker." It's big enough that we could last for a while and take it far out to sea. They're dependable, and I know them.

"Fine, I'll get the Sunseeker keys," Zane says, pivoting back to the box on the wall.

I head over to the Sunseeker. A crack sounds on the boat next to it. It's the one not on the lift. *Fuck.* I turn in time to see the engineer of the *Rosewood*. Turner, his engineers, had called him, the one I told about the battery leak. Turner and I lock eyes, and I have a few seconds to get to him before he radios for help.

But he throws his hands up in the air. "Don't take the Sunseeker. It's got a leaky fuel line. I've been trying to get it fixed, but I'm on the *Rosewood* forever and the guys here are lazy as fuck . . . Take this one."

I blink because I'm not sure what just came out of his mouth.

"Are you dumb? I know you're not dumb. You saved my damn engine room and lived on an island for a year. I'm coming dockside. Don't go knocking me in the drink." He jumps off the Axopar 37, nimbler than I expect him to be.

The boat he's just come off isn't as fast as the Riva, and it's smaller than the Sunseeker, but it's big enough and will get us across to another island. It also doesn't scream *look at me, I stole a boat*. And that's something we're going to need.

"What were you working on?" I nod to the boat he just got off. Because this could be a trap where he knows we won't make it anywhere but will end up sitting ducks for Ed's men to pick us off.

"Just routine stuff. I want to get to the fuel line on the Sunseeker, but with Ed's guys coming in tonight, I want to go back to the *Rosewood*." His face twists in a way that says *fucking assholes*. "You get on board. Controls to lower her the rest of the way are over there. I owed you. Now we're even."

It's like we're all frozen, and it takes us a minute to spring into action. Sam and Easton climb on board first.

"Grab that rope over there. I need you to tie me up. Oh, and you'll want to go south. There's a gun station to the north. And if you get caught, tell them you overpowered me. I'm just a little old guy." Turner winks at Haley.

Haley hands him the rope, and he hands it back to her. "Well, if I have to be tied up, I'd like a pretty girl to do the tying."

"Give me the rope, Haley." I hold out my hand.

"I've got it. I practiced enough knots on the island." She ties a really solid clove hitch and bowline. I watch them out of the corner of my eye. The controls for the lift are easy, and I lower the boat into the water.

By the time I'm back to the starboard side of the boat, everyone else is on board.

"Wait," Turner says.

I snap around, my hand on the gunwale, about to jump aboard. Sam's at the wheel, ready to turn over the engines.

"You can't let anyone know you're here. Not until you're out of the country. Z has agents throughout the area. You won't make it if you let anyone know," Turner says.

I stare at him. Because it's going to be a hell of a lot harder to get out of here without Easton making some phone calls, even with the cash we have. "The police? A consultant?"

The whizz of the outboard motors lowering screeches through the boathouse.

"He doesn't have them all in his pocket. But it only takes one call to have the rest of the elder Z's men called in with their guns blaring. Honestly, I don't want to be here tonight when they come in. Go."

I nod.

Fuck, I thought we'd just walk into the police station. I jump over the gunwale onto the boat with everyone else. "Thank you." Sam fires up the motors the second my feet hit the deck.

"You can thank me by not getting fucking caught. There's a dock to the south of the large city on the next island over. Treasure Resort. We have slips there. They would take the *Green Summit* without expecting a docking fee. Slips twenty to twenty-two," he yells over the engines.

I nod and push the boat off from the dock. Zane's got Dante working with him to get the bumpers pulled in.

"Did he say the fucking *Green Summit*?" Easton yells over the engines.

"Easton?" Haley puts her arm around his waist.

"Everyone down below before we pull out," Sam orders. "The *Rosewood* will be able to see us."

"I've got it, Sam. You should rest your leg." I stand next to him as everyone else moves below.

"I'm fine. And I look most like the engineer." He cocks

his head to where the guy is tied up in a deck chair. No one's going to believe we did that. I'm surprised Haley didn't get him a beverage and ask what he wanted for dinner.

"His name is Turner, if someone calls on the radio. Channel an inner Midwestern rage and you should be fine." I swipe a black stocking cap from the console and toss it at him. He pulls it low over the bridge of his forehead. I tap his shoulder and head partway down the stairs. Just a few steps though, enough that I can pop up if he calls for me. But enough to hear what's going on down below too.

Sam looks down the stairs at me as he pulls out. They've backed in all the boats, which makes for an easy departure for the owners. The roof of the boathouse vanishes and is replaced with inky black sky and stars. He turns the boat hard.

"Hang on," I call to everyone below.

When we're out a few minutes, the breakers have us jostling, and I grab both handrails on either side to keep from tumbling down.

Sam glances down. "I'm swinging port of the *Rosewood* now."

The radio squawks. I can barely hear it over the waves. I climb up a step to hear better.

"*Green Summit, Rosewood,* over."

I look up at Sam. He doesn't take his hands off the wheel.

"Turner, *Rosewood,* come in, over," *Rosewood* repeats.

"*Green Summit,* over," Sam says.

"Are you almost done? Over."

"I need to open her up. Clearing the fuel out of the lines. Over." Sam glances down at me.

Fuck, that was a fantastic thing to say.

"Good idea. Get your ass back over here before Ed's men arrive. Over."

"Heard." Sam has a faint Midwestern lilt. Maybe he should try his hand at acting. "You believe him? Turner, about the dock?" Sam calls down to me.

"Yeah, I do. This is one of his kids, and he'll want it back in one piece. But he's decent enough to pay back his debt to me . . . Or it could be a trap."

"That's what I was thinking too. I'm going to really open her up. It'll be at least ten minutes before we're out of visual range of the Rosewood. Go hang on."

"Thanks."

Below, Dante's pulling things out of the cabinets while Zane lies on the back berth, staring out the window toward the bay. Easton and Haley are sitting at a small table at the bottom of the stairs. A table that converts to a berth.

Dante tosses a tin of crackers on the table. "Bingo, charts." A book of charts thuds next to the tin. I'm at the charts as fast as I can be when Easton thumps his hand on the table.

"We are getting out of here. And when we do—I'm coming back and fucking killing Thayer Zambrano myself." Easton's eyes glow in the dim light.

Chapter 22

On the Water

Sam

I yank the stocking cap down over my ears and point the boat to the south, out of the bay. Fuck me. We need to get away. There's a drop in my stomach—I hate not knowing where I'm going. Squaring my shoulders, I push the throttle and really open her up. The twin Mercury outboard motors respond by lifting the bow up on the water. The damn 400's are smooth. Overkill, but that's standard for the Zambrano family.

Motors purring, we're making good time, but good time to where? Do I trust the engineer? It could be a trap. But the bit I heard of what Turner said to Calvin? I'm going with my gut. And my gut says the guy wants his boat back. Either way, we need to get gone.

The full moon is a blessing and a curse. The Rosewood's off my port bow. She's big but getting smaller by the second. And the mansion sprawls up the hill off my starboard aft. But what concerns me more is whether there are any guards who might already know it's not Turner taking the boat out for a test drive. A course is what I need—I flick on the chartplotter, changing it from the depth fishfinder to the GPS positioning and charts, and settle on the satellite view. A quick search along the moonlight dappling the hillside and I match the picture with the terrain. On the GPS, there's a blurred-out section on the top of the hill, and that's got to be the guard tower Turner told us about. It's off the starboard aft as well, as it shrinks on the horizon over my wake. But we're still in range. I've got it in my periphery, casually scanning it for any sign of movement. We've made it this far, and being sprayed with bullets isn't on my list of things to do tonight.

My heart slams in my chest as I push the motors as hard as I can. The mantra of getting away from everything to do with the Zambranos rings through my head. Even with more distance from the guard platform behind us, I'm not comfortable. I switch from the GPS back to sea charts and plot a course to the resort, Treasure.

There's a bang below deck, followed by a lot of loud jumbled words. I can't make out what they're saying. Easton's, Dante's, and Calvin's voices collide in the wind.

I lean over and shout down into the forward cabin, "Keep it down!"

Zane's head pops up. "Sorry, Cap. Apparently, this boat's named after some mountain at Emily's school. Easton's losing his shit." Zane's head is only a few inches above the deck. "I'll get them to quiet down. I was about to come up to ask you, what's that light on the horizon? I've been watching it get bigger. Looks like a boat from the berth, but it's hard to get a bearing on it."

I glance over at Zane and then back to the horizon. Sure enough, there's a dot of light coming straight at us from the big island. It's on the course I've plotted to the resort. "If I were a gambling man, I'd say it's the twenty of Ed's men Esmeralda was talking about."

There's more shouting below.

Zane nods. "I'll get them to be quiet."

"Better yet. See if there's anything we can defend ourselves with," I say.

"Right, Cap." Zane disappears below.

There's a pit in my stomach—for the dot speeding toward us and for Zane reverting to calling me Cap. But the boat approaching quickly has to be dealt with first.

"Find anything?" I ask after a few minutes.

Dante comes up this time. "A fire extinguisher, a dive knife, and twenty cans of kidney beans."

Calvin fills the rest of the stairs. "There's the boat hook on the port side."

"Dive knife and boat hook sound good," I say.

"I still have a fairly good pitching arm," Dante responds. "A can of beans to the side of the head can knock a guy out. Don't ask me how I know."

"Right, I still want to avoid them if I can. Shifting course twenty degrees." I take it slowly, like I'm drifting, not yanking the wheel.

"Sounds good," Calvin grunts.

Water sprays over the cockpit, and we bounce over a few rogue waves. Dante's and Calvin's heads sway by my feet.

"Fuck, the other boat just changed course." My hands are locked on the wheel, but I glance behind me.

"You want me to take the boat hook now, Sam?" Calvin asks.

"No, but be ready to. I'm taking the offensive. Let me try to talk my way out of this." I pick the radio mic. "Green Summit, Green Summit, over."

The radio crackles. "Hey, Green Summit, tell me there's still some dinner left?"

"Negative on that, you know Esmeralda." I shrug and keep my eyes off Calvin and Dante. The other boat might have a scope on me.

"What did she make? Over."

My eyes flick downward to Dante.

"She swore to the Philadelphia Eagles. She's an expat but been here a good time for as rapid as her Thai was," Calvin says.

"Thai cheesesteaks?" Dante raises his eyebrows.

I pick up the mic and repeat it.

"Fucking hell. We missed them?"

"Afraid so. Over," I say.

Their boat straightens out. We're going to pass, and pass far enough apart that we'll be able to see each other. But not close enough that, even with a Heisman Trophy arm, Dante would be able to knock somebody out with a can of beans. And having Calvin hit someone with the docking hook won't happen either. Bullets, however . . . bullets won't have the same problem beans do.

I rub the back of my hand over my face, covering my mouth. "Stay down unless I give you a signal. All the way down." I grab the wheel with both hands again and stare straight at my route. Veering off-course would be highly suspicious.

The five minutes waiting for the other boat coming our way has my heart slamming in my chest. Theirs is a converted fishing boat, but the way their bow is hitting the water, there's nothing standard about the boat. I'm betting they have Mercury 400's too. They might be trying to blend in, but even a tourist could see they're not trying to hook a blue marlin. There are a half-dozen guys sitting on the side of the boat with guns resting in their laps. I incline my head and keep going. The one steering gives a small nod back. And they're past my aft. My heart should be slowing, but it's not. One quick radio call from the boathouse and they're going to turn around and then . . . it's over.

"They're gone," Haley says, her shoulders squeezed between Dante's and Calvin's.

"Yeah, but don't come up. The last thing we want is for them to see."

"Right," she says. "You doing okay?"

"Yeah." But I don't mean it.

"I hear you." Haley reaches up and grips the top of my ill-fitting shoe. "You're doing great. We're almost home, and then you can give your niece and nephew a hug."

"Almost home," I repeat, but it doesn't feel real. There are still a hell of a lot of things standing between us and home.

"We're not docking where Turner told us to, are we? The resort?" Haley squeezes my toes again.

I glance down at her blue eyes. "That's what I've got plotted. My gut still says it's a good thing."

"The paper charts have a dock right after it. They're current," Calvin says.

"Maybe. But I'm not changing course. Not yet." Adjusting the GPS, I scroll through the map. "I see the other dock. Thirty minutes to the resort, thirty-five to the other dock. Let's see what we come up with when we get closer."

"He seemed like a nice guy. Not radioing when he found us. I just can't help but think it's a trap." Haley hangs on to Calvin's arm as we go over another rogue wave.

"Sassy, you've become cynical? I knew I could bring you over to the dark side." Dante laughs.

"Not cynical, practical. I've always been practical." Haley turns to face Dante.

Dante tilts up her chin and gives her a quick kiss. "Hmm, you say potato, and I say pommes dauphinoise, but sometimes I just want a French fry."

"I don't understand you. But I love you." Haley kisses the tip of his nose.

"Love you too."

"Take the love fest down below. Wait, belay that. We have thirty minutes. Be prepared to dock."

Dante laughs. "What do you think I was going to do?"

"I understand you completely," I say. Because I'd have the same thoughts he's having now.

"Never thought you didn't." Dante disappears below with Haley. But Calvin doesn't move.

"I think we should go to the resort." He looks up at me. It's an odd perspective. "I don't know why, but I trust Turner."

I nod. "I agree. But we'll still see what the traffic is like when we dock. If the marina's too full, we could ditch the boat near a beach and swim in."

"I'd rather not be walking around in wet, tight black clothing at midnight in a city we don't know. This might be a trap, but I believed Turner when he said that the Zambranos have an in with people in the city. It will be a hell of a lot easier to slip away if we come into a port and not a random beach that might not have services anywhere nearby," Calvin says.

"Yeah. You're right." My eyes are on the horizon. The big island is coming into view. Lights are twinkling in the distance, and there's a haze of light pollution above it. Not like Miami, but it's a big city for sure.

The port's quiet, being close to one a.m. I've shut the

motors way down. There are a few small boats on the way into port, fishing. The boats bob up and down. The fishermen have set up bright pink and orange lights under the boats. You don't have to speak Thai to know one of them has caught something. He yanks on the pole. His friend has the net at the ready. A large squid thrusts up on the end of the line and into the net. There's a pang in my chest. I miss fishing. I slow down more.

"This looks good." I yell down. "Zane, Calvin, come get the fenders." They hustle up on deck. Haley, Dante and Easton crowd the stairs. Turner was right. There are three empty slips. Zane jumps onto the dock and takes the line from Calvin. Dante's up and working lines too. We're tied off, and I turn the engines off. "All clear," I say to Easton and Haley. A marine attendant is strolling slowly down the dock as I grab the key and toss it into the map pouch below the wheel.

"Sam," Haley says, tapping my shoulder. "We need to go. We need to go now!"

"Move!" Zane yells.

Chapter 23

Dam

Haley

There's a boat whipping around the corner of the marina. A wake surges to the sea walls. One of the night-fishing guys wobbles back and forth while the other one has slid into the harbor with his plastic tub of catch with him. His friend is waving his fist at the boat. Oh, no.

I grab Sam's arm. "We need to go. We need to go now!" It's not the same boat we passed a while back, the one with Ed's guards hanging off the side. This is the speedboat from the boathouse, full of Thayer's men, Ed's men, not sure it matters anymore. We need to get out of here.

"Move!" Zane takes my hand and pulls me onto the dock. "Let's go, Little Bird. Everyone else will catch up."

I'm matching Zane stride for stride. It's not the first time I've run for my life in a marina. But the last time was because I had twenty minutes to find a decent bottle of rosé before the primary's mother-in-law lost her shit. It felt like life or death, but it wasn't anywhere near it. That's a lifetime ago. I'm not sure I can even relate to the girl I used to be.

"Slow down," a marina employee yells at us. He's waving his hands downward like a grandfather at a public pool.

I run by him. "Sorry," I shout over my shoulder, but I don't stop running. I don't even change my steps to a fast walk. Dante, Sam, Calvin, and Easton are behind us and quickly catching up. The dock bounces under our thundering feet. It's a big marina, but Thayer's slips are close to the harbormaster's house. The gate, of course, is closed. Not only is it closed, but it's a six-foot-tall chain link barrier.

Zane puts on a burst of speed and passes me. He stops at the fence and holds his hands out for me to step into them. "Up and over, Haley. Let's go."

I want to tell him no, I'll climb it myself, but that will take more time. I quicken my pace and run at the fence. My foot lands in his hands and he gives me a good boost. I grab the top bar of the fence. The metal rattle of the chain against the poles rings in my ears. Clutching the top rail, I hoist my leg over the other side and jump to the ground. I jumped off the living room platform on the island more than once, and this wasn't as far. But I land wrong, with a crunch. Grimacing, I push up from the crouch I've landed in. "Shit." I clutch my leg but keep hobbling forward. Two buildings make an arch in front of me. One's the harbormaster's house, and the other has a shuttered window, a snack bar. A few more feet and I have to stop.

Zane lands next on the ground behind me. The fence rattles behind us as the other guys come over. "You okay?"

"Yeah, yeah." I take another stride. I just need to walk—or rather run—it off. "I'll be fine." It's the same ankle I twisted back on the island. A tender shuffle forward and pain shoots up my calf and down my foot. It's more of a rocking hobble, but I'm moving.

Zane's dark eyes soften at me. "Haley," he groans and takes my hand.

There's a large thud on the ground behind us. Calvin's the last one over the fence. "You're not fine," he growls and sweeps me up onto his shoulder. "Hang on, Chiefie." His feet pound as we make it down the rest of the dock onto solid ground.

I can't see where we're going anymore. But I wrap my arms around Calvin's waist and hold on tight, pushing my cheek against his ass. The guards are coming down the dock. There are five of them, and even with my head bouncing against Calvin's ass, I can make out Holloway's scowl. He's the only one I can make out, though. I tuck my head in tighter and wish I could be more graceful. Twisting my ankle couldn't have happened at a worse time—Calvin carrying me has got to be slowing us down.

"This way," Zane says up ahead. The snack bar and harbormaster's house disappear behind us.

It's hard to get my bearings—things are sideways at best and mostly upside down. There's a long sandy beach to one side. Cabanas with blue and white striped roofs are buttoned up tight for the night. The moonlit beach has been raked to perfection. In the other direction, there's an alleyway of booths. Everywhere, the signs are in Thai and English. There's no one around. The boardwalk below Calvin's feet is polished teak. This resort has serious money. I clench my eyes tight from the sand flying up from Calvin's quickly moving feet. And when I open them again, we've taken a sharp turn. There's a large building along the side. It's darker here, quieter. There's no crashing waves, only the sound of the guys' feet.

"Here," Dante says, and we duck between two buildings. The moonlight is completely gone in the alley.

"Shh," Sam says behind me. He peers around the corner from where we came.

There's a squeak and a rush of cool air on my arms.

Calvin steps into a room.

"Can you walk, Sassy? Having the Viking carry you through the resort—" Dante says.

Calvin's growl cuts him off.

"Let me try. You can pick me up if I can't do it." I let go of Calvin's waist, and he eases me to the ground. Dante steps back to the door and yanks on it.

"It's locked," Sam says.

I wince when I put my weight on my foot. I take a step away from the door, where Calvin and Zane are doing something. My heartbeat echoes in my ears. We need to get out of sight; Holloway can't be too far behind us.

There's a loud thud, and Zane says in a hushed voice. "I've got it."

We're in a hotel, a hallway, but it's elegant. Wallpaper embossed with golden threads lines the walls, while the carpet is plush and sculpted. There's a framed tapestry on the wall behind Sam that's worth being the star of a room. "We need to keep moving. Holloway's not dumb. He's going to find us."

"You saw Holloway, not Ed's guys?" Sam asks.

"It was definitely Holloway. I didn't recognize any of the guys with them, though," I whisper. I take another step, but it's clear to everyone that I'm not fine.

"We've got this." Calvin drops to his knees and pulls my shoes off. "Here, Rockwell, hold these." He tosses my shoes to Easton before picking me up, this time in front of him like a bride. "Less I captured you, more I saved you from a poor footwear choice. Let's go." He leads the guys down the hall. "Hold on, Chiefie."

His strides are long enough to be the same speed as someone running. My arms are looped firmly around his neck, and I've got my head tucked into his chest. Up ahead, the hallway opens up into what I'm assuming is a lobby. Being in yachting, I've seen the inside of five-star hotels all over the world. Delivering forgotten designer sunglasses. Or picking up a special bottle of wine or a three-tier wedding cake. And this place? It's right up there with some of the finest I've seen in the French Riviera. We step out into the grand lobby. It soars up at least three stories. There's plush, overstuffed furniture arranged in conversation areas around the room. On the far side, there's a long, polished mahogany front desk with a wide-eyed attendant. I didn't see how the door we came in was opened, but I'm guessing it wasn't left unlocked.

"Can I help you?"

"Yes, you can," Dante says, his shoulders squared as he marches over to the front desk. "We were supposed to be picked up, but we were left to find our way here from the airport by ourselves. On top of that, we've lost our luggage and all we have to wear are these damn rags from our last gig."

"And you are, sir? I do apologize, but I didn't see that we had any guests coming in on a late-night flight tonight."

I have no idea where Dante's going with this because we definitely don't look like guests. All the guys have beards or scruff. My hair and nails look . . . well, like I've spent a year living on a beach. None of our clothes fit correctly. Calvin's are too tight, Sam's too loose, and I'm barefoot.

"Guests? No, we're staff brought in for the big wedding."

"Big wedding?" he repeats as he types. He stops and glances up at Dante, but Dante stands close-mouthed with that look of impatience in his eyes. The one he does so well. The agent types again. "Oh, the Freeman wedding. That's not until next week."

"Exactly, you know them. They want everything perfect. This isn't perfect, now is it?" He waves back at us. "Look at them? And now at me. We had three connections and twenty hours of flying. Do you have our rooms?"

"Rooms, right . . ." His fingers fly over the keyboard.

Anxiety boils in the pit of my stomach. There are five hallways around the space and a set of large doors that open out onto what must be the main entrance. "I see it here. Do you have your passports? You're three days early, but you're in luck, I have space. It really is going to be quite the event."

"Of course it is, but I told you we lost all our luggage."

"You put your passports in your luggage?"

"No, no one is that stupid. But we had to crowd together in one car, and the driver made off with all our luggage and carry-ons. We came straight from another event. You don't know how cranky you can be until you've worked a twenty-hour event for a billionaire and then had to go straight to the airport. Rich people, am I right?" Dante doesn't glance at Easton, which is a blessing.

The agent smiles. "I'll call the police immediately."

"What good will that do? He's probably already sold our passports and tossed our clothes in the trash. We'll straighten it all out tomorrow."

"Okay. I . . ." The guy clearly doesn't want to be an ass but knows there's something not right with what's happening.

"Put me down," I whisper to Calvin. And he lets me slide to the ground. I take a few tender steps to the counter.

"I'm really grateful that you're able to help us. It's been a horribly long day." I put on my best stew smile and pray I don't mess up what is an amazing con by Dante. But last year when I was working on Charlie's boat, we had a group of mid-twenty-year-olds take a week-long charter. Seven girls. The tab at the end of the week was just shy of a hundred thousand a piece, and the primary was named Stella Freeman. The rock on her hand would have made Candy swoon. "Stella's expecting everything to be just perfect. She's so sweet, but we wouldn't want her father to hear about any of this. Because he'll get upset at Stella's groom. It's such a delicate balance with him, you know?" And I only barely know . . . bits of conversations I overheard stitch back together for me. "An overbearing, righteous father who believes no one will ever be good enough for his daughter." I throw in a sigh. "But then she's really pretty great. And a really good tipper." I smile.

His eyes flick from his screen to mine. "'I've heard that too."

Champagne is going off in my stomach because I guessed right. This could have gone really wrong. Freeman isn't exactly Smith, but it's not far from it. "For the sake of keeping everyone's tips in place, I don't mind losing a bikini and a duffle bag of work clothes. We'll take care of our passports tomorrow. Do you think you can just get us a room? We'll come back and do everything properly in the morning." I turn quickly, taking the money out of my bra. "Stella gave me some money to tip the resort staff as we get settled for her." I slide a hundred dollars across the counter to him.

"Yes, please come back in the morning." He pockets the hundred and slides a card across the counter. "I've got you in the Freeman staff villa. I'm afraid things aren't set up correctly yet for the Freeman contractors. The beds aren't pulled apart." He takes a map of the resort out and draws a line to our villa.

"We'll manage. Thank you." I take the map. "Oh, and the guy who dropped us off and drove away with our bags? He's really tall. Almost as tall as my friend here." I place a hand on Calvin's chest. "Brown hair. I hope he doesn't come back. But maybe you could call the authorities if he comes around? Try not to tell him you saw us. He was making a pass at me. I was nervous. I think that's why he drove off."

"For sure!" Though he looks at the wall of muscle behind me and narrows his eyes at the guys. Like they weren't willing to protect me.

"Thank you. You're the best." I pivot on my good leg and widen my eyes to Dante. Holy crap. I want to squeal both for the pain in my leg and the excitement that it worked. I hand Sam the packet of keycards, and we're out the side door.

Chapter 24

Rough Water

Dante

I close the door behind Sam. Calvin's already placed Haley on the sofa. Zane's closing the curtains.

"You think Holloway will ask at the front desk if anyone has seen us?" Zane says, pulling another curtain shut. Calvin grabs a chair from a table and wedges it under the door handle.

They've got this. I sink down next to her. "Holy hell, Sassy. I didn't know you could lie like that!"

"I didn't either. Well, other than the occasional little white lie to a guest."

Rockwell sits on the sofa table and takes Haley's hand. "Damn, Firefly, how did you know who the bride was?"

"I wasn't sure but—"

"I was losing the desk clerk. You're the one who closed the deal." I give her a kiss on the cheek.

"On Charlie's boat last year, there was a group of girls. Remarkably easy to take care of—old money. A Vanderbilt,

Cabot, Winthrop, and some others. Stella was the primary. They just read, sunbathed, and drank their weight in skinny martinis all week. Stella was marrying into a shipping family from Thailand. It wasn't a sure thing, but . . ."

"Damn, you're hot when you're so smart. And telling the clerk that Holloway stole our bags?" I kiss the side of her neck.

"Thank you. You think it will work? It's going to work," she says to herself.

"I know it." I squeeze her shoulders and stand.

Sam's pacing by the window. Calvin's peering through the peephole insouciantly. And Zane's flipping through a wooden folder.

"What do you have, Zane?" I ask.

"We're going to need supplies. And if we're going to take the engineer's advice and not contact the authorities . . . Are you still sticking by that?" Zane's eyebrows raise. We went over it more than once below deck on the Green Summit.

"What?" Sam turns. "We go to the police. I don't believe the Zambrano family are all-seeing."

Zane pulls a crumpled file folder out of the back of his pants. "Bloody hell, it feels good having that out. Look at this, Sam, and you'll change your mind." Zane hands it to him.

"What is it?"

"Well, it's not straightforward. But it's a list of payments and debits. Off the books stuff. Look at the second page. Those are initials. Country codes."

Sam sinks into a chair. "It's global."

"Yeah." Zane pats Sam's back. "The twat has people in his ranks all over the world. Nowhere as secret as Rocky's journal. But . . . it would be a hell of a hard thing to sell in court. There's a ton of initials and records of debit and payments. Hopefully we can use it somehow to implicate him. Rocky's code was complex. This is simple but only if you know what each column actually means."

Sam flips pages. "There are hundreds of initials." He tosses it on the coffee table next to Easton, who picks it up.

"Yeah, mate. So no, we don't tell anyone until we're out of here and know who we can trust. Ed wants us dead. And there's a reason. A man with a list like that isn't going to hold back." Zane's attention returns to the wooden folder. "This is the normal 'what to do about town' folder. We need clothes and a way out of here."

"We're going to need passports. Fake ones. Good ones." I turn to Easton. "Don't suppose you have access to cash without an ID?"

"Not if we don't want anyone to know we're here," Rockwell replies.

"Right." I squeeze my eyes tightly closed and pinch the bridge of my nose. Because there's no way he's still here, running the same place. And if he is . . . can I trust the bastard? Haley puts her head on my shoulder. "Fuck, Sassy. Let me go get some ice for your ankle." I remove myself from the sofa and carefully stand. There's an ice bucket on the other side of the room. I take a keycard from the packet Sam left on the table. "I'll be back in a flash. I saw an ice machine not far from here. They must get a lot of Americans."

"Dante, don't go. My leg will be fine. It's not safe." She goes to stand, but Easton pulls her down onto his lap.

"You need ice, Haley. Dante knows what he's doing." Rockwell holds her.

"Thanks. I'll be fast." I give him a salute. Because I sure hope I know what I'm doing. We're already in trouble. And bringing the asshole I'm thinking of into the picture? It could be the dumbest thing I've ever done. And that's saying a lot.

Calvin moves the chair, and when the door swings shut behind me, I hear it being jammed back in place. It's quiet out. But it won't be where I'm heading. The last time I was there, I was slamming back shots of straight Thai whiskey at four in the morning. It's actually a rum, but whatever. It's sweeter and smoother and popular with the locals.

But first, I'm not leaving Sassy in pain. The ice machine is humming in an alcove between a group of villas. I fill the damn bucket to the top and run it back. I knock on the door. Calvin opens it. "Here." I shove it at him. "There's something I have to do. I know a guy. But I need to go alone. Make up a good excuse for Sassy."

Calvin narrows his eyes at me. "Don't fucking get caught."

"I've got this." I give the bucket at his chest a push; the damn Viking doesn't move. But he does close the door.

And I'm off. First, I need new clothes. You can only get so far wearing hand-me-down blacks. Though it's not bad for hiding in the shadows. I make my way to the front of the resort, staying clear of the marina on my way to the main building and out into the city streets. Where I need to be is more than a couple of miles from here. I'm about out of the gates when I hear a car coming out of the entrance. Fuck. I imagine Holloway coming down the road. It has my heart throbbing. I push myself into the tall, manicured hedge next to the road. A taxi passes. A flash of light illuminates the back seat. A man has his arm around a woman. I need to calm down. Jumping to the worst-case scenario hasn't been me since even before I got my stinking uncle out of my mother's life.

There's something there, though. My asshole uncle taught me a lot about getting what I want from people, even if they don't want to give it to me.

I remove myself from the bushes and run my fingers through my hair. Leaves drop from my shoulders as I do. I stride out to the sidewalk, a sidewalk that quickly disappears as you get away from Resort Treasure. The huge sign glistens behind me. Another car comes down the road, the driver's elbow out the side of his window. A flash of my hands at the driver and he slows. In my best French, I ask if he'll give me a ride into town. I ask again in broken Thai. He blinks and looks me up and down. Being here for four months, eight years ago, has left me more than a little rusty.

"Sure, why not? Hop in," he answers in English and taps the side of his car.

"Thanks." I round the front of his car, one hand atop his grill. Because you never know when someone might just run you over. You can take the kid out of the hood, but you can't take the hood out of the kid. I open the door and jump in.

"Where are you going?" he asks in English way better than my Thai.

"Yai's Place, in the Kathu." The car has a half-dozen air fresheners hanging from the mirror and a coke can full of cigarette butts in the glass holder.

"Ohh."

"You know it?"

"Yes, the best food in town. Also the best place to lose your wallet after dark."

"Exactly."

"You want to lose your wallet?"

"No, the food. I'm . . ." I hesitate to say friend of the chef-owner. Because I'm not. "I know Yai Anan."

He humphs but throws the car into gear and takes off. "He's an ass."

"You're not wrong."

"No, I'm never wrong."

I nod and watch the elite beach hotels fade into the real heart of the city where the locals live. The buildings get shorter and brighter. Pops of color glisten in the moonlight. Maybe it's having been away from the city—from people—for so long, but my heart's opening up like a world of possibility is out there again. There are fireworks exploding in my head. I don't remember every part of the way exactly, but it's coming back. Not that I spent many hours anywhere but in the bastard's kitchen.

"Here." He stops.

And I look at the other side of the street. A flood of late nights rushes back at me. It was hell and heaven at the same time. I learned a lot and slept not at all. I thought I was going to leave with a big roll of cash, but other than the money I had already sent to my mother, everything was gone. Because, well, Yai's an asshole. But right now, he's the only thing we have.

I hop out of the car and go around to the open driver's window. "Thanks for the ride." I fucking wish I had something to give the guy. If I'd thought this through better, I would have taken some of the cash from Sassy.

"It's a full moon. Bad time to die."

"I'll keep that in mind."

He peels off.

The fucking building looks worse than it did when I left

it. There's a crowd of people stumbling out the doors. Locals, mostly. A few tourists in the know.

I muscle my way through the crowd and inside. Fluorescent lights accost my eyes, but damn, the smells. My stomach growls, almost loud enough to be heard over the roar of the patrons in the place. Every booth is full. The bar is three deep. I make my way to the front counter. There's no one I know working there. Not that I thought there would be. A perfectionist jerk like Anan has a hard time keeping staff from turning over. I lean to the side where the counter lifts. I can almost see into the kitchen.

"Is Yai Anan here?" I ask in Thai.

"Yeah, who wants to know? He's busy," the counter girl says.

"The old fart's always busy. I'm an old friend." I bite my tongue on the word friend because, while he knows the whole city, I'm not sure he has a damn friend.

"Friend?" She humphs, and her raven black braid down her back sways. She tugs on her white T-shirt with the sleeves rolled up. Her eyes flick over me. "You a cook?"

"Yeah." I'm not going into the semantics of being a chef with her. When I was here, I was just barely a cook. The ass flipped my switch to being a chef.

I can hear him screaming in the kitchen. It's part Thai, a little French, and some English mixed in for good measure. There's a slam of a pot and a cloud of flames and vapor over the stove. He yells again—basically saying, "Get your shit together."

She lets the swinging door hit her, and I hear her telling him in rapid-fire Thai, "Some white guy says you're his friend. He can't talk worth shit."

The door flies open. "Dante!" he says with a shit-eating grin on his face. "Get back here and show this useless lump of flesh how to make Pad Kra Pao before I have to hurt him." He flips back the counter, making two of his customers grab their drinks before they are crushed. Somehow, he's not surprised I've shown up. But that's Anan.

I wink at the front-of-house bartender-server and follow Anan.

Chapter 25

Tango

Easton

Haley's lying in the bed, her leg resting on a pile of pillows. Her blue eyes follow me as I cross the room. "You need to get some sleep. I'll wake you when he gets back." I pull the blanket up over her body and tuck it under her chin. Just like I remember my mom doing when I was little.

"Don't you think someone should go after him?" She pushes up on her elbows.

Zane sits on the side of the bed. "No. He's worked here before, Little Bird. He's gone to get help. Or something."

"He could have told us what he was doing." She takes Zane's hand.

"Damn straight he could have," Sam says, pacing by the closed curtains.

Calvin's in the other room with the lights out and the curtains cracked so he can see the path between the center of the villas. "He didn't want you to worry," he calls back at us.

"Yeah, well, he failed at that." Haley tries to get up. And both Zane and I are there to help her. "I'm going to the bathroom. I can do it, but thank you."

"You should get some sleep, Haley," I say.

"Only if you do too."

I untuck her and help her out of bed. Holding her elbow, I steady her into the bathroom, then close the door and let her have some privacy. Zane and Sam have wandered out to the living room. Parking my ass on the edge of the bed, I wait for her to come out. This is so fucked. We should take our chances and head to the police. But then, I know enough about guys like Ed and his son. They take what they want, and damn the rest of society.

"You okay?" Haley hobbles out of the bathroom.

I rush to her side. "Shouldn't I be the one asking you that?"

"We're going to be okay." She squeezes my hand, and I help her back into bed.

I nod. Because I wish I could be as confident as she is. I click out the lights. "I'll be in soon."

I head back into the main room and sprawl over the far end of the sofa, glancing at Zane and Sam. Haley's not the only one angry at Dante. We're all fighting off sleep, but there's a buzz in the room. A pulse that says Holloway could find us at any minute.

"Dante's here," Calvin says. He thuds over to the main door and moves the chair from under the handle. He waits, bent over, looking out the peephole. The lock clicks and Calvin opens the door—Dante steps into the room. It's seven a.m.

"Where the hell did you go?" I'm the first to say it. We circle Dante; all of us have our arms crossed over our chests—a quartet of fathers about to give the misguided teen consequences for missing curfew.

Dante laughs—fucking laughs. "I've been out, Dad." He's got a black backpack and an armful of plastic grocery bags with paper bags inside them. "Here." He thrusts a fist full of bags at me. The contents smell fucking delicious. "To get what we wanted, I had to wait until the restaurant closed. And . . . where's Sassy?"

"I'm here." Haley emerges from the bedroom using various furniture pieces to get across the room.

"I've got some painkillers for your ankle and an Ace bandage."

"Thanks, but where did you go? I was really worried." Haley pulls the resort robe tighter around her waist.

"I went to the restaurant I worked at when I lived here. The owner is an ass, but he's just the kind of ass we need. He's got great food and stays open until there are no more customers. Midnight or five a.m., he doesn't care. Word got out I was there, and things got busy." Dante puts the other bags down on the table and takes off his backpack. "And it took a while for the place to clear out enough to ask Anan for what we really need."

"And that is?" Sam asks.

"Passports." Dante sits, and it's only now I realize he's wearing black scrubs instead of the security clothes Holloway gave us on the *Rosewood*. "Food, clothes, and maybe a way off the island. That part is still a little up in the air." He tosses some colorful Thai currency on the table. "But he paid my take for tonight, or last night, whatever it is. Don't get too excited. That 5,000 Baht is about a hundred and fifty USD." He pulls Haley into his arms. "I need to sleep." He kisses the top of her head. "Have you slept, Sassy?"

"No." She leans on him.

"Well, we all need to sleep. But maybe we eat first?" Dante takes containers out of the bag. There's enough to feed twenty people. He passes chopsticks around and tosses a fork at Calvin—who growls and grabs a pair of chopsticks from the pile.

Haley moans over the top of her container. "Holy hell, Dante. This is amazing." And the rest of us stop eating and watch her. She glances up. "You better eat, or I'll eat all of yours."

"There you go, Sassy. I love a woman that isn't afraid to eat something large," Dante says.

"No, you love *that* woman," I correct.

"Touché." Dante raises his container at me. "I stand corrected."

We all eat, trading containers until we can't take another bite.

Dante leans back. "Right, now we sleep, and then sometime this afternoon we need to take pictures and get them printed for our new passports."

Haley tilts over and places her head in my lap. I'm happily petting her hair away from her face when I turn to Dante. "Where are we getting these pictures taken?"

"Here." He pulls a smartphone from his back pocket and tosses it to me.

I turn it over. It's brand new, and it's on.

"It's not on a cellphone plan, but we can connect it to the Wi-Fi. You know, if you want to do a little deep dive into your family over the last year." He wiggles his eyebrows at me.

Haley sits up. "Are you ready?"

I'm still staring at the phone. Am I? I'm not sure. "What's the Wi-Fi password?" I say, looking at Zane. He's got the resort info book open again. He tells me, and I put it in. I'm shaking while I open a search engine.

"Where did you get the phone?" Haley asks Dante while she settles into the crook of my arm.

"Anan's got a drawer full of them. That was one of the only ones unlocked and charged enough."

I'm tuning them out as I type in Dad's name. The list populates the first few articles about things at Rockwell-Harding. But far down the page it goes into the *Rock Candy* being lost, and then there are the pictures I was hoping existed. My sister is wearing a life vest and being pulled onto a cargo ship. There are pictures of Dad too. But those are a hell of a lot scarier. He's strapped to a stretcher like they put you on after a car crash, and he's being hoisted above the water. It's a picture, but I can almost feel the stretcher he's lying in swinging back and forth onto the ship. Then there's a picture of him from a few weeks ago in front of the headquarters sign at the New York office. He looks old.

I close that article and click on one about Emily. That's a page down. She's standing in our dining room in Miami. There's a navigational chart behind her. It takes up the full wall. Attached to it are pictures connected with string, like she's on a murder mystery show. Emily looks like shit. Her hair isn't combed, and she has dark circles under her eyes.

"They were rescued," Haley says softly.

I hold Haley's stare. Her eyes are glistening. "Hey, it's okay." I skim through the rest of the article about Emily. There are a few more pictures. "Isn't this Shayla, the other stew?" I hold it for Haley to see. Shayla is sitting on the silk sofa next to Emily in the formal sitting room in our Miami house.

"It is. She looks so good." Haley stares at the phone.

And I know she's talking about Shayla because Emily looks like she needs to sleep for a month. Guilt washes over me. She's been looking for us, for me. Not that I was intentionally keeping myself from them. Not until now.

I squeeze Haley's hand and turn to Dante. "Your friend is going to be able to help us get out of here, and fast?" I need to get back to them. Let them know I'm okay. That they can relax. It's so tempting to just log in to my company email and shoot them a message.

"What are you doing, Rockwell? I see that look in your eyes. Don't get us killed." Dante reaches for the phone, but I angle it away from him and pass it to Zane.

"No. I'm not doing anything. My sister, my dad, the whole other raft was rescued. They were at sea for a long while. My dad took the hardest hit . . . other than Candy." They all nod. But Sam has the same scowl on his face when anyone mentions Candy. He has a good reason to be upset with her and my dad. They made Anders take the tender out when it wasn't safe. It's remarkable that Dad and Anders made it out alive, from what Calvin has explained to me.

"Anyone else want to check on their family?" Zane says, holding the phone up.

"Are you checking on your sister and mother? Or the soccer scores from last year?"

Zane lifts his head, his smile bright. "All three?"

"And how are they?" I ask.

"It looks like they're fine. I made a fake account on Insta. Anyone else want to check social media?" Zane holds the phone up.

"I've already checked in on the other raft and my sister and mother." Dante picks up Haley's almost empty container and eats the last bites before dropping it into an empty bag on the floor. "That's damn good."

"Because you're an amazing chef," Haley says and yawns. "Sorry, how are you not falling over?" She cocks her head toward me.

"You promised me you were going to go to sleep, Firefly."

"I'm asleep already. I have to be dreaming. I'm here with all of you in a nice air-conditioned resort with a big cozy bed." She nuzzles into my arm.

I extract her from my arm, stand, and carefully carry her across the room into one of the bedrooms off the living room. Zane pulls down the covers, and I place her in the middle of the bed. She pats the spot next to her. And there's nothing I want to do more than crawl in beside her. But Calvin's whispering to Dante in the other room. I'm not excited about trusting Dante's old boss. A guy who can get us fake passports and has a drawer full of cell phones. The kind of guy who runs a business until first thing in the morning. We might need him, but I don't like it. Zane kisses her temple and slips back into the main room.

"We'll be right in. I should clean up a bit," I say.

"You sound like me." Haley smiles.

"That's a good thing." I pull the door partially closed.

"Easton?" Haley calls.

"Yeah?"

"Get the truth out of Dante. I know he doesn't want to scare me. But anyone who's selling passports? That's the same sort of person who would easily sell us out."

"I know, Firefly. I know. I will."

"Good. Because I'm not as tired as I thought." She pulls the robe off from under the covers and tosses it on the ground.

"Haley," I growl. "Go to sleep." But I sure as hell hope that she's awake when I come back. I close the door, and four heads turn toward me. "Keeping things from her isn't going to help in the long run."

"He's right," Sam says. He's sitting in one of the dining room chairs pulled up to the coffee table.

Dante and Zane are on the sofa. Calvin's in the lone swivel chair.

"You trust this guy?"

"Anan?" Dante asks. "Enough. Passports aren't his money maker, more of a side hustle to his side hustle. He's a talented chef. He's been offered head chef positions at all the major resorts. Or at least that's his brag. He makes his money with gambling and collections and the restaurant—it's more than a front. It's his passion. Honestly, he's the only person I've ever met who sleeps less than me. He'd be bored without all the underworld shit he does."

"I don't like it," Sam says.

"Then we go to the police," I retort.

"No." Zane taps Ed's file with his foot.

"Okay . . . okay, no." I nod. I've been around plenty of rich assholes who think they can pay to get out of anything. Ed has firepower. "We get somewhere safer first. New York, Miami. Somewhere my dad can have hired guns to protect us."

Calvin's eyebrows shoot up. "Do we know your dad's not in on this?"

"Fuck you, Green. My dad isn't trying to kill me, or you. He might have been mixed up in some shit, but he's not a killer. He would never have hurt anyone. Especially Emily." I didn't like him with Candy, but he loved her. "You can see it by the look on his face. Back when she was alive and again by the haggard look of him in all the current photos."

"Sorry." Green holds my stare.

Sam picks up the folder. "Damn it, I don't like it. But this list is awfully convincing. Though there's a hell of a lot of lines with NY on them. Still, we should head home."

There's a twist of my stomach. We're going to get there.

Chapter 26

Home Port

Calvin

The sun streams through the blackout blinds as I crack my eyes open. Haley's ass is pressed up against my groin, and I have to suck in a breath to keep from rutting on her. Dante's on the other side of her. Easton, Sam, and Zane are sleeping in the next room. The bed's huge, and I'm shocked they didn't force their way in. Easton offered to take the first shift of watching the path and out the front door. Sam and Zane said they'd take the ones after that. I'd been on watch since we got into the room.

I haven't moved all night. I'm not sure I've slept this solidly or long in years—not even when I was in high school and had to bale hay all day. I crane my neck. The fancy clock on the nightstand says twelve. As in noon.

Haley rubs against me. I place my hand on her belly and pull her closer, inwardly groaning, and whisper, "You're awake."

"Hmm, not really." She grinds up against me, and fuck me. I'm ready to go. Brushing her hair away from her neck, my lips hover over the tender spot behind her ear. She tilts her head back. "Do it."

My laugh vibrates against her skin as I taste her sweetness. Her silky-smooth skin has my eyes drifting back shut. There's movement on the other side of her, and she moans.

I harden more as I wiggle into her, my cock settling between her butt cheeks. Her top leg moves and bends back into me. There's a change in her breathing, and she pushes hard against me. My eyes spring open. Dante has one of her legs over his shoulder, his face buried in her pussy. I freeze, taking it in. Damn, who would have thought I'd like watching the woman I love being devoured by another guy? Even after a year of it, I'm still in shock. Maybe it's being back in civilization. Running water, clean sheets, and all the damn strong smells—coffee, laundry soap, car exhaust, and cooking oil . . . the world's a weird place. But this is where I belong with Haley.

It's like a switch clicks for me. I never thought we were getting off the island, and then I thought I was going to die for her on the sun deck. But now? Fuck no. Nothing's going to stop me from getting her home. From introducing her to my family. This is what Haley Brewster is for me.

A feral need boils up from my stomach. I lick along the rim of her ear and turn her head to mine. Capturing her lips, I drink her in, brushing my tongue along the seam of her mouth, and she lets me in. Each kiss with her is a precious gift. And I want more. I hold her head to mine. She plunders my lips back. I'm kissing her knowing we finally have a future. We're not nearly out of the thick of it yet, but my body is shutting down my brain—fuck it. She's it for me, and I will protect her with every cell in my body. This won't be the last time I have her. She tastes of spice and warmth. But mostly of Haley. Home.

Her head falls to the pillow. Her back arches.

"You're close. So damn close," I say, watching her head flop from side to side on the pristine white pillowcase. Her tanned skin glows against it. She smells of exotic soaps, but under it all, it's her.

"Don't stop." Her right hand rests along my cheek. Her left hand grips Dante's hair, and he chuckles.

I hold her neck still and let her wiggle into my hand. "We're not going to stop, Chiefie. You have to take it. Take every last bit of it. Open your eyes."

Her blues flick open.

"You're in control, Haley. You have every last one of us." I mean it. I don't even fucking care that it doesn't seem possible. That the world might be against us. It doesn't matter.

I love watching her when she's like this. Having it drawn out for her. Keeping her from the high she's chasing but not letting the pressure too far off. My hand's on her breast, pinching her nipples. Doing it how I know she likes it. I suck on the skin around her hairline and pull her hair against it with even pressure. Her long moans fill the room. She's screaming our names. I move my hand from her breast to her neck.

She nods with the little room my hand in her hair allows.

"Do it, Dante," I command. I'm back to kissing and sucking at her ear and neck.

Haley's body shakes and she shouts, her side convulsing into me.

"There you go. Damn you're beautiful when you come." I keep my hand around her neck, letting her flail back and forth against me. When she stops moving, I yank my underwear off and throw them across the room. Dante's chuckling, and he hasn't let go of her leg. He did most of the work, but when I glare at him, he must see the determination in my eyes. I'm jumping the line. He switches places with me. His monster cock is erect and veiny.

"Hey, Sassy." He grabs her head and kisses her. "You taste amazing." Dante pulls back and runs a series of kisses down her neck. He's pumping his hand up and down himself. But I fucking don't care about him or any of the other guys right now. It's only Haley and me.

"I need you." It's a slow growl from deep within me. I've gone wild. I'd take down an army to get to her.

"Then take me." She turns from her side and sprawls her legs open. Her pink tongue flicks along her lips.

I'm on her, and I pull her legs up around my hips. I sink into her. "Fuck, Chiefie, you're drenched. Dante did a good job eating you out. But now I'm here for the main course."

"Damn, Green, don't go stealing dirty food talk from me." Dante laughs. He moves from her neck to her ear, spending time at the tender spot behind her ear.

Her legs clench around me, squeezing me tight until there's no ending of her or starting of me. Our eyes are locked, and Dante fades away until I can only see her. I'm bucking into her with everything I have. I'm lost.

"Roll her over," Dante says.

I freeze because, as far as I know, his giant dick hasn't been anywhere near her ass. The angle I'm propped up on my arm at has me hovering over her. Haley grabs me around my waist and flings us to the side.

"Well, I guess that answers that," I say.

She tucks her light brown hair away from her face behind her ears. Our eyes are locked. She moves her knees on either side of me—she sinks back down on to me. She's about to ride the hell out of me when I grab her arm. Her eyes widen.

"You sure about this?" I roll up and brush my lips against hers. "Your ankle's okay?"

"I'm good," she says before she plunders my mouth. She's riding me like she's being chased. I'm on fire. When she flicks back, I can see Dante behind her, his hands on her backside.

"You good?" I hold on to her shoulders, not sure what he's doing back there.

She nods and starts again. Haley's going. All I know is I want her to keep moving.

I thrust up and into her. "You're the one who needs to relax and enjoy the ride now."

She tilts her hips, pushing me deeper into her. There's a flicker of light across the bed, and the mattress at my feet shifts. I freeze for a brief second, but no one's yelling for her to stop. That we've been found. And damn her, when she rolls her hips, I have to silently count before I switch to running old football drills in my head to keep from shooting off. This is too good. I want it to last.

My hands grip into the soft skin on her shoulders. When I thrust up, her pussy vibrates around me. Reaching upward, I run my fingers through her soft, sun-kissed hair. "You're so beautiful." And damn. She doesn't wince or look away from the compliment this time.

"I love you," she says. "I . . . love all of you."

On the next inhale, I gasp. "Damn, I love you, Chiefie."

I've never felt love like this before. Like I could wreck the world for her. There is no other woman for me. Not now, not ever.

I grind up and take every bit from her that she's giving. Thrusting into her until her head flops back. She's a second away from exploding. I reach between us and send vibrations with my thumb on her clit.

I love my name on her lips. I've never heard a better sound than her screaming my name. This lasting is on my list of important things.

Fuck the neighboring villas hearing when she pulls me with her. I pull her toward me and take her lips to mine. It's only now that I confirm that Dante left. Wherever he went doesn't matter. Only Haley matters.

She collapses on top of me. Her head nuzzles between my neck and chest. My arms clamp around her. I can't move. I don't ever want to move from this spot again. Lightly, I run my fingertips down her spine. I was never a snuggler before Haley. And now I can imagine myself back at the farm on a lazy Sunday, just holding her while watching the field change colors with the moving sun.

"What are you smiling about?" Haley runs her fingers through my hair.

"You."

Her face lights up. "Well, right back at you, Green. I guess we should get up and shower?"

I anchor my arm around her waist. "Nope. Not yet."

She drops her head to my chest, and her fingers trace the tattoo on my arm, and gradually her breathing slows until I know she's fallen asleep. Asleep with my cock still in her. I close my eyes and try to go back to sleep, but as much as I want it to be that lazy day back on the farm . . . we're nowhere near Illinois.

The door to the bedroom opens. Sam stares at me, and his eyes flare. He puts his finger to his lips and cocks his head to the other room.

I nod.

He's saying we've got a situation. *Get up and don't wake Haley.*

Chapter 27

Dress Blues

Haley

I never meant to fall back asleep. But that's what happened, and it's not like I'm refreshed. Though, sex with Calvin in a bed—in a bed where we're so close to freedom—was absolutely fantastic. Easing off the bed, I test my ankle. It's better but not great. Gingerly, I clean up in the en suite bathroom. Hopefully, I will never take running water for granted again, but . . . I know I will.

"Hey, Sassy. I put some clean clothes for you on the counter." Dante peeks into the shower. "Damn, if we didn't need to get moving, I'd join you."

"We're leaving? Where are we going?"

"We'll figure that out soon. We need to get photos printed first."

"Right." I turn the shower off and step out. There's a bright orange and blue floral dress on the counter. "Thank you for the dress," I say, but I'm not sure how much I mean it. Picking it up, I shake it from the fold. It's not as bad as it appeared on the counter. It's not good but not horrible. I pull it on. It's short with a frilly hem. "It's . . . clean."

"You can find the positive in anything. We'll find you something else soon. That dress doesn't exactly say covert." It also doesn't say luxury resort.

I glance over at the loose black cargo pants and black T-shirt I wore coming off the *Rosewood*. "It's fine."

"We'll find something tonight." Dante straightens the strap of the dress.

My stomach lets out a loud rumble.

"We'll fix that too." Dante kisses my neck. "Sooner."

Now that I'm not as tired, there's a list of questions I want to ask him. I push away the less important ones, like how he came to work for a guy who sells black market passports. But then, he did work for a Russian mobster. Why did he leave? But the real question is: "Do you trust Anan?"

"Absolutely not. But the only people I trust in my life are my mother, my sister, and you. He'll get us the passports we need. I know that much is true."

I nod. "Okay, so photos?" I glance over myself in the mirror. Even with the fancy shampoo and skincare line in this bathroom, I still look like I've been run over by a tuk-tuk.

"Whenever you're ready." Dante kisses my other cheek.

"Let's do this."

The other guys are sitting on the edge of the sofa, all but Calvin. He's watching out the window, but he turns and smiles at me. I melt. The guys have on new clothes too. T-shirts of various colors and dark pants.

"Stand against that white wall, Sassy. Let me snap a few pictures."

"You sure you can do it, mate?" Zane puts his hand out with the cell phone.

"I've got it."

I stand next to the wall and do my best government non-smile as Dante snaps my picture. He holds it up for Zane to see, and Zane shrugs.

"Okay, you." Sam takes my hand. "As much as we would all like to keep our heads in the sand longer, we need to move. You and I are going to follow behind Calvin and Dante. Zane and Easton will follow behind us."

I nod. Sam's got his captain's take-charge voice on, and I have to squeeze my legs together. I hope he doesn't notice.

"You like it bossy, don't you, Little Bird," Zane says and kisses my cheek.

"We're taking everything. Because the front desk has probably already figured out our little trick." Dante puts on the backpack. It's a lot fuller now. "I have your spare black clothes, Sassy."

I nod. But I hope I never have to put them back on. Even though this dress is hideous, especially with the dark tennis shoes, it's better than the ill-fitting cargo pants. I look around the room. "I'm tempted to leave a tip but . . ."

"I'll send one after we're safe." Easton hugs my shoulders.

"Okay, let's do this." Calvin and Dante slip out the front door.

I glance up at Sam. "We have a meeting spot in case . . . ?"

"Yes. And I've got a map of the city. It's one of those tourist things. You want to hold it?" He hands me the map. There are several routes laid out and three starred spots. "Anan's, the police station if things go sideways, and a women's shelter if everything goes to complete shit."

"I'd put it in my bra, but that's where I'm keeping the

cash. And this lovely thing doesn't have any pockets." I do a little twirl.

"You make anything look good, Sugar." Sam takes my hand. "Ready?"

"We're ten minutes behind you," Zane says. "Love you. Be safe." He pulls the door shut behind us.

My heart is thudding.

"It's a bit of a walk, but it's a nice day and the clouds are keeping the temperature down." Sam smiles.

It's at least eighty degrees and humid. But I agree with Sam, no point in making it worse.

There are people walking around the villas. I'm keeping my head down or looking at Sam every time we pass a group of people going to the beach or pool. They're made up from head to toe, designer hats to top of the line sandals and wraps. I've got on this odd dress, black athletic shoes with a wrapped ankle.

Several older women with British accents slow as they pass us. "Good afternoon. Taking your daughter out to lunch?" one says as they pass.

"Afternoon," Sam says in a low voice.

I'm about to jump in and say something to them when Sam grabs my elbow.

"You don't look that old," I say, because he doesn't. The woman must need glasses.

"No, but your dress is more of a romper for a pre-teen."

"I suppose it is." I hold his gaze as we make our way past another villa. Another group passes us and slows.

"Haley?" a woman's voice says behind me.

My heart stops, then races. I glance over at Sam. I've already slowed, but we haven't stopped.

A hand touches my shoulder. "Excuse me. I'm sorry to bother you, but are you Haley?"

I can't breathe. I turn slowly, because running will make the whole thing worse. "I'm afraid you have . . ." It's Stella.

"You're Haley, right?"

"Stella, I'll see you at the beach." Her friend's eyes flick over me and linger a little too long on Sam before she pivots back in the direction she and Stella were going.

"You were chief stew on the yacht my father rented for my graduation from grad school. Come on, it's you. I saw that you were lost at sea. I was so worried. I'm so glad you're okay. I hadn't heard that you were found. The damn news can be so fickle. They only like to report bad stuff."

I take Sam's hand. This isn't flying under the radar. And down the path, I can see that Zane and Easton have stopped near a bench.

"Stella! Congratulations." I give her a hug while holding down the back side of the dress. "So, honestly . . ." I flick my eyes to Sam. He inclines his head. He's letting me make the call. "Right, honestly, we just made our way back to land. No one knows yet."

Her eyes go wide. Her mouth drops open.

"We're in a bit of trouble. More than a bit. This is Sam, Sam Miller. He's the brother of the captain who took you and your friends out."

"I see charming and handsome runs in the family." Stella smiles, brushing her hair from her face, and the diamond on her left hand flashes in the sun.

"Thank you. Haley's right, though. Let's talk about this, but not out in the open," Sam says as he turns, surveilling the area.

"My bridal villa is just up the path." Stella loops her arm with mine. "So, where have you been since—" She stops, waiting for a trio of staff members to pass us. "Let's wait until we get inside." She swipes her keycard and opens the door to a three-story villa. A crystal chandelier is centered over a golden table with a massive flower arrangement. The cavernous space smells like a floral shop. She sits and hands Sam and me a bottle of water.

I give her the shortest rendition of the last year, mostly the last week. But I come clean about pretending to be part of the wedding planner's crew, too. "But you can't tell anyone we're here. We'll pay you back for the villa fees. Please."

"I don't care about the fees." She waves her hand. "You really think this asshole can get you? We should go to the police." Stella has her phone out.

"No, please. I believe he can hurt us if we do. We just need to get out of the country and to better protection." I stand, ready to dive on her phone.

"This is going to sound . . . no, it *is* elitist . . . but I've not found a problem that a black Amex card can't fix." Her dark brown hair is swept up into an effortless updo. She's wearing a textured white one-piece bathing suit with black piping and a gold belt that doesn't have a designer logo on it. Because she doesn't need anyone to know she has money. She is money. "I'll just buy you all a ticket home on the next flight to JFK or wherever. Or you can wait a day until my mother gets here and take our private jet on its return trip to New York. It's scheduled to go back the tomorrow."

"Are you kidding me?" I clap.

"No, the jet has to go back and pick up some other guests anyway. It's just flying home empty."

I jump up and run over to her and throw my arms around her. "You are the best."

"You might want to rethink that?" Stella says, holding me at arm's length.

"Um, why?"

"Because I'm not letting you on my jet in that dress."

My laugh starts out slow and builds until I'm holding my side. "You're right. It's horrible."

"It is. But if you weren't wearing it, I wouldn't have noticed you. Do you want to borrow some clothes?" Stella stands.

"No, that's okay." I drop my arms to my sides and step back toward Sam. I have no idea where Dante found this dress. But seeing that I have the same amount of money I first put in my bra, he got what he paid for.

"Really, I insist. I overpacked, anyway. Krit, my fiancé, said I should leave most of it here anyway. We're moving to the mainland after the wedding. We'll live here half the year and New York the other half. We'll be right back. Help yourself to anything in the kitchen or bar." She gives Sam a cute shrug and takes my hand and leads me up the winding, open staircase to the primary bedroom. "Take anything you want. Well, not the wedding dress." She takes the sheet covering it off and laughs.

I pause. "Whoa, that's beautiful." Though the last wedding dress I held was Candy's, and it was a lot of things, but beautiful wasn't one of them.

"It's my dream dress, but even this girl with the black Amex had sticker shock when I saw the price tag. I picked out something lovely but not as expensive, but when Krit heard about it, he called the shop and had them special order me one."

"It's lovely." So lovely that even though I want to touch it, I don't dare in case I have oils on my hands.

"Here, try these instead. What size shoes do you wear?"

There's no way my boat feet will fit in her tiny shoes. "Huge." I laugh.

"Like this?" She pulls out a cute pair of flats. "My sister is coming from Scotland."

I change into lightweight navy blue pants and a crisp white collared shirt. Part of me wants to stay with Stella and be a girl longer. But Calvin and Dante have no idea where we are, and I can't imagine what they're thinking. Because I wouldn't have put together that I've found us a ride home.

Back on the first floor, Sam's chatting with Easton and Zane. Zane's eating an apple, and Easton's holding a sports drink.

"Nice to meet you, Stella." Easton gives her a nod, like nothing is out of the ordinary, and I can hear Calvin cursing rich people under his breath even though he's not here.

Chapter 28

Slackwater

Dante

"Where the hell are they?" I say to Calvin. We've been at the restaurant for twenty minutes. Enough time to give Anan the pictures. Even if they walked super slowly in the heat, they should have caught up with us by now. "We shouldn't have split up."

"No, we should have split up, but I should have stayed with Haley." Calvin finishes the rest of his bottled water. His eyes rove constantly between the door and the small front window.

My stomach churns. "We should go look for them."

"It's a big city. We stay here until it's time to switch to the next rendezvous point. We stick to the plan until we have to change. Fucking grow a pair." He pushes the empty bottle to the side of the table.

The server comes over. "You sure you don't want to order?"

"We're waiting for some people," I say in Thai. Last night, I felt at home in this shithole. Today? Today not so much. Bringing my family here? Yeah, I see what a dump it is. It's a dump with amazing food. World class food. It's on several lists of authentic places where you should eat before you die, if you follow the hyped-up bloggers. Which I don't. I shake it off. We're so close to being out of this that I'm getting ahead of myself. A limo pulls up out front. Thinking about bloggers just brings them out. The driver opens the door, and Haley gets out. Followed by Sam, Zane, and Easton.

When she strolls in, it's like the whole place spins for me.

"Dante, Calvin!" She zig-zags through the tables. It's not anywhere as busy as last night, but there's still a good bit of locals who look up at her. And look at her indeed. Because the horrible dress I bought for her last night has been replaced. She's dressed every bit the part to step out of a limo.

Haley slides into the booth next to me. "I'm sorry. I hope you weren't too worried."

"Me, no. Calvin, though, was jumping out of his skin, ready to burn down the city."

Calvin cocks a smile at Haley that says *you know I would burn down the world for you, but Dante's the real basket case.*

Haley reaches across the table and squeezes his hand without taking her eyes from mine. "We found Stella, as in the Freemen wedding. Or rather, she found me. Your dress attracted her attention. She's going to let us take her jet home. Tomorrow. And we can stay in the villa. She's going to arrange everything. She doesn't like it, but she's not going to tell the police."

"That's . . . that's amazing." I lift her chin and kiss her.

"I used the phone in Stella's villa and chatted with the harbormaster," Sam says. "*Green Summit* and the speedboat are gone. Left this morning."

"How did you get that information?" Calvin cocks his head. "Harbormasters don't pass out that kind of information."

"I said . . . 'I have the *Rosewood* coming in. And vant to make sure the slips are clear,'" he says in a Scandinavian accent. "Hawk would turn the accent up and down if he thought it might get the crew better tips. Guess I learned a thing or two. They told me the slips had been clear since this morning."

"That's brilliant. Anan says he'll have our passports ready by tomorrow. We'll owe him. He's made a big deal over letting me go on credit when I have none."

"We'll pay him. As long as he comes through," Easton says.

Haley leans back against the booth. "I can't believe it. We're going home. We have, or rather, we're going to have the paperwork. We have a way home and we also . . ." She turns to me. "I'm so excited we can stay in the villa, too."

"Whoa. Nice."

"Holloway's gone. We have a place to stay. As far as we know, Ed's men don't know we're here. We can relax. You could show us the city." Haley lets go of Calvin's hand and throws her arms around me.

The counter girl's watching us, but why the fuck do I care? I give Haley a kiss.

"Haley, while it's true the boats are gone, that doesn't mean Holloway didn't leave some men here to look for us." Calvin waves off the server, who hasn't been leaving us alone.

"You are Debbie Downer, Calvin. But you're right." Dante raises his eyebrows. "We'll have to be careful. I'd love to show you what I know here. Granted, I spent most of my time behind that door over there, in the kitchen, soaking up everything the asshole Anan had to teach me. Honestly, I could have stayed longer. The guy's a genius, but his side hustles made me want to get out of here." I'm about to order a late lunch for us when I have a better idea. "You're right, Sassy. One of the best things to do here is eat. And while you've already had some of the best food in the city, eating it on a stick in the market . . . it makes it better." I apologize to our server and pay her with some of the money Anan gave me last night. "Let's go."

"I'll be back tomorrow," I say in Thai and head out with Sassy's hand in mine. "You look good."

"She does," Easton says, inching up behind her.

"Thanks, I thought Stella's pants would be too tight for me, but they fit."

"No, they fit you, not her." Sam's eyes flick down Haley's body.

"Is it hot out here or what?" She fans her face with her hand.

"Nope, you're the only hot thing out here." Zane continues the compliments.

"I didn't see Stella, but I already know you're better looking in her clothes than she is," I add.

Calvin gives a nod. "Which way do we go, Chef?"

"Down the hill. On the way, there's a local Buddhist temple. It's not as big as Wat Chalong, but it's really beautiful." By the time we reach the bottom of the hill, we're all hot. We turn the corner and Haley gasps.

"It's amazing," she whispers.

This temple has two mythical creatures flanking the steps up to the temple. Wreaths of flowers are looped around their necks. There's a large bodhi tree a monk is sitting underneath, reading. We climb the stairs and take our shoes off, placing them in the line beside the door. Inside it's cooler, and the air is tinged with incense. My breath slows. I might have been raised Catholic, but I'm not a spiritual man. All the years in parochial school, I've never been moved. But this place has done it to me more than once. And now is no different.

"What do we do?" Haley whispers to me.

I take her hand and lead her to one of the woven mats off to the right. I sit down cross-legged, facing the large Buddha on the other side of the room, and place my hands on my knees. The sweet air fills my lungs. I glance over at Haley. The other guys have filed in beside her and behind us. Her eyes are shut, and there's a sweet close-lipped smile on her face. I don't know how long we sit, but it's long enough that I hear a slight snore from Calvin behind me.

"Wake up, mate," Zane says.

I cock my head to Haley. "You ready to go?" I whisper.

She nods.

Down the stairs, I turn back to her. There's a tear dripping down her cheek. "Are you okay, Sassy? Does your ankle hurt?"

"No, not at all. It was so peaceful and beautiful. Like when we were back on the other side of the island." She turns to Calvin and Easton. "It made me feel connected to the world. To all of you, to my dad and my best friend back home. It was like my spirit soared and was everywhere all at once. That's nuts. Forget I said it."

I take her hand. "Not nuts. You're connected to the

world and our conduit. You're special, Sassy. I'm not lying when I say I've never met anyone like you before. And I never will again."

"You never know." She smiles and rubs a tear from her cheek.

"I know. Because you're it for me. I'm done looking. There can be only one Sassy." We're back on the main sidewalk now.

"Are you quoting Highlander?" Sam laughs.

"Maybe. But I'm not taking any of you out with my sword. It's reserved for Sassy."

Easton groans, and Zane laughs.

"Just so you know, you come anywhere near me with your alien dick and I'm going to cut it off," Calvin says, but there's a twinkle in his eye.

"Noted."

"Where to next, Dante?" Haley takes my hand.

"Food. I couldn't hear the wind chimes over the growl of Zane's stomach," I say.

"I think that was my stomach." Haley bites her lip.

"No way, Little Bird, that was mine." Zane throws his arm over her shoulder. "Are you getting tired? I could give you a piggyback ride, like back on the island?"

"Not yet, maybe later." She places her hand in his and presses a kiss to his cheek.

The delicious aroma travels on the humid air a block away from the market. "Are you thirsty, Sassy? They make the best fresh fruit shakes." It's closing in on six. I didn't realize how long we'd taken at the temple. The colored, crisscrossing overhead lights are already on as daylight is on the way out. Vendors are stirring and chopping. And a good crowd has formed, but it's not enough to make even Calvin uncomfortable. You can see who's around us and who isn't, which is Holloway and his thugs. There's plenty of alley-ways where we could duck out of the way if he suddenly appears.

Damn, it's been so long. My eyes flit around, and not searching for assailants but from stall to stall. There are colorful displays of Thai desserts in exact rows. Sticky rice with mango and layered jelly cakes, the colors of a bright sunset and dragon fruit flesh. Across from that vendor there's a woman making fresh spring rolls with nimble fingers before she places them in sizzling oil.

"I want everything," Haley says.

"Me too, me too." I'm like a grand director gathering everything—from steaming bowls of tom yum soup with bright red prawns bobbing in a broth, a dozen egg rolls, and a plate full of meat skewers. Haley and Zane have found a picnic table and are chatting with a local boy when I drop off the first load.

"Whoa, this is bloody brilliant, Dante." Zane's inhaling a skewer while making up a plate of food.

"I love this place. The food is amazing, but it's the people." Haley waves goodbye to the young boy who's been called back to his family stand. "Everyone is so lovely."

When we've all eaten more than we thought possible, we start the walk back. It's only a minute before I see the same guy who gave me a ride yesterday.

"There you are, friend." He waves at me. "You need a ride?"

"There's more of us. I'm not sure we'll fit."

"All but the big guy." He points at Calvin.

I don't know if it's the one Thai beer I've had or if I just have a death wish. "We can fit, even the big guy. I'll even pay you this time, and for the last time too." I hand him money for last night's trip. "Here's for yesterday," I say in Thai.

"Thank you." He bows, and I return the bow. "Can we try?"

"Sure, big guy can push."

Calvin gets in the front seat, and somehow, we all fit.

Chapter 29

Can of Sardines

Sam

The car rolls up to the side road near our villa, and I let go of the door handle. It pops open like expected. My hand's cramping from holding it closed on the bumpy road. I unfold my legs from Zane's and step out onto the sidewalk.

"Here, Sam—pull." Haley waves her hand at me and laughs. I give her a good yank and she pops out, flying into me. I catch her and hold her up. "Is your ankle okay?"

"Yeah, but I have to go to the bathroom now from laughing so hard." She holds her hands to her sides.

The ace bandage has come loose. I kneel next to her and tighten it.

Straightening, I rub my ribs. "That's the last time I do something like that. Zane's elbow was in my kidney."

Haley chuckles. "I'm a one person, one seat belt kind of gal too."

"I know you are." I wiggle my eyebrows at her as the rest of the guys fall out of the car. Calvin, who comes out of the front passenger seat, is the only one who's not rubbing a part of his body.

Dante says something to the guy in Thai and hands him a wad of cash.

The driver waves him off, but Dante's insisting. Haley steps next to Dante and bends down to see in the front passenger window. "Please, you really helped us out."

"Okay, okay." He takes the cash. "Good day." He waves as his red car speeds away.

"What now?" Dante asks, stepping up to Haley. "You ready for a shower and a nice comfy bed?"

"That sounds good." Haley pauses. I'm not the only one who can hear the *or* coming.

"Or?" Easton adds for her.

"We could walk down to the beach and listen to the ocean. If we're really going home soon. This might be—"

"That's a great idea," I say. Hell yes I'm ready to go home. But I'm not ready for what I feel about Haley to end.

"I thought you might all hate it. I've had enough sand for life, but the sound and smell is something I think I'm going to crave forever." Haley latches onto my bicep.

"Exactly," Zane says.

Down at the resort's private beach, we wait for Haley outside of the beach restroom before continuing down the beach. There's only a few chairs and things not put away. We find a large ottoman-like chair that hasn't been covered up for the night.

"Here?" I ask.

"I love a cabana bed." Haley jumps into the middle of it.

"It has a name?" I crawl in beside her.

"If you can charge more for it, it has a name," Dante says, playing with Haley's hair. And I think about how nice it would have been to have one back on our beach.

The laughter from the car ride fades away, and we all turn silent like we were back in the temple. It's been an exhausting day. From the hotel phone ringing and Anan wanting to talk to Dante to finding Stella and her amazing deal to get us back home. The beauty of the temple and the amazing tastes of the market. Now . . . I pull Haley to my chest and close my eyes, listening to the crashing of the waves on the manicured beach. I can't help but think about our island and about Penny back with Esmeralda, but we wouldn't have been able to be here with Penny. We wouldn't have found a way home. I will bring Penny home, but first I need to think about Haley. And only Haley. "Penny would have loved it here," I say.

"You think Stella's going to keep her promise?" Zane asks Easton.

"Why wouldn't she? What would be in it for her to not keep it? She didn't come off as flippant or uncaring to me. Do you agree, Haley?" Easton places his hand on her leg.

Haley rolls onto her back. "I do. She was really kind when she was on Charlie's boat. What benefit could it be to her? If anything, it gets us out of the villa and away from her wedding without bringing in the press. Despite what Stella said about the media not reporting on positive things, we're going to have our fifteen minutes of fame. I'm not looking forward to it. There's bound to be all sorts of questions."

I grab her foot, and when I look around the cabana bed, all the guys are touching her in some way. She's not wrong. "I won't let them defame you, Haley. None of us will. What we are is no one's business but our own. We're a family. We lead with that," I say.

"A family," she repeats. "You're right. It's no one's business but our own. I don't have a family, but you all do. What are your parents and siblings going to think?"

"We'll cross that bridge when we get there, Little Bird. But I know my sister is going to adore you. And my mum is going to be glad that I didn't decide to marry a football."

Haley laughs. "You would if you could."

Zane shrugs. "But shite, I can get a real football now and show you how bloody brilliant I am." Calvin pushes at him with his foot, and Zane dramatically rolls off the cushion, then jumps to his feet and stands with his hands on his hips. "I've got the moves. I'm as fast as Harry Kane. He's a football player," Zane adds and nods at Haley.

"I know. You might have told me about him once or twice before. You definitely have all the moves, Zane." Haley laughs.

The sun dips below the horizon, and we head back to the villa. The room has a giant fruit arrangement on the table, like the one in Stella's suite. There's also a rack with six hanging clothing bags, each with one of our initials on it.

"Looks like Stella's been busy using that black card of hers," Easton says and unzips the one with an E on it. "Two shirts and two pairs of pants. There's also a small plastic bag of underwear and a blue tie. Fucking hell." He moves the rack, showing a tower of boxes of men's shoes. "Guess Ms. Freeman wants us to show up with a little bit of style to the airport."

"It's really nice of her." Haley takes her bag. "There's a note from Stella. It says she's arranged transportation for us tomorrow. It'll pick us up at three. We need to get her our passport names and numbers so she can get it to the crew by tomorrow morning." Haley looks over to Dante. "Is that going to be an issue?"

"Shouldn't be, Anan said any time after ten. Ten's morning to me."

Haley nods. "The rest is just her wishing us well."

"I'll send a nice wedding gift when we get back to the States." Easton kisses the top of Haley's head.

"That would be great." Haley flops into the swivel chair, her bag of clothes on her lap.

There's a lot of silent negotiation between the guys as to who's going to sleep where. Calvin's the first to crack. "I'll take the first watch. We might have a plan on what and how we're getting out of here. Doesn't mean that Ed or Z's men aren't still looming around the resort."

"I'll take the one after you." Dante sits on the sofa and spins the seat Haley's sitting in.

"I can take a shift." Haley crosses her arms over her chest.

"You should get more sleep, Haley. Make sure your ankle is healed," I say. My own leg is healing up surprisingly well.

"It's almost healed." She stops the chair from spinning with her good foot. "But I didn't think I was going to get a resounding yes from any of you. I'm going to choose to think that it's because I'm not one hundred percent healthy." She spins the chair the opposite way and immediately stops. "Yeah, I'm too old for the teacups now. I'm taking a shower and heading to bed."

Zane and Easton take off after her and close the door behind them.

"You're not going to the party, Cap?" Dante asks.

"I'll take the early morning shift. But I want to head out and check the slips, see if any of the Zambrano fleet are back." If I thought I could get away with calling again, I would. But the harbor master would be suspicious, seeing that the *Rosewood* didn't arrive yesterday.

My turn on watch drags on for two hours with not much but housekeeping carts and men heading to the dock for early morning fishing. When Zane gets up and takes over watching, I use the shower in the bedroom with the two double beds. An impulse strikes me when I see the shaving kit on the counter. I lather up and shave off the beard. Unlike my dad for my sister's wedding, I actually manage to not cut any veins in my neck. Man, my mother and sister were pissed at him.

With the new clothes on, I head out into the bedroom where Zane is watching out the window. "I'm heading out to the dock."

"No beard?" He nods, his lower lip shooting out in what I hope is approval.

I grab the keycard from the table and head outside. The castaway in me has been cleaned right up. This is the first time I haven't had a beard in ten years. I run my hand over my shaven face, hoping it's taken a few years with it. It doesn't matter to Haley. I know it . . .

There's a stillness to the air. It's going to be super hot today. But we'll be gone soon enough. I nod at the guard at the hut at the entrance to the dock. They should be looking for an ID, but I know how to carry myself in the dock. I got the I-belong-here walk down a long time ago. Long before I actually did belong.

I stroll down the dock that we ran down two nights ago and make my way down a side dock that should give me a clear view of the Zambrano slips. It's past the time most fishermen would be out and too early for pleasure cruising.

There are some large yachts in this section of the harbor. I'm trying to glance between them to see the next dock over when a deep voice comes from the deck of the yacht I've just passed. "Can I help you find something?"

"I'm looking for dock fifty-nine," I say without looking

up, taking a few more steps so I can see around his vessel. And fucking hell, the speedboat is back.

"You need to go down one more," he says. He has a European lilt to his English. Something French-like, maybe.

"Right, thanks." I glance up at him. He's middle-aged, with more gray at the temples than I have. And clearly not the crew of the yacht he's standing on—he's the owner. I wave over my shoulder. Then I stroll to the end of the dock, and when I'm sure he can't see me, I hightail it as casually as I can back to the villa. There's a rumbling in my gut. We need to get out of here, and we need to get out of here now. I open the door to the room, and everyone's awake.

"Sam? Your beard." From the look on Haley's face, this might be the only time I don't have a beard again.

"It's hair. It'll grow back. We've got a problem," I say.

Chapter 30

Riptide

Calvin

"The fucking speedboat is back?" I move to the window, where we have the curtain open a tiny sliver. It's the same view it's been for the last few days.

"It doesn't mean they know we're here," Haley says.

"No, but it sure as hell is going to make getting out to get the passports a lot harder." I glance away from the window.

"I didn't see anyone coming down the path who looks like one of Holloway's guys when I was on watch," Zane says. He took over after Sam, before I got up.

"Doesn't mean much. If the boat's here, they're here." I should have stayed up.

"They don't know we have any money. They might search the regular rooms." Haley puts her hand on my arm, and I breathe her in.

"You're right. It doesn't mean they know we're here. We need to be careful. We had planned out that we were all going to go get the passports and have lunch. But that's not going to happen now. Dante and I go and the rest of you stay here."

"No," Sam says. "You stay here. I'll go." He holds my stare. "You, Easton, and Zane stay with Haley. We'll be back as soon as we can."

Dante gathers his backpack, and Haley hands a wad of cash to Sam.

"You need to keep that," Sam says.

"No. If we're found, we're found. But there's always the chance that you might need it so you can evade them." Haley puts it in his pocket. "Now don't make me force you to take the money. Be safe." She runs her hand down the side of his cheek. And I'm considering losing my scruffy beard too.

Sam and Dante slip out the front, and we wait.

I'm shit at waiting.

Haley comes around and sits next to me. She doesn't say a word, knowing I need to keep all my attention on the path. Zane and Sam are watching out the front.

It's over two hours later when the lock clicks. Sam and Dante are back.

"Hey Sassy." Dante kisses her neck. "I'm glad you gave Sam the money."

"Really?" I tear myself away from the window.

"Yeah, Anan decided he wanted cash, after all. He took everything we had, but we've got them—the passports!" Dante holds up four passports from St. Kitts and Nevis. He passes them to Sam, Easton, Haley, and me. Zane and I are from Moldova, apparently. He tosses one to Zane and waves his around.

"I do love St. Kitts and Nevis," Haley says, flipping through her new documents. "I'm pretty sure I can answer at least basic questions about St. Kitts. I've been on charter there so many times."

Then we wait some more.

At 2:30, there's a knock on the door. "It's a limo driver," Easton says and opens the door.

I'm right behind Easton checking the driveway and front path, but both are clear.

The driver bows. "Freeman, party of six, for the airport?"

"Yes, we're ready," I say. I wait for everyone to file out of the villa to the limo. I grab an apple on the way. There's an intrinsic part of me that can't believe we've made it. We'll have to touch down and make our way to the police station in New York before I really believe it's true. I scan the resort beyond our door and jump into the limo.

There's a bottle of champagne and glasses waiting for us. But that's not something we should drink until we're out of here. It's open, though, and Haley picks up the wire cage that was around the cork and rolls it around in her hand.

The road to the airport is crowded. I'm sitting next to one door. Easton's across from me. Haley's in the center back, with her seat belt fastened, between Sam and Zane. The limo driver takes a sharp right.

"How far is the airport?" Haley says loudly to the driver.

"Not far. This is the fastest way. I know a shortcut." His brown eyes flash in the useless rearview mirror.

He takes a left and a quick right and stops short. Zane slides to the ground, Sam's arm holding him from going farther. Easton and I both hit the front seat with our shoulders.

"What did we hit?" Zane asks, getting up from the floor.

The door behind Easton opens. "Fucking hell, we didn't hit anything," Easton says.

Holloway's large head pushes into the limo over Easton's shoulder. "Good afternoon. You left without saying goodbye. Now, we can't have that." He uses the tip of his semi-automatic gun to wave Easton out of the limo.

The door behind me opens too. A guard I don't remember from the *Rosewood* yanks me out by my shoulders and pushes me against the limo. "Any problems with you, big guy, and we know who we'll be taking it out on," he hisses in my ear.

"Heard," I say back. But if he touches Haley roughly—I will kill him. I crane my neck, taking in what the hell happened. We're on a suburban street—local small houses on either side. Two SUVs block the path in front of us. Like they knew we would be coming. Someone sold us out. And I bet to hell it has something to do with my new citizenship of St. Kitts and Nevis.

Zane comes out the other side, and Sam stands and helps Haley out.

One of the guards binds my wrists with zip-ties. He gives it an extra tug, but I've got my wrists at an angle so I should be able to get out of them when I see a chance. Sam, Haley, and I are on this side of the limo. Dante, Easton, and Zane are on the other side with Holloway. He's giving orders, but it's hard to make out over the revving of the SUVs in front of us.

"Move it," one of Holloway's men says to me and grabs my arm.

A dog barks in the distance, but there are no people around. It's like they've cleared the street for their little operation. I've got my head turned back to Haley. But damn, I don't know why I expected to see fear in her eyes.

When her blues connect with mine, she's practically shouting, *do we make a run for it?* I shake my head. What are we going to do? Our passport maker sold us out.

The guard next to Haley isn't touching her. He turns his head toward me. And fuck, it's the asshole Collins. The one who shot at Dante. I want to break away from the scrawny guy holding my arm, but Collins isn't even touching her. He's not showing any anger. It's not what I would have expected out of a twat like him.

The door to the SUV closes and locks from the front. Haley's between Sam and me. The others are in the vehicle in front of us. Our driver isn't outside. I turn around, staring back at the front of the limo. He's slumped over the steering wheel. Dead or knocked out, I can't tell. To my relief, Haley doesn't look back at the limo. She's sitting at an angle, and her fingers brush mine. She drops the metal wrapping from the champagne cork into the palm of my hand and swings to face forward. Her eyes flick to mine. The edge of the wire cage is sharp. I run it up and down the plastic of the tie, making as little movement as possible. Damn, she is smart. I have enough slack that I could get out with force, but that wouldn't be taking anyone by surprise.

Holloway hops into the front passenger seat. He turns and narrows his eyes at me. "Do you know how fucking hard it is to keep you ungrateful assholes alive? I wasn't just talking out my butthole when I said if Ed's men find you, you're dead. For the love of god, stop being so damn difficult." He slams the door. "Go," he says to the driver.

"It might be easier to stop if you did tell us everything. Because from where I'm sitting with my hands zip-tied behind my back, your boss is looking pretty guilty," Haley says. And I've never been prouder. Because if any of the guys had said it, Holloway would have clocked us with the end of his gun.

"That's not for me to say." Holloway doesn't turn around. "You'll have to ask Z."

"So, that's where we're going? Back to the house."

"Fuck, no. You want to die? I can't take you back there." Holloway doesn't say anything for the next ten minutes.

I'm making a dent in my ties but nothing much. I've more scored them in multiple places than cut them. It might be enough to snap them if I give them a fucking good yank.

Haley asks how it's going with a raise of her eyebrows, and I shake my head. She frowns, and I rub the damn metal harder. Because if anything, I hate letting her down.

To me, it doesn't appear that we're heading back to the dock. Granted, I don't know the city that well. I studied our rendezvous places and locations around them. I've got a pretty good general sense of direction, and we're past where we should have taken a left to get back to the resort. I lean forward and look directly at Sam. He shrugs and shakes his head. Yeah, we're not going back to the resort. It's another thirty minutes in heavy traffic. Tuk-tuks, motorcycles, and bikes weave in and out of the car traffic in a dizzying pattern.

"Where are we going?" I lean forward and pass the metal back to Haley. It's then that the driver of the SUV catches my eye. It's Collins with a black baseball cap on. I didn't realize he was our driver. There are two more SUVs behind us. No one in the front seat answers me. "It must have been hard to get things timed just right to catch us. I'm surprised you didn't do it at the resort."

Holloway's shoulders twitch. Twitch. Like he didn't know we were at the resort the whole time. We spent a good two hours hanging out on the beach last night, talking about home and soccer. We were at the resort and not careful. My eyes flick to Haley and then Sam. Did they catch his reaction?

Haley makes a quick face. That's a yes. What the hell does that mean? If Anan didn't sell us out, who did? Someone at the hotel? Stella? But like Haley said earlier, what would Stella get out of turning us over to Z?

It's another ten minutes of silence. When we go around a corner, I check each time to make sure the SUV with Easton, Dante, and Zane is still behind us. A few minutes more pass, and the houses thin, turning to farmland. The SUV slows and stops. Collins taps his badge on the reader, and a gate opens and we drive through. There's a large parking lot in front of us, and the SUV takes a quick turn. Then I realize it's not a parking lot.

Chapter 31

Sky Sail

Zane

I've got my eyes glued to the SUV in front of us when we pull to a stop inside a garage. The door is yanked open, and a guard with the *Rosewood* anchor on his uniform glares at me and grunts, "Out."

I step onto the smooth concrete floor. The air smells of grime, and I tilt my head up. It's not a garage—it's a hangar. An airplane hangar. A long, sleek jet with wing-mounted engines sits fifty yards away from the three SUVs.

"Where are we going?" I bypass the guard next to me and yell at Holloway, who's talking with someone at a messy desk on the other side of the hangar. Calvin, Sam, and Haley are clustered in front of our SUV.

"Shut the fuck up." The guard next to me maneuvers me toward Haley and the other guys. Collins stands next to Haley, and I want to kick him in the balls. As if he can feel me glaring, he turns and glares back. I'm not one to hold a grudge. But that wanker can take a leap off Tower Bridge.

The guard holding on to my arm squeezes. "Keep quiet."

We're waiting—and I'm not sure what for. Holloway marches across the hangar and stands at the bottom of the stairs to the plane. The guard I don't recognize boards first. Collins positions himself across from Holloway and pulls a large diver's knife from his cargo pants.

Holloway points to each of us, but his finger lingers on Calvin. "We're taking off your bindings for the flight. But I'll put them back on—or my man who just went up is trained in giving sedatives. You muck about, and you'll find out how to take a little nap—either by fist or his drugs. Now sit back, relax, and enjoy your flight. Or some bullshit like that."

"Turn," Collins says to Haley. She does, and he cuts off her tie and drops it to the pavement. He does the same to Sam, who sprints up the stairs to join Haley.

Calvin turns and gives me a look. I normally understand Calvin's looks, but not this one. Collins cuts off his tie but shoves it in his pocket.

I'm next. Collins cuts mine off and drops it. I race up the stairs.

It's posh in here. Teak and mahogany. Leather captain chairs and a sofa. In the back, there's a table with chairs around it. A large screen takes up the whole rear, or one side of the plane.

There's no flight attendant—rather, the guard who went up first says, "There." He points to the chair at the table where Haley sits, her hands folded, resting on the polished wood. Sam and Calvin sit in chairs facing the screen.

"Zane." Haley squeezes my hand, and the angry indents on her wrist have me seeing red.

"Did they kill the limo driver?" she whispers.

"I don't know, Little Bird. One of the guards hit him in the head."

"Oh." She turns around, staring at the guard talking to Dante.

Damn, I want to tell her it's okay. But it's far from okay. Dante and Easton are pushed into bucket seats behind us.

"Sassy," Dante says, leaning forward.

"Stay in your seat," the monitoring guard says.

Dante flips him off.

"Dante." Haley cocks her head at him.

Dante smiles insincerely and nods at the guard.

Calvin tenses in the chair to the right of me, and I'm with him. This whole thing is odd. How did Holloway know where to find us? And this jet was clearly waiting—like we're some sort of VIPs. I've had to take guests to private airstrips before. Just because you own a plane doesn't mean you aren't on some sort of schedule. Planes have slots to leave just like big yachts have to dock.

Leaning toward the window, I see ramp agents standing on the far edge of the hangar, ready to get us out of here. I stare out the window at the trio of men in yellow vests, two of them with lighted orange wands in their hands. I wonder how much they're paid to look the other way. What other people have they seen stolen away in the night? I hope it's worth it for them. I hope Z is willing to pay them well enough to turn a blind eye. Hopefully, they can't sleep at night. I wonder what the going rate is for six lives? Maybe it's just some sort of steppingstone into the Zambrano family's society of people who can be bought off. A steppingstone in crime.

Haley puts her hand on my knee, and I turn back to her.

"Keep your hands to yourself," the guard barks.

Haley nods, and I place my hands on the table in front

of me. I don't get motion sickness, but facing backward on a plane is going to be a new thing for me.

Holloway's up the stairs. He ducks his head into the cockpit, and then he's back. He comes to the rear of the plane, one hand on Calvin's chair and the other on the table beside Haley. The large man looks tired, ragged, worn. And I can't help but give an inward chuckle about it. Good for him. Hope he sleeps well in hell.

A male flight attendant steps out of the cockpit. The stairs retract, and he does something to the door.

"We'll be off in a second. First, I have someone who wants to talk to you. Watch the screen. He can see you," Holloway says, and I'm not sure if he's talking about Father Christmas, God, or Z.

Z's face fills the screen. "Ah, there you are. The lot of you are quite troublesome." He's obviously in his mansion—the one we invaded a few days ago. Behind him is a dark bookcase that matches the one in Ed's office. The file is in Dante's rucksack—hidden behind the cushioning on the back and the back fabric. Thayer looks just like any other finance bro about to give a presentation on Zoom. "I would love to come with you, but my father is flying in. We have a wedding to go to—Krit Niran and Stella Freeman."

"Stella." Haley inhales Stella's name on a whisper.

"Krit Niran and I went to boarding school together when we were twelve in Switzerland. His mother and my father have a bond. He called me, and you're damn lucky. When I say that you'd be dead if my dad's men had found you, I'm not exaggerating. The man who raised me is many things, and one of them is single-minded. When he makes a decision, there's no going back. And in his mind, you all must die. I'm the only thing keeping you safe. And yet, you want to get away from here. That's fine. I'm taking you away, but you must not try to escape again, or your lives are worthless. If you let anyone know that you are alive, he will find you. You're just damn lucky I found you first—and that I was willing to pay . . . Now Holloway will give you more instructions. Be good. And stop trying to get yourselves killed."

Sam clears his throat. "So that's it? You expect us to just . . . what? Live as prisoners for the rest of our lives? Just to stay alive? Now that we're back in society, we're supposed to forget we have friends? Families? Jobs? Opportunities? You want us to remain captives? You should've just left us on the damn island. We were happy."

"Yes—except my father knew where you were. Trust me, I thought about it. Thought about faking it. Lying. Saying we didn't find you. But the freelancers he hired—the thugs—would've just kept coming back, again and again, looking for a new payday. That wasn't going away. So no, I couldn't leave you on the island.

"And now, I hope we can work through this. But you're going to have to wait until I can take care of my father. I don't know how long that will take. Could be months. Could be years. Trust me, I have no intention of keeping you forever."

"Wait," Sam says.

"Yes, Captain?"

Sam leans forward in his seat. "What if we issue a truce, a compromise?"

"What do you propose?" Z scowls into the camera. "From where I'm sitting, you don't have much to bargain with."

"We go along with your plan *to protect us*," Sam says with disdain. "And you agree to let us go in a week."

Z turns to the side. Is he looking at someone out of

frame? "Two weeks, and I'll do what I can to get you out of dad's crosshairs. If I can't, then my conscience is clean. I won't like being responsible for your deaths. But that's up to you."

I want to scream at the screen, *then turn your fucking father in*. But that's not the way his type works.

"Indeed." Sam turns, looks at each one of us in turn, and we all nod. Even Easton. His jaw is clenched and there's a feral look in his eyes, but he's resolute. "It's a deal. We give our word to follow Holloway's directions," Sam says.

"Good," Z replies. "Holloway?" Holloway steps closer to the screen. "You and your men have the plans. Stick to the schedule, and everything should be fine."

There's a weird pause, like Z and Holloway are trying not to argue. Z's jaw flexes, and Holloway's hand twitches at his side. Whatever compromise they reached must've been shaky. But we're here. That means someone gave in. The video call ends.

"You heard the man. Paul, tell the cockpit we're ready to get out of here," Holloway announces to the flight attendant in the front galley. "How do you turn these damn things around again?" Holloway's fiddling with a lever on Calvin's seat.

It takes a few minutes, but the flight attendant turns the chairs around to facing forward. He moves Haley and me to more comfortable bucket seats.

And then we're in the air.

Going somewhere.

Somewhere I have no idea about.

We're in the air for a good hour. I've been eyeing a tablet in the cubby in front of us. Haley nods toward it, then looks back at me. Holloway, Collins, and the other guard are scattered throughout the cabin, but it's been about an hour since takeoff, and none of us have broken any rules. There's no touching, no talking.

Behind me, Dante snores louder than the engines.

Since I have the window seat, I take the tablet while Haley leans forward, blocking any view of what I'm doing. I nest the tablet between my body and the cabin wall.

It's already connected to the plane's Wi-Fi, and there on the screen is our course.

My heart seizes.

I can't believe where we're heading.

Chapter 32

Turn About

Haley

My eyes widen when Zane turns to me. "London. We're going to London. FAM, that's the private airport south of the city, right?" I ask Zane in a whisper.

Hope soars—even after everything they've said, after the negotiations between us, Sam, and Z, and despite all that's still uncertain, it feels more like home. Like maybe . . . maybe we have a better chance of slipping away.

How deep do the Zambrano family's ties run? I can't imagine what's going through Zane's mind right now. It really is his home—or almost. Birmingham's only a few hours away. His mum, his sister . . .

My heart squeezes for him, and I hold his hand, hiding it from the guard behind us.

Our eyes lock, and I try to communicate as much sympathy as I can without saying a word.

We've got a lot of hours before we get there. Zane tries the tablet, checking to see if it's unlocked enough that we could actually send a message. I regret now that we didn't do more—something, anything. But I was still so hopeful that Stella would really help us.

Instead, she and her fiancé sold us out.

I wonder what kind of family favors they'll receive for their loyalty to the Zambranos. That's how the rich operate. It's all about networking—who you can help so they'll help you later.

It's disgusting, and I hate it.

It makes me never want to associate with anyone like that again.

Maybe I need a new job when all this is over.

That's the weird thing. I love what I do—so much that I can't imagine ever doing anything else, even after everything that's happened.

Maybe there's something wrong with me.

"You doing okay, Little Bird?" Zane whispers.

There's a grunt from behind us—from Collins. I don't know what he has against Zane. The rest of the guards seem indifferent.

I don't want to fall asleep. I feel like every second we get closer to London, something could happen.

But that's ridiculous.

I convince myself that sleeping now is for the best and recline the large leather chair and pop up the footrest. It's not quite flat, but it's damn comfortable—way better than the economy seats I usually travel in.

The flight's not as long as the one from Miami when I first went to meet Rocky and Candy. Back then, I thought I was going to be touring Asia and eventually helping reprovision the ship for a world cruise. Rocky and Candy were supposed to be popping in and out as the ship changed locations.

It feels so long ago now.

Now . . . here we are.

My guys. My new family.

On the edge of maybe getting back to whatever our new normal could be. That is, if we can convince Z that his dad can't touch us.

Maybe I'm being naïve.

But I don't understand why Ed cares so much.

I mean, I suppose it's great to have Z's protection—even if it feels like a prison sentence.

But I glance back at Easton.

The whole thing feels muddled and confusing.

And I want answers.

But I also want us to live—and not under the rule of Thayer Zambrano Senior.

We have rights. Or at least . . . we should.

I drift off to sleep.

My dreams are as jumbled as the situation. When I wake, there's a blanket over me.

Zane's grin flashes at me. "You hungry, Little Bird? Paul —the flight attendant—brought us dinner a little while ago, but he said he'd give you some when you woke up. It's not great, but I've had worse. Even Dante finished his."

I drink two bottles of water, finish off the food, and then —fifteen minutes later—the inevitable happens.

I'm not one of those girls who refuses to use the bathroom on planes. But I try not to. And it's been a long time since we left the resort.

I lean forward and get Holloway's attention, then point to the bathroom. He gives a curt nod.

I unbuckle my seatbelt and head that way.

Paul, the flight attendant, is sitting in his seat. "Can I get you anything?" he asks.

"I'm good. Just gonna use the bathroom."

While I'm in there, I wonder about him. Someone like Paul. When I come out, I lower my voice and ask, "So . . . how long have you worked for the Zambranos?"

"Long enough," he says. The way he lifts his chin tells me he has stories—and he's not about to spill them.

I give him a wry smile and head back to my seat. I lean over to Zane. "How much longer?" I whisper.

"An hour, tops," Zane says, giving my hand a quick squeeze before letting go—before Holloway or one of the guards can notice.

When we do land, it feels like the plane is actually driving us somewhere else. It's a good forty-five minutes before we come to a stop.

The door opens, and Holloway heads down the stairs while the other guard scowls at us and points at our seats.

After another long wait, we're taken off the plane—one at a time—and loaded into a sleek town car.

It's dark outside the hangar we've been parked in.

This time, we're all in one car. I'm sandwiched between Calvin and Sam again.

Across from me are Dante, Easton, and Zane, with the guys flanking him on either side.

The door clicks shut, and a small window in front of the car slides open. Holloway's face fills the opening. "Remember your promise," he says.

Then the window clicks shut again. I reach across and take Zane's hand. The guys are all staring at him too.

"I don't know what the hell you expect me to do," Zane mutters. "Just because we're in Britain doesn't mean I have any answers." His tone is sharp. It's surprising—but I get it.

We're all on edge. And Zane has to be even more so, being this close to his family.

Sam knocks on the window.

Holloway opens it again. "What?"

"How long before we get to where we're going?" Sam asks.

"Not that it should matter to you, but a little over an hour. Surreyham," Holloway says.

"Posh," Zane mutters under his breath. He lifts his head. "But I suppose that's their brand." He glares at Holloway, who shuts the window.

The windows are tinted dark, but when we pull through the gate of the walled yard, I'm blown away. It's a castle. Well, not a castle but a chateau. A nice primary in the south of France explained the difference to me. Castles are fortified and usually built before the 15th century, while chateaus are grand manors with no fortifications. Still, I can't help wondering, "You think there's a dungeon in there?"

"Not the kind of dungeon I want to take you to, Sassy."

"Dante!" I playfully smack the side of his knee.

"Don't make me take you over this knee." He grabs my hand before I can snatch it away and holds it there. The car stops, and we're escorted out onto the driveway of crushed gravel under a very un-British clear night. Behind us, the light pollution of London glows in the sky, but beyond the chateau, stars dance, not a cloud to be seen.

"This way." Holloway holds up his arm and points us away from the main entrance. We go beneath a rose archway to a smaller side entrance, and the path wanders between two stone lions standing guard on either side of it. Ivy trails up the side of the bricks.

The thick door we walk through has iron strapping on it. The floor inside is terracotta. There's a small flight of stairs to our right, and next to the entrance there are two sets of garden boots, one pair considerably larger than the other.

"Up you go." Holloway stands at the bottom of the stairs. Collins leads Dante, followed by Easton and then me.

Collins stops halfway down the red carpeted hallway. "You're all in here." He points to his right. There's a massive tapestry bed in the middle. "There's one bed, but you'll figure it out." He closes the door behind Sam, and it locks with a thud.

There's an attached bathroom. I'm busy looking around the room while Calvin's trying to open the windows. "They're nailed shut."

"We gave him two weeks," Sam says.

"You don't expect us to follow his rules?" Easton raises his eyebrows.

"Let's regroup in the morning." Sam slaps Easton on the back.

"I could sleep for a week," I say, salivating over the bed. It looks as soft as a cloud. I pool plunge onto the mattress, and it puffs up around me. Rolling to my side, I close my eyes.

There's a pounding on the door, and Holloway walks in. "A couple things." He's holding a bunch of straps in his hand.

"Those are the things?" Dante asks.

"Ankle monitors. You have free range of the house. Don't leave the walled gardens or we'll know." Holloway slaps them on us, one each. I hold out my good ankle for him. He looks up at me as he finishes attaching the strap. My other ankle is still visibly swollen and wrapped in the bandage. "I have someone who can look at that if you like?"

I'm about to tell him no, I'm fine. But for when we're

released, I should make sure it's not going to slow us down. "Sure, that would be great."

"The sofa pulls out; do what you want. Just don't be loud about it." Holloway pulls the door shut.

"Sleep, that's what I want," I say.

"And that's what you shall have, my lady." Zane pulls down the duvet for me.

I wake, and only Zane is in the room. "Hey Little Bird."

"You know, I used to be a morning person." I stretch and slide out of the bed.

"I know. I believe you."

There's a knock at the door, and Zane goes and answers it. "Holloway," he says. "Haley just woke up. I'm not sure we're ready to go to the dining room yet."

I hold the sheet up to my chest. Even though I have Zane's T-shirt on, I still feel exposed. "If you give me a few minutes, I'm sure I'll be ready soon."

"If you could hurry up, I'd appreciate it. There are not many of us here to watch you all." Holloway turns around.

I glance over at Zane. I guess that's my cue to get out of bed. I scoot out the opposite way from Holloway and high-tail it to the bathroom. A few minutes later, I'm back out into the main room. My wardrobe consists of three wrap dresses. Holloway and Zane are looking out the window together.

"Anything interesting?" I ask.

"I was just telling Zane about the grounds, since we're on new terms."

I smile and give a little nod. "I'm ready to go." I put my hand on my stomach.

"Good, because the chef here isn't as patient as Esmeralda."

At the mention of her name, it makes me sad, thinking about Penny and Pepper stuck back in Thailand. Sam and I have talked about how we need to make sure that we get them back. They're family, too. We will. "Well, let's not keep the chef waiting. I know how they can be." I smile at Zane.

"There's just not as much staff here. I really need you guys to keep up your end of the bargain. You need to really believe what he told you. It's a death sentence otherwise. I don't like that he . . ."

Zane and I wait for Holloway to continue.

"What?" I ask.

"Nothing. Collins used to work for Ed. I don't trust him. And you shouldn't either." Holloway nods. "But I never said that. After you." He opens the door and gives us directions through the complicated corridors and down a back flight of stairs. I'm going to need a map to know where I'm going from now on. We take another left from his directions and are in the grand entryway of the chateau. Heavy tapestry curtains line each doorway—tall potted palms are at equal intervals too. "Next right," Holloway says.

I take the right and jump. "Collins! Sorry, you gave me a fright." I clasp my hand to my chest. His eyes lock with mine, and it's weird. I feel like I should know him. But why? He's just the asshole who shot at Zane, the one even Holloway doesn't trust because he used to be one of Ed's men.

"My apologies." He waves me into the dining room.

"Sassy," Dante calls to me. "You're awake, finally. I

thought it might be dinnertime before we saw you." He pats the chair next to him. "I saved you a spot. It's not bad—the food that it is." He spears a sausage and holds it up. "It's still English food. This spot is the best because it's next to me."

"Mushroom, sausage, and tomatoes. I'm in heaven." Zane races to a chair next to Sam.

"Hey," I say and wave to Calvin, Sam, and Easton. When what I want to do is go over and kiss them all. But my inhibitions are back.

Dante serves up a plate of food for me from the covered dishes down the center of the table. But it's not long before a foot rubs the side of my leg. Only, whose foot is it? Easton's staring out the window. Calvin's eating, and Sam's reading a paper.

Chapter 33

Diving

Sam

I'm reading the section of newspaper that Easton's done with. I'm not even sure why. But it does make me feel like things might be edging toward normal again. Like there's an end to this that doesn't leave us buried in a ditch on a beach. That's enough, I guess. I'm not sure I've read a paper since I sold my half of the house to Jennifer. That's a million years ago. But the second that Haley sits down, diagonally from me? I stop reading and drop my slipper under the table, running my foot up the side of her calf. In my peripheral vision, I see her trying to figure out which of us it is.

"Do you not like the lunch, Sassy?" Dante asks. "It's not the best, but it's good for British food."

"Hey!" Zane says, then pauses. "You know what? You're right; I rescind my objection." Zane laughs over his mound of eggs. "How hard we had to work for just a couple of these." He holds his next forkful of eggs in front of his mouth. "Remember when we got the chickens?" He's looking at Haley.

"I remember when you got the chickens. Because you almost drowned, but then you asked me to marry you." She smiles at Zane.

"I did, and I meant it. You, me, and any other of these losers you want."

"That loser line feels like a winner's line," Calvin says.

"I'm in that line, too, Sassy." Dante takes her hand and puts it under the table. It doesn't take a strong imagination to think of where he puts it.

Easton looks over from the window. "I don't know what the hell you're talking about, but I love you, Firefly."

"Love you too," Haley says, her other hand emerging from under the table.

I lift my foot higher up her leg, and she twitches when I part her legs.

"Sam?" Zane elbows me.

"I'm busy," I say as if I'm entranced by the paper and not the silky leg under my toes.

"What are you doing?" Zane bends his head and lifts the tablecloth. "Ah," he says when he rights himself.

Haley's cheeks are a lovely shade of pink, and I drop my foot now that my game has been discovered.

"You started something, Sam. Now you need to finish it." Dante holds his napkin up and tosses it under the table. "Are you going to fetch the napkin under the table, or am I?" He leans forward into his challenge.

"I'm picking it up," I growl. But I glance over at Haley.

"You wouldn't want someone else to have to clean up after you." She smiles. And the guys' boisterous approval fills the room.

"Everything okay?" The third guard from the plane steps into the room. "I was walking by and heard a shit show loud roar."

Zane picks up the paper. "Sheffield United defeated Man City. Looks like it was a bloody amazing match. I can't believe it."

"Things changed in the last year. Man City isn't what they used to be. Okay, I'm down the hall if you need something." He ducks out.

"We're good, mate." Zane drops the paper.

I crouch under the table. It's a weird sensation, because the last time I was under a dining room table was probably the same year I was last under a bed, before the Rosewood. But this time, it's a lot more interesting.

On all fours, I crawl across the floor. Nudging her legs wide, I press kisses up the inside of her leg. My girl is going to have to slouch a little. I grip her legs, pulling her closer to me. But my assistant, Dante, pulls her chair out. His hand slides her to the edge of the chair and into my nose. She flinches when my tongue hits the side of her underwear. Damn, I do like this dress, the way it opens up with the wave of my hand. I tug her underwear to one side before I decide that it's too much in my way. I reach up under the dress with both hands and ease it down her backside. She lifts her glorious ass off the chair. It takes a bit of wrestling, but I manage to get her underwear down and off one leg. That's good enough.

I didn't declare my forever after with her, but she knows she's it for me. Dropping to my knees under a table? That's not something Samuel Miller has ever done before.

With one hand back around her ass, I hold her in place while my tongue circles her clit.

The guys are holding as normal a conversation as you can when you know the woman you love is being eaten out under the table. China teacups rattle above my head.

She's squirming in my hands. Her legs vibrate with each flick of my tongue.

"Hey there, Holloway," Easton says loudly.

I try not to chuckle because her legs have stopped vibrating and her knees are squeezing my head tight. But I've become as perverted as the lot of them. I fucking love it. I suck and lick away at her divine pussy.

"Where's Sam?"

"Bathroom," Zane says.

"Right, okay. Well, keep it down. Just know we'll know if you take off your monitors."

Haley's monitor is currently firmly against my thigh. And the pinch of the metal, her taste, and the pressure of her knees against my head has me hard enough I want to swipe the table clean to let me feast on her like the meal she is.

Heavy steps leave the room, and Haley relaxes. But I can't have that. I push two fingers into her in rhythm with my tongue.

"How you doing, Sassy?" Dante asks.

Haley makes a noise that almost sounds good. She's close. One of her hands snakes under the table. The other fists the tablecloth. A few more seconds and she shatters. Her knees push my head into the underside of the table, and she yanks on the tablecloth. The clinking of glasses covers the sweet noise coming from her mouth. Water drips through the fabric over my head. I give her a last kiss.

Dante laughs. "Haley's not the only one who's wet. How are you doing, Sam?"

I don't answer. Instead, I kiss the inside of her thigh and

help her back into her panties and pull them up before I crawl backward to my chair.

Easton and Zane are picking up the tumbled glasses while Calvin's blotting at the wet tablecloth.

I hold her beautiful blue eyes and take a bite of my leftover breakfast roll. "Delicious."

Four days. Four. Days. I'm going stir crazy. We're not being treated as captives anymore, more like restricted guests. But there's nothing to do. It's worse than being on the *Rosewood*. That was something I knew, even though we were captive. This . . . this is like being retired without hobbies. I come out of the bathroom, and Calvin is staring at Haley, who's sleeping. "Let her be," I whisper. "Unless you're actually going to take an afternoon nap?"

He shakes his head and paces the length of the bedroom before he leaves. I follow him. Out of everyone, he's going even more stir crazy than I am. "We should ask Holloway if he's heard from Z," Calvin says as we charge down the stairs together. We go out the back door. It's drizzling, but I don't care. Being inside makes it worse. I lead Calvin through the formal boxwood garden to a table covered with a wisteria trellis. It's mostly dry.

"He's not going to tell us anything," I say, sitting at the table.

"We need to get out of here." He sits next to me, and I lean forward to see his face.

"You think I shouldn't have made the deal with Z? At least we're not under lockdown. We can walk around."

"I think there's no honor among thieves, and he's not

going to let us walk out the door at the two-week mark. There's a reason he thinks he's protecting us. The evidence leads to not killing your ex-girlfriend's brother if you're still hung up on her. Honorable? Maybe. Fucked up, for sure. I don't feel a damn ounce of responsibility or respect for the ass. I say we find a way to get out of here. The bigger the better. Bring in the media. Let's just blow this out of the water."

"True, there's a reason that the bride and groom didn't want it to happen at the resort. It would have brought in tons of media and connected their wedding with us being hauled away." I nod because Calvin's onto something. "We don't need to walk into a police station and let them sweep us under the rug. We need to announce it to the world and let everyone know about the Zambranos and how they've been trying to kill us for over a year."

"And how are we going to do that now?" Calvin taps the monitor on his ankle. We've gone over them. There are no cameras, no sound. As far as we can tell, there's nothing monitoring us in our room. However, outside there are cameras at the doors and walls, normal equipment for a house like this. A few around the grand staircase.

I point at the potting shed. I'm the one who made the deal with Z. But that doesn't mean I don't like to keep our options open. I've been searching the house for something to cut the monitors off with. But there's nothing. The chef keeps the knives locked away when she's not in there. And when she is, she has the door locked. A butter knife won't do much. I've searched through every open drawer in any room not locked down. The library, as far as I can tell, doesn't have any secret passageways. The young kid deep down in me was hoping there were—but if there are, I haven't found them. The desk has stamps and a stapler older than my grandmother and nothing else. If the Zambrano family uses this estate, it's not often and never for long.

It's well-maintained, and the gardens have a crew of regular gardeners who come through. And there are at least two house cleaners who won't make eye contact with any of us—and Zane has really tried. When the gardeners are working is the only time Holloway locks us inside.

Calvin and I saunter over to the potting shed. It's a square brick building with a cupola on the top. A mermaid weathervane spins in the light rain. There's a brightly painted green door on one side, and on each of the other sides is a window. Calvin tries the door while I go around to the other side. It's farther away from the wall and possibly less likely to be covered by one of the wall cameras. Peering through the bubbled window glass, there's a neatly hung row of tools, mostly for gardening. On the opposite side of the shed, I spy a pair of bolt cutters. I push up on the window frame, and it opens. There's a stick on the inside windowsill.

"Door's locked," Calvin says before he notices the open window. "Awesome, you climb in. I'll hold it open for you. I'm not going to fit in that opening. Plus, you proved you can fit into small spaces earlier in the week." He smirks at me.

Inside the shed, I dust off my hands and step around a small hand-cutting mower, grabbing the bolt cutters. "These should do the trick." I hand them out of the shed and climb back out the window, closing it behind me.

Calvin has the cutters tucked in the back of his waistband. We're about to the side entrance when a car pulls into the lot. Things around here have been pretty regular. The cook comes and goes at the same time every day. The gardeners left when it started raining.

"Who do you think it is?" I ask.

Calvin and I round the corner. A tall woman with gray hair is getting something out of the back of the car.

Chapter 34

Sea Dog

Calvin

"Esmeralda?" I shout at the woman in the driveway. Her head snaps up, but it's the sound from inside the car that's more shocking. There's a loud woofing, and it's crazy to think, but I know that bark. It's different from any other bark.

Sam takes off running to the car. He knows it too. I'm not going to risk the damn bolt cutters sliding down my pants or stabbing me in the waist, so I powerwalk to the car. Penny's jumping up and down on Sam. When she sees me, she switches to jumping between us.

Esmeralda pulls a cat carrier out of the back seat. "I have your demon too." She thrusts Pepper's carrier into my arms. There's a small lock on it. "Here's the key." She drops a luggage key into my hand.

"I thought we were . . ." I stop myself from mentioning our arrangement. There's no need to out her if we're wrong about the microphones in our ankle monitors.

She pats the top of the cage. "This demon clawed up

269

the side of Z's leg. It's amazing that he didn't have her killed. I told the elder Z I loved them and if he hurt the animals, I'd walk." She puts her hands on her hips. "Honestly, I thought he was going to drown me. Instead, I've been transferred to this hellhole." She waves at the château behind her. "But better yet, you get to take care of them now."

Penny's jumping at Pepper's crate, and Pepper is doing a good job hissing back at her.

I hold the cage up and stare into it. "I've got you now." I wish I had a hoodie on. It would calm her right down to snuggle into my chest.

"What room are you in?" Esmeralda straps a backpack on, while a driver unloads several trunks and three large suitcases.

Sam tells her while crouching, scratching Penny's ears, and I set Pepper's box on the other side of my feet.

"Good, I want to be in another wing. And don't let the demon pee on the Oriental carpets." She marches to the front door. A door I've yet to see open.

I grab a suitcase and Pepper and follow behind. Sam's tugging two suitcases while the driver wrestles with the trunks behind us. Penny zooms between Sam and me.

"Put it there." She points to the bottom of the grand staircase. "Now where is Hunky Holloway?" She wanders down the hallway to a sitting room where Holloway and Collins watch sports on a tiny television.

"This way, Penny." Sam calls her back from following the chef. Her fluffy ears flap back and forth at us.

"She looks good. Someone has given her a haircut." I head up the backstairs with Pepper, and Penny with her coiffed curls races in front of Sam like she knows where she's going. Her nose is to the ground. She heads right to our room and paws at the door handle—opening it.

"What?" Haley cries. She is on the floor, rolling around with the golden-doodle by the time we get in. "Where did you . . . Is that Pepper?" She points to the crate.

"It is." I put it down, but I don't open it up. Esmeralda has a point. Pepper's not a house cat. She's a treehouse cat.

"Hey, Pepper." Haley crawls over to her on the floor and lies down, her nose inches away from the crate.

I toss her the key from my pocket. "The house manager from Thailand brought them. Apparently, Pepper attacked the elder Zambrano."

"Well, I knew I always liked that cat," Easton says, coming out of the bathroom.

"Hope she clawed his eye out." Sam's playing with Penny.

I pull the bolt clippers out of my pants and tuck them under the bed.

"What are those?" Haley's got a good view of it from the Oriental rug.

"It was our idea of freedom," I say. But how can we do it now? Penny and Pepper are family too. They kept us alive as much as we kept them alive. Heck, we'd probably still be yelling down to Sam on the *Rock Candy* if it wasn't for Penny. Easton would be singing out of the small opening in the rock for the rest of eternity. I glance from Haley to Sam and to Easton. It's easy to read that they're all thinking the same thing. We can't run away from them again.

"We'll figure something out," Haley says. She stands and picks up Pepper. "I'm going to take her out in the bathroom. We need to get her some supplies. Penny too." Penny jumps up onto the bed.

"I should tell her to get down, but I can't." Sam sits on the side of the bed and rubs her ears.

The house library doesn't exactly have the newest Lee Child book. But I'm working my way through a set of Agatha Christie's leatherbound mysteries. It's been four days since Penny and Pepper showed up with Esmeralda. The food has gotten a lot better. And Holloway is a heck of a lot scarcer. I'm not sure if he's hiding from the chef or with her. I don't care. It will make things a lot easier if Z doesn't hold up his side of the bargain and let us go in three days.

Zane comes out of the shower and sits on the bed. His feet are inches away from the bolt cutters on the floor. The bolt cutters that have been driving me crazy. I glance from him back to my book.

"So, what are you doing? Reading, right? Sorry," Zane says.

I've always thought of myself as the doer of the group. But we're all doers, even Easton. And it's interesting to see them all squirming. We need to get out of here. It's a prison. A really nice prison, but when you're a get-shit-done kind of person?

Zane stands and re-sits. "I've been thinking. What if we take them north?" There are most likely no microphones here. But we're all in the habit of talking in code after the *Rosewood* and we haven't dropped it. The "them" is Penny and Pepper. North—I'm guessing—is his mum's flat in Birmingham.

"What do you think will happen if we're followed?" I ask.

"Right, that's no good. I don't want to invite shit into their lives."

"Nope." I turn the page, though I haven't read what was on the last one. I want to be left alone.

"Why did Collins put your zip tie in his pocket?" Zane cocks his head at me.

I blink. I guess using a code is out the window. "I had almost cut through it."

"Right, that makes sense. But why didn't Collins tell Holloway or the other twat?"

"I don't know. I didn't know he had put it in his pocket."

"I've been playing it over and over," Zane says.

My head bobs because there's a whole ton of shit that I've been playing over and over for a while now.

"I'll let you keep reading." The bedroom door bounces closed behind him.

But fuck, now I'm looking out the window. Zane's more of a Hercule Poirot than I am. It sends my head spiraling. How did we get here . . . more like why? Who benefits from Easton, Rocky, and Emily being dead? Is this about the diamond or them? The more time that goes on and the more Ed wants us dead, the more I think it's not about the diamond. The diamond is expensive, but the *Rock Candy* was worth more. And if Rocky and Emily are living their merry fucking lives, it's just Easton.

Like a damn witch, Easton comes into the room. "You want lunch? Zane said to leave you alone."

"I could eat." I put down my book and follow Easton to the dining room. Zane's hidden behind the newspaper. "Yeah, I want lunch." I pull down the paper and flip him off.

"You were reading." Zane picks up the paper and straightens it. "And you were a bit pissy."

I glare at him. But he's not wrong. I've been shit for company lately.

"What the hell?" Easton takes the crumpled paper from Zane.

"Hey, I was reading that." Zane reaches for it back, but Easton angles his body like a point guard.

"I'll give it to you in a second. The Futures of Markets Forum is taking place in London. It starts soon."

"And?" I reach for the pitcher of water.

"And my Dad goes most years. He's virtual sometimes, but he likes London. I was supposed to go with him this year." Easton hands the paper back to Zane.

Dante hands me a platter of roast beef. "You want some?"

"No, I'm good."

"Haley, do you want some roast beef?" He wiggles his eyebrows at her.

"No." I say for her and take the platter. The last thing I want to watch while I eat lunch is Dante's face while Haley goes searching for her napkin under the table.

Haley's blinking at me. I know she's holding back the are-you-okay question.

"Yes, I'm pissy. I've been thinking . . ." I turn to Easton. "How much is Rockwell Tire worth?"

Easton opens his mouth.

I cut him off. "It doesn't matter. Is it publicly traded?"

"No." He takes a rabid bite of his sandwich and chews with vigor. I've pissed him off.

"Sorry, what I'm getting at is if you, your sister, Rocky, and Candy are dead, who gets the company?"

Easton puts his sandwich on his plate. "I own the tire company. It's worth around nine hundred million last time it was evaluated. Dad had it switched over to me. He knew I wasn't happy about him marrying Candy."

Zane stands and paces near the window. "What the hell, Rockwell? Why didn't you tell us that before?"

"We were on an island. And I could ask you the same thing, but I'm not going to because it's in the past."

"Fair enough. Right, okay, so if someone wanted to kill you to get the tire company, that would explain why they aren't going after Rocky." Zane bounces on his heels.

Haley puts her hand on Easton's arm. "Who gets it if you're dead?"

Easton laughs. "That's the thing I wasn't big on. My lawyer wanted me to update my will after the transfer happened. Fuck. But with the training and then making the decision to retire . . . I never did. Everything I have was to be transferred back to my parents. Rocky and—"

"Your stepmom, Susan." Haley covers her mouth.

"Fucking Susan," I growl.

Easton combs his hand over his face. "I . . . I've thought about this before. I've thought of every angle. But it's hard to think that she could do this."

"People do more for a lot less money," Sam says.

Easton nods.

"They hadn't been divorced long? Before Candy?" I ask.

"No. And Susan stayed on at Rockwell-Harding. She'd been dad's assistant with Rockwell Tire. She was part of our family before my mom died."

Haley has her arm around Easton. "If she did this, I don't think she was part of your family. We can find the proof."

"Money laundering for Ed and taking Rockwell Tire

out from under your family?" Zane says. "No, that's not family. That's greed."

"Did she go with Emily and your dad? That summer after freshman year, when you think Rocky met Ed for the first time." I raise my eyebrows at him.

"Yes, I mean, I wasn't there. But she went everywhere with Dad."

"Kind of hard to give up the jet-set lifestyle," Dante adds. "That's reason enough."

Easton winces.

"Whoa, whoa . . . I think we're jumping a few steps. We don't know if Susan did it or not. We don't have proof." Sam puts his drink down and glares at Dante.

"Sam, it's okay. She might have raised me, but her idea of raising me was picking us up from boarding school for the summer and driving me to swim camp," Easton says. "It's a theory, and it's not a bad one. And I'm fucking sorry if I'm the one who caused all of this."

"You didn't cause anything," Haley says. "Because you didn't update your will? What your stepmom did or whoever, that's not your fault, Easton. None of us will ever blame you." She wraps her arms around his waist and plants a kiss on his neck. Easton's eyes lock with mine.

"We're family. What we went through together can't be broken." I nod at him.

"Hear, hear." Dante raises his glass.

But the hurt on Easton's face is there. There's something more. He knows something else, and he's not saying it.

Chapter 35

Sharks

Easton

Closing myself off was how I got through my childhood. It's how I turned myself into a champion. It's how I can ignore my body when it's in pain. But what I can't ignore right now is the way they're all staring at me. Or the thoughts that have been churning in my head since Zane told me about the money laundering. My dad was involved with it, but like I just told Calvin, everywhere my dad went, so did Susan. For my entire life, until just a few years ago when he suddenly announced he was getting a divorce. I wasn't shocked outwardly, but inside? Yes, I was shocked. Damn shocked.

If she set up the sabotage of the *Rock Candy* to kill me, what else would she be willing to do? Susan was there when I was little, when my mom was so depressed. My mom had mental health challenges . . . I remember overhearing my grandmother—my mom's mom. My mom had promised her own mother that she would never hurt herself. But then she did. And I hated her for it. Hated her for being a liar. The what ifs pop in my head. Susan was the one who found her, the bottle of pills in her hand.

I raise my cup of tea. "To this family. We have each other's backs." I kiss the top of Haley's head.

With lunch over, we clear the plates and bring them in to Esmeralda. Unlike the last cook, she doesn't lock the doors during the day. Haley takes my hand. "I saw the gardeners leave before lunch. Want to take Penny for a walk with me?"

"Sure. Yes, I'd love that."

We're around the back of the château near a duck pond when Haley unclips Penny. The ducks have disappeared since Penny's arrival. We stroll around the side and sit under a large tree.

Haley touches the bark. "This is an English Oak."

I smile. "It amazes me you can remember so many plants and trees."

"It's a passion. I like knowing things about things I care about. And people. People like you. You know, you can tell me anything."

"I know." I bite at the inside of my cheek, and I'm a second away from shutting down completely again. But then I spill it all out in one long-winded breath. Everything about Susan and my mom.

Haley's blue eyes are full of tears, and for a second, I think I've said too much. Jumped too many steps.

"Wow . . . I don't know what to say. It seems like it could be. She wanted your dad, his money. She got them, and then she lost them . . . so she decides to take it out on you. On him . . . on all of us. It's ringing bells to me." She holds my hand, and we sit there for a long time, not talking. Just watching Penny chase leaves.

After a while, Haley turns to me. "What about the diamond? Or diamonds. Why were there two diamonds on the *Rock Candy*?"

I pull the diamond out of my pocket. Somehow, from the island to the *Rosewood*, the house in Thailand, the resort, and now here, I've managed to not lose the damn thing. "I'm pretty sure I've got the real one, but I'm not positive. I've been meaning to ask Dante . . . I have no idea. Maybe Susan was mad that Candy got the diamond, and she wanted it as a trophy. Maybe the saboteur was supposed to take it."

"Rockwell, Brewster," Collins yells. He comes jogging around the side of the house. "Get the dog." Unlike the last few days, he's got a large gun slung over his shoulder.

Haley whistles and Penny's at her side. I don't trust the asshole. He was willing to shoot at Zane. He's just the kind of asshole who would shoot our dog.

"Move around the side of the house." Collins is right behind us. "Faster."

"What's going on?" Haley's running with Penny at her side. Penny's butt is dancing around like whatever is going down is some kind of game.

"Get in the van," Collins shouts.

Dante, Sam, Easton, and Zane are leaning against the van. Calvin's wearing Pepper in a hoodie.

"I told you to get in," Collins yells. "Here." He hands Dante some wire cutters. Dante snips the ankle monitors off me and Haley.

"What do you want me to do with them?" Dante swings them sideways from his fingertips.

Collins takes them and throws them into the hedges on the side of the driveway. It's a long haul. He's got an impressive arm.

"Get in the damn van." We pile in, and Collins gets in the front seat. He backs out, handing me his phone. "Turn this off. You don't have any other devices on you, do you?" He swipes his badge, and the gate goes up. We're a hundred feet from the gate when Collins tosses his badge into the hedge.

I turn his phone off and hand it back to him.

"What's going on?" Haley whispers to Dante.

"I've got no clue. You want to tell us where we're going, Collins?" Dante asks.

"I'm trying to keep you alive. Just hang on; we'll be there in an hour. If we don't hit rush hour and don't run into the elder Z's guys. Or Holloway."

"Holloway? As in your boss?" Sam asks.

"I don't work for any of those criminals. Not really." Collins takes a sharp right and turns onto the M3. "Do me a solid and watch my six." He points to Calvin in the back with Zane.

"I'm not watching anything. I'm so fucking sick of that. You shot at me, Collins," Zane shouts from the back row.

"My name is not Nick Collins. It's Nolan Mitchell."

He's got the wheels of this van gripping the road with each car he passes and swerves around. Like he's a Formula One racer turned delivery driver. But there's something about him that's ticking at me. Why should we care about his name?

"Mitchell?" Haley asks. "Nolan Mitchell?"

"Yes," he says and cranks the wheel, passing a tour bus.

"Like Trent Mitchell, Mitch, from the *Rock Candy*?" Haley says, an edge to her voice.

Collins-Mitchell turns quickly around and catches her eyes. He nods and turns back to the road. "Yes. I'll tell you everything you want to know when we get where we're going."

I turn to Calvin and hold his icy stare. And I'm not the only one looking at him and then Sam. Finally, my eyes flick to Zane. He shakes his head. Not surprisingly, he doesn't trust the man driving us. He tried to kill him. He's one guy. Granted, he's one guy with an assault rifle.

"How are you related to Mitch?" Sam asks.

"He's my cousin. I'll tell you the rest when we get where we're going." A half hour later, Nolan pulls the van into an underground parking lot. He's wearing a large overcoat over his gun. "Let's go. Three blocks down this road, take a right at the fruit stand, look for 120. It's a green door. Wait in the lobby. Walk two at a time. I'll be right behind you. And I know it's tough to trust me. But please, please just give me ten minutes when we get to the flat."

Surprisingly, there's not a battle over who's walking with whom. Sam and Haley are first, Dante and Zane are in the middle, and lastly, it's Calvin and me. No one is looking at us. Which is shocking. I'm not short, and Calvin's a damn Viking with a cat in his hoodie.

We pass a pub, a bakery, and a small grocery store before the fruit market. The lobby at 120 has seen better days.

Our keeper, Mitch's cousin, unlocks the door to the inner foyer. "It's a walk up. Sorry, elevators have been broken for the last month."

"You want a lift, Haley?" Calvin asks.

"My ankle's good. I've been going up and down the stairs at the château."

"It's ten stories. Pick her up, caveman. We don't have a lot of time," Nolan says.

But I give Haley a cock of my chin and she throws her

arms around my chest, and up we go. My shoulder's long healed, and holding Haley makes me feel better.

"I've seen more of the world upside down than I've ever imagined." She holds on tight. We're flying up the stairs. A couple passes us, coming down, holding the hands of their child. "Training for the wife carry contest," Haley tells them. I can tell she must be waving as she momentarily lets go of my waist and moves on my shoulder.

"You want me to take a turn?" Calvin's beside me, step for step. I know he wants to take her, but he's carrying Pepper in his hoodie.

"I'm good." When we round the tenth flight, I've got to say I'm awfully glad to see the landing.

Nolan unlocks the door.

"What in the hell?" Sam says. Whatever it is can't be good, as Sam doesn't shock easily.

I haven't seen what he's referring to, as I'm helping Haley get her equilibrium back. "You good?" I ask when her feet are settled on the floor.

"Yes, thank you. I swear I didn't injure myself just so you all could carry me." She winks.

"I'll carry you for no reason, any day, Little Bird." Zane's focused on Haley too.

And when I turn around, I see what Sam means. There's an arsenal of weapons on a plastic folding table. Behind it is a wall of maps, photos of people, mug shots. And places. We're all drawn to it like Penny is drawn to a tennis ball. We gather around the wall. Penny jumps on the threadbare, secondhand sofa, and Calvin's locked Pepper behind the door to the side of the sofa. Which I can only guess is a bathroom or bedroom.

My eyes flick over the photos.

"This picture is just like the ones we found on the *Rock*

Candy." Haley pulls the push pin from the black-and-white photograph. It's the one with the girl sitting on the cot with a cross behind her. She holds it up to the light.

"That's my sister, Kiera." Nolan points to the college student photo. "This is Trent's sister. Our family called us the twins. Because I'm the same age as Trent, born two weeks apart. And our sisters were born on the same day, five years later." Nolan takes the photo from Haley. "These two photos are how our personal hell started." He taps one of Mitch-Trent's sisters. "Before he left to pick up the *Rock Candy*, someone paid him a visit in Miami. They made it sound like they had a job opening up for him, when what they had done was take Kiera. She was at school in Paris." His voice trails off. "They told Trent to not tell anyone or they would kill Kiera. And the stupid fucker believed them. It might be true. She might already be dead. I still haven't found her."

"Mitch . . .Trent did it all? Everything to the *Rock Candy*." Sam's growling.

"He did. Though I never got a chance to talk to him. I don't have proof, but I'm sure he's dead."

"Oh." Haley clasps her hand over her mouth. "I'm sorry."

"Thank you," Nolan says.

I'm not sure how I feel about him being dead. The kid could have gone to the police. He could have said no. And then maybe both he and Candy would be alive. We wouldn't have been on an island for a year. I wouldn't have Haley, my family, the guys. "If you haven't talked to him, how do you know all this?"

"Trent thought he could handle it. But he had a backup plan if he couldn't. A month after the incident—"

"Incident?"

"Yes. His interference with the ship was planned. But comparing his notes to the press briefing, something happened. A month after the incident was to have happened, he had an email scheduled for me."

"You? Why not the police?"

"I've got some skills . . ."

Chapter 36

Prime the Engine

Dante

"**S**kills? Who the hell are you, Liam Neeson? This isn't a fucking movie." I step up to him. I don't fucking care that he has a gun. He could have a machine gun pointed at my head. I've had enough.

"Dante Jones." Nolan shakes his head. "I'm not an idiot. I've told the police. But since my sister vanished and withdrew from school without evidence of foul play and she's an adult, the French police say there's nothing they can do."

I glare at the douche bag. I'm not changing my opinion of him now. He shot at Zane. He's a damn talented actor if his wall of evidence is true. "I don't care how good of an actor you are. You don't have skills."

"Eight years as a SEAL, four in spec ops. I've been in two wars that you don't even know about. I've got skills." His green eyes peer at me, then he turns to Sam. Fuck I thought he was like twenty something. But looking at him now, I can see he's well over thirty. "I joined up with Ed's team undercover. I had to do a ton of digging, but I found

285

Ed's men. I worked my way in through some contacts and joined Ed's guys. I was with them for eight months. He's into a lot of shit: drugs, money laundering, and human trafficking. The crew he uses for trafficking is the most senior. I wasn't making any headway. I had to move. The teams on both sides are fucking loyal and close-mouthed. It's what keeps both the Zambranos safe. Keeps their men safe too."

He sinks onto the edge of the sofa. He's still looking at the picture of his sister Keira—while his other hand is running over Penny's ears. She's got her head in his lap. Good thing she doesn't work for Ed's crew. She jumps sides with a scratch behind her ears.

Nolan tosses the picture on the table. "I heard the *Rosewood* had a trafficking locker, and since the younger Z's been hanging out on it, it made the most sense. What I didn't realize was that there's quite the rift between the two crews. It's a divide the elder Zambrano's men don't know about, but Thayer's men? Fuck, they hate the other crew. They weren't going to ever tell me anything."

"So that's why you busted us out?"

"No, I know a couple of guys in Ed's crew who were more sociable than the others. They never told me anything useful, but we'd chat about football and shit. They're doing a fantasy football league and told me they were going to be at the château later today. But not to let it slip."

"You blew your cover to save us?" Haley sits on the other end of the sofa.

"Yes. I can't be responsible for the deaths of six people to save one. One that might already be dead." He picks up the picture again.

"Let's go to the police now," I say, glaring down at him. I know I've got that damn folder of Ed's in my backpack. Zane moves to get it from where I dropped it near the door.

"No." Nolan continues to pet Penny's ears like that's enough explanation for the children who know nothing.

I glare at the folder. Because cool, he's got a CSI wall and a lot of facts. But I don't need to believe everything he says. I shake my head, and Zane holds the folder at his side.

"Give us a good reason we shouldn't?" Sam asks.

"You know, Holloway is right. You all are exhausting." He rubs a hand down his face. "Because the elder Zambrano has friends in high places. All over the world. It's actually more dangerous for you to drop into a police station here than in Thailand. Paris? Fuck no. New York is even worse. I've got a friend, but he's on day shift and I'd rather not call him into work and have to explain what's going on over the phone. We hang here until nine a.m. Sorry it's not up to the château standards. There's a dog relief area on the roof. Up two flights. I'm going to go get some pizzas. I'm locking you in. Is the dog good for an hour?" Nolan stands.

"She'll manage," Sam says.

"Good. Don't touch my shit." Nolan pulls the door shut.

Calvin and Easton stare at the wall. Haley joins them, and I glare at the locked door with Zane beside me.

"Why didn't you want him to know about the folder and the evidence we have on Ed?"

"Do you believe all of that? Do you believe all that stuff on the wall too?" I ask.

"Why would he lie? What does he get out of taking us away from the château?" Zane sits where Nolan was and rubs Penny's belly.

"Maybe he's into human trafficking. Maybe he wants to keep us here until his buyers arrive." I know that sounds ridiculous. But I'm still mad. I fucking hate not being in control. I hold my hand out and take the folder from Zane and flip it open. I drag my finger over the page until I get to the UK section and what appears to be London. It's mostly initials. I count the accounts. "Nolan was right. There are twice as many names or initials for England as there are for Thailand."

"Twice as many?" Sam asks.

"Twice as many." I toss the folder over to Zane and walk over to the board. There's an entire section of Rockwell family pictures and some from their website of Harding and Rockwell. It's the first time I'm seeing a picture of Rocky's partner. He's the same age as my uncle and has the same scale of knowing everything that my uncle has. I have an instant disdain for him. I tap the picture. "Are you sure that Harding doesn't have something to do with it?"

"I don't think so. I'm pretty confident it's Susan." Easton drops his head and snaps it back up. "Do you remember what we saw in the paper about the Futures of Markets Forum? Good chance Rocky will be there, along with a hell of a lot of media and security. Big and splashy. That's what we need to keep Ed and his men away. Getting on camera that the *Rock Candy's* stranding was no accident? And that we're back? No sneaky operative of Ed's will have the chance to come after us. Not if we're on the evening news."

We've got some proof. "Hell, if we get to the cameras of the resort in Thailand before Zambrano's team does, there'll be evidence of us running out onto the dock."

"Those tapes are long erased." Calvin grips the back of the sofa. "But I like the idea of crashing the Futures of Markets Forum. Did you ever see where it's going to be held, Sam?"

"The Saint Redford."

"Swanky," Zane says.

"How far are we from there?" Haley asks.

"It's on the other side of town, but by the tube it takes thirty minutes." Zane puts his arm around her shoulders.

"It starts tomorrow." Easton crosses his arms over his chest. "We don't know if Rocky will be there. He might videoconference in. But it doesn't matter. We can still crash the cameras. There's always a group of protesters outside."

We're spread out on the tube but all in the same car. I'm still shocked Nolan agreed to the plan. Well, he agreed after he changed almost every detail we'd worked out. But we're on our way. It's an amazing feeling. It feels like we're almost free. Almost home.

Haley's holding on to the railing in front of me. Zane stands behind me. He's definitely got the I'm-home swagger, the *I belong here.* I can almost picture him with earbuds and a cell phone in his hand. Even though I can feel this is almost over, I . . . I don't want it to be right now. It's just us and Nolan, but in a few scant hours we're going to be put to the test even more so than running from the Zambranos. We're gonna be tested by societal norms. And I fucking hate it. I do a good job not caring. But I know Sassy is going to care.

Haley changes handholds to the strap above my head and, with her other arm, gives me a quick hug. "Are you doing okay?"

I pull her back to my chest. "When you're next to me, I'm always good."

"That's so sappy. But I feel the same way."

Zane taps me on my arm. "Nolan says this next stop is

ours." He takes Haley's other hand. "We've got this, Little Bird."

"Yeah, we do," I say.

There's a coffee shop across the street from the Saint Redford London Hotel. There are five-star hotels and then there's the Saint Redford. I'm pretty sure the damn thing costs $1000 just to look at. I've never been inside. And the plan is for us to not go inside now but to stay in the coffee shop across the street.

Nolan came up with a plan to get Easton onto the camera. Hopefully, he can get a reporter to turn around without having to beg. At this point, I'd cross a road of glass to get us out in the clear. I need Haley out of this mess.

We walk along the platform, trying to keep anyone from recognizing Easton before it's too soon. Though this is London and he's an American Olympian. Still, he's a missing billionaire. We come out into the gray morning with people bustling about to their jobs. Just living their normal lives, not dealing with the craziness that has become our daily life.

Nolan nods and enters the shop. There's a guard at the front who mutters at us as we bypass the front counter. "You have to buy something to use the tables."

Chapter 37

Bilge Water

Zane

The coffee shop's bright and modern. I fucking hate it—it's soulless, and it doesn't fit in with the classic Victorian architecture of the Saint Redford across the street. The security guard glares at us on our way in.

"Oi, mate, let us put our shit down." I incline my head at him.

"Get to it." The old man scowls at me. "You have to buy something to use the tables." He repeats himself to the couple coming in behind us.

Nolan hands Calvin a wad of cash. "Here, go get us some coffees."

It's fucking hysterical, the look on Calvin's face. "Me?"

"Yeah, or Dante. Everyone has a role to play," Nolan says. He lifts his eyebrows. And it's clear he thinks Dante and Calvin don't have important roles in our plan. But they are making sure that nothing happens to Haley, and that's the most important thing to the five of us.

"I'll come with you." Haley links arms with Calvin, but

he has to let go so they can zigzag through the tightly packed tables. Dante follows along behind.

Nolan makes his way to an empty table by the window, with Sam, Easton, and me following. It's busy here, a real mix of people. If I stop and watch, I'm sure I can pick out a half-dozen reporters, a dozen protesters, and twice as many assistants to the financiers going to the meeting.

"Are you ready?" Nolan's watching the door and the street. When I glance back at Calvin, he's doing the same, but his eyes are following Nolan. The fact they are so much the same and can't see it makes me chuckle and shake my head.

"What are you laughing about?" Sam asks.

"Nothing. Yeah, I'm ready. You ready, Sam?" But it's Easton I'm worried about. He's going to go on camera and accuse his stepmother of attempted murder. Or murder. Because Candy wouldn't be dead if Susan hadn't arranged the whole thing.

Sam, Easton, and Nolan sit facing the window, and I'm across from them, looking out at the room. Nolan's gone over the plan so many times I can't listen to it again. And thankfully, he must know it. He stares over my head. His part of the plan is simple—keep us safe until the action starts. He's going to vanish into the ether again to go searching for his sister as soon as it starts. He knows what a lot of Ed's guys look like, so he's keeping watch. Nolan's not going back to the Zambranos; he's going to need to protect himself from retribution if what he says is true.

My stomach's in a twist, so I'm playing a game to keep myself from losing it. I glance at each table and decide which of the categories they belong in. The table right behind us, it's four women, two with pink hair, and T-shirts that read, "Down with the one percenters." Not much of a question there. Protesters. The group beside them is a little more difficult: business attire but nothing too fancy, two of them on their phones. A dark-haired man puts his briefcase on the chair next to him. It's worn from years of use. He's writing on a yellow pad, but when a younger man comes along, he's got two phones and a tray of coffee and sweet bites. He arranges them on the table. The guy with the yellow pad is the boss.

I do this for three more tables, scanning between Little Bird in the queue and back at the scowling trio on the other side of the table from me.

On the far edge of the café, there's a couple. They're not in one of my three categories: boss, protestor or admin to a boss. I'm about to skip over them when I pause. There's a blonde with her back to me, but the guy looks familiar. Really familiar. And I'm wracking my brain as to where I know him from. School? The club? But the guy doesn't look like a football player. He's American. Was he on a yacht with me? Not a bosun for sure. He's got that I-don't-do-work look about him. The guy leans across the table and kisses the blonde. It's quick, then he goes back to slouching and drinking his coffee. I'm staring, but I don't fucking care.

"You good, Zane?" Sam asks.

"Behind you by the window on the far side of the café, there's a guy with a blonde. I know him from somewhere, but I can't remember where."

"Don't all go looking at once," Nolan says under his breath while still staring out the window. Sam and Easton turn together. "For fuck's sake," Nolan growls.

The guy by the window kisses the blonde again, and Easton drops his fist on the table.

"You okay, mate?" I ask.

Easton's up and charging through the tables. I'm right

behind him. When we get to the table, the guy is so focused on the girl in front of him, he doesn't look up. But the girl does, and I finally see her face.

"Bri?" I don't mean to say it so loudly, but the occupants of the tables around us turn and look. It's Bri, the stew Sam had to fire for cutting Shayla's hair. Bri, the girl Easton had a restraining order against. I take a longer look at the guy. It's easier because Easton has pulled him out of his chair. It's Brick—Emily's fiancé.

"What the hell are you doing, kissing her?" Easton doesn't glance down at Bri.

But the whole coffee shop is looking now. And the old guard is weaving his way through the tables.

I glance back to where Nolan was, but he's gone. Fuck, I don't blame him. That was the plan the whole time, that he'd get clear of us when we started the show. And the show has started. Not how we thought, and this might just be a preview. But it's a darn entertaining one.

"Sit down," Calvin growls at Brick.

"It's a little hard to do when Easton's holding me up. How the hell did you get so big? When did you get back? How did you get back?" Brick's jabbering, while Bri's mouth is hanging open.

There are two empty seats at their table, but the table jammed up next to theirs cleared out when Calvin marched across the café—giving us ample space to sit. And when we sit, the security guard inclines his head at me.

"We're sound, mate. Just having a laugh."

The man grunts, but I can tell he doesn't want to have to kick us out.

"Let him down, Easton," I say, and like I'm a horse whisperer, he does.

Easton sits on one side of Brick, and Sam takes the

other. When they're sitting, Calvin plops down next to Easton. I wave at Dante and Haley to stay in line. The last thing we need is to be kicked out. The guard continues to give us sideways glances.

I'm in the chair next to Bri. She still hasn't said a word, and when I look over at her, she looks like she's about to hyperventilate. "You good?" I don't care, but my mother raised me correctly. And it's always been one of my rules—care for those in need, even if they don't deserve it.

My rules. Huh, I haven't thought of them in a hell of a long time.

Bri shakes her head.

"Why are you kissing her?" Easton spits out at Brick. "Where's Emily?"

"Emily? Right, you really haven't been around, have you? Emily and I broke up . . ."

"And you're dating Bri?" Sam leans in.

"Yeah, listen I . . . I came here to come clean, do the right thing, and move on with my life. I've been living with . . . I know you don't care, but my life has been hell for the last year."

"You were rescued after what, ten days?" There's a chill in Easton's voice.

"That's not—"

"Clean start, that's what we're here for." Bri's voice shakes, and she doesn't look at anyone but the cowering man across the table from her.

"Clean start, right? Fuck. Promise to not hit me?" Brick stumbles over his words.

"Sure." Easton's eyes flick to Calvin, then me. I'm not making any such promise, and damn straight you know Calvin isn't.

"Emily broke up with me after Candy died."

"Why would she . . . " Easton's eyes flare, and I'm not working out whatever he's figured out. "You were with Bri the whole time? You were dating Emily for her money, just like Candy was dating my dad?" Easton growls.

Brick puts his hands up. "No, I—you won't hit me, will you?"

Haley and Dante join us. Haley places the tray on the table in front of me and sinks into the seat next to mine.

"I already promised," Easton says flatly.

"I was with Candy. Candy came up with a plan to take the Pink Phoenix, and her diamond-encrusted wedding dress."

"Brick." Bri's voice has stopped shaking. "You're leaving too much out." She turns to Easton. "My aunt loved your dad, at first. But she couldn't take the threats. She was scared for her life. She just wanted out."

"Threats?" Haley says.

Bri closes her eyes and pinches her nose. "That's why she got me a job on the yacht. She wanted me to protect her."

"From whom, Bri? Why?" Easton smacks Brick's reaching hand away from the pastries Haley bought.

"Rocky's ex," Brick says. "She was threatening Candy. Candy came to me because she thought the threats were too subtle for Rocky to take seriously. That's how we . . . how we ended up being together. With me comforting her."

I turn away because if there's one thing I don't want in my graphic imagination, it's an image of Brick doing whatever he thought was comforting Candy.

"Why are you here? How is this your clean start?" I ask.

"Rocky's at the forum across the street. He won't take my calls, and the office won't let either one of us get close to them. I need to give him something. In person," Brick whispers.

"What? What could you possibly need to give a man after you slept with his fiancée who is now dead? Why would he need anything from you?" Easton asks.

"Well, he does," Bri says.

"I have something to give him." Brick pulls something out of his jeans pocket and puts it on the table with his hand over the top.

Easton lifts Brick's hand, revealing a sheet of paper folded in thirds with Rocky's name on it. "What is that?" Easton points.

"It's a letter," Bri whispers.

Chapter 38

Swab the Deck

Easton

"**A** letter? What the hell does Rocky care about a letter from someone who cheated on his daughter with his fiancée?" I fucking yell it because the vultures surrounding Rockwell-Harding have taken my family to a place of terror. And I don't mean only Emily and Dad, but Haley and the guys too. This letter ignites my fury.

"Please, it's important, Easton," Bri says. "Your father will want to see it. And Candy had the whole thing planned out, how we were all going to make a new life away from . . . Honestly, they didn't mean for it to happen. Take the letter. Please. Give it to your dad. It's important." She waves it at my face.

I snatch the letter from Bri. I'm about to tear it in half when Sam plucks it from my hand. The damn thing isn't even sealed or in an envelope. It's just a piece of paper folded in thirds. Fucking thing is probably written in crayon, anyway.

"The wedding dress with the smaller diamonds and the Pink Phoenix were Candy's escape plan?" I say. "Not that it worked. She ended up dying anyway."

A fat fake tear rolls down Bri's cheek.

"Easton." Haley touches my arm, and I look up. The security guard is back, muscling his way between Calvin and Dante.

"You all need to go," he says.

"We're sorry. They're old friends," Haley says.

"If one of my mates grabbed me like that, he wouldn't still be my mate. Off you go." The guard points to the door. Outside the window, across the street at the Saint Redmond, there are now a lot more people and a lot more police. "Here you go. You can go be a giddy aunt outside." The guard unlocks the side door and motions us out. Haley's the first to go. Calvin and Dante are right there with her.

I'm glaring at Brick, seething. He's vermin, hurting my father and sister at the same time. I don't care what excuse he has. What excuse Candy had. That she felt threatened? Fucking bonkers. Zane's beside me, but Sam's over my left shoulder.

"You, too. Out you go," the guard says, and I assume he's talking to me as I step out onto the sidewalk. But the older man is leaning over the table with Bri and Brick.

Bri holds up her hands. "We didn't do—"

"Save it for the coppers. You've not bought a thing, and you've been yappin' too long. Out. Plenty of coppers out there in front of the swanky Saint Redford—go cry to them."

And with that, all of us are out on the curb. The door slams shut behind us.

Bri puts her hand on my shoulder, and I jump back out of her touch. "Give him the— What are you doing?

You can't read that! It's addressed to Rocky," Bri cries at Sam.

"It wasn't sealed, and you need to— No, fuck it." Sam shoves the unfolded paper into his pocket and swings his fist in a perfect right jab into Brick's face. There's a snap, and Brick screams.

"Holy shit, holy shit." Brick clutches his nose. "You hit me. He hit me." Blood drips between his fingers onto the sidewalk.

"You better get moving before the rest of them read that fucking scribble." Sam takes a step toward Brick, and Brick backs away, holding his nose.

Bri's screeching. "Why did he do that?" She turns to me and then to Brick. "Why did he do that?"

"He's nuts, feral." Brick shakes out his hand, and droplets of blood fly onto the pavement.

"Sam?" Haley's eyes are wide.

I look between Sam and Brick, wishing I was the one to do it. And I don't even know what the letter says, but I trust the fuck out of Sam, and there's no way he would have done something like for no reason. There's damn straight more to it than Brick sleeping with Candy.

Fuck my promise. I punch Brick in the gut. The wind rushes out of him, and he holds his stomach. I want to do it again. But I step back.

"Let's go," Sam says, nodding across the street. "Now."

Sam takes Haley's hand, and we make our way across the side street to a larger crosswalk leading to the Saint Redmond.

"What the hell, Sam? That's something the Viking would do. Nicely done," Dante says. "What does the letter say?"

Sam stops short of crossing the street and glances back

at the side door of the café, but Brick and Bri are already gone.

"Let me read the letter," I say.

"Not now. I don't want any of us to be tried for manslaughter. We need to get over to the hotel. We still have a plan to follow through with."

I want to see the letter. But it's in Sam's pocket.

"Later. Later," he states a second time when I take a step back toward the café. He puts his hand on my shoulder. "We need to get across the street."

There's an officer directing traffic that has come to a standstill. The crowds are getting larger. Many demonstrators and even some of the forum attendants leaving the hotel have noticed us. And two beefy private security guards are making their way across the sidewalk toward us.

"Fuck. Incoming," Calvin says.

"We wanted to draw attention to ourselves. Just not like this." Zane's back goes straight, and he steps in front of Haley.

But then the guards part, and my dad's behind them. He's using a cane to walk.

"Rocky!" Haley's the first to move; she jumps in front of Zane and beelines for my dad.

"Haley Brewster, how in the hell did you get here? Boy, I can't wait to tell your dad."

"My dad? You know my dad?"

"I've talked to him every week since Emily and I got back. Same with Charlie and your mom, Sam. And Dante's mom and sister. Yours too, Zane. I'll be damned, all six of you are here. And there's my boy." Tears start rolling down his cheeks. He takes a few wobbly steps and steps onto the curb. A security team surrounds us, but I barely notice. My dad's not the only one crying.

"Mr. Rockwell, we need to get you out of here. You're drawing too big of a crowd," a guard says.

"Right, we'll walk back to the hotel."

"No sir, the way is blocked."

"Easton!" People are yelling my name. There's shouting, and when I look to the side, there's a camera crew filming the whole thing. And fuck, Haley's in the middle of it. We wanted to save her from the circus we knew we had to create to announce we're back.

There's lots of shouting.

"Have you been in London this whole time?"

"How did you survive?"

"Where's the diamond?"

Two black London taxis pull up. "Get in, Mr. Rockwell. We'll drive around to the back entrance."

It's quick, and in an instant the five of them are pushed into one cab while I'm in another with two guards and my dad. My insides hollow out, and panic rises up my throat. It's been a year since I've been without them. Without Haley.

My dad grabs my hand. "You're okay, son. You're home now."

There are so many things I should be saying, so many things I've dreamed of saying to him for the last year, but I'm having a hard time gathering any of my thoughts. It's also damn near impossible to keep me from jumping out of this car and running after the next one.

"I've been home. But it's fucking amazing to see you."

"What, to Miami?" Dad asks.

I shake my head, realizing he's never going to fully comprehend the year I've had. How an island with no running water or electricity could be better than the civilized world. "We just got back to civilization three weeks ago. It's a long story."

"How the hell did you end up in London? I was standing at the top of the stairs in front of the Redmond, about to give a two-minute update to the BBC finance radio, when I saw you punch someone. At first, I didn't trust my eyes. You were so far away, but I asked the Rockwell PR person beside me if he thought that hooligan looked like you, and he gasped and said he would bet anything it was you. And that the rest of the surrounding people were the missing crew from the *Rock Candy*. He's been working really hard to keep your case in the media so people didn't stop looking for you. But you found us. That's . . . It's so . . . Damn it, Easton, I'd say I've never cried this much, but you haven't seen me for the last year. Em! Does your sister know? We need to call your sister."

"Not yet. We will, Dad."

The car stops around the side of the hotel, and a valet yanks the door open. I'm out of the car, and the second I see the others getting out in front of us, I turn back to my dad and hold out my hand.

"I've got it. I've got it. The cane's just for show." He shakes me off. But I know he's lying.

There's a face I recognize standing next to the car. Someone from Rockwell-Harding. "Mr. Easton Rockwell, welcome home." He holds out his hand. "I'm making arrangements to get us up to Mr. Rockwell's suite as privately as possible."

"Actually, for our safety, we need to make our arrival as public as possible," I say, turning from my dad to the PR guy and back again. "You need to trust us on this."

"I can do it in public. Do you need it right now?"

"We've got a start," Dante says. "There were a few people filming with their phones."

"I'll arrange a press conference." He stops and squares his shoulders. "Or a deep interview with the reporter of our choosing? A one-on-one with the six of you. It will be easier to control the narrative. I'm Mike Hastings." He nods to us.

"That sounds good," Sam says.

"Follow me." The doorman opens the doors for Mike and my dad, who step into the elevator. The six of us crowd in around the two shorter men. I've never thought of my dad as short, but I think he's shrunk an inch or two. Even Haley is taller than him, and she towers over the PR guy.

The elevator opens on the top floor, and we're ushered into a multi-room suite.

"Easton!" One of my dad's two assistants runs at me. She's waving her phone in her hand. "It's true. I've got your sister on FaceTime." She pushes her phone into my hand.

Em's holding it close to her face, so all I can see is her nose. And I can't make out a thing she's saying because she's screaming into her phone. "Em . . . Em?" I look up at Haley, who's smiling from ear to ear. "Em, I love you, but I need to talk to Dad. It's so good to see you. Well, your nose."

She's crying so hard she's hiccupping.

"It's okay, Em. The six of us are in London."

"Good, good," she manages.

"I need to talk to Dad."

"Okay."

"Here, talk to my sister." I hand Haley the phone.

"Emily, it's Haley." Haley waves into the phone.

"Haley . . ." Em starts sobbing again.

I should clear the room. Have the PR person step outside. But I don't fucking care anymore. Appearances don't mean a damn thing to me. My whole life has been about appearances. Don't let anyone know you have an injury—metaphorically or physically. Don't show your weaknesses, in business or the pool. Swimming might look like an individual sport against the clock, but who you're swimming against mentally changes everything. If the last year is going to mean anything, I need to clear that out of my DNA.

"Dad, what the hell are you doing? Why were you doing business with the Zambrano family?"

Chapter 39

Eye of the Storm

Haley

Emily's full-on ugly crying.

"We're okay. I'm so relieved you are too. And your dad looks great." It's my stew voice. I wish I meant it. Rocky looks like he's aged a decade in the last year.

"You do too. I like your hair short."

"Uh, thanks. Your brother cut it rather quickly." There's a click, and the memory of Easton cutting off my ponytail flashes in my head. "I've been meaning to even it out." The right side is longer than the left. But honestly, I hadn't really noticed until we touched down in London. I've been missing fiddling with my ponytail. Something I've always done when I'm deep in thought. Though, over the last year I think I've hardly done it at all. When Calvin and Easton were missing, and a few other times. But not much at all. "I think I might keep it short." It's just below my chin. Easton did the best he could to protect me from the pirates.

There's a shift in energy in the room, and everyone goes silent.

"What's happening?" Emily asks. I'd dropped the phone to my side, forgetting I was even on with her.

Easton takes the phone from me. "Em, can I call you back? I'll tell you everything later."

"Sure, I love you. I can't wait to hug you and then smack you for not telling me you were okay the second you got back."

"Love you, too, Em."

"Wait," Em screams out of the phone.

"What?" Easton cocks his head to the side. It's adorable. I can't wait for the two of them to see each other again. Because I have every confidence that she will give him a kiss and hug and then smack him. I feel horrible that she's been so worried. And it comes at me that Rocky said he's been talking to my dad every week? That's . . . that's crazy.

"Dad, don't let him out of your sight," Emily says.

"I won't," Rocky says. "Promise."

"I'm counting on that."

"Bye, Em."

"Bye, Jerk Face," she says, half crying and laughing. Easton sets the phone down, and I sit in an empty chair on the side of the sofa. Five sets of eyes glare at me. But I can't do it. I just can't do it. I can't let Rocky see how much I love my guys.

Dante stands and grabs my hand, and he pulls me over to the sofa and squeezes me in the six inches between him and Easton. Rocky's brows furrow, and my pulse races. I stared at the ceiling of the treehouse more than one night with Calvin's arm pinning me to the mattress while I was nestled into one of the other guys. He sleeps so poorly I never want to wake him up. So I'd lay there thinking of what it would be like to be back home. What I would eat— not that I obsessed about it, but I'd let my thoughts wander, and it would always come to a moment like this. Looking at the parent or relative of one of the guys as it slowly sinks in what we are to each other. How our relationship is more than friends.

My stomach flips, but I'm strong enough to do this. I'm strong enough to love them and push away what other people think. In Dante's words, *fuck them*. I straighten my shoulders with as much space as I have. Because I'm comfortable here.

"There's room over there," Rocky says, pointing at the love seat on the other side of the room.

"She's good here. Aren't you, Haley?" Easton takes my hand and intertwines our fingers and rests them on his lap.

Rocky's eyes trail from our joined hands to where Dante has a hand on my knee. He turns to Mike the PR person, who visibly swallows and nods at Rocky—like they're telepathically linked in dealing with business issues.

"We have a lot to talk about, Dad. Some of it is going to be difficult for you to accept, but it's my life. But the first—"

"Why don't you tell me what it is before you make me judge and jury? I doubt I'm going to care. You're alive, and that's all that matters. But you've got that look on your face. You want to ask me something?"

"You didn't answer my question about the Zambranos." His voice doesn't waver.

But me? I'm Jello inside. The PR guy is typing on his phone faster than a teenager with good gossip, and he keeps glancing at me. This place is putting me on edge. I've been to plenty of nice hotels before. A few of the yachts I've stewed on make a five-star hotel look like a roadside motel. But I'm climbing out of my skin. I don't belong here. Only Dante's hand on my leg and Easton's interlocked fingers keep me from bolting.

"Sassy," Dante whispers in my ear, and I'm pulled back from my racing thoughts.

I close my eyes. I can do this. I want to do this. I'm not that same little girl who was scared when her parents fought. I haven't been her in a darn long time.

Dante squeezes my leg. I'd like to say that my insecurities vanish with a wave of a magic wand. But they're in there. I know they're going to come out again. I stare over at Rocky and at Sam, Zane, and Calvin.

Rocky's staring at Easton. His chest rises and falls. His lips stretch into a thin line, and I'm not sure he's going to admit to it. After a long while, he stands. "It's complicated. It's complicated in the most horrible kind of way. And . . . what are you saying? Where have you been?"

"Right, we're going to need more than that," Sam says, standing too. "I don't have any right to know what's going on in your business. But your dealings with the Zambrano family put my crew and the vessel I was in command of in peril."

"How—"

"What happened with the *Rock Candy* wasn't an accident. A deckhand, Trent Mitchell, sabotaged the boat. He was blackmailed into doing it. We believe the Zambrano family took Mitch's cousin."

Rocky walks the length of the room and back. "No. I . . . How did you find out? And how did Sam end up with the rest of you?"

"The *Rock Candy* drifted on the same current as their raft. I arrived on another part of the island weeks after they did."

"So you fixed the ship and—"

"No, Dad. It's not as simple as that. Pirates stole the *Rock Candy* when we had her tied up. They came back to kill us months later. That's when it takes a twist. We fought back, and Thayer Zambrano came in on his yacht."

"And he brought you back?"

"Sort of. He went back on his father's orders to kill us. Instead, he held us captive," Zane says.

PR Mike sinks to the empty sofa. His eyes are even wider than Rocky's.

"Why . . . why would he want to kill us? He's been using . . ." Rocky glances at where we came in. "Is she over there?" he asks Mike.

"Ms. Blanche?" Mike asks, and Rocky nods. "I believe so."

"Susan kept her maiden name," Easton says to us. "And why the hell is she here?"

"She never left the company. You know she has too big of a stake in Rockwell-Harding." Rocky wrings his hands in front of him.

"Honestly Dad, is she the one who brought the Zambranos into the fray?"

"Yes. It took me a while to figure it out. It's why I divorced her. But I didn't have complete proof. And then when you were missing, she was so . . . fucking helpful. Damn it. She was helpful because she knew where you were the whole time?"

"I don't think the whole time. But for the last four months? Most likely."

"She convinced me that it was Roger Harding who had gotten the laundering going. Right before we left for the trip. I thought about selling my shares, but I couldn't get a lockdown on the right price for the total company. I thought I could walk away and get rid of the whole mess. Instead, they decided to get rid of me."

"I don't think they were trying to get rid of you, Rocky, but Easton."

"I never changed my will. Half of Rockwell Tire would have gone straight to her."

There's a red tinge to Rocky's face. Dante, Easton, and I lean forward because I'm worried he's going to have a heart attack. Rocky sinks down next to Mike. "We need to get her on tape. You've got twenty minutes to figure out how to keep this from sinking both companies and landing both me and Harding in jail. We need a film crew and a reporter who has enough clout to make this go big. I want Susan and the Zambrano family to go down in flames. Jail's too good for them, but I won't settle for less."

Easton's leaning forward, and I can tell he wants to bring up his mother's death. I squeeze his hand. He squeezes my hand in return and leans back on the sofa. "There's more, Dad, but let's start with this for now. Mike's going to need more than twenty minutes."

Mike laughs. "I've been with Rocky long enough to know what twenty minutes means. Do it fast and right. No worries. I have a team back in the States working on things already. This is going to sound insensitive—"

"Then don't fucking say it," Easton growls.

"What?" Sam asks, at the same time.

"I'm sure it's not needed, as I can tell you all have a tight bond. But as crew for Rocky's ship, you are still beholden to the NDA you signed last year."

"Shut it." Easton lets go of my hand and stands, thundering across the room in two steps. But I'm right behind him as he's inches away from Mike's face.

"Easton?" I put my hand on his arm. "Your family is our family now." I turn to the rest of the guys, and they nod. "We wouldn't do anything to hurt you, Rocky, or Emily."

"Now, about Susan . . ." Calvin stands. "Are you sure she's still around? If she gets wind on social media that we're back . . ."

"I've got a security guard at her door, and her assistant messaged me that Susan is taking a nap after this morning's meetings," Mike says. "I'm stepping out. I'll be back when I have the exact time of the interview." He stops at Calvin. "Forty-five long?"

"Forty-five along what?" Calvin cocks his head to the side.

"Your suit coat size, Calvin," I say.

"I'm not wearing a suit coat. There's a reason why I became a ship engineer."

"For the camera crew?" I ask. And it's the first time I take the six of us in with the perspective of someone who hasn't lived on a beach with almost nothing for the last year. We've got a feral edge. Or maybe that's just me with my chopped hair.

"Nothing says a unified front more than a uniform," Sam says.

Mike snaps around, eyes suddenly alight. "I can do that."

"I'd like one too," Easton adds.

Rocky puts his hand on Easton's shoulder. "I'm going to need you to explain what the hell is going on with the lot of you, Easton. And I'll leave my judge's robe in the closet."

Chapter 40

Making Port

Calvin

It's the fucking tone that Rocky's laying down. It makes my skin crawl, and I want to put my fist into an iron plate. Or his face.

"Dad." Easton stands. "We've been through a lot. And we're together now. It works for us."

Rocky's eyes flick around the room, stopping on each one of us. "That's . . . As long as it works for you and you're happy." His head bobs.

I want to believe he means it. While I was on Rocky's old boat for a couple of seasons, I wasn't out and about in the owner's area much. But I've always gotten the sense that he's the kind of guy who says what he means.

"You want Mike to come up with the verbiage?" Rocky points to the door the PR guy walked out of.

"No." Easton's quick with an answer.

Haley stands. "It wouldn't hurt to see what he comes up with. As long as we have the final say."

"You are as smart as your father says, Haley Brewster."

"You really talk to my father once a week?"

"Yes. To begin with, it was a couple of times a week. We had big online video calls with all the family members. We still do that once a month."

"I should call my mum. But first I want to make sure that Ed doesn't go trying to get revenge through my mum and sister." Zane crosses his arms over his chest.

"Once Susan is under arrest, Easton can get his will changed. Then there's no reason to go after any of you anymore." Rocky holds out his hand, and Zane shakes it, but then Rocky pulls him into an embrace. He's a lot frailer than last year. And when Zane squeezes him back, I'm afraid he's going to cut the old guy in two. "Your mom is going to be thrilled."

"She's going to go mental," Zane says.

"I don't claim that I understand what all this is, Easton. But I know all of your families. And they're good people." Rocky's lips thin.

A knock vibrates the door Mike left through.

"Come in," Rocky says, emotion lingering in his voice.

"I've got Henry Goodstone coming up here in thirty minutes. He was about to leave for Paris, but he's delayed his flight until tonight for exclusive coverage of the castaways' return. I've given his producer a few things to not ask. Personal relationships and the like. The guard is still at Susan's door."

Rocky nods. "Good. Thanks, Mike."

"The clothes will be here right before Henry gets here." Mike pivots and heads out of the suite.

The front door to the suite opens, and Mike ushers in ten people. Two Rockwell private security guards stand next to the door, watching everything that comes into the room. "We'll set up over there," Mike says.

"And you all can get ready in this room." Mike ushers us into the second bedroom space.

"Let them get ready in my room, Mike. I'm ready from the press conference earlier. There's not much you can do with this mug, anyway," Rocky says.

Mike nods and pushes through the cluster of people coming into the suite. The crew moves furniture and sets up lights on the other side of the room.

"This is Rina. She'll fix your hair and put a little powder on you all." Mike steps to the side, and a middle-aged woman wearing a BBC jacket and pink pants appears from behind him.

"Oh, this lot won't take much work. A good-looking group." Rina walks around each of us. "Right, we'll have to find you a chair or me a ladder if I'm going to powder that nose." She pats my arm like a grandma. Her gaze lands on Haley. "Oh, you're lovely. That's an interesting haircut. I don't think I've ever seen one like it before."

"I'm afraid that's my fault." Easton puts his hand on Haley's shoulder.

"You let this handsome devil cut your hair? I guess I might have too. Is this something you like?" Rina's brown eyes flash at Haley.

"I don't hate it. But if you wanted to tidy it up a bit . . ."

"Anything you want. I've done it all. I gave Darlene Smootworth a fantastic touch-up last week. You know she's on *The Garden Flat.*"

Haley smiles and nods. If she knows who that it is, I'll be surprised. I don't have a clue.

"Didn't she win *Sunset Cove* a few years back? It's a dating show," Zane says, handing me a shirt.

"Exactly, love," Rina says.

"Oh, yes. A little symmetry would be nice." Haley pulls on the ends of her hair.

"I'm just going to close the door to keep out the distractions." Rina pushes the bathroom door shut, and I bounce backward into Sam. Dante and Easton are on my other side.

"Oi, it's weird, right?" Zane elbows me.

"Weird?" I ask.

"Yeah, I feel like a little kid. Like I don't mind you all, but sharing Haley with even the makeup gal has me itching, you know?"

"I suppose I do." With some effort, I tug my fingers through my hair. It's a bit different for me, though. I'm sure Rina is nice, but I don't want her touching me.

I open the door and watch what's going on in the living room. Lights and cables are being moved around. This is far from some guy holding a video camera. I close the door and peer out the window. We're on the top floor, and far below, the crowd of protesters marches around with their home-made signs. Nolan's long gone. Though we've got the key to his apartment. Honestly, I think I prefer that shithole to this place. At least there you know what you're getting. Out in the other room, we have no idea what will happen. Will this Henry Goodstone make us out to be a bunch of lunatics or tragic victims?

"Rockwell, do you still have your dad's phone?" I ask.

"Yeah, catch. You going to call your mom?"

My shoulders hitch, because I wish I was. "Not yet." I dial his number—or what was his number the last time I called him. Before I blocked him. It rings once. There's a large part of me that wants it to go straight to voicemail.

"*Hello.*" But of course the fucker picks up. The one time I don't really want him to pick up.

"Jared, it's Calvin—"

"That's not funny."

I hold the phone away from my ear. Because only my damn brother would think I was lying. "It's me, Jackass."

"Oh, my god! Calvin?" There's scrambling, then a bang as he drops the phone. Muffled, I can hear him talking to someone. Probably Trisha. "It's Calvin. Give me the phone back."

"Calvin?" Trisha says.

I have the very strong urge to hang up. But that's not going to get what I need done. "Trisha, hand the phone back to the jackass."

"You're alive." She breaks out into crocodile tears. There is no way that piece of trash was mourning me. Me being dead would make holidays a hell of a lot easier for her.

"Just hand the phone back to him."

There's more fumbling. "Calvin," Jared says, "where are you?"

"London. Can you go over to the farm and—"

"We live on the farm now."

My heart squeezes in my chest.

"Mom and Dad are fine. Dad wanted to retire. They built an apartment in the old milking shed, but they spend most of their time in Florida. But they're here for the kiddo's birthday."

"Oh, right? Tell her happy birthday from her favorite uncle."

"Now I know it's you. You're her only uncle, but Trisha's sister is dating someone."

"I like competition." I look up to see the four guys watching me.

"Yeah, you do. How did you get to London?"

"Listen, Jackass, I don't have much time. Can you get Mom and Dad to watch the news tonight? I'm fine. And I'll be home for a visit at some point soon."

"I've missed you."

"Of course you have."

"Thank you for forgiving me."

"Who said I forgave you?"

"You haven't called me Jackass since Trisha and I got married. Only Jared."

I stop and stare at the floor. Have I really forgiven him? I guess so. I don't give a shit about Trisha anymore. But there's not that rock of hate in my chest when I think about her now, either.

"Just go tell Mom I'm alive and I'll call her tomorrow."

"I will. I love you, Cal. You're the best brother I could have ever had. And I will—"

"I said I never want to talk about it again. Let's move forward, Jackass."

"I can do that."

I end the call. And turn back to the window. Not that I mind the guys seeing me tear up. Or Haley, if she was done with the makeup girl. But I don't want to talk about it now. Later, when we have more time. There's a twist in my gut, because I actually think I will bring it up later.

"Anyone want the phone?" I ask.

Sam puts his hand on my shoulder. "Yeah, I think it's a good idea. I'm going to call my sister and have her be with my mom." Sam takes the phone from me and sits on the bed, staring at the phone. He's wearing one of the polo shirts that was dropped off while I was talking to Jared.

"What's up, Sam?" Dante asks.

"I can't remember my sister's number. I'll call Charlie."

He stands and paces, walking into the giant closet next to the bathroom. "Charlie. Where are you? . . . Fair enough. I'm in London. We're back. I—"

The bathroom door opens. "Who's next?" Rina shouts.

Sam pulls the closet door shut behind him.

"Look at you, Sassy. You look amazing." Dante gives Haley a twirl. The makeup artist has Haley's hair in a fluffy cut that hangs just below her ears. I don't know what it's called, but she looks hot as hell.

"Thank you." Haley gives Dante a kiss on his cheek.

"I'll go next, not that you can do much with perfection," Dante says.

"There's room for two more." Rina waves at Zane and Easton. "You put your shirt on." She points a finger at my chest and pulls the door shut.

"You look good, Chiefie."

"Thank you." She tilts her head, and her hair swings. "I'm nervous, though. Are you nervous?"

"I hadn't given it a thought. Nervous about the cameras?"

"Yes, but no. All of this. Our families. Your families more than my dad. I've never been on TV. Once there was a clip of a yacht I was stewing on, and you could see me for half a second. My friend went nuts over it. But that's about it."

"Just be yourself." I yank the shirt I have on over my head and pull on the new one. It's tight—tourniquet tight—from my shoulders through my chest. "It doesn't fit."

"It looks okay." Haley smooths her hands down over the fabric.

"It's not okay. It's a crop top at best. If I move, I'm going to bust out of this shirt like a rotting watermelon." I try to peel it off, but it doesn't budge.

Haley laughs. "Here, let me help you. Sit on the edge of the bed."

I do. I hold my hands up in the air like one of my nieces. Haley tugs on the hem of the shirt, and it gets stuck on my pecs.

"Pull harder," I say, and she does, but it doesn't move. She straddles my legs and yanks, and when the fabric comes off the top of my head, she flies forward. I tumble backwards onto the bed, and Haley lands on top of me. My hands surround her waist on impulse, pulling her tight against my chest. Even with the too-tight shirt wrapped around my face, I can't help but hold her against me.

"Calvin," Haley says, with a chuckle. "We've got to get ready for the interview."

The bathroom door opens, and Dante's laughter fills the room. "We've got a few minutes. You look perfect, Sassy." Dante jumps on the side of the bed.

"There's no way in the world we are doing anything here. Not after that nice woman did my hair. And Easton's dad is out there." Haley gives me a quick kiss on the top of my head and rolls off me.

Chapter 41

Calling Shore

Sam

I hang up from talking to Charlie. He's in shock. To him, I've come back from the dead. He gave me Sis's number, but he's going to call her now. There's no way I have time to do it before the interview.

"You want to phone next?" I hand it to Zane. He stares at it. "Do you need a number? I could have Charlie look it up in my records." He's got my backup laptop at his apartment. In fact, he's got everything I own at his place. Which is a considerable bit less than when I left last year—he apologized over and over for giving away a lot of my stuff. Charlie never apologizes. Charge-ahead-Charlie, my mom calls him. He packed up my apartment after I'd been missing six months. My clothes have been tossed. Though he said there's a few boxes of things our sister wouldn't let him throw away in her basement. I don't care. It's just stuff. Replaceable. We're here and alive. Haley's alive . . . all those days alone with Penny on the *Rock Candy*, that's all that mattered to me.

What comes next? That's been something I've thought about my whole life. What's next? And now I don't care. Just as long as I have Haley and Penny somewhere safe. Together. I want us to be together. Though I don't have unrealistic expectations that it will be the same as on the island. No fucking way it could be the same. But with a hell of a lot of work, it might be better?

"I don't need the number," Zane says. "I know Mum's and Ruby's, the pizza joint, fuck, I know the number from my best mate's old landline from when I was a kid. Numbers I've got stored in my head forever. I'm just nervous about what to say."

"Nervous? From everything you've told me, they're going to be thrilled."

Zane twists around, and Haley grabs his hand. "I know . . . I know—" There's a knock from the main room.

"Yeah?" I check behind me to make sure everyone's decent before I open the door.

Rocky's got his hands in his designer suit pants pockets. "We're ready when you are. Hank will be up here soon." Of course Rocky knows Henry Goodstone well enough to call him Hank.

"Do we have a minute?" I ask. "Zane and Dante haven't called their families yet."

"Of course." Rocky nods at the phone in Zane's hand. "Your mum's a lovely lady. Ruby too."

"Yes, they are. Thanks." Zane stares at the floor, then back to the phone.

"What?" Rocky asks, before I can.

"It's nothing. I was sending money to Ruby for school. I know they're going to be thrilled with me being home. I just feel guilty about not being able to help them for the last—"

"I hope you don't mind, son. I know how important it can be to take care of your family yourself. But I— Or rather, I had a team making sure your families were taken care of. I made the calls, though. Ruby's schooling was paid for. She's been sending in her marks to the office. It's rather adorable. We never asked her to do that. She's smart. So smart we've offered her a paid internship in the Birmingham office this summer."

"You're shitting me?" Zane's smile returns.

"Uh, no." Rocky puts his hand on Zane's shoulder. "It's the very least I could do."

"Thank you, Mr. Rockwell."

"It's Rocky. And thank you for being such a good friend to Easton."

"He's family to me now. We're all family."

"It's nice to have more sons." Rocky tips his imaginary hat at us. "I don't mean to rush such an important phone call, but Hank's on a time limit."

"Of course," Zane says.

"You want to go first, Dante?"

"Sure, toss it over." Dante catches the phone. He punches in a number. "Hey, Shortstack." A scream comes out of the phone, followed by a loud cry and an unintelligible jumble of words and loud music.

"Yes, I'm alive. No, I didn't disappear on purpose . . . I'm safe and can't talk long. But I'll be in touch as soon as I can get a phone of my own. Tell Mom. Gotta go. Hug those rugrats of yours for me." There's a long stream of mumbling. "I've got to go. Everyone needs to use this phone." The screaming stops. "Yes, everyone is alive . . . yes, Zane is alive . . . yes, he's going to call Ruby if you let me go." Dante looks at the phone. "Well, Zane, I'm using your sister as an excuse to get off the phone with my sister from now to the end of time. I guess she likes Ruby. Catch." Dante tosses the phone back across the room.

"I'll be as fast as I can." Zane gives Haley a hug and ducks into the large walk-in closet that I talked to Charlie in.

The bright lights shining down on us are hot. And despite the efforts Rocky's team went to get matching polos, the news producer had us change out of them. The white was too much for the integrity of the shot. And Calvin's didn't fit, even with taking a slice out of the back of it to give him some room to breathe.

We're lined up on the sofa, Easton, Haley, me, and then Zane. Calvin and Dante are behind us on tall bar stools that have appeared from somewhere. Rocky's in a chair next to the sofa, next to an empty chair. Henry . . . hasn't shown up yet, and it's almost an hour from when we were supposed to start.

"I really like your hair, Sassy. It's sassy to a T." Dante fluffs the side of her hair.

The eyes of the production assistants weigh on my shoulders as they skim over us. Easton gave Haley a kiss on the cheek when we came out of the primary bedroom. It's easy to see the wheels in their heads turning. And I remind myself again: I don't care.

The door flies open, and Henry strolls in by himself. I figured he'd have an entourage behind him. He's wearing khakis and a bush jacket, complete with epaulets and a dozen pockets. When it sways open, a linen shirt flashes. He looks more like he's going on a safari than interviewing castaways and billionaires as he beelines across the room. "Rocky, amazing to see you. Thank you for sitting down with me to have this chat." He shakes Rocky's hand and pivots on his heels toward the sofa. His eyes focus on Haley.

"There's the gal who lived for a year on the island with all these blokes." He laughs. "How was that? I bet you're looking forward to a spa day? Haley Brewster, correct?"

The mention of a spa day has me spiraling inside, remembering the spa day I gave her. My eyes flick to her cheeks that are turning crimson. She's remembering it too.

"It wasn't bad. Sure, there was a lot of rain. But we managed. Island life wasn't the problem. It was leaving the island that we'd like to talk to you about."

"Yes, say no more. I want to capture everything you say with a fresh reaction to inform our viewers." He nods like he's curing world hunger and points at each of us. "Calvin Green, Dante Jones, Easton—good to see you alive and kicking. Captain Samuel—"

"Sam."

"Noted." Henry gives a curt nod. "And our hometown boy from Birmingham?"

"Stourbridge."

"Ah, a lovely village, yes. Right, then, let's get this show moving. Such a lovely piece."

I turn to Haley beside me. Her eyes go wide. *Lovely piece*, she mouths.

"Hank, your producer told you about—"

"Things like this I want to go in fresh." He plops down in the chair next to Rocky's. "Knee's giving me fits. Nigel, are we doing this or what?"

The producer puts on his headset, and the lights flip from glaring to supernova and back down again.

A camera person focuses on Henry. "Almost a year ago, the mega yacht *Rock Candy* was lost at sea. One raft containing *the* Rocky Rockwell, his daughter, another guest, and some of the crew was found after a short time. The yacht and a second raft containing Olympian swimmer

Easton Rockwell and more crew were never found and presumed lost at sea. That's clearly not the case. Welcome to the long-lost gold medal winner Easton Rockwell and the missing crew."

I can feel Easton's disdain rolling off him.

The camera pans over us, and Henry introduces each of us before turning to Rocky. "You must really have been waiting for this day? Your big announcement at the forums market and now your son is home. This will be a day you never forget."

Easton cocks his head at his dad, and I'm more than wondering what announcement was made at the forum.

"Yes, it's an exciting day. I'm damn happy to have them all home." Rocky crosses his legs.

Henry's off. "How did you end up in London, Captain Sam Miller? Belay that order." I want to slap Henry. He's sounding more like an early morning talk show host and less like the award-winning hard reporter that PR Mike sold him as. "Can you introduce us to your crew?"

I straighten myself on the sofa and give a quick introduction to people I know Henry knows the names of. He's rubbing me the wrong way, and I'm losing hope quickly that this is going to do anything but make us look like a bunch of helpless victims. ". . . and Easton," I say, and it feels darn awkward.

"Right, well, of course we all know the water genius of Easton Rockwell. Did you pull the raft to the island?" Henry asks Easton.

"No." Easton looks back to me. He's boiling.

"We really appreciate you talking to all of us today. Because what happened to the *Rock Candy* wasn't an accident. And we need to go on record with what did happen," I say.

Henry's eyebrows shoot up, and he butts in before I can say anything else. "What do you mean? It was malicious? Sabotage? That's fascinating . . . unless you didn't live through it, I suppose." He straightens himself and looks into the camera. And now I'm wondering if good old Hank has had a couple of mimosas this morning.

"Yes, we're incredibly lucky that there weren't more fatalities," I say.

"Yes, Candace Abbott. What a tragic loss. She fell out of the tender when it was put in. There was an inquiry into your first officer for it."

Now it's my turn to raise my eyebrows. My stomach clenches. Anders was doing his best to get the primaries off the boat. I don't know for certain, I didn't see it, but I can imagine how hysterical Candy must have been for him to break protocol.

"He was cleared of all wrongdoing," Rocky says.

"That's right, he was."

"The first officer did his best to keep her safe. But she was hysterical. She kept screaming *my wedding dress, my wedding dress*." Rocky shakes his head.

Easton's hands are clenched in fists between his and Haley's legs. That dress was Candy's way to escape from Rocky. Or I suppose escape from Susan.

"We'll be doing a full investigation as to who the guilty parties are for what they did to everyone on the *Rock Candy*. And we thank you for letting us announce to the world that my son and his friends are back."

"Back from the dead," Hank says, mugging on his face. And now I'm sure he had a few glasses of champagne on the way back from the airport. "Any speculation on what happened?" He turns to me.

"That's best left for the authorities to decide." And as

much as I'd like to spill the beans about Susan, it's best that she's taken down by surprise. Mike and Rocky had a call with the lawyers while we were waiting to start filming. They advised against bringing her in on camera.

"Spoken like a true captain." Hank nods at me. Whatever the hell that means. "How did you find food, Calvin?"

I turn to see Calvin better.

"We fished," Calvin grunts. He's glaring at Hank, and I'm not the only one who doesn't have a good opinion of the anchor.

"I would love to hear about how you survived all those days on the island. What did you do for shelter, Miss Brewster? And food other than fishing?"

"The guys are really rather resourceful," Haley says.

"We all are," I add. I'm not going to let her not take credit for our survival.

"Yes, my knowledge of plants came in handy. Zane's building skills, Calvin's archeology degree and his hunting skills, Sam's maritime knowledge, Dante's ability to turn lacking ingredients into a five-course meal, and Easton's attention to detail—we kept each other alive. It really wasn't all that bad."

"You didn't miss your cell phone and television?" Hank turns to the camera again.

"No, we told stories. Or rather, Zane did. He's a movie buff and a great storyteller . . ."

Chapter 42

Fog Horn

Easton

Hank asks most of the questions I would expect, like how did we pass the time? Dante handles that one with ease.

When the blaring production lights flick off, I blink into the darkened suite.

"Hope that helps, Rocky. I expect you to give me the real scoop when all of whatever is going down finally clears." Hank waves his hand around the room like we're all some sort of dog shit.

"I will keep that in mind. I'll have Mike be in touch with . . ." Rocky trails off while shaking Hank's hand.

"I've got your assistant's contact info." Mike nods at Hank. "We've arranged a limo for you to the airport."

"Wonderful." Hank spins on his heel. "Which way out? Ah, this way." He heads for a double door closet.

"This way." Mike takes his arm and walks him out of the room with a security guard.

"Don't worry about the furniture. We'll move it back,"

Calvin says to the producer. The rest of the camera crew vanishes within minutes, and then it's just Dad and the six of us.

"I'm not sure that went how we wanted it to." I cross over next to my dad. "It's proof that we're alive, and that's a start. It should put Ed on a new warpath."

There's a click at the main door. Mike's back. "I've got your legal team back. They'll be on a call in ten. Their first look says there's not enough evidence to have Susan arrested yet. But they suggest—" There's another click at the door behind him, but it doesn't open. It's followed by a knock and a pound.

"Don't stand there. Open the door." I'd know the voice on the other side of the door anywhere. My stepmother was never a quiet, wait-around kind of gal.

I'm not ready to see her. The woman I trusted for so much of my life, even begrudgingly, but I did. Her and dad cheered me on from the stands. Though Susan was more likely to come to my televised meets than the general ones.

"You want me to let her in?" Mike asks Dad.

"Let her in. There's a few things I want to say to her," Dante says.

Mike doesn't stop looking at dad, though.

"That's up to all of you. Sam, Calvin, Zane, do you want to meet her here or in a courtroom first?" my dad growls.

"Haley has a say," I correct.

"What would the lawyers say?" Haley asks Mike. She moves between him and Sam to take my hand.

"Open the damn door, Rocky." Susan pounds. "I can hear you in there."

"That talking to her without council could cause—"

"I fucking hate lawyers." Dad interrupts Mike and pulls the door open. "Get in here and sit your ass on that sofa."

My former stepmother has changed quite a bit. Her platinum blonde hair is now a shiny silver. She's lost a hundred pounds. She's always worn business suits, but the one on her now is designer and new compared to the ones from the nineties she wore when she was married to Dad.

"Easton. You're not dead!" She opens her arms and comes at me. It's the way she says it. There's a fake surprise in her voice. My eyes flick over to the security guard behind her. He's one of ours from the Miami office. And I hope to hell he heard the tone she said it in.

I hold my arm out straight, stopping her from reaching me, and she runs into my hand. "No, sit down."

"When did you get back? I can't believe you're here. What's all this?" She motions to the furniture moved about. "Media? And you didn't wake me up? Rocky," she says in a scolding tone.

"Yeah, that's not going to work." Dante loops his arm over Calvin's shoulders. I'd been busy taking in Susan. I didn't notice his furrowed brow or clenched fists.

I nod down at Haley. She gives my hand a squeeze and moves over next to Calvin. Good. The last thing I want is for Haley to have to visit Calvin in jail for manslaughter.

There's a boiling hate taking over me. I bottle it down. I need justice for Haley, for the guys. They've all suffered enough over the last year.

"Sit, Susan," I say.

"I liked it when you called me Mom." She smiles, sitting on the edge of the sofa.

I hold her gaze. She doesn't deserve an answer. Doesn't deserve anything but a cold jail cell. I wiggle my fingers. The feeling of Haley's touch lingers. I thrust my hand in my pocket, and the damn diamond's there. I pull it out and put it on the coffee table. If she wanted me dead for the company, then she sure as hell had to have been damn mad about the diamond. Baiting her—it's foolish of me, but I want her to know all the things she doesn't have: Rockwell Tire, the Pink Phoenix, and soon anything to do with my family—especially my dad. She never wanted a divorce. Maybe her civility during their split boiled over inside of her. She wanted what she could no longer have. Finding another way to have it, killing me . . . She's crazy, that's for sure. And having the Pink Phoenix out on the table? I'm poking the bear, seeing that Candy's the one who made Dad buy it. But there's a tingling telling me Susan will be just as interested.

"What's that?" She leans forward.

But Zane's there. "We look with our eyes, not our hands." He's sitting on the sofa's arm.

"You know what that is," Sam says, his tone gruff.

Susan purses her lips and leans back on the sofa, her arms crossed over her chest like a scolded toddler.

Behind me, Mike had vanished, but he's back, this time with a laptop in his hand.

"Who's that?" Susan points at Mike. "Legal?"

"Susan Blanche. This meeting is being taped," Benson Walsh, a senior member of Rockwell-Harding's legal team, says from the laptop screen. Benson's voice boomed from my dad's home office on conference calls long before video calls or cell phones.

"That's not necessary, Benson." She clasps her hands in her lap.

"You know it is," I say.

"What do you know about the operations of James Zambrano, AKA Ed and Mr. Z?" Benson asks.

"You mean the dad of Emily's high school ex? He has a nice house in Switzerland. We had a lovely dinner with him, didn't we, Rocky?" Susan cocks her head. She's not dumb. I've never thought of her as dumb. Calculating? Hell yes. But dumb, no. She's not going to answer anything. And she's definitely not going to answer anything without her lawyer present.

"What else do you know about him?"

"This is feeling like an inquiry, Benson. Is this an inquiry? Because I think I want my lawyer present if it is. Is Abigail around?"

"Ms. Stewart will no longer be able to represent you due to a conflict of interest in the firm," Benson says.

"We'll see about that." Susan smiles like she's not batshit crazy. "Is there anything else you'll be needing?" She slaps her hands on her legs and stands. "Because you'll not be getting it from me. If you're worried about Ed, you can ask him yourself. I'm sure you'll find him more than willing to cooperate. He loves lawyers." She giggles. Honest to goodness giggles.

Haley drops her hand from Calvin's shoulder, and he steps closer to the sofa.

"Really, Winston, it's not like you to result to brute force. You must be slipping, dear." Susan turns, and I don't know who wants to kill her more: Calvin, myself, or my dad. No one pulls out Dad's given name. I'm not sure I've heard anyone use it in years.

She stumbles next to the sofa but quickly rights herself. "I'll be checking out of the hotel. No worries. I'll find my own way home."

Dad stands. "Obviously, you're fired."

She smirks back at my dad. "You can't fire an owner of

the company, darling." Her designer suit pants swish when she walks out the door. The guard looks at Rocky.

That's not true. Her seat on the board will be gone as soon as we can call a meeting.

"Make sure she leaves the suite without stealing the bedsheets and the whole mini bar," my dad growls.

We're all standing staring at the door when Mike circles around the room with five members of Legal on the video call.

"We'll sign off now, Rocky," Benson says. "We've got a full team on it. Our lead investigator will be calling you first thing in the morning. Mike sent a prospectus with the information he's gathered. Obviously, we'll want to interview each of you as soon as you get back to the States. That being said, get back here as soon as possible. I want this to go through our courts. Not that I don't think the London team could handle it. But the Zambranos have a home field advantage if we leave it in the UK. I'll talk with you soon."

"Thank you, Benson, I hope we didn't wake you." Rocky nods at the computer screen.

"I'll sleep when I'm dead." Benson ends the meeting.

Mike closes the computer. He nods at Dad. "That went better than I expected. The interview with Hank was a little rough, but you guys did a good job." Mike puts the computer down on the dining room table. "What do you want to do for lunch, Rocky? Do you want me to order in?"

Dad nods, and the two of them leave the room for the side room where Mike and another member of his team have an office set up. When the door clicks shut, I feel the collective sigh of relief from everyone that it's the six of us alone again.

"Dante, you did an especially good job handling Goodstone." Sam nods at Dante. "Nice recovery when he went on the prowl about how we spent our nights."

Haley paces on one side of the room, and I cross the room to be with her. "Hey." I pull her in for a hug.

"Well, old Hank needed to mind his damn business, and well, lying to people full of shit comes easy to me. Don't forget I went to an all-boys Catholic high school. And then there's my uncle. I got lots of practice lying to that piece of shit." Dante plops onto the sofa and pats the cushion next to him. When Haley doesn't sit down, he jumps up and pulls her to him—and I follow. "I hope you didn't mind my little white lie, Sassy. You know how I feel. And the world is full of assholes who won't understand how things work for us."

Haley loops her arms around Dante's neck. "No, I get it. I was tired of him putting me on the spot. I thought he might come right out and ask me about my sex life."

"The media here is a different beast." Zane sits on the coffee table. "Wait, what the bugger? Did you take the diamond?" Zane's eyes go wide, and he stands. The table's empty. "Fucking twat took it." Zane rushes for the door. But I beat him to it. The guard that followed Susan into the room is gone.

"You're telling me that a sixty-eight-year-old woman gave seasoned security agents the slip?" I'm holding Dad's phone because he's too angry to speak. "Find her. She didn't have this planned. Follow her finances; you'll find her. And make sure you coordinate with Benson Walsh's teams, both in London and New York." I turn the phone off and hand it back to my dad. He's pinching the side of his head.

"We'll find her," Mike says.

"Mike, do you mind giving me some time with my dad alone?"

"Not at all, Easton." Mike and his assistant step out into the main part of the suite.

"I don't care about the diamond. I have you back. If she wants the diamond, she can have it. She can have Rockwell Tire as far as I'm concerned." Dad tilts his head up to mine. His eyes are full of tears. "I've made some horrible choices. And you and your sister have paid for my faults."

"No, Dad. You were set on a course by a sociopath. She manipulated you."

"Susan?"

"Hell yes, Dad, Susan."

"A sociopath?" Dad sits on the tufted stool that Mike had pulled up to the makeup table to use as a desk. "She wants power, but that's not saying she's a—"

"She got in deep with Zambrano, dragging both of your companies and you with her. And when you suspected something was up and divorced her, she tried to kill me. It's not the first time, either." Fuck, it slipped out. I had no intention of confronting Dad with the accusation that Susan . . .

"First time?" He tilts his head at me.

"Were you having an affair with Susan when Mom died?"

"No." He over-squares his shoulders. It's his tell.

I widen my eyes at him.

"I never touched Susan when your mother was alive."

"But you spent more time with her than Mom, right?"

"She was my assistant, and I was growing the business. Of course I spent more time with her than your mother. She never wanted to go anywhere."

"Because . . ." I wait for my dad to fill it in.

"She was raising you and Emily. Yes, yes, but I didn't touch Susan."

"Who found Mom?"

"Susan, but that doesn't mean . . ." Dad looks over my head, and his mouth goes slack.

There's a hole in my chest. I've already processed the idea. But watching Dad do the same thing? That's a whole different level of hurt.

"She didn't want me to read the note." Dad grips the side of his face.

"Note?" Because that's the first time I've heard mention of a suicide note.

"Susan. She read it for me."

"And what did she do with it?"

"She kept it. Said I could read it later. But anytime I asked over the years, she said it would send me into a spiraling depression. And I fucking believed her."

"It's not your fault, Dad. There's no way we'll ever know." My stomach clenches, but I mean it. I'm not going to hold him responsible for my mother's death. The evidence is long gone—or maybe it isn't. That's a good use of Dad's money. I pull him into my chest in a tight hug. The same kind he used to give me as a child.

Chapter 43

Mother Harbor

Zane

"That's the pitch I played on growing up." I point out the window, and Haley leans over my lap. There's a group of lads kicking a ball around, and it reminds me of me and my mates as a kid. The rain has cleared, and the grass glows an iridescent, electric green.

"It's so lovely. Just what I imagined. Bet it feels good to be home?" Haley squeezes my hand.

And I laugh, because there were a damn lot of nights I thought about this moment. Seeing my old neighborhood. Being on these streets. "This isn't home to me anymore, Little Bird. It's special; don't get me wrong. I'm thrilled to be seeing my sister and mum soon. I might jump out of the car before we park. But this isn't home. You're home, and I don't care if I sound like a proper headcase. It's sappy, but it's true. I love you."

The car stops at the building next to my mum's, like I asked it to.

"I love you too. Now let's go meet your mother and

Ruby." Haley has her hand on the door handle, but Sam's already out and on the sidewalk, Penny beside him.

"Haley," Sam says, taking her hand in one of his own, Penny's leash in the other. I tumble out after her. Easton and Calvin somehow got stuck in the rear. Calvin's holding on to a crate containing a piss-angry Pepper. The lot of them head up what I've always thought of as my street. I'm a few steps behind them, watching the chaos I've learned to love walk away from me.

Haley stops short. "Zane, you coming? Is everything okay?"

"Everything is more than okay," I say, catching up to them. There's a short ball of energy running from the lobby of the building. "Ruby." I catch my sister and pull her into a giant hug.

She lets go of me and playfully smacks the top of my head. "Did you get taller? I can't believe you're here. It's like a dream. A dream I never want to wake up from." Ruby's hazel eyes blink up at mine. She looks so much like Mum. She pinches me.

"Ow." I hold the side of my arm even though it didn't hurt. "Mum home?"

"Is Mum home? Are you having a laugh? She hasn't left home since you said you were coming. She's been crying and cooking. Well, not at the same time." Ruby waves back at Haley. "The food's not contaminated with tears or anything."

"I've cried in more than one sauce." Dante holds out his hand, and Ruby shakes it.

We do a quick round of introductions, and then we're up the three flights to my childhood flat. The place where I had the last dinner with my nan and my dad. Where I told my mum I was going to go work on yachts instead of going to uni. And it will be the place where I tell her how important Haley is to me. How she's my girl. Things might not look like she'd imagined them. But I'm . . . I'm not afraid she's going to reject me, Haley, or the guys because of how things are.

"They're here," Ruby sings as she opens the door for the group of us to enter.

"My boy." My mum tackles me, and I stumble back into Calvin who, along with Pepper's crate, holds us up. "Sorry, sorry. I'm more than a bit excited."

"And well so," Calvin says and shakes my mum's hand.

She pulls him into a hug with a lot of force, and when she's gone through everyone, she pushes us into the lounge and makes us sit. It's weird but wonderful to watch my worlds clashing together.

"Lunch will be ready soon. Sit and take a load off. I don't need help, so don't any of you ask." She picks a spoon up off the counter and waves it at us. She's never hit me with a spoon, but she did tell me the stories of how her mother used to smack her with one. I'm on the sofa with Haley at my side, the other guys peppered around the small room.

"I tried to tell her she didn't have to cook, that we could go out for curry, but you know Mum." Ruby's sitting on the arm of the sofa, and her eyes skip over everyone. Clever has nothing on my sister. She's figuring things out. She jumps up. "You need to see Zane's room. It's like a flipping museum. I mean . . . I'm glad we left it alone now." Ruby pinches my arm, and this time I don't react. She'll keep the pinch-me game going if I do.

"Your sister wants to make it into a Taylor Swift room. No respect," Mum yells from the kitchen.

"No, I don't," Ruby hollers back and grabs Haley's hand

and pulls her down the hallway. "Really, I wouldn't have done it. I missed him tons. Just don't tell him," she says to Haley, loud enough for the entire flat to hear.

"Stay put." I point at the guys.

"No way in hell. I want to see what a young Zane's room looks like." Dante laughs and is up after us with the other guys trailing. The only saving grace is that there's not enough space for Easton, Sam, and Calvin to fit into my room. It's just wide enough for a single bed, my old school desk, and a dresser.

Damn, the walls are still covered with the posters from my cringe GCSE era. One wall's got footie flags from school tournaments, a signed Villa kit, and a dozen posters of Lamborghinis. We're good as long as Ruby doesn't close the door—which is why I'm leaning up against it.

"This is exactly how I pictured it." Haley squeezes my hand.

"Are you two an item, then?" Ruby asks, sitting on the side of my bed.

"Yes," Haley says.

"Oh." Ruby looks out the door to Calvin. When we walked up to the flat, Haley gave Calvin a kiss on his cheek. Which is totally fine. It's not like I'm not going to tell my mum and sister that I'm not in a traditional relationship. There's been nothing traditional about the way I've lived for the last year.

Except maybe there has been. Not having a phone, very little electricity, and nothing from the outside world to bother us. Maybe people would be a lot kinder to each other if they were allowed to find their own way instead of following what society tells us is normal.

"Ruby, we're all dating Haley." I thought there might be an easier way of telling her. Easing her into the idea. But I don't have time. We're taking off tomorrow morning for Miami. And telling them over the phone or in an email? That's not the way my family does things.

"Whoa, that's . . . You're okay with that?" Ruby asks.

"Yes." I stand, and the door bounces behind me.

"I wasn't asking you. I was asking Haley. You've always been a little off." Ruby turns to Haley. "And by off, I mean . . . I mean that in a good way. Zane doesn't give a monkey's arse what people think of him. But when that bully took the piss out of me in my year nine, Zane absolutely flattened him. He's protective, proper loyal to the ones he loves. So yeah, you picked a good one. Well—at least one good one."

"They're all good ones."

"I was going to make you look at the poster behind the door, but that's nothing on what . . . Sorry, it's going to take me a minute to . . . Bloody hell. All of them?"

"No worries. I completely understand. It took me more than a minute to realize what was happening and to be okay with it," Haley says.

"Ruby, let me tell Mum."

"Can I be there when you do it?"

"No," I say.

"I had to try. It's going to be epic."

Sam leans into the room. "I don't know, Ruby. I think your mom loves Zane an awful lot and she'll be able to see that he's happy."

"Oh yeah, but that doesn't mean she's not going to do a bunch of yelling first—and go a little mental. And the golden child here never gets yelled at. So you can't blame me for trying. I've got some bits and bobs in the lounge. You know Mum, when she says lunch is almost ready, that means anywhere from twenty minutes to an hour." Ruby bounds out of the room down the hall, but Dante has to go and move the door, revealing the Miss December poster from ten years ago. Damn, I never realized how much she looks like Haley. If Haley had on a fuzzy white negligee and a Santa hat.

"I know what I'm going to buy you when we get to Miami. I guess Zane here has a type," Dante says, and he pinches my arm. "Can I be there when you tell your mom?"

"No!" Haley and I say together.

I'm sitting next to Haley again on the sofa my dad used to watch the telly on after a long shift. It's weird. There's a vibration going on around the room. It's like my dad is here with me. I miss him so much. He taught me everything. My rules started with him. And now I can hear him say, *Trust your gut. When you find the right girl, you will know. It won't matter who she is, what she looks like, or what she does. If she treats you with kindness, respect, and love, you'll know she's the one.* Trust myself—rule . . . I don't need the rules anymore. I've got my family, and that's everything.

"How are your classes going?" Haley asks before taking a cracker with pub cheese on it.

"Good," Ruby says, without any further explanation, which means they're far from good.

"Really?" I ask.

"Yes, really. I could bore you with the strategic management goals and consumer behavior in a bullish market. But I'm not going to." Her eyes go wide, and she cocks her head to the side.

"I don't know, it sounds interesting," Easton says, taking a cracker.

"It's not. Well, it is to me, but not to the average bloke. You're not eating crackers?" Ruby glares at me.

I shake my head. "The entire time on the island, my stomach didn't hurt. But the second they started feeding us sandwiches on the ship that found us, my gut wanted to crawl out of my body. When we get a quiet moment, I'm going to pop in at the GP."

"Oh, cousin Abby has Celiac, found out about it a few months after you went missing."

I nod. "I've already figured out that I might have it."

"What?" Haley takes my hand.

"There's plenty of options now for gluten intolerance. I'll be able to handle that with no problem."

"Are you all going to work together again on another yacht?" Ruby glances toward the kitchen. She said it a lot louder than I wish she had. It's not a large flat. Big enough, but not a mansion for sure. And now Mum's in the room, standing on the middle of the rug.

"You're doing what? You just got back here, and now you're going to go back on a yacht? We don't need your money, Zane. We need you." She points a large wooden spoon at me.

I was so concerned about telling her about Haley and the guys that I didn't think about how she was going to take me going to live in Miami. "I need you too, Mum. And I'm not going to go straight back to working on a yacht. I'm going to go back to the States with Haley and the guys."

"Are you now?" My mum's five-foot-four stature feels Viking-sized right now. Penny gets up from in front of the sofa and heads over to Mum. Penny puts her head on Mum's feet and gazes up. "No fair using the cute dog to win me over." Mom scratches Penny's ears with her free hand.

"I am. But I'll be back for visits."

"Will you now?" Mom diverts her attention from Penny. She's asking a question, but it's not a question. It's a heavy layer of guilt.

"I can't imagine what this year was like for you and

Ruby. After what happened to Dad. I'm not going to pretend to understand. But I didn't do it on purpose—it was a fluke. I'm not going to be in danger again. Not like that."

"How do you know? That boat—" Mom points at Sam. "That boat was brand new, and it left you floating in a raft in the middle of nowhere."

"It's not that simple, Mum." I stand and walk over to her. First, I remove the wooden spoon from her hand. It's a quick reach back into the kitchen to place it on the counter. I look down and then back up at her. I don't want to tell her this because I don't know that it's completely true myself. But it's the only thing that will make her happy. And perhaps it's taking the easy way out of softening the blow of the other two things. "I'm going to go to school."

There's a gasp from Haley behind me.

"Really? What for?" My mum stands firm, but there's a twinkle in her eyes. Really, I'd expected her to jump.

"Architecture. Eventually, I think. Maybe not right away. I'm going to do some undergrad online first."

"Is this true?" Mom asks Haley—not me.

"I . . . If Zane says it's true, it's true." Haley nods. I hate that I've blindsided her too.

Mum clings to me in a long hug. Her eyes are sparkling with tears when she pulls back. "You're good for him. All of you." She picks the spoon back up and points to Haley and the guys. "I listened in on what you told Ruby in your room through the vent." She shrugs. "You do what you want. Just be happy and alive. And with a degree? Yes, your dad would be so proud. Me too."

"He doesn't have it yet," Ruby says.

"But he will. Just like you." Mom pulls Ruby to one side, and I, unfortunately, get the other—the one with the spoon, but it doesn't stay there for long. Penny jumps and takes it from her hand. A tinge of smoke comes from the kitchen.

"Oh, no." My mum runs to the stove.

"Let's go get that curry now," Ruby says as Mum turns the cooktop off.

Chapter 44

Dry Docked

Haley

"I like flying in your private jet a lot more than Z's." I grab Easton's hand. We've got another hour before we land in Miami. But the memory of being on Z's jet, locked up and not knowing where we were going, won't leave me anytime soon. Really, there's a lot that's going to take a while for me to process. The only thing I know is that I love the men on this plane with me.

Penny's sitting in the chair on the other side of the aisle. She jumped up the second Sam headed to the lavatory.

"Get up," Sam says from the aisle next to Easton.

"You're not going to make Penny move," Easton says with a laugh.

"I was talking to you." Sam cocks his head to the side.

"Fine. I need to use the loo too." Easton closes his book. I give Easton a quick kiss.

"That's the bathroom now that we're almost in Miami," Zane says from the row behind me.

Easton growls and heads off.

Sam drops into Easton's seat. "How are you doing, Haley?" He takes my hand and kisses my thumb.

"I'm . . ." Honestly, I don't know how I am. We've told Zane's mom and sister. Easton's dad knows, but that's it. Dante assures me that his mom won't care. She didn't care when he came out as bi. She won't care about this either. As long as we are all kind to her son. Calvin said the same thing.

That leaves Sam's family and my dad. There's also the very large question of where we're all going to live and what we're going to do to survive. There've been little details discussed. But a lot of things have changed about me in the last year. More than having five boyfriends, a dog, and a cat —but the one thing that hasn't changed is that I like certainty. I like knowing what's going to happen and how it will be done. It's one of the things that made me a great stew. I like the prep work. And I love a good list. A list!

"What?" Sam says softly, giving my hand another kiss. "Your eyes are sparkling with excitement."

"I need some paper." I search the pocket in front of my seat on the wall, but there's nothing there but an airsick bag. "Good enough."

"Do you want this?" Sam hands me a pen. And I start scrawling across the top of the bag.

Sam leans back, his eyes closed, his hand on my leg. That's what I love about Sam. He's so easygoing he doesn't ask me a thousand questions about what it is I'm doing. He knows when I'm ready I'll tell him.

I fill the whole bag with my list, front and back, before I open the inside and use it too. "That's what I needed," I say, absentmindedly. The bag flops over and rubs Sam's arm.

"That's a lot of something." Sam leans over to me.

"It's a list." I need to copy it over, but it's exactly what I need. "A list of what I'm going to tell my dad. Because he's not going to cry and hug me like Zane's mom. He barely spoke to me before I left on the *Rock Candy*. He's not going to like . . . well, us."

"Parents love me, Haley."

"You know what I mean."

"I do. May I look at it?"

"Yes," I say and almost instantly regret it.

"A list of reasons why having all of us in your life is better than just one of us?"

"No. Yes. Not really. It's what I love most about each of you. It's . . . I'm not going to read it to my dad. But I wanted to have my points blocked out in my head for when he comes at me."

"At you? You don't talk about your dad much. But I don't like that phrase. You're an adult. And he can't make you live your life the way he wants you to live it. That part of your relationship is over. He had his say."

"No, my mom had her say. Even when he was there, he wasn't really there. It shouldn't matter what he thinks."

"But it does." Sam nods.

"That's really infuriating. You know, I wish I could be more like Dante sometimes."

"'Blunt, forthright, honest, culinary genius,'" Sam reads from my list. "Let's not ever show him this."

I laugh, and he continues, "'Hard worker, has a soft interior and a sarcastic exterior, can make me laugh even in the bleakest of times, protective, and cares about others more than himself.' I might agree with a few of those. But you forgot hung like a horse. The world can't handle more than one Dante."

"I suppose you're right. On both accounts," I say with a laugh.

"Calvin." His eyebrows raise. "'Protective, responsible, skilled survivalist, reader, hard worker, loyal, and committed to those he trusts. Is willing to change even if he doesn't know it. A gentle soul.'" Sam nods. "Easton."

Easton turns his head. "What?"

I grab my list back. "Shh." Not that there is anything I wouldn't want the guys to read or know.

"What you got there, Sam?" Easton asks, and Calvin leans around the seat from behind.

"I'm a gentle soul," Calvin says.

"Maybe remember that the next time you punch me." Easton unbuckles from the window seat and crouches next to Sam.

"You okay with sharing, Haley?" Sam asks.

Dante's standing behind me, hanging over my seat. "That's a dumb question to ask now." He laughs and leans down far enough to give me a kiss on my neck. "Speaking of sharing, we could all join the mile high club."

"What's the list about, Haley?" Zane crowds in next to Easton.

"Yes. I . . . okay, I'm nervous about talking to my dad. So I want him to know how great you all are."

"Dad? Well, that's a buzzkill, Sassy." Dante gives me another kiss. "What does the list say about me?"

"I already read yours. You know, impossible, loud, a pain in the ass," Sam says with a straight face.

"Sounds like you've finally learned the truth, Sassy."

"It doesn't say that." I cock my head at Sam.

"I'm reading Zane's next. 'The most positive, optimistic person on the planet without being a Pollyanna, charming, dependable—'"

"Sounds like Penny." Easton rubs Zane's head.

"I'll take it," Zane replies.

"There's more," Sam continues. "'Supportive, a visionary, a master builder, an incredible artist, funny without being mean-spirited.'" Sam points a finger at Dante.

"What? I'm not mean." Dante holds his hand over his heart, and the guys moan. "I'm not mean to Sassy."

"True." Sam nods. "'A quick thinker in emergencies, able to adapt to any situation, respects boundaries, and thinks before acting.'"

"I've got to disagree with that last one, Haley. Remember when he dropped the WaveRunner off the side of the *Rock Candy?* That wasn't thinking," Calvin says.

"I did the math, and it worked. We would have been a lot worse off if I hadn't taken the risk." Zane smiles.

"I'll add 'risk-taker when it matters.'" I take the paper back from Sam and scribble it on the bottom and hand it back to Sam. Zane gives me a wink. And my stomach flutters.

"Brilliant. Here, Sam, let me read the next one." Sam hands the paper to Zane. "'Easton: vast medical knowledge that saved us over and over on the island. Brave, willing to stand up for what's right. Smart, humble despite his accomplishments. Willing to work hard and get dirty. Compassionate and protective of his family and friends. Is more than his money.'"

"I put that in there because my dad is rather shallow. Honestly, you could be . . . well, let's just say that more than once he told me I should seduce a guest on a yacht that I was working on." I reach across Sam and squeeze Easton's hand, but he leans forward and grabs my neck, bringing me in for a kiss while we're stretched across Sam's lap. His tongue sweeps through my lips. He tastes of whiskey and salt. And I end up moaning into his mouth.

"You keep making sounds like that, Sassy, and you're going to be on the board of directors of the Mile High Club." Dante's fingers skim down my neck, and I pull back.

Dante's not wrong. My heart races, and despite the insinuated warning from PR Mike as we got on the plane at the private airfield south of London, I'm a second from ripping off all of their clothes. I shake it off. Because the last thing we want is to be outed by the press and have that take some of the heat off the Zambranos or Susan. They'd be chasing our story instead of our justice. Sex will sell more copies of magazines and boost more ratings of shows than greed. Though greed can't be that far behind.

I take the list from Zane. "I'll read Sam's." I know he's already read it to himself. But I want to read it out loud to him. "'Self-sacrificing—he was willing to give his life for us to get out a distress call.'"

"Didn't work out, though," Sam says.

"That's not the point. 'Smart and calm under pressure. Brother to Charlie.'" I smile at Sam. "My dad met Charlie last—two years ago and said he was a stand-up guy. So I thought I should add it."

"Charlie is a stand-up guy. And I'm happy to have it on my resume of assets."

"Resume of ass." Dante laughs.

"I'm not done." I scrunch my eyebrows at Dante.

"Don't give me the disappointed teacher look, Sassy. It makes me hard."

I grab the list with two hands, fully aware that my face is turning crimson. "And . . . 'Sam is thoughtful, considerate, loyal to family, friends, and his dog. He will always put my safety first.'"

"Like Superman without the cape," Easton says.

Sam's easy smile lights up his face. "And when I tell my family about you, I'll say you're passionate about life. Observant of others and their feelings. Funny and wise."

"Detail-oriented," Dante adds.

"Kind." Zane grabs my hand.

"Modest. You still have no idea how amazing you are, do you?" Easton stands.

"Calvin?" Dante says.

"Right, my turn. I was going to say hot as fuck. But that's not something I should bring up around the Sunday dinner table when we visit the fam. So I'll go with being brilliant and resilient. You knowing so much about plants really helped us. But know when I say it to people it also means hot as fuck." Calvin tugs on my short ponytail.

The flight attendant, who's been giving us our space, comes out from the galley. "We're getting ready to land in Miami."

Sam leans over to me. "Thank you, Haley."

"Thank you? For what?"

"For being you. This . . ." He taps the paper on my lap. "You don't have to defend us to your dad. But that's up to you."

I nod and take Sam's hand in mine. "You're right. I'm an adult. He's made a lot of choices in his life. Most of them didn't include me."

"That's what you said on the island. You can hear him out, though . . . but your relationship with him isn't just up to him."

I wrap my arms around Sam, and the seat belt and armrest frustratingly keep me from getting as close as I want. Because it's true I don't have to wait for my dad, or play by his terms. It's such a simple thing, but it's not something I've accepted as truth before. Now it's like a light has flicked on. My dad can take me or not. It might make me sad if he doesn't want anything to do with me, but I'll be okay.

"I love you," I say.

"I love you too," Sam says and squeezes my hand.

Chapter 45

Course Change

Calvin

For such a modern, open, Floridian house, there's a lot of hallways. I inch around the corner to the foyer.

"Calvin," Maya, the house manager, says. Though she's less manager and more dictator. She stabs the last flower into a giant arrangement by the front door and turns to me. "Can I get you anything to eat? You should eat."

"No, thank you. I'm good."

"No, you're not. I'll make you a snack." She fluffs the flowers one last time and hustles off toward the kitchen, leaving me and my no thank you in the huge foyer. That's when I hear Haley and Emily in the living room. I pivot my way to the sprawling room with the floor-to-ceiling windows that overlook the Atlantic ocean.

"Hey." I wave to Emily and give Haley a kiss on the cheek.

"You're finally up. I thought I might have to call Dr. Titus." Haley smiles. Dr. Titus is an overrated quack who charges two thousand dollars an hour to come out and treat yacht owners on their boats so they don't have to leave the boat. "How's your book?"

"Done. I've missed reading." I sink down next to her, our legs touching. "Where's everyone else?"

"Dante's out at the market. Zane and Sam are visiting Charlie, who pulled into port last night. Easton's . . . I don't know where he is. Do you know, Em?"

"I'm not supposed to tell. But he'll be back soon." Emily stands. "I've got to get going to the airport."

"Oh," Haley's voice drops. "Where are you off to?"

"I'm going to New York. I hope you don't mind, but I've given Maya a vacation. And she promised me she would really take it. It's been a whirlwind for you guys, and you could use some time alone. I better get going. My ride's due in ten minutes." She stands, and the leather swivel chair she was sitting in swings back around to face the ocean. Emily puts a small beaten-up backpack on. "Do you think I need a coat?"

"In April in New York? Maybe," I say, and Emily dashes off down the hall to her bedroom. I put my hand on Haley's knee. "You doing okay?"

Her nose crinkles up. "I'm okay. I'm resilient, remember?" She is, but it sucks that her dad is being an asshole. Haley had a long chat with him on the phone the day after we landed in Miami. He's too busy to come to Florida. So she told him about all of us on the phone. He cut her off and now won't return her calls. Easton had Rocky call Haley's dad, but he hung up on Rocky too.

"You are." I need to change the subject. She's twisting the short hairs above her ear. I grab her foot and squeeze. "This is the longest I've not had a job."

Her eyes widen. "A year?" she asks.

"Fuck, no. Two weeks."

"Since you were eighteen."

"No, like ever." I shake my head.

"But when you were little?"

"Chores on the farm from the time I could walk. I started feeding the chickens when I was three. I suppose I was helping my grandmother feed the chickens, but still."

"What type of job do you want to get?"

"I . . . I don't know. It felt weird taking the back pay that Rocky put in my account, but it's there, and with us living here for now, I don't exactly need any money. How are you feeling about it?" I have an idea, but I need to wait for Sam.

"I've had at least one job since I was sixteen. I had two in college. Waiting tables and work study . . . Zane suggested we both take online classes together. Though I'm not far from graduating. I need a little over a semester of credits. But I don't think I can take the level of classes I need online. Most of them are upper-division classes. And it would be hard for me to do. Unless I can get a waiver."

"So we move to Pennsylvania to your old school until you're done."

She nods but stares at the floor, and I can't help myself. I pull her onto my lap. "We'll make it work."

"You think Sam's going to move inland?"

"For seven months? I think Sam would do anything for you. And we won't know until we ask him." There's a flutter in my stomach. I want to tell her now. But Sam and I agreed we'd talk about it with everyone at the same time.

She nods again.

And I take my thumb and tip her chin up to me. Her blue eyes twinkle in the setting sunlight.

"I'm leaving now. I see nothing," Maya yells from the entrance to the room.

I crane my neck to see her. I'm not lying when I say I'm

a little scared of the five-foot-nothing fifty-year-old. Four-star generals have nothing on the Rockwell house manager.

"Goodnight, Maya," Haley says.

"Goodnight. I will see you tomorrow." Maya pivots on her flats.

"No, you won't. You're taking five days off." Emily slings her arm through the crook of Maya's elbow. "Now, let me give you a lift home on the way to the airport. Bye, guys." Emily waves.

"Bye," Maya says. "He isn't going to use my kitchen."

"He'll clean up after . . ." Emily's voice trails off, and the front door slams shut.

"We're alone." I run my hand down her back. My mouth is hovering over hers when a door slams.

"Was that my sister in the car, driving away from the house?" Easton comes down the hallway from the garage.

Haley gives me a light kiss before she leans back. "Yes, she's off to New York," Haley projects into the hall.

Easton rounds the corner. "Hey guys." He gazes out onto the lanai. "Maya's gone?"

"Yes," Haley says.

"Thank fuck." Easton drops down on the other side of Haley, his hand on her leg. He leans over and kisses the nape of her neck. "I'm not wrong in thinking we're alone?"

"No, you're not wrong." Haley turns in my arms and kisses Easton. "I'm glad you're back."

"Me too. I fucking hate lawyers." Easton pulls off his suit coat and tosses it on the arm of the sofa. "Almost as much as I hate these straitjackets. It's ninety degrees out there." He undoes his tie and throws it at his coat, but it misses and tumbles to the floor.

"World-class athlete." I laugh.

"Swimmer," he shoots back.

Haley relaxes back, her head on my chest.

"I shouldn't have to put one of those on again for a while. My will is completely updated and in a private trust like I should have had it all along."

"That's good. Another step toward getting Susan out of our lives." Until the trial. When they find her. I pull Haley closer to my side.

There's another slam from the foyer. "Honey, we're home," Dante yells. "I've got enough groceries for the weekend, and I've brought pizza for tonight. Both gluten-free and gluten-full." Dante pokes his head around the corner, a tall stack of boxes in his hand. "I got Emily's text. Is the kitchen Czar gone?"

Haley tries to jump up to go help Dante, but I wrap my arms around her waist and hold her on the sofa. Easton's on the same train of thought as I am. "You'd be the same way if it was your kitchen."

"That's different, Sassy," Dante yells on his way to the kitchen.

Easton stands. "Stay there. I'll be right back."

Zane and Sam pass by the living room. "Don't worry, Viking, we've got the mountain of food from the car."

"I'm doing something important, Zane." My fingers roll around Haley's shoulders, and she moans but quickly covers her mouth. Not quickly enough. Heads appear in the opening.

"Sorry," Haley says and points back at me.

"Never be sorry for making that sound, Sassy. We'll be right back. Move." Dante bosses Sam and Zane to the kitchen. It's not long before they return with the pizza, beers, and plates.

"Hey, Little Bird." Zane hands her a beer and a plate

with pizza before dropping in front of the sofa and pulling one of her legs over his shoulder.

"Where's mine?" I ask as I'm getting up to get it myself. I was hoping to eat something else. I glance over my shoulder at Haley. She's turned a lovely shade of red. And I'm hoping she's thinking the same thing.

"I've picked out the movie. And no criticizing my retelling when we watch this one. I did my best." Zane turns on the TV.

"Yes, but you missed the whole subplot. You told it as an action movie, and it's really a love story." Haley runs her foot down the side of Zane's arm.

"Potato, potato," Zane says, turning up his British accent. "This is good pizza, mate. I can hardly tell it's not real."

"It's real. You have to reframe the way you think about food, Zane." Dante sits on the floor next to him.

Sam's the last in the room. "Excuse me." He pushes between Haley and Easton.

"I kind of miss the days where you had to have your personal space." Easton laughs but moves over.

The sun starts to set beyond the television. There's a massive blackout curtain, but we've never pulled it. Having the crashing waves outside the lanai makes me feel more relaxed. It's still hard being here. We've gone out a few times, but the second we're recognized, we all want to head home. At first it was just Easton being noticed, but we've been on enough media now that we're all getting it. The ones that survived, they're calling us. And *Gilligan's Island*, which is even worse. But whatever.

I haven't told anyone other than Sam about the email I got today—it said that they were offering it to him too. But we didn't have to negotiate as a group. I'm still not sure I want to do it. Though it sounds interesting.

There's a lull in the movie. I'm not telling Zane, but he made this one way better than it is. Maybe he shouldn't go to school for architecture but for script writing.

Sam leans forward, his eyes connecting with mine, and I give him a nod.

"Pause it for a second, Zane," Sam says. When the movie is off, Sam rolls his shoulders. "So . . . today Calvin and I got an interesting offer."

"Really?" I can hear the dread in Haley's voice.

"It's nothing bad, Chiefie. It's good. In fact, really good. Sam and I have been offered a publishing deal to write a survival guide. Well, I'll do the part on surviving off the land, and he's doing the marine section. Two books."

"That's fantastic." Haley turns to me and then back to Sam.

"Amazing," the guys echo.

"It is, but there's a catch: they want to put our faces on it and use all of us as marketing."

"Oh." Haley nods. "That's fine. It's something we'll get used to. Right Easton?"

"Uh, you never get used to it. But it will be different as time goes on. I think it's a great opportunity if you want to do it." Easton stands. "This calls for the good stuff." He vanishes down the hallway to the wine cellar, which isn't a cellar because this is Miami, so it's a room off the dining room.

"Do you want to do it? I think it's fantastic, but I don't want you doing it just . . ." Haley trails off.

"Haley, I want to do it," Sam says. "Zane and I chatted in the grocery store about the two of you going to school. We can move back to the ocean again later. Plus, Pittsburgh has rivers. You and Zane can go to school. We'll write the books, and Dante—"

"I know at least three restaurants that would love to have me. There might be one or two that I'm not allowed in as well." Dante takes the bottle of champagne from Easton. "Let me do that."

"And I can work from anywhere." Easton picks up his tie from the floor. "Even better if we don't have an office in the city. Though we have a Pittsburgh branch."

"Then it's settled." Haley raises her glass of champagne and sips from it. "Whoa, this is good."

"I know something that's going to taste even better to celebrate with, Chiefie, but you're going to need fewer clothes."

Easton grabs a remote, and the blackout shade makes its first appearance. I hate waiting to pull her shirt off, but early last week, Maya pointed out a photographer floating in a speedboat. They took off when one of the security guys headed outside.

When Rocky left for New York last week, we sent most of the guards with him. There were too many people around. Funny, I would have said the same thing about right now a year ago—four other guys in the room with me and my girlfriend.

"What are you smiling about?" Haley runs her finger over the shell of my ear.

I huff out a laugh. I didn't realize I was. There are bubbles in my stomach, and I haven't had a sip of champagne.

Chapter 46

Prime Slip

Sam

Calvin's laugh rumbles the sofa, and Haley turns to him.

"I'm happy, Haley. I know it's not a common look on me. But that's what it is," Calvin says.

My fingers grip the side of her hip, and her head tips around to me. "Me too. At least, that's what I think this fluttering in my chest is."

"At your age? Could be a heart attack. You better move over, Sam, and let me take your spot." Dante taps the side of my foot.

"Stuff it, Jones. You're not that much younger than I am."

"True, and you're in better shape. So move over—who knows how much longer I have?" Dante's amber eyes widen like Penny's when she's trying to get out of something she did wrong.

"I'm not moving." I lean forward and plant a kiss on the

side of her neck. She tilts her head, giving me better access while she's kissing Calvin.

There's a scraping sound as the heavy sofa table is moved out of the way, and the clinking of glasses being set down. The lights are dimmed, and music replaces the sound of the silenced movie.

Easton carefully removes Haley's watch, and there's nothing that could take me out of this moment. The soft hairs on the back of Haley's neck rise. Her shorter hair gives much better access to the soft skin along her spine. I kiss along the thin chain that graces her neck. It's so strange to see her wearing jewelry. But the delicate chain suits her. I remove it and hand it to Easton to keep safe.

My fingers run down her arm to her waist and over the edge of her shirt. "Lift your arms, Sugar."

She does, and the shirt comes off over her head— severing her kiss with Calvin. I toss it to Easton, and he flings it on top of his suit coat.

In my peripheral there's more clothes flying across the room to the growing pile. I tug off my own shirt. Calvin lifts her to his lap, her legs straddling his, their lips tangled together.

My fingers run down her back to the clasps of her bra. With a flick, it's loose around her shoulders. Dante guides one hand through one strap, and I pull it down the other side. Zane takes it and shoots it across to the pile of clothes. When she's leaning forward, I stop and gaze at her. I don't know how I got so damn lucky. It's weird. But this is more than I could ever have thought possible.

"You're so damn gorgeous," I say.

"Lift your delicious rear, Haley." Dante taps her behind. "We need these shorts gone."

And when she does, I see it as my opportunity. With

one leg lifted to get the shorts off, she's unbalanced, and I pull her into my lap. She's facing outward now, her back to my front. But it's all the better for my hands. My fingertips trail down the front of her chest and around her soft breasts. I work each of her nipples into even harder diamonds.

Zane lifts her legs up, pulling off her black panties. He flings them across the room. Haley's head flops back onto my shoulder. With my thumb and forefinger, I turn her head toward me, capturing her sweet lips. Our tender kiss escalates into a fast-paced frenzy. She pulls back, gasping for air. A sweet moan fills the room as her head rolls around on my chest, under my chin. Her ass grinds against my dick. It's begging to be freed.

Easton knocks away my hand from her breast—he sucks on her tit. My arm's captured between her leg and his chest. There's not enough room to move a hand down to her leg. She's closing her thighs around Zane's head. Zane's working away on her pussy, his fingers pushing into her.

"It's good. So good." She turns to me, her blue eyes wild with need. Her lips are on mine again. She's close already. I'm gripping her thigh, keeping it open.

There's a thud on the other side of the room. Our kiss breaks, and Dante jumps down the last few stairs, our new box of toys in his hand. "Is this what you want?" Dante holds up a silver butt plug bigger than any of the others I've ever seen. "I know you do."

"Holy fuck, Jones," I growl.

"No way, you're not breaking Haley so you can—"

Dante cuts Easton off. "That's up to Sassy, now, isn't it?"

"I can always say no, if it's too much." Haley twists around to me, and she shrugs.

"I suppose. It's your body. That's one thing, but the thing holding it?" Calvin growls.

"For fuck's sake. I won't hurt Sassy, and you all know it."

"You better have an extra-large bottle of lube," Zane says with a laugh. But he opens the case and takes out a smaller plug. "Let's start with this one first. It's been a minute. Ready, Little Bird?"

"Ready."

I steady her. With one hand on her hip. I place the other on her waist, prepared for when she reflexively pushes back onto me as the smaller plug enters her.

But Zane stops and nods at Easton. "How about now?"

"Now, now is good. I'm ready. Let's go—"

"You've become so needy, Sassy. And I damn well love it." Dante laughs. "Easton bought you a surprise. Well, he bought us all a surprise."

"And I've got a couple of ideas as to where to start." Zane stands, and in true Calvin style, picks Haley up and throws her over his shoulder. He takes off down the hallway and up the stairs like a wild boar is chasing him again. There's a dash of naked bodies flying up the stairs behind him. The door to the bedroom next to ours is open. It's been closed other than the first day we were here. Zane carries Haley into the room, and I don't know where to look. It's a complete sex room. Not a dungeon. It's bright and white and has an oddly Miami vibe to it.

Zane places Haley on the edge of the bed, larger than any I've seen before. It's the star of the room directly in the center. But around the wall there are straps and a swing I want to see Haley in. There's a masseuse-like bed and another stand with adjustable legs and places to buckle down her legs and arms. Even a hole in the headrest.

"Whoa. How did you get this all done? Does Maya know this is here?" Haley's eyes are wide.

"Maybe, but all our new toys fit in the closet. And unlike our resident lock picker, Maya won't open a locked closet," Easton says, glaring at Dante.

"What? You can't hide anything from me. I was a juvenile delinquent. This room was wide open and empty except for a boring bed frame when we arrived. And a locked door? Yeah, I'm shit for secrets. But anytime you want to keep more secrets like this, I'm game."

Haley stands beside the bed and pulls the duvet from it and begins folding it. "This is really lovely. It's huge."

"That's what she said." I get it out before anyone else does and grab the side of the cover. The impulse to ball it up and throw it in a corner is huge. But we all know that it would bother Haley if we did. Zane takes the other corner from her.

"This ought to be good," Haley laughs, then reclines on the bed, one leg bent up. Zane and I fumble to get it done. "Interesting job. I don't think I'm going to hire either one of you as second stews, though. Maybe you can start as fifth stews down in the laundry room." She reaches out for me, while Zane takes the duvet to a bench near the closet.

I take the spot on the end of the bed, nudging my head between her legs. Her fingernails go straight into my hair. Damn, I love it when she scratches me deep on my scalp.

There's a click of the door as Easton locks it. It may be only us here, but we're all aware of how we need to protect Haley.

"You feel so good, Sugar." I spread her open and lick around her clit. Her body twitches in anticipation. Her breath hitches as I take my time, tracing patterns with my tongue, teasing her. Calvin leans down, kissing her deeply, swallowing her moans. Her hips try to rise, seeking more friction, but I pin her down, keeping her at my mercy.

Easton's on the other side of the bed, his hands exploring her breasts, rolling her nipples between his fingers. She gasps into Calvin's mouth, her body writhing under our combined touch. Dante watches, his eyes dark with lust, stroking himself lazily as he waits for his turn.

Zane returns from the closet, a silk blindfold dangling from his fingers. He raises an eyebrow at Haley, a smirk playing on his lips. "Let's heighten a more important sense than sight, Little Bird," he says, his voice low and seductive. Calvin breaks their kiss and holds up Haley's head.

"Yes," Haley whispers.

Zane leans down and places the blindfold over her eyes, securing it gently at the back of her head. Her breath hitches again.

I hold on tight to her bouncing legs. "Shh, Sugar," I murmur against her thigh, my hands stroking her smooth skin, soothing her.

"We've got you." Calvin trails his lips down her neck, his hands joining Easton's, lavishing attention on her breasts. Her back arches slightly, pushing her closer to their touch.

Dante places his hand on my shoulder. "Let me do the honors, Cap."

I twist enough to see the glistening smaller plug in his hand, ready for action. "Not this time." I take it from him and touch the cold lubed metal to her clit, circling it around. Haley's hips buck slightly, seeking more. I slide the plug lower, teasing her entrance before moving it back up to her ass, pressing gently against her.

"How are you doing, Sassy?" Dante's voice comes from over my shoulder. He's stroking himself. I press the plug against her again, feeling her resistance give way as it slips inside her, her body closing around it.

"Oh god," she moans, and her spine rises in a slight arch, adjusting to the intrusion. I keep my movements on her clit slow and steady. I add a finger to her pussy, allowing her to adjust to the plug in her ass. She gasps, her chest heaving beneath Calvin and Easton's touch.

"That's it, Sugar," I coax, my voice low and soothing. "Just like that." I continue to lick and suck at her clit, my fingers gently pumping above the plug. Her hips move in rhythm with my pace. "You want more, don't you?" Damn if the chef isn't making me a perverted bastard too.

"Yes!" she cries.

"You look so sexy like this, Little Bird. All laid out and open for us. Taking what we give you." Zane's on the other side of me. His hand traces the curve of her waist, his thumb circling her navel. "You're doing so well, Haley."

Her head thrashes slightly, her breaths coming in quick pants. "More," she begs, her voice a husky whisper. Easton and Calvin move away slightly, their hands still roaming her body, but their eyes are on me, waiting.

I slide another finger into her, scissoring them gently to stretch her. Her little mews fill the room. Her body writhes beneath us. Dante moves closer, still stroking himself, his eyes locked on where my fingers disappear into her.

"Please," Haley begs again, her voice desperate. "I need more."

Zane looks at me, a question in his eyes. I nod, and he moves to the closet, returning with the larger plug Dante showed us earlier.

"I'm ready now," Haley says, though there's trepidation in her voice.

Calvin and Easton are quick to distract her, their

mouths and hands lavishing her with attention. I slow my pace, allowing her to focus on the impending sensation.

Zane hands me the larger plug, his eyes never leaving Haley's writhing form. I remove the other one. We've taken our time playing, but I'm wondering if it will be enough. I ease out the first one and replace it with the new one. She gasps as I do.

"Easy, Sugar," I murmur, my voice steady and reassuring. "We've got you."

I increase the pressure, the plug slowly entering her. Her body stretches. Every second I push it in, I'm searching to make sure she's okay. Zane works her clit as I take my time.

Dante moves closer, his eyes locked on hers, even though she can't see him. "You still with us, Sassy?" he asks, his voice surprisingly tender.

She nods, a small smile playing on her lips. "I'm good."

"All right, then. Time to up the game," Easton says. He nods at me to move beside her and then uses the hand gestures we practiced back on the island to ask if I'd rather use one of the new pieces.

I answer him by changing positions with him, running my hand along Haley's side.

"Sam?" she asks.

"You ready?"

"So ready."

"Straddle me."

In a smooth motion, she untangles her arm from Calvin. Her hands trace over my chest and arms. And damn, just her rubbing my biceps has my dick twitching. She hovers over me. One knee on either side of my hips.

I take my dick in my hand and rub it at her entrance.

She lowers herself onto me, a slow, delicious descent that has us both groaning. Her body envelops me, tight and hot, and I can feel the plug adding extra pressure, intensifying the sensation. My hands grip her hips, guiding her as she begins to move, rolling her body against mine in a rhythm that's purely her own.

This woman is more than I could ever have hoped for. "Damn, Haley. Fuck, I love you so much."

"I . . . yeah, me too." Her head flops to her shoulder. "I love you, Sam." Her hands fling around, and she smacks Calvin's chest. "I love you, too, Calvin." She bites her lip. And pats at the air like a sexy version of Marco Polo. There's the cutest little grunt of frustration from her when she doesn't make contact with any other skin. "Where are the rest of you?"

Easton's deep chuckle comes from her left. "Right here, beautiful Firefly." He takes her hand and places it on his chest, leaning in to kiss her shoulder.

Zane's voice comes from behind her. "And I'm right back here, Little Bird." He trails his fingers down her spine, making her arch into his touch.

Dante takes her other hand, placing it on his cheek. "And you know I can't stay away for long, Sassy."

With all of us connected to her, Haley starts to move again, rolling her hips in a rhythm that has us all groaning. I can feel every twist and turn of her body as she rides me, the plug in her ass adding a whole new level of sensation. It's not just sex—it's a dance, a rhythm that only the six of us share.

Her rhythm picks up, but I drop my hands to her waist and bring her to my chest. "Take it slow, Sugar."

"More." She kisses my chest.

"You're going to get more." Behind her, Zane has rolled a condom down his length. He meets my eyes, a silent question, and I nod, holding Haley still for a moment. I hear the plug being pulled out.

Chapter 47

Cooking with Heat

Dante

Haley's on Calvin's cock now, her short hair bouncing with her tits. The blindfold's gone. Easton and Zane have been where I want to be. But if she so much as winces, I'll stop. I put one hand on her waist and trail the other hand down her ass crack. She's come four times, but I know we can get a fifth out of her. We've done it before.

I've got a condom rolled onto my dick.

"Here, use more." Zane hands me the bottle.

"Any more lube and I'll be declared an oil slick. Let Sassy be the judge. You ready, my good girl?"

She drops her head onto Calvin's chest, and her blue eye blinks at me. Her skin glistens with exertion. I'll try to take it easy on her, but I don't know if I can. I'm wild with want.

I catch Calvin's eyes, and he nods. Not sure he's happy about it, but that's enough consent from him for me. It's Sassy I care about. I lay my hand on the hollow of her back.

Her smooth skin glows in the dusky Miami evening light coming through the sheer curtains. It's darker in here than out on the water, but still. "Get the blinds, Rockwell."

Easton rolls from the side of the bed where he's been watching. Going first has its advantages. But I prefer her this way. Her skin's hot to the touch, her short hair sweat-damp and clinging to her neck. I run my fingers through it, gripping gently to hold her steady. She grinds against Calvin, her breath coming in quick pants.

"You good, Sassy?"

She twists her neck as her blue eyes flash at me. I'm not the only one with a wild need. "What are you waiting for? Plate the damn dinner."

I huff out a laugh. My dick smacks her in the ass as I do. I'm not the only one who thinks our needy girl is hilarious. Zane laughs so hard he has to catch himself from falling off the far side of this massive bed.

I take my time pushing into her. Even so, she lets out a breath, and that has the room jump.

"You can stop if you want to," Sam says.

I'm ignoring the other guys. But it's hard to not pick up on the glare Calvin gives Sam. Our Viking likes it too.

"No," she moans.

"Fuck, Sassy," I groan as her body squeezes me.

She gives a low, guttural groan, sending shivers down my spine. I move, slow and steady, and let her body adjust to me. Calvin has stopped moving altogether. He's learned a thing or two in the last year.

"Move already. One of you. I can't. There's no way—no room." Haley shakes her head.

Calvin matches my rhythm from below, his hands gripping her hips tightly.

Haley's moans fill the air, her body writhing between us. Easton returns to the bed, his eyes locked on where our bodies join. He reaches out, his fingers finding her clit, rubbing in slow circles, matching our pace. Zane leans in and captures her lips in a deep kiss. Sam mirrors Zane. She's surrounded, consumed by us, and it's exactly where she wants to be.

Her moans turn to gasps, her body tensing as we drive her higher and higher. I can feel her tightening around me, her body already on the edge. Calvin's fingers tense on her hips, his own breaths coming in ragged gasps.

"Close," she whimpers, her body shuddering. "So close."

Easton increases the pressure on her clit, his fingers moving faster. Her body trembles around me. Zane and Sam have dropped away, watching from the side of the bed. Easton, with a final swirl, moves away too. Giving Calvin more room to push up.

"Come for us, Sassy," I growl, my own control slipping. "Take what you need. We love you, Sassy. Never, ever doubt that." I'm speaking for us all. Something I never thought I'd do. Men are scum. But somehow not Sassy's guys. "You own our souls."

Her body convulses, and the orgasm rips through her like a storm. She screams out, her body clamping down on us, pulsating, as wave after wave of pleasure crashes over her. Calvin grunts and bucks upward, his own release triggered by hers. He pulses within her, intensifying her orgasm and sending her into another wave of spasms.

I grip her shoulders, my own climax building quickly. Her body is slick with sweat, her skin hot to the touch. I lean forward, my chest pressing against her back, my hips moving faster, chasing my own release. Calvin's hands roam her body, his touch gentle now, soothing her as she comes down from her high.

Her breath hitches as I pound into her. She's pushing back into me. That she can take this, me . . . She's insatiable, always craving more, and I'm so here for it. I piston my hips faster, the sound of our skin slapping against each other filling the room. Zane and Sam watch with hungry eyes, their hands stroking their own lengths that have grown hard again. Easton moves to her side, his lips finding hers in a passionate kiss, swallowing her moans.

Calvin slows his movements, his body still trembling from his release. He supports Haley's hips as I grow even quicker. My fingers dig into her soft hips, my body tensing as I reach the peak.

"Fuck, Sassy," I groan, my cock pulsing as I come hard, filling the condom. Her body draws every last drop of pleasure. I slow my movements, my chest heaving as I catch my breath. I rest lightly on her back for a moment before pulling out.

I'm about to stumble across the room to get things to clean her, but Zane, Sam, and Easton are already on it.

I roll to the side and take her hand. I kiss each knuckle. "I love you."

"Love you." Her blue eyes flutter closed.

If someone had told me that after working around the world, I'd be back in Pittsburgh cooking at an overrated restaurant on the hillside of Mt. Washington, overlooking the city skyline, I'd have pushed them off the incline. But here I am. Well, not working at a glorified prom and cheap wedding venue but a food truck.

It's the best damn food truck, well, this side of the Allegheny River at least. I'm working on getting a permit for some other counties. It's only for a year. And fuck if my favorite thing isn't parking my truck outside of one of my uncle's job sites so he has to see the bags with my name on it every time he pulls up in his oversized little-dick truck.

My food truck is a mixture of everything I love. A good amount of recipes come from Anan's restaurant, but there are lots from all over the place. Fusion at its best.

This was just going to be a hobby. One to keep me from having to babysit my sister's kids every damn day. I don't mind watching them. But Sassy loves them and stops studying to play with them every time they're over. And they love her even more than me . . . but Sassy needs to study. She's too much of a giver. Not that I minded last night. We bought a few duplicates of our favorite things from our room in Miami. Damn, now I'm getting hard.

I turn to my new truck manager. "You've got this?"

"We're good. Get out of here while you can. I don't want Calvin coming and looking for you again. He scares the shit out of me." Todd finishes up an order and puts it in one of our compostable containers.

"He's not the one you should be afraid of," I say.

"He's not?" The kid looks up, fright in his dark brown eyes.

"Nope." I'm not telling him who, though. That our billionaire has become extraordinarily possessive of all of us.

"Okay. Well, have a good night, boss." He nods and grabs the next ticket to wrap up.

There's four people in the truck now. And we could use a

couple more if there was room. In the last two months, I've been approached by two restaurateurs, but that's not what I want. We've only landed here temporarily. A year and a half in total. Zane's only taking classes that transfer back to Miami.

I open the back door of the truck. There's a healthy line from the window on the sidewalk.

Movement catches my eye from a few picnic tables down. We move the truck at night to a lineup of trucks in a park.

I quickly step toward the bench. "Who are these two little monsters?"

My niece and nephew are covered in ice cream. It drips from their chins to their knees.

"What did you do?" I turn to Mario, the owner of the ice cream truck behind us. He laughs and waves. "Did he dip you in the chocolate fountain?" I pat the top of each of the twins' heads. I look around, but I don't see my sister. "Where's your mom?"

"Grandmom brought us," Mary says.

"She's talking to Haley over there. Told us to not move a muscle or this is the last ice cream of the summer," Michael adds, his eyes going wide.

"Yeah, don't believe everything Grandmom says."

"She said you'd say that." Mary licks her fingers. My niece is too much like me.

I step away from the sticky, adorable second-graders. Damn, how did that happen? I walk toward Haley and my mom. I don't like the body language going on. Haley has on her stew face, and Mom is talking with her hands. Her back's to me. Haley sees me approaching and her eyes widen.

"Dante!" Sassy pulls me close.

My mom's been cool with everything. Honestly, she's

thrilled I'm alive but even more thrilled that I'm not going to die on my own. But most of all that there's the possibility that there might be more grandchildren in her future. When I told her we were moving to Pittsburgh, she cried so hard she had to hang up the phone and call me back.

"Mom, what are you doing here?" I ask, kissing Haley's temple before turning to face my mother.

Her hands freeze mid-gesture, and she turns to look at me, her eyes wide with surprise. "Dante! I was just . . . catching up with Haley," she says, her voice a little too cheerful. I know her well enough to know she's hiding something.

"Catching up about what?" I ask, my eyes narrowing as I look from her to Haley, who seems to be studying the ground intently.

"Oh, you know, just girl talk," my mom says, waving a dismissive hand. But I can see the tension in her shoulders, the way her eyes keep darting to Haley. Something's up.

"Girl talk about what, Mom?" I press, not willing to let this go. My mom can have a one-track mind. It's either about babies or staying in the 'burg.

"Fine, there's this house that came on the market. It's one street over from where your sister lives." She pauses. What she means is its two streets over from where Mom lives. "And it's big. Like really big. Huge master bedroom."

"Primary suite," I correct.

"Yeah, well, it's big. And there's a nice fenced-in yard for my grand-dog, Penny. Pepper needs fresh air and birds to watch out the window. There are no birds forty stories up in your current place."

"Mom, we're not staying. We've gone over this."

Her head tilts back like a toddler. "I know, but with all

your roommates, you can afford it. Pittsburgh's an inexpensive place to live. You can have your Miami house and—"

"Temporary, Mom. Until Haley graduates."

"What about your trucks?"

"I'll sell them when the time comes. Or have someone run them for me."

"Have someone run them for you?" Mom laughs. "It doesn't hurt to just go look at the house. Your place now is nice, but it's so small."

"It's a luxury condo."

"It's tiny."

Haley's just watching my mom and me go at it. She's biting her lip to keep from laughing.

"Well, we need to get going home. Sassy has homework."

"She finished it," my mom answers for Haley.

Haley laughs.

"You think this is funny?" I grab her hand and kiss her knuckles.

"Yeah," Sassy says, sounding like my mom. "We have an appointment to look at the house."

I cross my arms over my chest. "Now?"

"Of course now. Why do you think I'm here?" My mom nods in a make-it-so kind of way.

I look over at the sticky kids. "We're going to need a hose first."

Chapter 48

Sunken Treasure

Easton

I step out onto our covered suburban porch for the tenth time in the last hour. Penny comes out with me every time. Her head cocks at me like I've totally lost it. And I probably have.

"Can you even see them coming up the street?" Sam asks when I come back in. He's sitting at the smallest desk ever made, next to the front door, typing away on his computer. We made two huge offices upstairs with giant monitors and anything any of us would need, but Sam still sits down here. I don't blame him.

They're deep in edits, and Calvin does a lot of swearing, talking to the editor's comments on the page, but their yacht and land survival books are almost done.

I settle into the sofa and pick up my laptop again, my knee bouncing. And Penny jumps up on the sofa and puts her head as close to my computer as possible. Things are going smoothly, and I want them to continue this way. But I can't help lingering on *what do we do after Haley graduates* thoughts.

I check my email, and I have to blink. There's a message from Dad. One I've been waiting a while for. I'm about to interrupt Sam and tell him the good news, but it can wait until Dante's here. He's due home before Zane and Haley. He's got a call with the manufacturer of his latest truck. This will bring his fleet up to four. I'm nervous. About my original news, that is, and I'm wondering if I should have told them. When I asked Haley before, she said it's up to me. So I did it. I close the email and try to settle in to work in the meantime.

The door slams when I'm in the middle of a report.

Dante sinks into an oversized leather chair opposite me. "You wanted to have a meeting?"

"Yeah. Zane and Haley should be home soon." When we moved farther away from their school, I wanted to arrange for them to have a car service or at least buy them parking, but they both insist on taking the bus.

Dante leans back, his fingers drumming on the armrest. "All right, what's this about? You've been edgy all week."

I take a deep breath, setting my laptop aside. "I've been thinking about our future. All of us. We've been in Pittsburgh for a while now, and I know we've talked about going back to Miami, but—"

Dante's eyebrows shoot up, and he stands. "But what? You want to stay here? Not to jump too hard into a no, but fucking no." His nose crinkles, and he holds the side of his head. It's the same way he did the day I tried to fill in for a sick cook on his truck. "I grew up here. And if there was one thing I didn't want, it was to stay here." He blinks twice. "Fuck." His shoulders drop.

"Dante?"

"I mean fuck in a good way. I hate to admit it, and I'm never going to say it again, but I kind of like it here. I like knowing the neighborhoods and having people I've known since I was an asshole teenager come and eat my food. Shit. I actually like it here." He flops back into the chair.

Before I can respond, the sound of the front door opening catches our attention. Zane and Haley walk in, their laughter filling the room. They're both dressed casually, Haley in a pair of jeans and a sweatshirt, her hair slightly windswept, and Zane in his usual dark jeans and a fitted tee.

"Have you started talking?" she asks.

"Yes and no." Dante's eyes flare. "I'll go get the Viking." He takes the stairs up two at a time.

"Hey, what's going on?" Zane asks, taking a seat on the arm of the sofa next to me. Haley slides in next to me. Sam closes his computer and moves over. The stairs creak, and soon we're sitting in a circle.

My throat goes dry. "I've done two things. And I hope none of you are mad."

"That depends what they are," Dante answers.

"Right, I sold Rockwell Tire. It will be announced tomorrow."

"Whoa, Rocky and Em . . . ?" Haley asks.

"I got their blessing, of course, first."

There are nods around the room.

"Congrats." Calvin slaps me on my back. "But did you think we were going to be upset or something? That's your money. Do what you want with it."

There's more nodding.

"Right, mate. What's the second thing?" Zane crosses his leg over his knee.

"That one is a present of sorts. I've made a trust with

the money. And the trust has made a purchase." I take the envelope out of my bag on the floor. "Here, Haley, you open it."

Zane leans forward, brows furrowed like he's trying to read the future through the envelope. Calvin props his elbows on his knees. Even Sam is quiet, waiting. Haley's hands tremble just slightly as she slips her finger under the flap.

She licks her lips. "I feel like I'm on an award show with all of you watching."

"You'll be graduating soon. And Zane's able to take classes online—"

Haley's eyes bulge. "Is this . . ." She turns the page to the map and holds it out for everyone to see. "Did you buy our island?"

"I did."

"Shut the front door." Haley jumps. "This is . . . this is fantastic." Her voice cracks, and I see it—tears she tries to blink away. "I didn't think we'd ever get back there," she says softly. "It was ours, but it never felt real. Not until now."

"And after you've graduated, we can take a trip." I pull her into a hug.

"I can't wait," she says into my shoulder.

"There's more."

"Damn, Rockwell. You don't need to bottle up secrets," Calvin says.

"This isn't a secret. Rocky sent me an email a bit ago. They found Susan. In Switzerland. She's being held on one count of murder and numerous accounts of attempted murder. They're working on her extradition now. Since the *Rock Candy* was flying under a Bahamas flag, it's a complicated process. The trial might end up in the Swiss courts."

"I'm just relieved to hear they caught her." Haley leans against me. "Oh, I have news too. It's not as big, but . . . Stella Freeman never went through with the wedding with Krit. She found out about how he sold us out to Thayer and called off the wedding. She friended me on social media, but I've been staying off my account because of all the weirdos out there."

"There are some weirdos in here too." Dante stands. "A business sold, a killer caught, a loser dumped, and an island bought. I'd say this calls for a celebration! What do you want to do, Sassy?"

"I've got a big test tomorrow . . ."

"Rain check it is. But how about I deliver some study snacks to your desk?"

"Yes, please." All of us meet in the middle of the living room in a big hug.

"You sure you want to go here?" the local captain we hired to bring us here asks. Our island is a speck on the horizon, but we're getting closer. "It's not a lucky place."

"Lucky's a matter of perspective," Calvin mutters, gripping the rail. "Or memory." He turns to me. And the time on the other side of the island flashes back to me. The village was decimated by the greed of someone.

"We'll be good." The back of the boat is loaded down with things we don't need but will be nice to have. I put my arm around Haley. "You doing okay?"

"I'm nervous. It's been a long time, and it's not going to look the same, you know?"

"It's true, the jungle will have taken back a lot of land in the time we've been gone," Sam says and gives her a peck on her cheek.

"Change is hard, Sassy." Dante comes up behind her. His hand around her waist, he pulls her to him. "Much like I am. But damn, I'm looking forward to seeing you in your bikini again. Can we all agree that this weather is much better than Pittsburgh in winter?" He gestures to the approaching beach.

"I don't know. I kind of like snow," I say.

"Me too. But this is nice as well." Haley tilts her head to me.

"Honestly, I thought being inland would drive me batty. But I've adjusted. You guys want to give me a hand loading up the tender when we get there?" Sam asks.

There are many piles of supplies. Tubs of clothes, coolers, solar panels, tools, tarps, tents, fishing gear, and snorkeling equipment stand next to our four new WaveRunners. Tethered to the big rock is our hard-sided tender. The only thing missing is Penny and Pepper. They're back with Dante's mom. Hopefully, the next time we come, they'll be with us.

After everything is secure and undercover, the captain of our ride stands with his hands on his hips in the surf. "You're sure?" he asks in his thick accent.

"Abso-fucking-lutely," I say with a smile. "Next Monday, the contractor and his team will be waiting for you. Call me if your plans have changed."

Calvin and Zane have been double-checking the satellite phone the whole way to the island. And with the right targeting, we've been able to keep a clear signal.

"I will. You're sure you don't want my men to take your things farther inland?" He glares at our mound of supplies.

Zane's moving another box. "I didn't know how much I missed some physical labor." He flexes his biceps at Haley.

She laughs. "We're sure. Thank you, Captain," Haley answers for us. She snakes her arm around my waist.

The boat captain gives us a salute and heads back to his tender. The other guys come over and watch him leave.

"Are you ready?" I ask Haley.

She jumps and claps. "I am."

"Are you going to tell us all the names of the plants you didn't know before?" Zane playfully bumps her with his elbow.

"Abso-fucking-lutely," she mimics me from earlier.

The path to the treehouse isn't completely overgrown, but vines and ferns are reaching for each other.

At the first peek into the clearing around the treehouse, Haley gasps. "It's still here. Overgrown a bit." She rights one of the chairs. "But it smells right, and it feels like home."

I touch her elbow, and she turns to me. Her blue eyes shine in the dappled jungle light. "I didn't know what I was searching for when I boarded the *Rock Candy*. My professional athletic career was over, and I was floundering. But somewhere between the storms and the secrets, I found a future I couldn't have dreamed of. And it started right here. You know wherever you are is home. But being in the spot where I learned what love is? Where I became whole again? It feels damn good." I pull her into my arms and kiss her.

When we break apart, everyone is staring at us. Zane's next. He kisses her, and when he finishes, he gives her an extra peck on her neck. It feels like an hour later when Dante's the last to dip her and we continue our exploration.

The table Sam and Calvin made has a pile of branches on it. I could have sworn it was turned over when we left.

"Holloway must have picked it up," Calvin says and

walks a few feet down the still visible path to the stream. "There are no current tracks around."

"Stove is still here." Dante pats the hunk of cast-iron. The makeshift roof over it has collapsed, though.

"Our treehouse looks solid." Sam's the first one up on it. "You going to finish the bathroom now?" Sam calls down to Zane, laughing.

"I think we might start over." Zane has got his sketchbook under his arm. "I don't have my degree yet, but I've got some ideas."

Haley wanders to the far side of the camp. She pulls at a stick in the weeds. And out pops our Christmas tree. "Whoa, it made it!"

"So did we." I help her pull ferns from the driftwood branches.

"All right, we've got some serious work to do before the sun goes down," Sam says.

"Aye-aye, Cap," we all answer back.

Chapter 49

North Star

Haley

The sun's beaming through the window. The frangipani tree brushes lightly against the glass like it's checking in on me—gentle and persistent, like one of my guys. It's weird being here and having glass windows, but I'm not going to complain. Glass and screens mean less bugs and water in your bed at night.

I stretch my fingers above my head. I should get up. There's a soft breeze coming through the open balcony door, carrying with it the scent of saltwater and something sweet, maybe frangipani. I can hear the distant hum of a boat motor, probably Calvin and Sam out for an early morning fishing trip. There's a clicking coming from the outside kitchen. Dante uses his old potbelly stove as much as our newly finished industrial kitchen. Easton has been up with the sun, working out in the gym on the lower level. And Zane, well, he's probably off sketching somewhere, planning yet another addition to our ever-growing island home.

I've been awake for hours, but I don't want to get up. It's the fresh air and finally having the house complete, I keep telling myself. But I've got a garden to attend to . . .

I swing my legs over the side of the bed, the cool bamboo flooring grounding me as I stand. Our bedroom is simple, adorned with artwork we've collected from various islands and bits of driftwood art that Zane has made. On the balcony, I look through the jungle palms to the crystal blue water that surrounds our home. There's a coffee carafe and a covered bowl filled with fruit. Dante must have brought them up when I was asleep.

The tang of pomelo and papaya makes my mouth water. The smell reminds me of our first few weeks back here—sticky fingers, barefoot mornings, and laughter echoing through a modern campsite.

The sound of footsteps echoes up the staircase, and I turn to see Easton, his skin glistening with sweat from his workout. He grins at me, his eyes softening as he takes in my naked torso where my shirt has splayed open. "Morning, beautiful," he says, walking over to press a gentle kiss to my forehead. "How are you feeling?"

I smile up at him, leaning into his touch. "Hungry," I admit with a laugh. "And excited. Nervous too, mixed with a little bit of sad. I'm not ready to go back to the States yet. Two more weeks here doesn't seem like enough."

"I know what you mean. But the rainy season waits for no one. We could stay if you want to . . ."

I devour the fruit bowl in seconds.

"No . . . we need to visit people. They're going to think we dropped off the planet, and I miss Pepper."

"She would like the new house, but I know she wouldn't like the plane ride."

"She's happy staying with Dante's mom."

Easton kisses my neck. "I'm going to shower if you want to—"

There's a thud on the bedroom door. "Are you ready?" Zane calls.

"Ready?" I wipe my hands on the cloth napkin that Dante left for me and stand. "Ready for what?"

"Oh, we've got a surprise for you." Zane raises his head to Easton.

"That's today?"

"Yup, today's the day. The equipment arrived from the mainland an hour ago." Zane's back in the bedroom, rummaging in my drawer. "This should work." He holds out one of my swim shirts and trunks. The big ones I use when we go snorkeling, when the water's a little rougher.

"Snorkeling?" I ask, taking them from him. I pull off my pajamas, forgoing a shower if I'm going out into the ocean.

"Something like that." Easton wiggles his eyebrows.

"What's the equipment that arrived?" I turn to Dante in the hard-sided tender. Because there was nothing on the beach. We're all here. Calvin's piloting the boat, and we're pointed in the direction of chicken and pomelo beach. "Is it something to do with pruning the trees again?" We had a small crew out last spring to shape them up and teach us how to do it.

"Nope, nothing about the trees. But we could stop by there and get some fruit after if we have time." Dante kicks his legs up on the bench in front of him. One hand is on my leg, and with the other he holds on to the side of the tender.

We pass the sheer cliff, and when the bay where the *Rock Candy* was anchored for so long appears, I see the equipment. It's the flatbed barge they used for laying our pier. It's anchored near the mouth of the cave. A large crane is attached to it.

"The box!" I cry out. "We're going to bring up the box?" My breath catches. That box was the ghost of everything we endured, searching for Easton and Calvin. And now it's going to rise like something out of a dream.

"You ready?" a man with a British accent calls out from the barge. "We've got it all hooked up."

"Ready whenever you are," Zane says. "You're sure I can't film it from underwater?"

"Not when we're moving it. I've got my diver down there, though. He can tape it if you're willing to let him use the camera. If you don't mind helping? I've only brought my long-time diver and myself, as you requested."

The diver surfaces and gives us a wave. Calvin, Sam, Easton, and Zane move over to the other vessel, following the barge captain's directions like they've been working together for years.

The box erupts from the water, a reinforced net supporting it, and when it's slowly placed on the deck of the barge, the barge sinks a good six inches into the water. I catch a look on Calvin's face. Could it really be treasure?

I grab Dante's hand. "It must weigh a lot to displace that much water."

"Gold weighs a lot. Though, so do rocks." Dante laughs.

"Come on over, we're going to open it," Sam yells with cupped hands.

I jump in and swim the short distance to the barge. The memory of arriving here and having the *Rock Candy* gone washes over me with each stroke. The horror of thinking I'd never see either Easton or Calvin again shook me into realizing what I wanted. It was a real turning point in us becoming a family. Calvin leans over the barge. I take his hand, and he pulls me out of the water.

Forty-five exhausting minutes later, the crowbars and the guys' muscles finally beat the box.

"Well, I'll be damned," the barge captain says. "I've heard the legend. I just never thought it was true."

Thayer had told me the legend. More than the island being unlucky or cursed. He said, *"The villagers who lived there years ago were massacred. Apparently, one of them went to the mainland and got drunk. Said they found treasure, and they were set for life as soon as the elders divided it up. Instead, a horde of greedy men attacked the island, killing them. But no treasure was found."* Until now.

I shudder. I haven't thought about Thayer in a long time. While Susan landed in a Swiss jail, nothing happened to Thayer or his dad. Their lawyers got them cleared.

"Ready to watch?" Zane sits next to me with a bowl of popcorn on his lap.

"Ready," I say. Even after being there when they brought it up, it gives me goosebumps. Our house isn't extraordinarily large, but we did splurge on a movie room. We're all snuggled on a large sofa.

Calvin hits play.

A crowbar creaks against the waterlogged wood, and the camera zooms into the golden glowing box. We now know most of the artifacts are from the Zheng empire. Calvin's voice booms on the recording as he tells everyone not to touch anything.

The barge captain left it for a week but then arranged secret transportation back to the mainland, where a museum is curating and preserving it.

The video switches to the museum curator, talking about the major pieces. He stops at the handful of coins from 1972. Whoever sunk the box had a good idea they weren't going to open it again. The video has the curator talking in detail about each piece in depth. Dante's snoring, his head in my lap, when the video turns off.

"Wake up," Calvin growls, and he slaps Dante's foot.

"I wasn't asleep." Dante sits up, his eyes flicking to the drool spot on my shorts. "Sorry, Sassy."

I laugh.

"Right. We have a decision to make. The museum has offered to buy the collection outright from us." Calvin passes his phone around with the letter from the museum director.

"Damn, that's twice what we paid for the island." Zane holds the phone in his hand. I've got to admit, I love that he's finally using terms like "we paid." The majority of the time we were in school, he had an aura of guilt for not having a job while he was taking classes.

"It is." Easton hands the phone back to Calvin.

I rest my head on Calvin's shoulder. "We should start a foundation. Help people like Rodel get back on their feet. Help people recover from being trafficked." We've been through storms, both on the water and in our lives. If we can use this gold to help someone else find their way through a tough time? I'm all for it. Without Rodel our time aboard the pirate vessel would have ended differently.

"That's an amazing idea, Sassy." Dante cuddles up to my side.

Easton turns up the lights and opens the blinds. The room fills with the light from the night sky.

"We should take a night stroll." I squeeze Dante's hand.

Dante jumps up, but Sam beats him to my side. He

grabs a flashlight, and we head down the path to the beach. It's so bright we don't really need it.

The big log is still there, shining in the starlight. I'm about to sit when Easton takes my hand. "Or we could take a swim?"

I'm the first to rip off my clothes and race for the surf. It's quiet tonight, but soon with the rainy season coming, it will change. Our island changes constantly, just like we do. But we adapt.

I never thought I'd survive that shipwreck—let alone build a life from the wreckage. But here we are. Whole. Loved. Free. I didn't think I could give my heart to one man again, let alone five. But I did. And they gave me theirs in return—fully, fiercely, without fear.

There's splashing behind me. Easton's the first to catch up, rolling onto his back and pulling me into his arms. "Got you."

Sam's next. Then the others. Soon, we're our own floating island, bobbing in the dark water, tethered to each other.

We're going back to the States soon. But part of my heart will always be right here.

This beach is where we landed, broken.

It's where we healed.

And where we learned how to love.

Thanks of reading! Want to know what happened on the other raft? Visit https://BookHip.com/BTGSQDR to register for my newsletter and I'll send you a collection of micro episodes about Emily's days floating in raft number two.

Savage Vow: Sneak Peak

Emily

I'm shaking as I swipe the keycard and push the button to go to the penthouse of the Saint Redford and drop the card into my purse. I'm nervous. Which is ridiculous. He kissed me goodbye when he left my hotel to come back here. It stopped raining, but I accepted the car service he sent to pick me up. That doesn't mean I'm not quivering inside. When I was with him, a feral version of myself was unleashed. One that wants more. And if I'm not going back to Miami tomorrow, can I forget about the guys back there? There's a stirring in my stomach. Tonight's dangerous, because I'm putting myself out there. *Light and fun. Light and fun.* I repeat it to myself. Guys do it all the time, dating more than one girl. There's absolutely no reason I need to play by some outdated grandma standard. I did that, and it left me heartbroken five times over. Light and fun. This time I'm going to take all the orgasms and leave my stupid, easily won heart out of it.

I adjust the strap on my dress. It's vintage, one shoulder Dior. It's my go to when I want to be sexy. I don't even know why I threw it in my bag, but I'm glad I did. It's rayon and clinging to my curves. Best of yet, it doesn't wrinkle.

I'm not a princess, but when he winked at me, my stomach fluttered. "We'll have more fun tonight," he said.

The elevator stops on the top floor, and I check my phone for the room number again. I pause at his door and straighten my dress before I reach out to knock.

I'm jerked backward. Hands grab me from behind, one over my mouth, the other around my waist. I twist my head, ready to ask him how he snuck up behind me, when I realize the hand over my mouth doesn't look like his and the linen musk scent that I huffed from his wet jacket before I had it sent out is missing. My throat closes, panic rises up my chest, and it takes me a second before I remember any of my training. I stomp on his foot, and it lands. Hard. But it lands with a hollow thud. Steel-toe boots.

I slam my elbow backward into his ribs, and he doesn't even grunt. He's a brick wall behind me. I throw my head back. The crown of my head thunks on his chin. He swallows a few swear words and tightens his grip around my mouth. I spit in his hand.

"Stop. You're coming with me. I'm not going to hurt you. And neither is my boss." The man has a Midwestern accent. He's quick, and in the next second, a gag is in my mouth.

Fighting back isn't working, so I drop all my body weight and go limp. But the brute's ready for it. He throws me over his shoulder. It doesn't matter. My brain fizzes, and I'm out.

Darkness takes me.

．　．　．

Savage Vow, Summer 2026
Available for preorder.

Also by Ellie Pond

Dark Wing

Resisting the Bear

Claiming the Wolf

Courting the Bear

Redeeming the Dragon

Tempting the Bear

Defying the Dragon

Chasing the Wolf

Dark Wing Series, Hidden Valley Wolves

Hidden Heart

Brilliant Heart

Bewildered Heart

Mated (completed series of Hidden Valley Wolves)

Mermaid Why Choose—Enchanted Elements

Wicked Water

Rugged Rock

Western Winds

Fire Falls

Veiled City

Captured by the Dark Commander

Tempted by the Forbidden Mate

Caged by the Ruthless Thief

Bound by the Golden King

Seduced by the Mermen: Men of Stele

Claimed by the Mermen

Dark Wing Series, River Divided

Crafting Love

Fighting Love

Dark Moon Rising

Guard

Protect

Honor

Wrecked

Adrift

Uncharted

Unmoored

Wayward

Revenge and Surrender (Emily's series coming summer 2026)

Savage Vow

Stolen Promises

Scandalous Devotion

About the Author

Ellie's had many professions, including costume designer, contract archeologist, organic farmer, fabric store owner, and airline gate agent. She's happy to be a full-time writer now. She lives in New England with her three teenage sons, husband, and father. It's a lot of testosterone. When time allows Ellie likes to travel. You can follow her on social media for her travel adventures, and more.

www.ingramcontent.com/pod-product-compliance
Lightning Source LLC
Chambersburg PA
CBHW070235200726
48293CB00005B/1626